BLACK CHALK

Christopher J. Yates

BLACK CHALK

Harvill *Secker*

LONDON

Published by Harvill Secker 2013

2 4 6 8 10 9 7 5 3 1

Text designed by Richard Marston

First published in Great Britain in 2013 by
HARVILL SECKER, Random House
20 Vauxhall Bridge Road
London SW1V 2SA

www.rbooks.co.uk

Addresses for companies within The Random House Group Limited
can be found at: www.randomhouse.co.uk/offices.htm

The Random House Group Limited Reg. No. 954009

A CIP catalogue record for this book is available from the British Library

ISBN 9781846557279 (hardback)
ISBN 9781846557286 (trade paperback)

The Random House Group Limited supports the Forest Stewardship Council® (FSC®),
the leading international forest-certification organisation. Our books carrying the FSC label are
printed on FSC®-certified paper. FSC is the only forest-certification scheme supported by the
leading environmental organisations, including Greenpeace. Our paper procurement policy
can be found at www.randomhouse.co.uk/environment

Typeset in Scala by Palimpsest Book Production Limited,
Falkirk, Stirlingshire

Printed and bound in Great Britain by Clays Ltd, St Ives plc

For Margi

Because without you
nothing

Never trust the artist.

Trust the tale.

– D. H. Lawrence

I(i) He phones early. England greets the world five hours ahead of us and I answer before my day has gained its groove.

Before long I have agreed to everything he says.

Don't worry, he says. I promise you, it'll be fun.

It'll be fun. Pause. Click.

Yes, that's what we said about the Game all those years ago. It'll be so much *fun*!

I hold the phone to my chest for some time after the call has ended. And then, crossing the room, I open my curtains for the first time in three years. Because now he has found me, tracked me down, and there remains no good reason to stay hidden any longer. For three cloistral years the quantity of time I have spent inside this apartment has averaged twenty-three hours and fifty-nine minutes each day. I am a hermit, as pale as my bones, as hairy as sackcloth. But now I intend to grow stronger. I must ready myself for the impending visit of the ancient friend.

Because the timing of the call was of course no coincidence. In five weeks' time, fourteen years to the day since last we saw each other, this hermit turns thirty-four. And let me state from the outset that, whether I win or lose, I hope this story will serve as my warning to the world. A cautionary tale. My confession.

I stand by my window staring out at the city. Everything is storm-light, the bruised palette of the sky. Manhattan, mid-April. Down below on Seventh wheels rush and slosh water to the sides of the road.

I push my forehead to the glass. If I am going to win, then before he arrives I must undergo a transformation. I will embark upon the journey of the recovering warrior, just like in the boxing movies. Months of hard work before the comeback fight, the washout trying manfully to resurrect his career. And from the hermit's chrysalis there will emerge a proud fighter. Except the strength I will need for the coming battle is all mental. I begin to wonder what might be the psychological training equivalent to sprinting up museum steps, pounding sides of beef with bare fists, quaffing raw eggs. I begin to hum inspirational music, I wave my fists feebly in the air.

Perhaps I could start out with a gentle stroll.

Yes, I'm going to do it, the hermit is going to go outside. And he may be some time.

I(ii) But I am sorry to report that I did not make it outside. The glasses stopped me, all six of them. Please believe me, I had absolutely no choice in the matter.

It surprises me every morning how much there is to remember, the fuss we must wade through before life becomes *life*. The eating and the drinking and the cleansing. The cleansing especially. Every day I question whether such cleansing has a purpose – for a hermit especially. But I have learned to trust my routines. When I lose trust in routines, bad things can happen.

I pick up a water glass and routine saves me again. Saves me from languishing in thoughts of the Game. Nudges me back to the present.

———

II(i) It had taken an act of immense bravery for Chad to befriend Jolyon.

Chad and the other Americans in the year-long programme had arrived in England a week before the British freshmen. At Pitt they called them freshers but at least the words were similar. Chad would have drilled into him far greater lexical oddities than this while studying at Oxford. (The cleaners they called scouts, the bills they called battels, the tests called collections . . .)

And during that first lonely week, as was his habit, Chad failed to make friends with his countrymen, a habit that made him feel awkward and defective. There were six of them and they had been garrisoned together in a narrow terrace house a few streets below the river, a fifteen-minute walk from Pitt College.

Coming to Oxford was the número uno bravest thing Chad had ever done. And he had come for adventure, so he didn't see how spending time with his fellow Americans would benefit him. Because adventure wasn't a vain search for some decent *frickin* food in the city. Adventure wasn't a sweatshirt with your university name emblazoned proud and blue across the chest. And the truly adventurous surely had access to more than three adjectives when describing the architectural splendour that surrounded them. Cute, cool, awesome.

Around these Americans Chad knew he would never escape that part of himself from which he longed to break free. The shyness, the gulping and blushing and smiling at people when the more honest reply would be *bullshit*.

Although sometimes Chad wondered if his shyness was actually a secret defence mechanism, an evolved shield. Perhaps biting your tongue was the only thing that kept the worst parts of you hidden from the world. But what if shyness was simply a curse and in the world beyond his sealed lips a whole better life awaited him, the real Chad?

And so he resolved to act, to do something entirely

un-Chad-like. He had pushed himself into adventure and now he needed to push himself just one more time. He would force himself to make friends with one British student at Pitt. Because any friendship was a path and paths always led elsewhere. To more paths and new places. Maybe even a better kind of life. And then, if he could only find a new world, Chad would skip down its lanes. Wherever they took him.

II(ii) Chad reasoned that freshmen would be the most open to new friendships. He should strike early on in the game before impenetrable circles and cabals began to form. This was a lesson learned from the errors Chad had made in his first year at Susan Leonard. A semi-lonely freshman, a barely social sophomore. He had hand-delivered the application to spend his junior year abroad on the day they began accepting submissions.

And so at the end of that first week in England, Chad spent two hours standing in the front quad of Pitt College. Two hours, and every minute becoming more forlorn, his temporary resolve dwindling by the second.

Yes, throughout those two hours a steady trail of freshmen did indeed appear. But they arrived not alone, not companionless as they had been imagined. Instead they came accompanied by coteries of parents. Proud, harbouring parents. Besuited parents. Parents swarming their beloved children and buzzing with manifest pride.

Over and over Chad watched the same routine unfolding. The freshman's first entrance through Pitt's front gate in the painfully assembled clothing that best summated his or her desired image. The ageing father's insistence upon carrying the heaviest loads. The mother's hand fluttering proudly upon her décolletage, resting only to stroke the stone or locket of her finest necklace. Then later the return from the freshman's room, their child's new home having been located and inspected and the luggage all unloaded. And finally the farewell. The freshman awaiting the moment when the final thin twine of umbilical cord would at last and forever be cut.

The arriving families would pause here and there as they made their first turns around the perfect lawn. Shoulders were squeezed. Fingers pointed out the Gothic glories of the college buildings, the gargoyles and the diamonds of lead that latticed the windows, the uneven staircases spiralling up from the squat arched doorways. Dark stone passageways that promised more of Pitt's pleasures beyond front quad. The gardens and their ancient tree with tired limbs held up on crutches. Back quad with its wilder lawn, its meadow airs. The *thunk* of mallets striking croquet balls. The shadow of the sandstone wall washing over the grass toward students sprawled around their books and drinks.

Pitt College had been founded in 1620, the very same year that the *Mayflower* had dropped anchor in Plymouth Harbor. Chad would spend eight months in the city and the marvel of it all would never rub smooth.

But what was he to do? He couldn't approach an entire family. One human being at a time he found difficult enough.

And then just as Chad had accepted the abject failure of his plan, his ideal target had arrived. Alone. Male. Heavy bags. Yes yes yes.

Chad forced his legs to start moving before his mind could round on the plan.

Part one was simple, a greeting. And then Chad would ready himself for part two of the plan, to listen out for a name, to actually retain it – a vital stage of meeting people and a hurdle he usually failed to clear, his nerves like so much white noise. And then, part three, Chad would offer to help with the bags.

'Hi, I'm Chad,' said Chad.

The ideal target put down his bags. And then he looked up at

Chad, his lips tight against his teeth, and said, 'Who on earth names their son after a Third World fucking country?'

▬

III(i) Why did the presence of six water glasses prevent your narrator from enjoying a gentle stroll outside? Yes, I should explain. Rewind.

III(ii) When I turn away from the window, I see six glasses staring back at me from the floor of my apartment. As part of my routine, every night I place six water glasses very carefully in the middle of my living-room floor.

They make for an arresting image, six glasses arranged in two ranks of three. And this of course is the point of these glasses. To arrest me, to stop me on the spot. So I stand and I think and then I look up at the clock. Lunchtime. Seven hours have passed since the phone call. Which means I have lingered at the window all morning, the words of the phone call playing, rewinding and replaying in my head. And six glasses means I must not have not drunk any water today. Not one single drop.

It would seem that the phone call has already caused some considerable disruption to my routine.

Allow me to explain. Those six glasses are, to use a common phrase, an aide-memoire – although I prefer my own term, physical mnemonic. The physical imposition of the glasses helps me remember to drink six glasses of water a day. Because there was once an occasion, over a year ago now, when I forgot to drink any water at all. This liquid lapse continued for a dangerous length of time. The effects of dehydration, I soon discovered, can prove somewhat debilitating.

So now that the glasses have jolted my memory, I pick one up and head to the kitchen. Upon my arrival I see three plates lined up on the chequered linoleum floor. Which means I haven't yet eaten any breakfast. (Nor lunch nor dinner of course.)

Next I find that in the kitchen sink and hindering access to the faucet there sits an inverted salad bowl. With a Pavlovian twitch I glance down, whereupon I spy my genitals. Yes, I would appear to be entirely unclothed.

What ludicrous notion first caused me to make the mnemonic link between salad and genitals? Every morning I find the connection vaguely disturbing. I would like very much to change this memory prompt, I should replace the salad bowl with a heavy rolling pin or magnum of champagne. But alas, meddling with routines is a dangerous game.

I stand in the kitchen drinking my water, considering my limp lettuce nakedness for a short time, and then head to my bedroom. I leave the salad bowl and empty water glass on the bed. I find shorts and a T-shirt beneath my pillow.

Now clothed, I return to the kitchen. In the sink, and previously hidden by the inverted salad bowl, sits an old marmalade pot. So now I know what comes next. I go to the refrigerator for bread to make toast for my breakfast. But in the refrigerator there hangs a single red Christmas-tree bauble. Which means I haven't yet taken my morning pills. So I swallow my pills, put the bauble in the marmalade pot and slide the bread into the toaster. I open the cutlery drawer for a knife so I can spread peanut butter on my toast . . . And staring up at me is a Halloween mask of the Wookiee Chewbacca from the *Star Wars* movies.

So I put on the Halloween mask with the elastic under my chin but the Wookiee's face atop my head, eye-holes pointing to the ceiling. (It might prove somewhat tricky for me to breakfast through Chewbacca's mouth-hole, so I wear him thusly.)

Hungrily I eat my toast and peanut butter. And then, when I finish, I turn on the shower. Which means I can now take off the Halloween mask, its purpose having been to remain uncomfortably on my head until I remember to turn on the shower. (Although what a hairy Wookiee has to do with cleanliness, I could not possibly say. Sometimes my mnemonics make sense, sometimes they do not. Often this is the result of what lay at hand when the need to place another element in my routine arose.)

So I shower, stumble across more mnemonics, drink another glass of water and read the newspaper (whose presence, outside my door, a pair of sunglasses dangling in the shower closet alerted me to). This all takes about two hours of my time. And then upon the completion of morning tasks, I sit down at my dining table on whose uncluttered surface there rest only three objects. My diary, whose last entry was written some fourteen years ago, my laptop and an old yellow tooth. The diary has been patiently awaiting this moment for some time, the moment at which I would begin telling my story, and I will open it soon. But first the tooth, an old molar that rests on top of my laptop. The tooth has become my lucky charm, a reminder that I cannot be beaten. So I pick up the tooth, hold it clenched in my fist and close my eyes. And feeling warmed by this mnemonic of strength, I open the computer to record the morning's events. But then I can't remember the order in which I just performed my morning tasks. (You might at this point be forgiven for making the following observation – it may require more than one gentle stroll to propel me back into the world of normality.)

I sigh an enormous sigh, leave my computer again and head to the bedroom once more where I stand, hands on hips, staring at my bed. Every night when I try to climb into bed, I find I cannot get under the covers because an assortment of glasses, plates, bowls and various other gimcracks and gewgaws block my way. And so every day ends with the same laborious task. Each night before sleep I move around the apartment carefully replacing all of my physical mnemonics in their correct positions to establish the next day's successful routine.

Today I rearrange my mnemonics early, taking notes as I go, so that I can type out for you the details of my morning routine. A morning routine that, today, failed to attain completion until gone three in the afternoon. Which means I now have to shift my afternoon routine to the evening and my evening routine close to bedtime. But never mind, I refuse to allow minor setbacks to hinder my recovery. And were it not for my ingenious system of physical mnemonics, nothing whatsoever would have been accomplished today.

All of this thinking about mnemonic ingenuity puts me in a delightful mood. Yes, my thoughts will be sharp once more. I will spend every day in training. Slowly I will regain my strength, the very best of my mind.

Suddenly my mood becomes so fresh, so clear, that something wonderful jumps right into my head, something I have been unable to recall for the last three years – the mnemonic significance of the salad bowl. Ha, no, not any sort of unkind reflection on the size or health of my genitals. Yes, something so obvious.

Dressing. Salad: dressing!

I have five weeks.

———

IV(i) Jolyon rubbed his bag-strangled hands. Yes, he was feeling crabby. But he was feeling crabby because several second-year students had been posted at Pitt's front lodge precisely for the purpose of helping freshers carry bags and find rooms. And two of them were currently assisting a boy whose entire bearing suggested he came from a life of perpetual privilege. The boy's father – Admiral? Lord? Sir? – had commandeered a luggage cart which was now piled high with enough bags for a maharaja. So in fact the second years were lolling behind carrying nothing at all. Instead they were listening politely to the boy's mother who was telling them about little Toby's recent summer, half of which had been spent gaining impossibly valuable work experience in the offices of the Foreign Secretary, a personal friend, and the other half in Argentina participating in a polo tournament.

Jolyon meanwhile had been carrying his heavy bags alone all day. A twenty-minute walk to the station, a train journey, a Tube journey, a second train journey, another twenty-minute walk to Pitt. For months his separated parents had argued over which of them would drive him to college. As their shots ricocheted around him, Jolyon detected in the smell of the gunpowder the true nub of the problem, the unspoken question – which one of us deserves more credit for the cleverness of our son? Neither of his parents would submit and no fraction of the credit seemed attributable to Jolyon himself. And then the date for his parents' divorce hearing had come through. That date was today. Problem solved.

So now, while his parents were no doubt being physically restrained by their lawyers, Jolyon found himself carrying a large and heavy suitcase and, over his shoulder, a sports bag full of as many books and cassettes as he could cram inside. His shoulders ached and his hands and arms now hung at his sides utterly devoid of blood and strength. And the sight of little Toby had confirmed for Jolyon everything he feared this place would be. So yes, he was feeling crabby. More than a little maybe.

But despite his ill mood Jolyon had warmed to the American as soon as he had spoken. Jolyon had taken a year off travelling before college, finding odd jobs as he made his way around the world, always worried the money would run out and he would have to return home to his feuding parents – parents who couldn't send him any money because they worked as schoolteachers and were both using what little money they had to pay their divorce lawyers. During his travels, Jolyon had liked all the young

Americans he'd come across. In Vietnam he had taken up with a group of friends from New Mexico, including the smartest, most beautiful girl he'd ever met. He had planned on sticking with the pack as they headed west to Cambodia, even though he had just come from Cambodia himself. And that's when the smartest, most beautiful girl had told him about her boyfriend back home. No, more than a boyfriend – she took a deep breath and revealed a ring that she kept in her pocket. Her fiancé.

So Jolyon scuttled away to Thailand instead. He found a job in a beach bar and barely thought about his feuding parents at all, only about the girl, the feel of the sand between their dovetailing fingers when they would walk ankle-deep through the surf.

Months after Asia, while travelling around Europe, Jolyon had once again made sure to stay close to backpacking Americans. They had such an easy manner and he felt comfortable and safe around them, especially whenever a situation felt hazardous. Americans believed in their rights and standing up for them vocif-erously. Jolyon always felt secure in their constitutionalist company.

One night in Venice he had been crossing the Piazza San Marco, the whole experience like wandering through the jewellery box of a wealthy duchess, and next to him a Montanan named Todd had gasped at the view and said, 'Man, that's it. I'm seriously moving to Europe when I'm done with the whole college shitstorm. All the best Americans end up in Europe anyway.'

The notion that all the best Americans ended up in Europe appealed to Jolyon and Jolyon liked to cherish and cultivate the notions that appealed to him best.

And this Chad looked like one of the good guys. Jolyon had teased him about his name only to indicate that potentially he liked him. But then Jolyon remembered that, unlike the British, Americans tended not to initiate their friendships this way. In his head he now ran over the words he had spoken aloud. 'Who on earth names their son after a Third World fucking country?'

Yes, perhaps his crabbiness had made the words, intended as a welcoming joke, sound a little severe.

IV(ii) 'I wasn't baptised Chad,' said Chad. 'It's from my middle name – Chadwick.'

But Jolyon couldn't abandon the joke, he had to follow through to show it had been only a joke in the first place. He tried to sound playful. 'So you actually *choose* to be named after a Third World country?'

The English had such a sarcastic way with their vowels. To Chad's ears everything for those first few months had sounded biting or wry. I'm going to the *sooh*-permarket for some *booh*-ze and *cheeh*-se. It was like living submerged in an ocean of Oscar Wildes.

He couldn't think of an immediate response to the Third World quip. Everything had gone wrong in the span of mere seconds. To have approached this foreign stranger in Pitt's front quad was the número dos bravest thing he had ever done. But now courage felt like foolishness. He felt the blood climbing toward his cheeks, the patter of its hot little feet.

'I'm sorry, I'm a little tired and I didn't mean to . . . I'm Jolyon,' said Jolyon, offering his hand. 'Like Julian but pronounced jolly, which might seem ironic right now.'

Chad initiated part two of the plan. 'Jolyon,' he said, pronouncing the name carefully, *Jolly-un*, so that he would not forget it. And then Chad abandoned the plan completely, still smarting despite the apology. 'Sounds like a country and western singer,' he said, 'You know, with suede tassels and big hooters.'

Jolyon considered the foreign final word, its alien vowels and consonants. *Hooh-durrs*. What did it mean? But then the universal gesture of men the world over, hands cupped above the midriff, gave the game away.

'Jesus, you're right, Chad,' said Jolyon, taking absolutely no offence. And then, laughing and leaning in, Jolyon pointed over Chad's shoulder. 'You see that guy over there?' he said.

Rounding the other side of Pitt's front quad and being helped by his parents and two more second years was yet another freshman. He was wearing a businessman's blue pinstripe shirt tucked stiffly into black jeans.

Jolyon leaned in further. It made Chad feel like his most trusted confidant and together they were about to embark upon an act of heroic subversion.

'That guy's name is Prost,' Jolyon whispered. 'I met him in the bar when I came up for interview. You know how most people, when they take a year off before starting university, visit Asia and come back as Buddhists? Or try and sleep with as many Scandinavians as they can while backpacking round Europe?'

Chad nodded for want of a better or more truthful response.

'Well, Prost over there took a year off and you know what he did? He worked for a bank. I swear to God, a major bank for an entire year. Commercial loans division. I bought him a pint and he told me all about it like he's so much better than everyone else who, you know, maybe just wanted one last scrap of fun before entering the big, bad scary world of adults.' Jolyon leaned back and raised an eyebrow. 'The guy's a one hundred per cent, grade A, total fucking cock.'

Chad laughed, his splutter too loud so great was his sense of relief.

Jolyon clapped him on the shoulder. 'You know, now I come to think of it, Chad's a cool name. The incorruptible cop, the sheriff who stands alone against the band of outlaws.' Jolyon smiled. It was the sort of smile you longed to earn. And then he said, 'If you help me with my bags, I promise I'll buy you a pint.'

'Sure,' said Chad. 'You know, I kinda planned to offer anyway.'

'Excellent,' said Jolyon.

So they were going to be friends. It was agreed.

Jolyon had decided.

————

V(i) Something someone once said all those years ago has stuck in my mind. Although I can't actually remember who said it.

Someone else had come out with that old line about winning not being everything. Probably Emilia, that's exactly the sort of thing she liked to believe. And then one of us replied . . . perhaps even me, I'm not sure . . . one of us said, Of course winning is everything. Why else do you think we call ourselves the human race?

V(ii) But tell me, what did we do that was so wrong?

We played a game. That's all. *A game.* Isn't this how we teach children the ways of the world? Are we not all supposed to learn early in life how to cope with defeat?

But then there were the consequences, the price paid for losing.

Ah, the consequences.

Yes. We went too far.

Well of course we went too far. Why else would I be living in this dark hole, hands shaking as I dare to let in the sunlight for the first time in three years? Obviously we went too far. But no one was supposed to get hurt.

When a boxer dies in the ring, whatever our views on the sport, don't we accept that the boxer knew the risks? We don't blame his opponent. In law there exists a doctrine that covers this. *Volenti non fit injuria.* To the consenting person, no injury is done.

Yes, *volenti non fit injuria.* That should serve as my defence. But, instead, I stare at the blood on my hands every day and allow the guilt to suffocate me once more.

We went too far.

I went too far.

But it was never supposed to be that sort of game.

———

VI(i) The bar was underground and stone and ancient. From his seat at the middle of the crowded table Chad gazed around him and savoured once more the mustiness that gave the place a taste of the religious. Interconnecting rooms dimly lit. Wooden tables and benches like pews.

Throughout Chad's time in Oxford, they would frequently find something to raise their glasses to at Pitt. It was 3 October 1990, and Germany had been officially reunified since midnight. So that night they drank to the end of the Cold War, which had not been announced by the world's powers but inferred by Jolyon. And Jolyon had insisted on buying drinks for the whole table to celebrate. They toasted each other '*Prost*' and '*Zum Wohl*' and Jolyon taught them a drinking song he had learned in Munich. A boy named Nick teased Chad about his German pronunciation and Jolyon wagged his finger at Nick over the table. 'You do know that Chad's fluent in Spanish, right? So how's your *Español, Meestah Neeck*?'

'No, fair point, Jolyon. It was all Latin, Kraut and French at school. Sorry, Chad. Fluent, huh? That's actually pretty amazing.'

Chad wasn't fluent in Spanish. And Jolyon knew this, they had already compared tales of their schooldays on different continents. Chad had only studied Spanish at high school for a few years. '*Salud!*' he said, raising his glass to Nick.

While Nick returned the glass-raise with a respectful nod, Jolyon tugged at Chad's elbow. 'Come on, Chad, let's go, I can't breathe down here any more.'

Jolyon believed the world was becoming impossibly

overcrowded. But Chad already had a deep understanding of his new friend and it was clear to him that Jolyon believed the world was becoming overcrowded because he was so frequently at the centre of a crowd. Jolyon was like a fireplace in wintertime, people liked to warm their souls around him.

'Cocktails? Your room?' said Chad.

'Absolutely,' said Jolyon. 'And just the two of us tonight. I need some space.'

Chad's adventure was only eleven days old and already a success. And the número dos bravest thing Chad had ever done was the número uno reason why. Because even after knowing him for only a few days, Chad's friendship with Jolyon made him feel immensely privileged. Everyone who had met Jolyon in those first few days at Pitt already seemed to crave time with him. And yet Jolyon chose to spend most of his waking hours with him, Theodore Chadwick Mason. Such an embarrassingly lavish name for a poor small-town boy. Theodore felt too grand but Ted and Teddy had always felt too gentle. Chad was the lesser of several evils. And better still for the fact that Chad was his father's least favourite of the available options.

Chad finished his beer, hiding his grimace inside the mouth of the pint mug. His American taste buds had been trained on Bud and Coors, great lawnmower beers said his dad, although the farm didn't have anything resembling a lawn. It would take Chad several months to wholly acquire an appetite for English beer. Yeasty sweet yet at the same time bitter like burnt nuts.

A good-looking boy named Jamie called after them. 'Jolyon, Chad, don't leave us this way.'

'Back in a minute,' said Jolyon.

Jamie winked, made a gun shape with his fingers, a clicking sound with his tongue.

VI(ii) The bar's steps brought them out by the fine bulbous rear of the Hallowgood Music Room. They walked around back quad, moonlight shrouding the tallest of Pitt's towers, its proud flagpole stripped for the night. Some of the students referred to the tower as Loser's Leap because, as Jolyon had recounted to Chad, five years ago a girl had thrown herself from its battlements having failed an exam. Since then the tower had remained locked and chained. Chad couldn't help himself from peering down at the gravel whenever he passed by, as if he might spot a bloodstained stone underfoot.

As they made their way toward staircase six, Jolyon shared with Chad entertaining facts about the crowd they had just been drinking with. 'That attractive girl, Tamsin, with all the fake fur – she has a phobia about the sound of other people vomiting. She had to move from her room near the Churchill Arms in case she might hear the customers throwing up as they left. Jamie and Nick, meanwhile, they like to masturbate in adjacent stalls in the toilet while they talk about sports. And all of this is why you should always feel proud rather than embarrassed you don't come from a wealthy family, Chad. The evidence is overwhelmingly stacked up round here.'

'How do you know all this stuff? I was at the same table, I didn't get any of this.'

'People just tell me things,' said Jolyon.

They reached the door marked VI and Chad savoured the kiss of cold stone on his palm as they climbed to the top of the narrow staircase. Inside the room, Jolyon reached for the cocktail bible they had bought from the creaky used bookstore on Martyr Street, near the Oxonian Theatre whose name was another of the university's peculiarities, Chad learned – the Oxonian 'Theatre' was used for ceremonies, music, lectures . . . but never for plays. Jolyon turned the book's pages with reverence and great care, the brown-taped thing nearly thirty years old. They had bought it after their first night in Pitt's crowded bar, Jolyon having felt quickly crushed and unable to hear Chad though the din.

First they had made Manhattans in honour of Chad's heritage and decided they liked them on the sweet side of perfect. The next night came rusty nails, Drambuie with whisky, which tasted of heather and honey. Chad and Jolyon would spend the rest of term turning their gins pink or into gimlets and Gibsons, making concoctions for the delight of their names. Monkey glands, weep no mores, corpse revivers.

The liquor collection was clustered on Jolyon's desk. He had spent hundreds of pounds from his student grant to acquire what their book called 'the basics' and refused any offer of money from Chad. 'What goes around comes around,' Jolyon had said.

On the coffee table stood an unopened bottle of framboise. 'Ah, that reminds me,' said Jolyon, 'I bought this so we could try Floradoras tonight.'

'Twist my arm,' said Chad.

VI(iii) Jolyon's room looked best in the lamplight at night when the stark walls glowed and the ceiling beams cast dramatic shadows. The towers and domes of the city became obscured by the windows' inward reflection but there was time enough to enjoy towers and domes in the daylight.

As they sipped their Floradoras they returned to their favourite topic, an idea for a new kind of game that had been amusing them for several days already. When Chad finished the last of his cocktail he turned in the armchair to hang his legs over its side. He let out a long sigh, his inner bliss now drifting around him like smoke.

Jolyon seemed to have been asleep for the last minute but then he opened his eyes. 'I think those girls really liked you, Chad. Tamsin and Elizabeth. I could tell.'

Chad blushed, hoping Jolyon wouldn't notice. He had always wondered if behind his teenage mask there was someone worth looking at. 'Liked me?' said Chad. 'It was you they spent the whole night talking to.'

'Talking's easy. You could program a computer to say the right things to make people feel special. If I had your looks, Chad, your softness. That's real charm.'

Chad would cherish the warmth of this compliment for the rest of his life. Better even than his adventure made him feel. Lighter yet than the cocktails.

'I'm starving,' said Jolyon. 'How about we order some pizza?'

'No, let's go out. Hey, we should go back to that kebab van. What was it you made me get? A doner and cheese with the works and extra chilli sauce. Man.'

Jolyon was lying on his bed, limbs spread and belly up, a starfish gazing absently at the plasterwork and timbers. 'I have no legs,' he said. 'Really, not even jelly, just a complete nothingness.' Jolyon wallowed in the pleasure of his total immobility. 'Come on,' he said, 'they'll deliver pizza to the lodge and I'll pay if you'll pick the thing up.'

'I don't even like pizza,' said Chad.

Jolyon lifted his head and looked quizzically at his friend. 'Who on earth doesn't like pizza?' he said. 'No one doesn't like pizza.'

'I don't like pizza. I just don't.'

'Is it the tomatoes?'

'What does it matter why I don't like pizza?'

Jolyon let his head fall back against the bed again and Chad relaxed, his fingers having been clenched to the armrest from the moment that word had been spoken. And then when the topic seemed to have receded, Jolyon spoke again. 'I've seen you eat tomato sauce,' he said. 'And cheese. And bread. Which means it's logically impossible for you not to like pizza.' He raised himself onto his elbows and stared curiously at Chad.

Chad turned again in the chair, gathered his knees and hugged them in his arms. 'It's not about the taste,' he said. He couldn't find a good place for his limbs. He dropped his knees, crossed his legs.

'What is it?' said Jolyon.

Chad felt a ballooning sensation in his head. The alcohol, the surprising urge to tell. 'Oh, shoot,' he said, uncrossing his legs. 'OK then, you see all this?' he said, tapping a finger across his brow and down past the bridge of his nose.

'All what?'

'Scars!' said Chad. 'Craters and pits.'

'I hadn't noticed,' Jolyon lied. He squinted and pretended to see for the first time.

'I was the first kid in class to get a zit,' said Chad. 'Thirteen years old, a big yellow sucker right between the eyes. It's hard not to notice when everyone at school stares you right between the eyes.'

'Every teenager gets spots. I had them quite bad for a while.'

'No, Jolyon –' Chad's tone became full of voluminous certainty – 'you didn't have what I had or you wouldn't be you. Trust me, that just wouldn't be possible. Anyway, within a week I was covered. They grew fat and yellow and when they faded turned red. A sea of red, here and here and here.' Chad dabbed at his chin, his cheeks, his forehead. 'And there was always a fresh batch growing on top of the red sea, bright yellow bubbles.' He paused, his body stiffened. 'So when I think about it now,' he said, 'I guess Pizza Face is a pretty accurate nickname.'

Jolyon sighed and shook his head. 'Kids are cunts,' he said.

'Yes, they are,' said Chad. He nodded over and over. 'And it didn't stop at Pizza Face. There was Pizza Boy, Pizza Pie. Oh, and Chuck E. Cheese, which soon became Chad E. Cheese. And when I came into the room, invariably someone would ask, *Who ordered delivery?* I couldn't even stand hearing the word . . . *pizza*. I don't even like saying it now. And if a commercial came on TV, I'd start to burn with shame. And there are a lot of you-know-what commercials on American TV.'

Chad laughed, so Jolyon laughed too. 'How long did it last?' he asked.

'I still get the occasional zit,' said Chad, 'but throughout high school was the worst, the names never went away until college. I guess over the last two years it cleared up. Perhaps it hasn't looked so bad for a while.'

'Didn't you use anything? I thought they had good stuff for acne nowadays.'

'Yeah, they do,' Chad said. 'Only this wasn't acne, this was bubonic *frickin* plague.' He lowered his eyes. 'I had some liquid stuff from a doctor, made my face stink and turn green. Loads of different pills. I tried a flesh-coloured cream but someone at school said I had make-up on. Or rather he shouted it out in the hall and everyone came running to see. Anyway, none of that crap really worked. Except the fleshy cream made me look better but I didn't dare use it after the first day.'

'So you really don't like pizza at all?'

'I guess maybe I liked it before I was thirteen. I don't remember exactly. But in my head I've convinced myself now I can't even stand the smell.'

'So let's order one,' said Jolyon. 'What better way to exorcise a demon than to tear him apart with your teeth? I promise you'll like it. And if you don't, I will personally trek to the kebab van and buy anything you like. With extra chilli sauce.'

VI(iv) They sat around the coffee table and ate from the box. Neither of them said anything until the last slice was gone. When he was done, Chad fell back into his chair and placed his hands upon his belly. 'That was great. I feel great,' he said. 'Thank you, Jolyon.'

———

VII(i) A new day. I stand at my window looking down along Seventh, as restless as a barn-sour horse. It feels as if I am poring over the pages of an atlas. The sun topples into the room, further urging me to leave this dank hermit's cave.

In five weeks' time we play again, our fourteen-year hiatus will be over. Did I really think I could escape? And if I can't escape, if I have to play, I must be ready. Because if I can't even face the outside world, what chance do I stand against the Game?

So yes, I will go out now in broad daylight. For three years I have left this apartment only in narrow daylight, the thinnest hours of the morning. Fleeting 6 a.m. trips every two or three weeks to drop garbage in the trash and walk to a small bodega at the corner of my block. Enough to satisfy my needs. Not so many needs. Thin needs. Milk and coffee. Bread and tea. Tea to remind me of England, Lipton in brash yellow boxes, impossible to brew strong unless you use two bags but the double expense feels excessive. Jif peanut butter. Cans of chilli, boxes of rice. Confectioner's sugar which I eat by the spoonful to help me through occasional energy emergencies. If you suck it just right, the dust in your mouth turns to smooth sugar frosting. And whisky as well, my one extravagance – although of course whisky cannot be bought from a bodega. Or anywhere else at six in the morning. But for the twenty-first-century hermit, the world of online shopping caters conveniently to almost every need. And yet I keep a thin oar in the water of life – I continue to visit the bodega because if it ever feels safe to emerge from this cave, I must be ready to face the real world.

I look down at the street where cars drive by, half of them taxicabs, sliding and stopping as the traffic lights perform their duties in long lazy blinks. A flurry of pigeons blows past the window, whoosh, then wheels to the left and settles on the lip of a roof.

Yes, this is what the world has always looked like. Wet, dry. Bright, dark. Blue, grey.

I find this enormously reassuring. Yes, I'm going to do it. The hermit is going outside.

VII(ii) I leave the apartment in something of a trance. For three years my only human encounters have been with delivery men beyond the crack of my front door or at the counter in the bodega. The thought of more contact than this makes me edgy, so I hum my inspirational music, the boxer beginning his training. I imagine the tooth clenched in my fist, strength and warmth radiate through me. And then at the bottom of my building's front steps, I turn not right toward my bodega but left with a skip toward the unknown, the forgotten.

I remember now what a city of light and shadows New York becomes when the sun beats down and the tall buildings toss out their cool grey capes. I move from darkness to heat, then back into shade, smiling as the sunshine tickles my arms.

And then arrives my first test of strength, people walking toward me, she in her forties with a shaved head and dressed in pink hospital scrubs, he wearing denim overalls above a Hawaiian-print shirt. He weighs in at maybe two-twenty with a bulldog jaw and cropped black hair. He looks like a children's entertainer who could knock out your teeth.

Oh deh bay-bee, Frank, deh baby, she says, you should have seen deh baby. (Frank is nodding, he can imagine the baby just so.) Oh but the clothes on him, Frank. She whistles. Not like we and you and me, Frank. This baby they dress *beaudy-full*.

I repeat her words within and mentally confirm what she said. We and you and me, yes, what a wonderful slip of the tongue. The real world has welcomed me back right away. I am not twenty steps from my apartment building and already I have swallowed the first vitamins of my new training regime. We and you and me. The imperfections of the world, its daily beauty. Yes, I can face this. I can do it.

I walk on toward a building covered in scaffolding. Underneath the poles and planks, the ground lies flooded brown with a liquid like old blood, the sidewalk stained where yesterday's rainwater has fallen rusty from the girders. And I love everything I see. The rust, the angular graffiti, the water as it drips brightly through sunbeams. All around me life swirls with a fresh beauty, three years of darkness extinguished in the light. This is love rekindled, the world my old flame.

I keep walking and beyond the end of the block I see swathes of green, the cool greens of plants and shade and filtered sunlight. Yes, I remember now, the park is here.

I wait impatiently to cross the street, I long to roam beneath the trees in the wine-bottle light. The sign at the corner reads Avenue A. The world pours in.

I look up past the street sign and spot three letters in the distant blue, H and E and L. A small airplane is skywriting, scratching the air with its smoke, with its loops and its swoops. Two more white letters are drawn in contrails across the shallow southern sky. I stop where I am and stare in amazement. H E L L O. Next comes an N and I applaud myself when I realise the airplane must be spelling out the message HELLO NEW YORK. I feel victoriously happy – an E forms in the sky – not only am I newly acquainted with the world but alert again to its futures.

I stand and I wait but nothing more arrives. Disappointed, I guess to myself that the pilot, in error, has drawn out his letters too large. Just like me he is simply in training, he must have run out of fuel and returned to base.

And then I nearly fall to the ground as my legs become weak. H E L L O N E, reads the sky. HELL ONE.

I run back to my apartment as fast as I can.

VII(iii) What a terrible omen. HELL ONE, like the zip code of my life. Or the title of its first episode, maybe. A movie featuring me fourteen years ago, my life in the Game, and in five weeks' time, look out for the sequel. *Hell Two: The Game Strikes Back.*

But I will go outside again. Tomorrow. Yes, I'm fine now. Baby steps, several minutes. Long enough for me to remember how much there is in the world to recommend it, enough for me to gain a little strength. And my tormentor was only an airplane running low on fuel, that's all, nothing more.

To calm myself while I write this all down, I make a cup of tea which I am currently finishing. And to hell with the expense – I used two bags so that the tea tastes good and strong. The tea soothes me, makes me think of England. Small hands around a mug, itchy warm in wintertime.

And then I start to laugh. I laugh for the first time in years as I picture myself running from words in the sky. Eyes wide and my beard and pale limbs flailing wildly. Not exactly a poster boy for the advantages of the hermetic lifestyle.

And when I stop laughing I realise that humour is a wonderful thing, a very good omen with regard to my comeback. In five weeks' time I have no doubt I will have rediscovered the better parts of me. I can win this thing, I truly believe I can.

So as part of my training regime I must head outside into the world every day. There are delights as well as demons beyond my four walls. And soon I will slip back, free and willing, into the warm and numb beauty of American life.

———

VIII(i) They gave the academic terms quaint names over there. Michaelmas, Hilary, Trinity. But a week before Michaelmas began there came Freshers' Week, a time to settle in before the onslaught of academia. And every night throughout that week the two of them found some time alone in Jolyon's room. Cocktails and liberty. Justice and nubs of cannabis resin. The world rejigged and smoothed and social inequality banished forever in their chatter, their grand world schemes.

Chad unloaded himself more and more in Jolyon's presence, spoke ever more freely, and to hell with his twitchy mental censor. One day he thought he might even talk to Jolyon about his father, the daily look in his eyes that said there was something disgusting and wrong with his son. And Jolyon would do nothing but listen and shake his head. And then perhaps they would eat a whole pizza together.

Toward the end of that first week, with smiles and mock indignation, they began to argue pleasantly over whose idea the Game had been. Just days after the first spark, Jolyon began to claim the credit. Chad, however, became convinced the idea had been his own. Both sides vigorously submitted their evidence but neither would admit defeat.

Had they argued about the Game many months or any number of years later, then neither of them would have fought for the credit. They would, both of them, have bitterly ascribed blame to the other.

For almost a week they had only a vague idea of how the Game would be played, just a few principles. A large financial reward for the winner. Numerous consequences for losing – like teenage dares – at first just embarrassing, later on mortifying. Sizeable deposits to ensure the performance of consequences. A gradual escalation. And the dares had always to remain purely psychological, nothing physically dangerous. A game of the mind.

But the large reward for winning quickly became an insurmountable issue – Chad the farm boy on a scholarship and financial aid, and Jolyon, the product of divorced Sussex schoolteachers, only moderately better off than his American friend. The precise make-up of the Game hardly seemed worth pinning down while funds remained an obstacle.

VIII(ii) 'Oh, that's a face I would definitely never tire of seeing on the end of my cock.'

Jolyon and Chad already knew which girl Jack was referring to without having to follow his eyes.

Jolyon sighed. '*Jah-aaaack.*'

'What?' said Jack, turning to see two disapproving faces. He bunched his shoulders and held out his palms. 'Don't you dare judge me. You think it. I just say it.'

The cliques and cabals were already forming at Pitt. In each case there was a central core around which the groups formed, a heart dense enough to begin the accretion of human mass. Often a group would take shape around a shared interest such as rowing or rugby or studying *Beowulf* in its original Anglo-Saxon. Or a clique might orbit around qualities such as money or beauty or pretension. But Chad couldn't describe his own group's defining feature. He felt it peculiar that he could label every other clique but his own. Perhaps Jolyon was the only thing that defined them. They were all the sort of people Jolyon liked – the normal ones at Pitt, Jolyon would have said.

They had met Jack a few days earlier and the customary introduction had included the information that Jack was studying history. A couple of mathematicians arm in arm had passed them by where they stood in the shadow of the college tower. She in severe skirt, he in severe sweater. Michaelmas term wasn't even yet under way and already they had found love. Jack began to joke about how he imagined mathematicians might have sex, nasally reciting the instructions for the missionary position in terms of computer subroutines such as, 'Thirty, insert penis. Forty, withdraw penis. Fifty, go to thirty.' And when he finished the skit he said, 'Because I have every right to judge, of course. Historians have always been known as the sex bombs of higher education. Maybe that should be our motto – historians, the scholars who put the *stud* into study.'

Jolyon thought self-mockery was perhaps the best of Jack's redeeming features. At least while laughing at the world Jack knew himself to be very much a cog in the grand comedy of life. And Jack was always happy to exaggerate his own flaws and shortcomings if he thought his own distortion might entertain those around him.

Now the three of them were standing together in the crowded university examination halls, students chattering, stirring the air with excitement and dispute. Around the edges of the hall were arranged a number of stalls side by side.

'Oh please, we just have to go and speak to those laughing boys!' said Jack.

They were at the Freshers' Fair, an event run to showcase for the new students the diverse multitude of thrilling societies they could join – newspapers to write for, sports clubs to join, debating groups to conquer. There were societies for aspiring actors, tiddlywinks players, communists, morris dancers, Francophiles, genealogists, knitters, hunt saboteurs, homosexuals, lesbians, chocoholics . . . There actually existed an agricultural society offering students the opportunity to plough for the university. Jack, being interested only in approaching stalls representing the sorts of societies he would never join, had asked them how one could possibly plough for the university. Did the university require farmhands? Was there a university flock and did they supply wool to the radical knitters three stalls down? Did they own an abattoir? Could a cash-strapped student earn extra money slaughtering ungulates for his university?

It was really very simple, they responded, pitying Jack with their looks and tone. Regional and national ploughing contests took place and if you proved yourself a good enough plougher then you could plough for the university.

Ploughing contests. Of course! Jack had slapped his head, apologised for his ignorance and made his exit.

The nomenclature of each society invariably concluded with the word *Soc*. So there was Drama Soc, Footy Soc, Tennis Soc and Weather Soc. Psi Soc was stationed in one corner, and not far away, their eyes filled with hatred for Psi Soc, were the representatives of Physics Soc. There were two socs for players of Dungeons & Dragons. Jack interrogated both to establish their differences which transpired to be that while one group favoured dressing up as wizards and orcs to act out their fantasy lives in the local countryside and caves, the other group insisted that games remained confined to the snugs of ancient pubs or cosy college rooms. Each soc utterly abhorred the other.

Meanwhile, Jack's latest target was locked in his sights. He stood with his hand to his mouth, pointing at a sign that read 'Sock Soc'. Above the sign was strung, between two broom handles, a blue nylon washing line. And fastened to the line, using old-style wooden clothes pegs, hung a large collection of different varieties and colours of socks.

Jack started striding purposefully toward Sock Soc's stall. 'Look at these two laughing boys,' he said over his shoulder, 'Tweedledum and Tweedle-fucking-dee.'

In fact, the two representatives of Sock Soc appeared only slightly overweight and wore name tags, one reading 'William' and the other 'Warren'. The name tags were designed in a sock shape with the names curling unevenly around the heels.

Upon arriving at the stall Jack leaned his elbows on the counter. 'Please, my friends, tell me everything I need to know about Sock Soc. I find it such a fascinating proposition,' he said. 'The name . . . it's . . . it's ingenious.'

'Sock Soc is a society for the discerning socker,' said William.

'We don't, however, meet regularly,' said Warren.

'The meetings are rather . . . *ad sock*,' giggled William.

'When we do gather, we like to discuss philosophical matters.'

'By which Warren means we engage in . . . *sock*-ratic dialogue!'

'I am the president of Sock Soc.'

'But I am the true power behind the throne,' said Warren.

'Some people have called it . . .' (now they spoke in unison) ' . . . a *sock-puppet* regime.'

Warren, having just about contained his laughter behind ballooning cheeks, then continued their pitch. 'Naturally you do receive certain guarantees as a member of Sock Soc,' he said, trying hard to appear serious now.

'Yes, we promise never to give anyone the sack,' said William.

Warren concluded with a smirk, 'No, we just give them the sock!' he said, producing from nowhere a pink-and-blue argyle to illustrate his point. Now they were both smiling and they held the pose together for several seconds while looking immensely proud of themselves. The scene reminded Jolyon of a holiday photograph, a humorous tableau snapped on a seaside pier.

For the first time since they had entered the Freshers' Fair, Jack had been rendered speechless. He stared in shock at the pink-and-blue argyle and turned very slowly around.

Chad, whose attention had been focused elsewhere for some time, sensed the movement and his mind snapped back to his friends. He looked toward Jack, who was walking away gingerly, and became concerned. Perhaps something was wrong.

When he had tiptoed the length of a tennis court away from Sock Soc, Jack finally allowed himself to laugh, an explosive outburst, his body creasing and tears squeezing from his eyes. 'Sometimes I wonder why the fuck I came to this place,' he said. 'You know, there *are* normal universities in this country, places full of normal people. I could have gone to one of those.'

Chad wondered what he had missed. Sock Soc had seemed such an innocent proposition. But he soon lost the thread of his friends' conversation.

Jolyon shook his head solemnly. 'Learning is about more than just books, Jack. And I think we've all learned an important lesson today.'

Jack nodded. 'The abortion procedure remains very much undervalued by the interbreeding classes.'

'Thank God I met you, Jack. I could have ended up with friends who consider garment-based puns the highest form of wit.' Jolyon clapped Jack on the shoulder and looked profoundly grateful. 'Just what in the hell do you think is going on with those two?' he said.

'I think it's pretty obvious,' said Jack. 'Tweedledee won't admit to himself he's gay. Not until he's fifty-five, been married for thirty years and is the Member of Parliament for Sutton and Cheam. Meanwhile Tweedledum will be dead in ten years' time after a tragic accident involving an adventurous bout of autoerotic asphyxiation. His latest beard will find him cock-out and lifeless in a cheap hotel room with a dog-eared copy of *Bodybuilders Monthly* and a sock stuffed with satsumas inserted most of the way into his mouth. Probably the pink-and-blue argyle.'

'I don't know if I can really laugh at people like that,' said Jolyon.

'I can,' said Jack. 'It gets me through the dark self-loathing hours. Well, that and alcohol. On the subject of which, anyone for a pint?'

VIII(iii) The reason Chad had not followed Jack's encounter with Sock Soc was because he had become distracted. Instead of witnessing William and Warren's duologue, Chad's attention had been snagged by the next stall along. Its sign was much smaller than most. 'Game Soc', it read, the words handwritten on a piece of paper no larger than a golfer's scorecard.

Game Soc's stall was not manned by grinning sophomores. Instead, behind its counter there stood three older students, postgrads perhaps. And not a single one of them was wearing a name tag.

Earlier Chad had watched from a distance as two boys had approached Game Soc. The encounter hadn't lasted long. Although Chad hadn't heard the conversation, he had seen Game Soc's reaction – the tallest of the three, his eyes distant and uninterested, shook his head three times and mouthed the words no no no.

Now two girls were approaching, the sort of girls whose appearance Chad imagined might soften the hearts of Game Soc's stony representatives. He moved a little closer to hear.

'Hello,' said one of the girls. 'We saw your stall, and we were wondering what sort of games you play at Game Soc.'

'What sort of game did you have in mind?' said the tallest. He said this with no trace of suggestion, not even a hint of innuendo in his voice.

'Well, I like party games like Twister,' said the second girl.

'No,' replied the tallest, looking away.

'Any party games at all?'

'No.'

'Board games then?'

'No.'

'Well, what sort of games *do* you play?'

It was the second tallest member of Game Soc who spoke next. 'I don't think you're quite Game Soc material,' he said to the girls.

'But you don't know anything about us.'

Game Soc's two shorter representatives exchanged glances. They seemed to communicate something wry, or perhaps something condemnatory, it was hard to tell.

Finally the shortest member of Game Soc spoke. 'Let's none of us waste any more time now,' he said.

'Well, I think you're all tremendously rude,' said the second girl. 'There are all sorts of societies who showed a great deal of interest in us.' She waved a stack of handouts to prove her point.

'You don't even have any leaflets,' said the first girl. 'No one's going to join your stupid little soc anyway.'

Game Soc's three representatives remained motionless, their expressions unchanging, and said nothing more.

The girls left, nodding to each other as they went, outwardly very much in agreement. Game Soc was for losers. But Chad also saw in their movements a sense of defeat. Two sails limp at sea and the air short of breath.

For a brief moment Chad admired the cruelty of Game Soc, even felt some small and vicarious enjoyment. If only he could be so . . . But then he performed a quick mental check and shifted his sympathy wholly to the girls.

Jack and Jolyon were moving away down the hall. He followed them, several steps behind, only half listening as they talked. Something about abortion, puns, satsumas. Chad couldn't stop thinking about what he had witnessed at the Game Soc stall.

'Well, the college bar's closed so how about the Churchill Arms?' said Jack.

'Let's go,' said Jolyon.

'No, wait,' said Chad. 'I just want to visit one last stall.'

—

IX(i) I am still abuzz from my time spent outside. (I will try to forget the ugliness of its ending.) I now feel so fresh in my mind that I barely require mnemonics to perform my afternoon routine. I use these precious hours not only for writing but also in preparation for less lucid days.

I go to the cake tin in the kitchen and dole out three weeks' worth of pills. (I have only a limited supply of ice-cube trays in which to keep daily doses.) I delight in unlocking child-safe lids and tearing open new boxes. I ease pills from their foil-covered trays with my thumbs, a diversion as pleasurable as playing pop with a fresh sheet of bubble wrap.

I have accumulated an impressive pharmaceutical collection. Diazepam, lorazepam, Codipar, diclofenac, Vicodin, dihydrocodeine, OxyContin, Percocet . . .

I adore the strange names of these drugs. I think the exoticism forms part of the appeal, like the philatelist's enjoyment of stamps issued in strange and distant lands.

Of the many collectors' stratagems I have devised over the last fourteen years, simple blackmail has often proved the most effective. A naive doctor, an older gentleman, usually. Doctor Proctor is nearing the end of his career rainbow, his retirement gold awaits. You lead him gently into overprescription and soon you have him where you want him. Your requests increase, new varieties, everything in greater bulk. He says this is not possible, you start throwing names at him. Medical councils, local politicians, newspapers. Being a journalist, you tell him, you can always claim you were carrying out a sting. He is already in over his head, the risk is all his.

Your collection grows.

IX(ii) I stop typing to take in a lungful of world, to breathe in its scents as I stand by my window. And that's when I see something wonderful. Small and fading in the southern evening sky, I catch the returning airplane's loops and swoops just a moment before they start to melt away. HELLO NEW YORK, reads the sky. And then a few seconds later, when its first-written letters have faded, O NEW YORK.

I clap my hands and the air in my soul turns bright.

And while I have been describing to you this propitious sight, its cryptic significance has dawned on me. Yes, I must stop taking my pills. I am in serious training, the outside world is my medicine now. I must wean myself off them.

And I promise. I won't forget. Starting tomorrow.

■■■

✗ They were arranged in height order with the tallest at the left. He wore a single-breasted jacket, woollen and greeny-grey, and beneath this a crisp white shirt with only the topmost button unfastened. The shirt was tucked into jeans with a snowy fade to them, half a decade or more out of date. Tallest's haircut was short and neat, the hair parted to one side. He wore spectacles with large teardrop lenses like those of an aviator's sunglasses. He had about him the air of a young London accountant dressed for a weekend in the Cotswolds. Twenty-five but going on fifty.

The other two were similarly dressed with jeans and tucked-in shirts but without jackets or glasses. Middle had black hair both on top of his head and sprouting from his nose like frayed electric cables. Shortest was a fading blond. They looked like science postgrads, serious types when they weren't quoting from Douglas Adams or Monty Python.

Chad was normally so nervous but now he was leading from the front, first up to the stall and planting his palms with intent. Jack had seemed ready to say something but Chad snatched away the opportunity. 'I have a proposition for you,' he said, 'for an entirely original and inventive game.' No one from Game Soc flinched. 'But I can turn straight around right now, if you don't think original and inventive ideas are your thing.' He lifted his hands and made to leave.

'Continue,' said Tallest.

'Six people, a number of rounds, each one separated by a week. A game of consequences, consequences which must be performed to prevent elimination. These consequences take the form of psychological dares, challenges designed to test how much embarrassment and humiliation the players can stand. Throughout the rounds players who fail to perform their consequences are eliminated until only one is left standing.'

Jolyon moved forward to stand shoulder to shoulder with his friend. 'The game takes place in utter secrecy,' he said, joining in and feeling it was important to mention secrecy early on in the sell.

'Yes, complete secrecy is vital,' said Chad.

'Success within such a game would rely upon a mixture of luck and skill,' said Jolyon, 'just like in the real world.' And then he reflected upon the analogy, this being the first time he had thought of it. Yes, he liked it, a game of life.

'Each player will be asked for a security deposit,' said Chad.

'Yes,' said Jolyon, 'failure to perform a consequence results in loss of deposit, which has to be a not inconsiderable sum. And any lost deposits get added to the grand prize.'

'Stop,' said Tallest, raising his index finger. And then he said, 'Name please,' while looking at Chad.

'Chad Mason.'

Middle took a small pad from his jeans, then a pen from his shirt pocket and wrote something down.

'Name please,' repeated Tallest, looking at Jolyon this time.

Jolyon said his name and again Middle made note of it.

'Continue please,' said Tallest.

'And I'm Jack,' said Jack, 'Jack Andrew Thomson, no P in Thomson.'

Middle made no movement of pen toward paper.

'Continue please,' said Tallest again. 'And tell me in more detail about these consequences.'

Jolyon looked to his friend. They had not discussed the Game all the way down to its dots and crosses.

'They start out as humorous dares,' said Chad hesitantly.

'Yes, humorous dares,' said Jolyon, playing for time as he tried to snatch some ideas from his mind. 'And it would fall to all the players as a group to finalise the details, but in the early stages consequences would prove merely entertaining, only a little embarrassing. For example, you would agree to advertise to the entire college – using posters, a note in the weekly newsletter and so on – that you would perform a solo singing concert at a certain time, in a certain place.' Tallest's expression did not alter. 'Or a magic show,' said Jolyon. 'Magic's so passé, don't you agree?' Tallest continued to look unaffected. 'It wouldn't stand a chance of going down well at Pitt,' said Jolyon.

'Or something as simple as turning up to one of your tutorials bare-chested or maybe wearing a bikini top if the consequence were drawn by a girl.' said Chad. Briefly he pictured a particular girl in a blue bikini top. He imagined the lines of her shoulder blades nuzzling the leather armchair in a tutor's room, an essay resting lightly on her lap like a starched white napkin.

'Or the opposite,' said Jolyon, slightly desperately now. 'You have to wear a suit and tie for a month.' Jolyon looked at Tallest and felt a sense of the sand in an hourglass falling too quickly away. 'And not only would you lose your deposit for the non-performance of a consequence but you would also lose your money if you revealed to a single person outside of the game why you were behaving in such an eccentric fashion. As we mentioned, secrecy is vital.'

'And then round by round the consequences would become tougher,' said Chad. But then he paused because to continue speaking, his imagination would have to venture into territory they hadn't yet explored.

'We don't intend to put anyone in danger and we wouldn't ask anyone to do anything excessively illegal. It's not that sort of game. But like Chad said, the consequences would become tougher and more embarrassing. But for me, that's one of the most interesting elements of the Game. Embarrassment is in the eye of the beholder, don't you agree? Personally the idea of singing in public would terrify me so much I might throw in the towel and forfeit my security deposit on the spot. Other people might have no problem with singing, the person who drew such a dare might even be a great singer. It's all definitely very psychological rather than physical. And that's one example of the element of luck involved.' Jolyon was playing for more time, hoping some appropriate escalation would simply appear wholly formed in his mind. 'You might, for example . . . you might ask someone to run naked three times round front quad.' Jolyon flinched inside. Like drunken rugby players, he thought, how painfully unoriginal.

'Or put on an art exhibition,' said Chad, regretting the words as soon as he spoke them.

Tallest leaned back a little. The interest that had thrust forward his shoulders had begun to wane. He looked away from Jolyon and Chad as he readied himself to speak.

Jack quickly cleared his throat. 'We had some more thoughts as well,' he said, although this was in fact the first Jack had heard of any such game. 'Ideas such as having to propose something highly illiberal in front of the lefty student union, having to forward a motion that could be interpreted as racist or sexist . . . Those are the hot-button issues that fire them up most of all. You can't beat a good bit of lefty rage for entertainment.

'Or you could give a lecture on Margaret Thatcher,' Jack continued, 'and claim that rather than her being a villain, she's your personal heroine. You have to tell a crowd of smug liberals how vital it was to kill Argentines in the Falklands and she saved the economy by giving the nation's miners a really good kicking.' Jack grinned as he became more and more amused by the thought. 'And then you lean on the lectern and watch the crowd just fucking explode like you've kicked over their cosy little anthill,' he said. 'Just imagine the liberal pandemonium. There's not a single person in college would *ever* speak to you again.'

Now Tallest appeared interested once again. 'Any more?' he said, his tongue emerging speculatively from his mouth.

'Oh, *fuckloads*,' said Jack. 'And it gets darker, much darker. But that's enough to give you a taste.'

Tallest turned to his left. 'Take down his name,' he said.

'No P in Thomson,' said Jack while Middle scribbled a third line on his pad.

'So why, may I ask, are you coming to us?' said Tallest.

'Funding,' said Chad.

Game Soc's representatives exchanged looks, then quickly and silently reached their decision. It was the first time any of them had smiled and now all three of them were smiling unanimously.

'How does ten thousand pounds sound?' said Tallest.

'This is not an unconditional offer, you realise,' said Middle.

And then Shortest added, his voice careful but nonetheless keen, 'We would have to see a more formal proposal. A side of A4 should suffice.'

'I'm sorry,' said Chad, 'ten thousand pounds? You said ten thousand, right?'

'Yes, that's something like twenty thousand of your American dollars, Mr Mason,' said Tallest. 'So long as you provide us with a more detailed proposal. And so long as we approve that proposal.'

Chad tried hard not to laugh.

'And we would have to insist upon one further important condition,' Tallest continued. 'At all times, and for the entire duration of the Game, at least one of the three of us would have to be present. This would remain applicable both during every round and for all consequences, where practicable. This condition couldn't be dispensed with. We would never interfere. We would always act as nothing more than silent observers unless some fundamental breach of the rules should occur. And one last thing, we feel your proposal should concentrate to a large degree on those consequences.'

'We like –' Middle consulted his pad – 'we like Mr Thomson's initial ideas,' he said.

'You might want to flesh out your plans in Mr Thomson's direction,' said Shortest.

Tallest then fastened the buttons on his jacket. 'We don't hand out money to any Tom, Dick and Harry, Mr Mason. It requires something rather special. But we feel your game has potential.'

Middle took down the small Game Soc sign while Shortest removed a blank business card from the back pocket of his jeans and wrote something down. 'This is the only number at which we can be reached. It's a mobile phone number, so I wouldn't waste any time trying to trace it to a college or any other establishment.'

'Mobile phone,' Jack snorted. 'Fancy rich fuckers then, are you?' The only student at Pitt who owned a mobile phone was a viscount and potential heir to one of Europe's largest fortunes.

Tallest took the card from Shortest, reached conspicuously past Jack and handed it to Chad. 'You have until Monday,' he said, 'and let's say no later than noon. You choose the venue, just call and let us know.' He rapped his knuckles twice on the ledge of the stall.

Chad thought he could see in Middle and Shortest's demeanours a sense of relief, or perhaps even gratitude. Tallest nodded to his shorter colleagues and they left together, Tallest first, mother duck leading the line. Very soon only one of their heads was visible above the throng of the crowd.

XI(i) I am woken by the sun today. I must not have closed the curtains last night, distracted by the thrill of my walk, my first day of training. (Must take more walks.)

For three years, since the onset of my hermitage, I have awoken only to sounds, the same dim hydraulic hum of the garbage trucks at work every morning, the Sisyphean task of removing the trash from the city.

But today I awake to the pleasure of an exciting new discovery.

Allow me first a brief explanation, some background. My apartment is a railroad flat, to use the local parlance. The name refers simply to the fact that such apartments are long and thin. Mine consists of three slender rooms, one after the other like the coupled carriages of a train. The kitchen is located at the back, the living room at the front and the bedroom in the middle. There are doorways but no doors and windows only at each end. And while the light from outside bleeds into the kitchen and living room just a little, my bedroom forms the heart of darkness in this railroad flat.

So this morning when I awake and find, for the first time in three years, my bedroom half lit by the sun, I discover the presence of a large closet at the foot of my bed. And I feel almost as if this closet has suddenly blinked into being. Yes, of course I suppose I remembered the presence of a *large* closet at the foot of my bed. I may no longer have a wife but I am not divorced entirely from my mind. However, my curtains and blinds have remained shut for such a long time.

Furthermore I am not an enthusiastic switcher-on of lamps or overhead lights. In the bedroom there are absolutely no working light bulbs. Because what else do I do in the bedroom but sleep? In the dark! In fact, for use in the gloomiest hours, I carry around a flashlight fastened to a loop of string that allows me to hang said flashlight from my neck. And when I need it, I use it. When I don't, I preserve its batteries. I use lamps or overhead lights only when a task requires two hands.

But I have become distracted from matters more pressing.

Yes, this morning in the lengthening sunlight, I notice a closet and the following thought occurs to me – I have not opened the closet for so long I have forgotten its contents.

I am leaving you here on the table a moment. Discovery calls out to me. I will report back immediately, I promise you.

XI(ii) A kind of hell. Nine, ten, eleven hours ago I descended into some circle of hell. That large closet is nothing but a vault in Satan's armoury of evil.

When I slide open one of the doors and swing my flashlight's eager eye across the closet's contents, I find the following: Monopoly, Chutes & Ladders, Buckaroo, Chess, Guess Who?, Clue, Operation, Risk, Backgammon, Connect Four, Scrabble, Yahtzee, Electronic Battleship, Uno, Checkers, Mah-jong . . .

At first I feel so happy to have stumbled upon such a treasure trove. I feel like Ali Baba in a cave of riches. So many games. So much training equipment. A mental gym, no less.

First I pull out that old family favourite, Monopoly, and choose my foes, Hat and Car.

I roll first and buy buy buy. I give my imagined opponents inferior strategies and trade properties at prices advantageous to myself. But even so I lose. The dice are against me, I couldn't buy a roll in a bakery. Such a stupid game with so much luck involved. Such a stupid fucking game that I don't even finish. I throw the board across the room and the paper dollars into the air. I tear up the Chance and Community Chest cards so I will never, ever have to play that stupid fucking game again.

I decide next to select a game that relies less on luck. I remove Scrabble from its dog-eared box, place the board gently on my bed and sense the excitement building again in my chest. I decide to make this a game for just two. (Not stacking the odds, you understand, merely improving them.)

I always play a tight and controlled game of Scrabble. Employing this strategy for myself only, as we near the end of the game I have surged almost a hundred points ahead. My crown awaits. And then . . . Which part of my brain despises me so? I see my hateful opponent has the letters IERGOAG. I sneer loudly when I realise these letters form an anagram of the word GEORGIA. Such a shame, I say to my opponent, that proper nouns aren't allowed. Maybe down in Atlanta they'd give you the points for the sake of state pride. But up here in Yankee New York, well, what can I say, old friend? Rules are rules.

My imagination idly picks up the word GEORGIA and allows its letters to swim above the board. And then . . . Am I really so deserving of so much misfortune? I see a floating GEORGIA winding itself around the letter P (from my superbly played PRETZEL). Yes, I look on with horror as ARPEGGIO appears. A fifty-point bingo and a double-word score to boot.

I can barely type these words I feel such rage. I hurl away the Scrabble board where it can languish in hell with Monopoly.

And how does my luck improve next?

It does not improve, that's exactly fucking how.

I unbox Operation and prepare to cure Cavity Sam of his diseases. I try to remove the wrench from his wrenched ankle and the pail to cure his water on the knee and the butterfly from his stomach. But every time the tweezers descend toward Sam, my fingers start trembling, very soon I twitch and . . .

Away, rapidly away, goes Operation, Chutes & Ladders, Backgammon . . .

Finally fate intervenes to save me. The batteries in my flashlight fail halfway through a woeful game of Buckaroo. Darkness has fallen outside, it transpires, so I jump off the bed and run into the living room intending to turn on the lamp. But something hits my toe and a split second later I hear the sound of breaking glass and feel a stabbing pain in the sole of my foot. I hop across the room and fumble for the lamp. When finally my fingers find the light switch, I see in the middle of the floor four empty glasses and the icy slick of a single broken glass. Blood is seeping from my foot.

I hop back to the bedroom and begin fumbling around for the game Operation. When finally I find it I return to the lamplight of the living room where I use my teeth to gnaw away the tweezers attached to the board. I grimace and then proceed to tweeze a large shard of glass from my foot. Due to my shaky hands, the procedure proves rather difficult and takes some considerable time.

And then with a great sense of relief, my foot hurting like hell, I remember my painkillers. I hop on my good foot into the kitchen where I see all my mnemonics untouched and in place. So it seems I have achieved nothing today. No water, no food, nothing at all. (Perhaps this explains the shaky hands.) I snatch up a pill but hesitate to pop it in my mouth, staring at this little blue caplet as if there is something wrong. And then I shake my head briskly, my mind cloudy, my foot stinging and throbbing. Quickly my painkillers become the first achievement of the day. And thus, soothed by my meds, I lie on the bed and close my eyes, holding my sore foot and thinking of all those losses. Thinking that, after HELL ONE, this day of defeat is a second poor omen. I have to be better than this. I must grow stronger.

███████

XII(i) They spoke of nothing but Game Soc all the way back to Pitt. When they passed through the lodge they saw Mark wandering down one side of front quad, yawning and wearing socks but no shoes. He had on a pair of headphones plugged into a Walkman that was clipped to his belt. When they approached him he pushed off the headphones and let them hang from his neck.

'Mark, there's no tape in your Walkman,' said Jolyon, pointing.

'Oh dear,' said Mark, 'is it that obvious?'

'And the play button isn't pushed down either,' said Jack.

'It's worked so far though,' said Mark.

'What are you doing awake so early, anyway?' said Jolyon.

'Can't sleep,' said Mark. 'I thought a walk might help. But there are some people round here I'm not so desperate to talk to.' He unclipped the Walkman and waggled it.

'Would a Hemingway daiquiri help more?'

Mark blinked serenely in the sunlight. 'Indubitably,' he said.

XII(ii) Mark was the cleverest person at Pitt, Jolyon had told Chad. Chad wasn't sure how Jolyon had judged this. Jolyon said the cleverest people were never aware of their genius but Mark seemed barely aware of anything. Always groggy, a voracious sleeper.

Jolyon had taken Chad on a mission of mercy one evening to awaken Mark so he wouldn't miss dinner a third night in a row. They eventually roused him, Jolyon having to resort to stealing his covers. Mark had been sleeping for sixteen hours straight.

He then yawned his way through dinner and subsequently drinks in the bar. In Jolyon's room that night he had catnapped between hash tokes and sips of gin rickey. Mark's lips made small murmurous movements while he napped. Perhaps, thought Chad, he was reciting equations, formulating new theories in his sleep. Mark studied physics. And like all of them in their circle, his area of study came in some ways to define Mark in the collective thoughts of his friends. Physicist, genius, mad scientist.

His hair stood in vertical coils, the effect somewhere between untamed bush and bedsprings. And he had a nose ill-suited to lethargy, it being pronouncedly aquiline. Whenever Mark's eyes began to droop, his gaze would drift down the slope of his nose and settle for a moment on its tip. And finally, with a gentle flutter, the eyelids would shut.

XII(iii) In his room Jolyon apologised for false advertising, he blamed his poor memory. It was not the right day for Hemingway daiquiris, the ingredients for Singapore slings were already arranged on the coffee table.

Chad listened in awe as Jolyon then discussed physics with Mark. Although Jolyon was studying law at Pitt, his knowledge encompassed everyone's choice of subject. Chad had heard him talk often to literature students about numerous obscure novels, which Jolyon always appeared to have read more of than they. He spoke knowledgeably with PPE students about politics, philosophy and economics. He chatted breezily with chemistry students about Mendeleev and the aesthetics of the periodic table. No topic seemed beyond him.

Mark spoke breathlessly about time being born in the instant of the Big Bang, other universes beyond the tails of black holes and how space was in fact composed of ten dimensions. To Chad it all felt like a high-speed thrill ride and you didn't have to understand the mechanics of the vehicle, you just sat back and enjoyed the view, the new worlds blurring by beyond the windows.

And that's when Chad realised Jolyon was right. Mark spent his life thinking on an entirely different plane to the rest of them and it was the immense weight of his thoughts that tired him out so quickly. Now the latest whirl of worlds was taking its toll. The creator of many universes was rubbing his eyes, apologising for yawning and stating that the time had come for his afternoon nap. 'Thanks again for the cocktail, Jolyon,' said Mark, raising himself wearily from the armchair.

'I'm coming to get you again tonight,' said Jolyon. 'You're not missing dinner again, not on my watch.'

'Thanks, Jolyon,' said Mark. 'Forgive me if I put up a fight again,' he said. 'I'm a terrible riser.' Mark left the room, stretching his limbs and scratching his head as everyone said their goodbyes.

Chad wondered if, when he left and headed home, he might find Mark curled in a quiet corner somewhere like the dormouse from *Alice in Wonderland*. Or like Alice herself, dreaming of extraordinary worlds beyond the ends of rabbit holes.

XII(iv) The three of them remained to discuss Game Soc.

They agreed they would sleep on the question of who the other players should be. But Mark would definitely be invited to fill one of the six spots. And Jolyon had no doubt Mark would accept. 'You heard him. He's desperate for something interesting to do.'

'And how about Emilia?' said Jack.

'Oh, she's great,' said Chad.

'She is, isn't she?' said Jolyon.

'That's five then,' said Jack. 'Why did we tell them six players?'

'I don't know,' said Chad. 'Six just felt right. Something to do with dice?'

'We need one more then,' said Jack and they all stopped to think.

But instead of thinking about a sixth player, Chad began thinking of Emilia, allowing longed-for scenes to loop and spool slowly through his favourite daydream.

XII(v) They had met Emilia while waiting in line for the cursory medical exam they all underwent before term started.

Jolyon and Chad and Jack stood together in the line. Mark came from the nurse's room and as he passed by they asked him what the procedure entailed.

'It's pretty basic,' said Mark. 'An eye test, a stethoscope, one of those cuffs for measuring blood pressure.'

'You mean a sphygmomanometer,' said Jack.

Emilia turned slowly from her spot ahead of them in the line. Her look fell piteously on Jack.

'What?' Jack complained. 'That's just what you call it.'

'And just what do you call someone like you?' said Emilia.

'Oh, so now I'm the arsehole for having access to a vocabulary, am I?'

Emilia responded with a single blink of her big green eyes.

Jolyon laughed. 'I'm Jolyon,' he said, 'and this is Chad. And that one's called Jack and I absolutely promise you he's way better company than first impressions suggest. And you are?'

'Emilia,' said Emilia.

'And what are you studying?'

'Psychology,' she said.

'Psychology's an amazing subject,' said Jolyon. 'I just finished reading some Fromm. I couldn't believe how political he is. The guy's a genius.'

'So you're studying psychology? I thought I'd met all the first-year psychology students.'

'No, I'm studying law,' said Jolyon. 'I was just interested in Fromm.'

Emilia's eyes narrowed and she cocked her head. And then she said, 'You know, you're one of the few people who, when I mentioned studying psychology, didn't say, *oh, so tell me what I'm thinking right now.*' Jolyon peered hard at Emilia. 'Is something up?' she said.

'Oh, nothing. No, it's just . . . you remind me of someone I knew for a short while.'

'Someone good, I hope,' said Emilia.

Jolyon seemed to slip away for a moment and an awkward silence fell over them.

Chad jumped in. 'What made you choose psychology, Emilia?' he said.

'That's a very good question, Chad.' Chad felt the familiar heat washing over his cheeks. 'I don't know,' said Emilia. 'Perhaps that's one of the things I'm hoping to find out before leaving here.'

XII(vi) While Jack drummed his fingers against his cheek, thinking through possible candidates for the sixth spot, and while Chad thought about Emilia and lingered in his daydreams, Jolyon was thinking of little else but Emilia as well. Or at least his thoughts began with

Emilia. Because soon he began to think about his month in Vietnam, the American girl with the same white-sand hair, the same sea-green eyes. The similarity was striking. They could have been sisters. The same coral lips.

———

XIII Games have awoken in me unpleasant memories of my divorce. Those boxes represent the only shared belongings I held on to when I left Blair four years ago. I even took the childish games we bought for the visits of her nieces and nephews. My ex-wife chose not to contest the ownership of Chutes & Ladders. Games had always been one of the sore points in our relationship, I couldn't bear to lose even the friendliest of contests. And Blair deserved better, she only ever wanted to fix me. Poor Blair.

But never mind yesterday, yesterday was merely a blip. I have bagged up the games with the garbage, there will be no more frivolous pursuits. And today has felt better. My resolve remains undiminished and my story progresses. My evening routine is complete. The evening is a season unto itself, Keats's autumn, all mists and mellow fruitfulness.

Chilli and rice. Check. Small nip of whisky. Check. Glass of water. Check.

Disrobe, brush teeth, take meds. One pink pill, one yellow, one blue.

And a spoonful of sugar helps the medicine go down.

Life is a game of balances. Work, play. Wake, sleep. Stimulant, narcotic.

My snug skin, my cosy mind, the gentle hum of me. Check.

———

XIV Chad knocked on the door. He could hear the faint sound of creaks from within, the groaning of floorboards as Jolyon moved closer. Chad sense a tightness in his chest. Was he nervous? That would be foolish, he wasn't here for any particular reason, only to hang out with Jolyon. At lunchtime perhaps they would go to the Churchill Arms. Maybe they would buy second-hand books beforehand or just sit and drink coffee and talk about the Game. So perhaps the feeling in Chad's chest wasn't nerves but a thrill.

When Jolyon opened his door, he smiled. He didn't say anything, he only turned around and moved toward his bed where a newspaper was spread out, every inch of the blanket covered but for a small spot to which Jolyon returned.

'I bumped into Prost at the bottom of the stairs,' said Chad, 'and he asked me to give this back to you.' He waved several sheets of paper covered in handwriting.

'Thanks,' said Jolyon, 'just leave it on the desk.'

'What's Prost doing with an essay on Roman law written by you?'

Jolyon looked confused for a moment. He picked up a page of newspaper and prodded it. 'There's a great story in here,' he said. 'Mikhail Gorbachev is being hotly tipped to win the Nobel Peace Prize next week.'

'Jolyon, I thought you said – and let me get the words just right – that Prost is a one hundred per cent, grade A, total *frickin* cock.'

Jolyon sighed. 'Look, when I finished my essay yesterday, I found him slumped over his desk in the library. It was midnight, he had nothing but a few torn-up attempts. His tutorial's today, the guy was panicking. So I lent him mine.'

'Even though he's a total *frickin* cock?'

'It seemed like the right thing to do,' said Jolyon.

'You mean you felt bad for him?' said Chad.

Jolyon looked even more confused than before. 'What's that got to do with anything?' he said.

Chad snorted. 'Never mind,' he said. He dropped the essay on Jolyon's desk and took the chair next to the coffee table.

Jolyon tore the Gorbachev article from the newspaper, placed it to one side and then turned his attention to Chad. 'Now then, would you like me to make you some breakfast?' he said.

Chad looked around the room. There was a toaster and an electric kettle. 'You mean a piece of toast?' he said.

'No,' said Jolyon, 'a real breakfast.'

Chad was doubtful. 'Sure then,' he said, 'go for it.'

Jolyon grinned and turned on the kettle. He went to his desk, opened a drawer and removed two eggs and a tablecloth. Chad watched in silence as Jolyon smoothed the tablecloth over the coffee table. Round and white, made of delicate lace.

'How do you take your tea?' said Jolyon.

'How do I what?' said Chad. 'Take? In a cup? What does that mean?'

'Milk? Sugar? Please don't say lemon.'

'I've never had tea in my life,' said Chad.

'Good,' said Jolyon. 'Then you take it the same way as me. Strong, no sugar, just a thimbleful of milk. Excellent.'

When the kettle boiled, Jolyon poured two-thirds of its water into a glazed brown teapot that he took from beneath the coffee table. He then removed the lid of the kettle and lowered the eggs inside with a soup ladle. Returning the lid to the kettle, he looked at his watch. Then Jolyon went back to his desk and from the same drawer as the eggs, found two thick slices of white bread and lowered them into the toaster.

He started to describe something he had recently finished reading. Jolyon made everything that interested him sound so wonderful. Chad said he'd love to read the book as well, so Jolyon went to his shelves, took out the book and handed it to Chad.

And then he said, 'Please keep it if you like it.' Jolyon looked at his watch. 'Five minutes exactly,' he said. With a pair of tongs he fished two tea bags from the pot then covered it with a padded tea cosy embroidered with bright bluebells and leaves. Then he started the toast. 'He was an alcoholic,' said Jolyon. 'All of the best American writers were.'

Chad looked at the book and felt ashamed that he had not heard of Raymond Carver. He read the back cover. It described Carver as one of the greats of American literature and here was an Englishman lending the book to him. Chad flicked through the pages, reading the names of the stories at the top of the pages, titles that were simple yet rich.

Jolyon was sitting by the kettle, staring at his watch. 'Nine minutes and twenty-seven seconds,' he announced, and then working fast he removed the eggs from the kettle with the soup ladle. He put the eggs in a cereal bowl and took them over to a cupboard door while he started to call out names. 'Faulkner, Fitzgerald, Steinbeck.' He opened the door, behind it was a mirror over a small washbowl. 'Hemingway, obviously. Hemingway was king of the writer drunks.' He put the eggs beneath the cold faucet and let the water run over them. 'Cheever and Carver. Truman Capote.'

Jolyon lifted the eggs from the water. He rolled them in the washbowl to loosen the shells and peeled each one quickly and skilfully, first removing a strip of shell from the middle of each egg as if whipping a belt from a pair of pants, then easing off their fragile hemispheres of shell. 'You go back a bit further and you've got Poe and Melville.'

As Jolyon finished the peeling, the toaster went *chunk*. He took two small plates from beside the washbowl. The plates were old and the glaze was cracked in places, he held them up for Chad to see as if displaying a brace of pheasants. 'From my grand- mother's tea set,' he said. 'She died just a year ago. I called her Grandma Fred until the day she died because that was the name of her dog when I was younger.' The plates were patterned with autumn leaves. Jolyon placed one slice of toast on each then crowned the toast with the eggs.

'You know the best thing about eggs?' said Jolyon. 'And it's not the fertility thing,' he added. 'An eggshell is like a chrysalis. But what's inside could be anything when it comes out, there's so much potential.' He held one of the plates at the level of his nose and stared lovingly. 'Think of everything an egg can do,' he said, 'the countless possibilities.' He turned the plate around and around on his fingertips.

'And you forgot to mention, they taste good,' said Chad, but Jolyon seemed not to hear and Chad felt embarrassed.

Also beneath the coffee table were stored a number of teacups and saucers. Jolyon took two of each and placed them on the lace-draped table. The cups had pink rims, the saucers pink borders, and both were patterned with roses and cornflowers. The cups rattled faintly on their saucers as Jolyon lowered them slowly to the table.

'OK, so perhaps with eggs it's the fertility thing just a little as well,' said Jolyon. 'You know, I always want to eat eggs the morning after sex. I really crave them. Do you think there's something deeply disturbing about that?'

'You mean Freudian disturbing?' said Chad.

'Maybe,' said Jolyon.

'Probably,' said Chad. They both laughed the same laugh, a small puff of air from the nose.

Jolyon climbed onto his bed to reach his window. On the ledge outside was a jug that matched the teacups. He brought the jug to the coffee table, removed a piece of foil from the top and poured milk into the teacups. Then he poured tea. The spout of the pot extended from a hole in the tea cosy.

'If I were a condemned man,' said Jolyon, 'I'd definitely choose eggs for my last supper.'

Jolyon put the breakfast in front of Chad. The egg was white and pure on the perfect golden toast. He handed Chad a fork and put a small wooden dish of pyramid-shaped salt crystals on the coffee table between them. Then Jolyon went at his own egg with a fork, mashing it and spreading it over the slice of toast. The yolk was a bright orange, halfway between liquid and set. 'Now this is important,' said Jolyon. 'And I'm never going to tell this to anyone but you.' Jolyon gave Chad his conspiratorial look. And then he said, 'It's the twenty-seven seconds that's the secret.' He finished by crumbling salt across the smeared egg and raised the prize up. 'English bruschetta,' he announced, and took a large bite.

Chad copied the procedure. He had no idea what bruschetta was. But the whole thing was delicious, it was perfect, and for a moment he chose to believe that twenty-seven seconds really was the secret. He could tell that Jolyon had meant it very much in earnest.

XV(i) A sudden thought. The spring air feels so fresh I should enjoy my breakfast on the fire escape outside my window. I hope you can excuse the insertion of an aide-memoire at this point in the tale. I prefer physical mnemonics but if I do not somehow mark things the moment they occur to me, they tend to slip away through the cracks.

Note to self: Must remember to place some trinket on the breakfast plate to remind me to breakfast al fresco.

Yes, a very good idea.

XV(ii) My intercom buzzes. Delivery.

I let him into the building but open my front door suspiciously and only a crack – I don't remember ordering anything. I sign his piece of paper and ask him to leave the box where it is in the corridor. When I am sure he is gone, I open the door wider and heave the large box into my kitchen.

A dozen bottles of whisky. I pull them out and line them up on my kitchen counter beneath the three bottles of whisky that stand on my shelf. Why did I order more whisky before I got down to my last bottle? And why so many?

I go to my computer to check. And there it is, my order confirmation from yesterday. Yes, I did indeed order twelve bottles of whisky.

I go back to the kitchen and shrug as I line up my bounty on the shelf. This is not exactly an unusual occurrence. I ordered more whisky than was strictly necessary – so what? Or perhaps some part of me yesterday was thinking more clearly than today. And when I think it through again the ordering of so much whisky makes more and more sense. Yes, there is much work to do writing my story. And then there is my recovery, my training. Long days of hard graft lie in front of me.

Twelve green bottles. Work work reward. A squirrel hoarding nuts for the pitiless winter ahead.

▬▬

XVI(i) It was the usual night-time scene, young bodies strewn around Jolyon's room, it was only ever the numbers that varied.

It was midnight and the bar had been closed for an hour. Jolyon, Jack and Chad, the three of them waiting, cherishing for now the secret of Game Soc. Emilia, Mark and Toby, sipping Tom Collinses as they chattered. The music from Jolyon's radio cassette blew over them all. The Stone Roses, 'I Wanna Be Adored'. An ascension of guitars and then breathy vocals like the cigarette smoke in the room, curling, climbing.

Toby reached for the ceiling and yawned. 'Well, I think that just about does it for me. Thanks for the cocktails, Jolyon.' But Jolyon seemed not to hear him, was scribbling something on a scrap of paper resting on his thigh. Toby shook his head briskly. 'Tutorial at two tomorrow and I have only half an essay. Love to stay longer otherwise.' He stood up and found his jacket. 'See you later.'

They all replied except Jolyon, who continued to scribble.

Emilia waited until Toby could not possibly remain within earshot but she spoke in a half-whisper anyway. 'What on earth have you got against Toby, Jolyon?'

Now Jolyon did look up. 'The guy's dad owns a racehorse,' he said, 'a thoroughbred.' Emilia shrugged. 'You know Toby went to Eton.'

'What does that matter? It's not Toby's fault.'

'I totally agree, Emilia. But it's a fact that at places like Eton they train their pupils to get into this place. Show of hands, did anyone in this room receive any special intensive training for the entrance exam? The interview?' No one moved. 'A good friend of mine, the brightest guy at our neighbouring school, got turned down here. No training. He froze in the interview. I only scraped through because I think Professor Jacks, my law tutor, is some sort of undercover Marxist on his own mission to even up the score. So I got lucky. And my friend got unlucky. And Toby got trained, just like his father's thoroughbred racehorse. Us here in this room, we're just the old nags. So we all need to stick together, that's massively important. Just like they do with their hereditary titles, their exclusive schools and old boys' clubs. So anyway, there's no way I was getting out the hash until Toby left. If he wants a smoke he can invite us to his room. And he can use some of his stabling expenses to buy the stuff.'

'But Toby's sweet enough,' said Emilia, 'he doesn't rub it in your face.'

'You're right, Emilia, sorry. I have nothing against Toby himself.

It's just he's not right for . . . I'll explain later,' said Jolyon, crossing something out on his piece of paper. 'OK then, Jack, second drawer, you can roll tonight.'

'Why can't Chad roll? I rolled last night.'

'Because last night was *best-looking-guy-in-the-room* night and tonight it's *funniest-guy-in-the-room* night. The honour's all yours again, Jack.'

Emilia looked over at Chad and he glanced down quickly. He had watched Jolyon roll a joint and memorised the procedure. But his own fingers had never heated and crumbled resin or curled cardboard into a roach. The licking and sealing and packing seemed like a process for practised hands.

'Jack's sister has a pony and you seem to like him,' said Mark, not opening his eyes. He was lying on the floor, his Tom Collins resting on his chest in the V of his T-shirt. To manoeuvre the drink from there to his lips was a model of efficiency.

'But I never had a fucking pony,' said Jack. 'Don't go labelling me some kind of pony owner. You know the quality of present I received when I was my sister's age? When *Stars Wars* was massive and everyone had a lightsaber and battalions of stormtroopers, I got a *Star Wars* jumper for Christmas.'

'That doesn't sound so bad,' said Emilia.

'Really? Well, for one, my mother knitted it herself. And then, two, she can't even fucking knit. The thing ended up looking like it read *Straw Arse*.' Jack rubbed the back of his neck. 'If I shaved off my hair you'd see thousands of scars left by hundreds of pairs of Doc Martens on my scalp.' He pretended to choke back tears, pestling the socket of his eye with his fist for effect. 'I had it tough. I know about tough.' He swatted his hand toward Jolyon, who was sitting on the bed. 'Tougher than Little Lord Fauntleroy up there on his throne.'

'It's my room,' said Jolyon. 'And anyway, you're welcome to sit here if you like.'

'No, I'm good in the cheap seats here,' said Jack. He bounced on the desk chair to make the thing squeak. 'My parents might not be schoolteachers but they taught me to know my place.'

'Do you have any idea how little a teacher in this country gets paid? Your dad is some kind of manager. You tell everyone he works for the Post Office so they'll imagine him plodding the streets with a sack slung over his shoulder. Meanwhile he's in his London office making scores of workers redundant every day.'

'He earns less than two teachers.'

'No he doesn't – he just bought a pony.'

'Fine, fine. We'll just call it a draw then.' Jack peeled a skin from its orange packet. He licked and split a cigarette, then started to burn the corner of a thumb-long piece of resin, chasing its snakelets of smoke with his mouth, nothing wasted.

Mark's eyes had been closed since his goodbye to Toby but he opened them now. He drained his drink and rolled onto his side, 'Have any of you been summoned to one of the warden's meet-and-greets yet?' he said.

'Yes, I'm due up this Sunday,' said Jack. 'You too, Emilia, right?'

Chad looked over at Jack and tried not to feel bitter toward him. The Americans were slated to meet the warden together as a group in three weeks' time.

'I'm subpoenaed next weekend,' said Jolyon.

'Well, one thing that makes it worthwhile, at least the wine's good,' said Mark. 'But the trouble is, the only topic of conversation the warden has any interest in is what your father does for a living.'

Emilia shook her head resentfully.

'So I was talking to that posh girl Elizabeth,' said Mark, 'when up he sidles in his weekend woollens and leatherette slippers. *Hellay*, he says, I'm *Rafe* Wiseman, Warden of *Peett*. How *jew doo*, and how *jew doo too*. And *jew* are, and *jew* are? Tell me now, what is it that your father does? So I told him my father works in a bookshop and my mother . . . Before I could say anything else, he'd already spun away, a blur of old bones. And then he says to Elizabeth, and *high abite* your father?' Mark looked around the room, their eyes all upon him. 'Well, it turns out the lovely Elizabeth's father is a judge at the Court of Appeal. Old Ralphy promptly led her away by the elbow. I don't think he said another word to anyone else at all.' Mark rolled onto his back and closed his eyes again.

'We're not keeping you up, are we, Mark?' said Emilia.

'No,' said Mark. 'Honestly, this is the time of day when I most come alive.' He repositioned the pillow beneath his head and became motionless again.

Chad tried to think of a recent injustice to share with the room but nothing came immediately to mind. And then he did think of something Pitt's liaison officer had said about preferential access to the computing suite, the computers there having been purchased with donated American dollars. But Jolyon spoke before he had time to weigh up the tale's worth. 'OK, Jack. I bet you a tenner Wiseman shows less interest in my teacher dad than your Royal Mail executive father. Assuming you don't lie and say postman as usual.'

'Come on,' said Jack, 'you have to allow me postman. Just to see him sprint away like he's bumped into a pigeon-toed leper.'

'God, you should hear yourselves,' said Emilia. 'Little boys turning this into some kind of game. My dad's not this, my dad's not that, but your dad's definitely the other.'

It had taken Chad some time to adjust to their ways. While Chad felt ashamed of being a farm boy, his new friends all seemed proud of their lack of breeding, everyone trumpeting their poor upbringing or the inadequacies of their high schools. Pitt College felt like America turned back to front and maybe also on its head. But gradually Chad had come to understand his friends, they had all made it to Pitt because of intelligence. They had, every one of them, proved themselves the cleverest at their schools. But intellectually they began here as equals, not one of them could yet be identified as top of the heap.

What they did have was background and so lack of privilege or money became the medals of honour they polished in public each day. They were the brightest of the blooms that had sprung from the harshest soils, like a long-distance runner from Kenya who had trained in the dust with no shoes. A natural. Each of them yearned for the great status that disadvantage could bestow, because in truth they all felt scared, fearful they had slipped through the net and they really didn't belong there at all.

Even Emilia played this game. She tried to sound weary of the boys, their public breast-beating, their peacock displays. They might as well have hung their disadvantages out from their jeans and compared lengths. She was like a schoolgirl disparaging schoolboys fighting dustily in the playground but then dating the one to emerge with the best of the scalps and the scars.

'Look,' said Jack, 'Mark's dad might just work in a small bookshop but he does *own* the bookshop. And his mum is a lecturer at LSE. And if you're a teacher like Fauntleroy's parents, you have at least been to university. My dad started on the counters, sixteen, straight out of school. No one from my family has even been to university.'

'You're just a bunch of soft southerners,' said Emilia. 'And you all lose, by the way, not that any of it matters.'

'Just being from Yorkshire doesn't automatically entitle you to win,' said Jack. 'But come on then. Let's hear it, blondie.'

Emilia lifted one of her legs and propelled the sole of her boot into Jack's shin.

Jack cried out in pain. 'Jesus, that *fuckingwell* hurt,' he said.

'That's right,' said Emilia, 'and next time you call me blondie I'll punch you in the face.'

'All right, all right,' said Jack, raising his palms in surrender. 'Go on then, tell us your tales of northern fucking woe.'

'My dad was a miner,' said Emilia.

'Oh Christ but that's perfect,' said Jack.

'What do you mean?' said Emilia, readying her foot.

'Nothing, nothing,' said Jack, waving furiously at Emilia's boots. 'Really, nothing bad. We'll explain later. We are going to tell them later on, aren't we, Jolyon?'

'Absolutely,' said Jolyon. He folded his piece of paper in half and placed it on his bedside table. 'A miner. That's . . . really fascinating, Emilia.' He had wanted to say cool but cool might have sounded insensitive. 'So what happened to him when Thatcher felt like going to all-out war on the working class?'

'He lost,' said Emilia. 'They all fought and then they all lost.' She glanced down and swallowed. 'He's fine now. It took a while but he's working at last. He fits kitchens. On and off. But the fight destroyed my parents' marriage.'

Chad sat quietly in his armchair pushed up against the wall. From this angle he could look at Emilia without turning his head, needing only to shift his eyes so she wouldn't catch him staring if she glanced his way. He kept telling himself to meet her gaze and hold it for just a moment too long.

'But how about you, Chad?' said Emilia. 'These little boys won't be happy until everyone's played.'

'I'm American,' said Chad. He shrugged. 'What do you think?'

'That you're culturally inferior,' said Jack, 'and you brazenly stole most of the glory of winning the Second World War from us.' He lit the joint and used it to gesticulate, trying to sound tough in his best American accent. 'Yo, *Emeel-yah*, Chad is from the *muddah fuhkin ciddy* of *Noo Yoick*.' He laughed. 'Sorry, that's the worst accent since Dick Van Dyke doing cockney.' Jack rehearsed his accent a few more times, then became quickly excited. 'Oh, I know,' he said, 'here's an idea. We should all fly out and stay with Chad for the summer. And make mine a pastrami on rye, even though I have absolutely *nofucking* idea what that means. And I'll eat mine on top of the Empire State Building. Like King Kong.'

Chad had quickly discovered that the British could think only of Manhattan at the mention of New York. But he didn't correct Jack. Chad hadn't told anyone in England about the farm on which he grew up, a world away from Manhattan. Except for Jolyon, of course.

Manhattan, that shred of land at the bottom of the state like the immeasurably modest penis of an ancient sculpture. Chad had visited only once as a child, a four-hour drive from the farm, the swine-stead upstate between the Catskills and the Adirondacks. And even four hours north of the city was only halfway to Canada. No, the British didn't understand that when you said New York you were speaking of an area the size of England. So Chad played the Manhattanite whenever prompted by false assumption. Although the role hardly suited him.

'Hey, of course,' said Chad. 'You're all invited. And pastrami on rye is a sandwich, Jack. Cured beef piled high between two slices of rye bread. And in New York City they're the size of your head.'

Jolyon smiled at Chad and chose to say nothing. If this was how Chad wanted it then Jolyon would play along.

But it seemed a great shame. Jolyon's own modest past felt like an unfair advantage when he had listened to Chad a few nights ago, both of them sipping Brandy Alexanders. And as Chad revealed more and more of his past, Jolyon had begun to envy and admire his new friend. The boy from the richest country on earth, a pig farmer's son. The smell of the family business smeared every day on his clothes. The morning wait for the school bus, standing in the too-still breeze with the sweet

62

and sickly shit-scent clumped in his hair. The green-tinged muck forever . . .

But perhaps Jolyon had over-varnished the story, added in detail that would allow him to cherish the tale even more. Because to Jolyon the notion of the peasant triumphant represented a romantic ideal. Chad, the boy who had risen from the straw and the sties to become his high school valedictorian. The straight As, the scholarship, his escape.

But if Chad didn't want to share the story with anyone else then perhaps there was something more, something Chad didn't want any of them to know. Not even him.

Jolyon slapped his thigh. 'So it looks like Emilia wins,' he said.

Chad wished that he had been the one to have declared Emilia's victory. He sucked on the joint and decided that marijuana tasted of sage and burnt toast, his mother's Thanksgiving stuffing. He blew the smoke hard and tried not to splutter. It felt like a bright balloon was inflating in his head.

Emilia's eyes had shut for a moment, it was safe to look at her, to linger a while. Chad felt soothed by her face like he might by a sunset. Emilia's blonde hair had fallen onto one of her cheeks and he imagined lifting the hair and hooking it behind an ear. The thin down of her face gathered the light at one corner of her jaw. He would be gentle and she would tremble, she would make sweet sounds of soft pleasure. Then she would roll into his arms, her nose nuzzling his neck.

Chad wondered if he must be lacking in testosterone because it was thoughts of closeness and clinches that dominated his desires. Perhaps his father was right about him. Perhaps real men had thoughts more carnal than these. Which was not to say that his puberty had passed by entirely without erections and bathroom ceremonies. But he had tried to limit himself. There seemed something wrong with *self-abuse* (why did his brain even use such a terrible, loaded phrase?), something disrespectful toward an unknown and future wife. Right now, most of all, he wanted to hold Emilia in his arms and kiss her gently.

She opened her eyes and smiled at him and briefly he smiled back. Then Chad let his gaze slide quickly away as if continuing a journey around the room. He hated himself for his pitiful spine-lessness. In that moment he vowed one day he would tell Emilia he loved her. But the setting would have to be right and the words ready. Just the two of them. Candles, good music. Billie Holiday, Chet Baker. And inside of him a half-bottle of wine, warm and inspiring.

XVI(ii) Jack passed the joint to Mark and then started to play with Jolyon's possessions, picking them up and absently moving them around the desk. There was a mug holding a bottle of aspirin, a toothbrush, a plastic fork and a strip of photo-booth pictures of Jolyon. The mug stood on Jolyon's diary and a thin volume on Roman law. And both books were balanced on two water glasses. In the bottom of one glass lay a thimble and also the small dried bud of a rose.

'Don't touch that,' said Jolyon. He hadn't noticed Jack's toying at first. He jumped up and snatched the mug from Jack's hand. 'Just leave my stuff alone, all right?'

'What is all this, a fucking art installation?'

'No, his daily to-do list,' said Chad and then, seeing Jolyon's lips draw back against his teeth, wished he'd said nothing at all. 'Don't ask,' he added. 'It's nothing important.'

Jack drew away from the desk and then wheeled himself back on the chair as Jolyon, muttering, began arranging everything back in its proper place.

Emilia tried to defuse the sense of tension now filling the air. 'So, Jolyon,' she said, 'when do we get to hear whatever it is you've been saving up for us all night?'

Jolyon turned his head, his lips softening then forming a smile.

'Right now, Emilia, straight away,' he said. He dropped the bottle of aspirin into its correct place in the mug and bounced back over to his bed.

XVII Let me clear one thing up. It has not been my intention to trick you, that is absolutely not the purpose of my story.

But I have just spent some time looking over everything I have written and it seems I might not have properly introduced myself. This failure was merely an oversight. Or perhaps it was my subconscious intention only to illustrate the distance I have travelled from my youth, another continent. So now a proper introduction. Hello, my name is Jolyon Johnson. And I am very happy to make your acquaintance.

And I have also realised there remains something else I have failed to explain. This story should serve not only as a warning, my confession. I am writing this story because I need to understand the real Chad, the one he kept hidden. Because if I can understand the real Chad, then maybe I can defeat him.

XVIII(i) Jolyon told them the tale but he allowed Jack to embroider its telling with colourful detail. The ploughers and Sock Soc. Impersonations of Game Soc that cast them as the witches from *Macbeth*.

'Count me in then,' said Mark, his eyes drifting with the hash smoke in the room. He was still lying on the floor but to indicate enormous enthusiasm he had hoisted himself modestly onto his elbows.

'Just like that,' said Emilia, 'you're in, Mark? No questions?'

'It's an interesting idea,' said Mark. 'There aren't many interesting ideas going round.'

'And just think of all those opportunities to humiliate Jack,' said Chad.

Emilia scowled. 'How can I possibly humiliate Jack any more than he already humiliates himself every day? With his own words.'

'No, that's fair enough,' said Jack, 'although it shows why the psychology student wouldn't stand a chance going up against . . . *History Boy*.' Jack mimed tearing open his shirt.

'Maybe he's right, Emilia,' said Jolyon, shooting her a provocative look. 'What if Jack can't be beaten?'

'Of course Jack can be beaten,' Emilia scoffed. 'Humour's his shield. All you have to do is work out what it's shielding him from and he's . . . *history*.' She winced. 'Pun intended. Very sorry.'

'See,' said Mark, 'the sweet-seeming psychology student's already one step ahead of the rest of us.' Mark let his elbows slide until his head was back on the cushion. 'Now *that's* interesting,' he said.

'Ten thousand pounds, Emilia,' said Jolyon, whistling. 'And wouldn't it be fun? It would probably bring us all closer together. We need to stick together, remember.'

Emilia shifted uncomfortably in the armchair. 'Well, it wouldn't be about the money for me,' she said.

'No?' said Jack. 'But think of all those pretty shoes you could buy, Emilia.'

'Just shut it, Jack.'

'Come on, Emilia.' said Jolyon. Chad recognised the edge in his tone, Jolyon's *don't disappoint me* voice. 'Just say yes, at least for now.' But Jolyon always seemed unaware of the weight in his words. Chad supposed he wouldn't be half as persuasive if his methods were only a trick. 'For all of us, Em.'

Emilia glanced down at her feet and then looked around at her friends. 'Fine then,' she said. 'I suppose I'm in. But I would like to know more about this strange little Game Soc before we go any further.'

Mark, his eyes closed, took a last puff of the joint and waved it in the air. 'That's almost the most interesting part of all,' he said, as Jolyon plucked the offering from his fingers.

'Well, I don't know who Game Soc are,' said Jack, 'but I know who they certainly aren't. They're not those closeted homosexuals of Sock Soc.'

'God, that's so homophobic, Jack,' said Emilia.

'What's homophobic about that?' said Jack, playing his outrage forcefully. 'Is it homophobic simply to recognise another man for what he is, a closet gay? To look at him and see in his eyes that he hides his true self from an uncaring society? Don't you first need to understand who a person really is before you can begin to sympathise with him? Is it really homophobic to notice when a man is suppressing his true hungers and desires? His dreams, his yearnings. His all-consuming love of long, hard man-cock?'

Jolyon coughed on his smoke, it rushed out of his nose and his eyes filled with tears.

'See,' said Emilia, 'you find homosexuality amusing, Jack. You joke about it constantly but there's nothing intrinsically funnier about gay sex than straight sex. It's all just trains and tunnels. Humour's your defence mechanism against anything that scares you. And it clearly does scare you. Fear, Jack, that's what a phobia is.'

'Listen,' said Jack, 'there's no question of fear. I for one happen to love the gays. Plus, I think we could all get along a whole lot better. Why can't we cooperate to reach our goals? I mean, take women for example. We want to fuck them and the gays love talking to them. Neither of us has any interest in the other act. So surely we could come to some kind of mutually beneficial arrangement.'

'I think they're spies,' said Mark, sitting up suddenly. 'Oh, sorry, Jack, not gay men. Game Soc. Which is not to say my thread's infinitely more interesting than your little stand-up comedy routine.' Mark and Jack exchanged looks like duellists appreciating the sport of the contest before Mark continued. 'It's well known that this university was for a long time, and probably still is, a recruiting ground for the British secret services. And by the way, I hear that your history tutor, Jack, is one of their talent scouts.' Jack nodded as he mouthed the words *it's true* to the room. 'Maybe Game Soc are on the lookout for young people with intelligence and initiative. And then this game, whatever we come up with, becomes our recruitment process.'

'But if they're British intelligence, why would they bother listening to me, an American?' said Chad. 'They rejected everyone else who went near them in about one second flat.'

'What, so you think Britain doesn't spy on America?' said Mark. 'And no doubt America spies on us. And much better, I bet. Maybe they see you as a potential double agent.' Mark finished his drink in one enthusiastic gulp. 'Look, we're all friends in this room. But that doesn't mean I expect us to tell the truth about ourselves all the time. And I'm sure it's the same with Britain and America's so-called special relationship. Anyway, who else might want to throw ten thousand pounds at us?'

'But we haven't even seen the money,' said Emilia. 'It might be a hoax, someone's idea of a student prank.'

'I know who has enough money to afford it,' said Jolyon. 'That secret society Toby was telling us about the other day. What are they called?'

'The Saracens,' said Jack. And then answering Emilia's enquiring look, he added, 'A posh rich-boys-only club. Remember those passport photos you sent in along with the room question-naires and forms a few months ago? Apparently the Saracens somehow get hold of the pictures of all the female freshers and sift through deciding which ones to invite along to one of their champagne-and-coke sex parties.'

'Elizabeth told me that at the warden's drinks,' said Mark. 'She said she received an invite to a mysterious champagne party just a week ago.'

Jack studied Emilia's reaction. 'Don't worry, Emilia,' he said, 'I expect your invitation just got lost in the post.'

Emilia raised her foot but Jack was ready. The desk chair had wheels and this time he scooted clear of the danger.

'Like I'd want to be leered over by a bunch of boys with dicky bows and Coutts accounts,' said Emilia. 'Stupid wankers.'

Emilia swore rarely and there was a short silence as if an amen had been spoken.

'But the trouble with it being the Saracens,' said Mark, 'is they don't sound like they have the imagination to spend their money on anything better than booze, coke, chasing girls and paying for repairs after they trash the restaurants they meet in.'

'And Game Soc's three didn't look much like they're into debauchery,' said Jolyon.

'Well, it doesn't have to be the Saracens,' said Chad. 'Aren't there plenty of other rich people here?' he said. 'And thousands of clubs. Or how about a psychological experiment – don't they often use students in those things?'

They all looked to Emilia. Although they had been at university for only a short time, already they deferred to each other on issues that might one day lie in their area of expertise.

'It wouldn't be considered ethical nowadays,' said Emilia. 'Not like back in the days of Milgram or the Stanford experiment.' She swatted the air between herself and Jack who was reaching over to offer her a joint. 'Get that thing away from me, Jack,' she said.

Jack shrugged. 'You might as well give in now, Em. Because you know we'll corrupt you one day. The bookies aren't even offering odds. You absolutely know we will.'

XVIII(ii) 'The most important thing to do first,' said Jolyon, 'is decide who else we invite to play. We need six. Right now we're only five.' He waved his piece of paper, a list of over twenty names and every one crossed out. 'I can't think of a single person,' he said.

'Why can't we plan the consequences first?' said Jack.

'Because this game is going to be fair and democratic. We won't decide anything else until there are six of us. Every player has to be present and we vote on everything.'

'Oh, so we're a democracy?' said Jack. 'And you just decided that on your own, did you, Jolyon?' He shook his latest cigar-like creation to better distribute the resin. He twisted its end and threw it to Mark who was holding the lighter.

'Jack, tell me, who came up with this whole thing?'

'I'm just saying,' said Jack. 'It's a joke, OK?'

Mark toked hard on the joint and puffed his cheeks as he held the smoke deep. After each exhalation he tried calling out a different name, another candidate for the last spot.

But none of them were right. Too rich or too full of themselves. Too pretentious, too smug. Jolyon's lips tightened with every rejection. 'Well, I can't think of anyone else,' he said.

Emilia looked around the room. 'We definitely need one more woman,' she said. 'Whoever the last spot goes to, she has to be female.'

'Agreed,' said Jolyon. 'Absolutely.'

'Then how about Cassie?' said Emilia. 'She lives next door to me.'

'Who the fuck is Cassie?' said Jack.

'Oh, you know who she is,' said Mark. 'Cassandra Addison. It's just that you know her better as Dee.'

'Oh, fuck me, not Dee,' said Jack. 'My first day here I arrived the same time she did and I nearly told my dad to drive me straight home. I got out of the car and she walked past carrying a stuffed rabbit. And I don't mean a toy, I mean a once-living once-carrot-munching *wascally wabbit*. And she was wearing some tatty old second-hand wedding dress. It looked like it must have been fifty years old.'

Jolyon pointed excitedly. 'You mean Havisham,' he said. 'Chad and I always call her Havisham. Big Dave – you know the Scottish guy with all the hair – he asked her out for a drink and she turned up at the Churchill in a wedding dress. He said he's going to need years of intensive therapy before he can even ask another woman so much as her name.' Jolyon picked up his list and his pen.

'Jack, why do you call her Dee?' said Chad.

Jack put down the book on which his joint-rolling assembly line was arranged. 'She's into writing poetry,' he began. 'I mean, I know half the people here think they're poets. But Dee's different. Dee Addison's on a mission. She says that when she's written five hundred poems – you're going to love this – as soon as she inks the final line of the five hundredth verse,' his legs bounced excitedly, 'she's going to kill herself.'

Mark blew the smoke out of him as fast as he could. 'Shit! No way,' he said. 'Mind you, if you ever catch me writing five hundred poems, you have my permission to shoot me.'

Emilia sighed. 'That's just not true,' she said. 'God, you can all be so tiresome.'

'It's absolutely one hundred per cent true,' said Jack, slapping his thighs as he spoke. 'Rory told us and he's her *Beowulf* tutorial partner. He went to her room to go over some notes and she was working on one of her poems. So he asked her what she was doing.'

'Why should we believe Rory?' said Jolyon.

'Look, no one could make all this stuff up,' said Jack. 'There's a whole lot more.' He leaned forward in his chair. 'She uses red ink and she has this big book with special parchment pages. Also she numbers each poem with large Roman numerals before the title. And that's why Rory calls her Dee. You know, Roman numeral for five hundred. And maybe she chose five hundred as her suicide target precisely because it's a D, right? D for death. I'm telling you, she's a proper fruitcake.'

Jolyon wrote Dee/Havisham on his piece of paper. 'And what number do we think she's up to now?' he said.

'I don't know for sure. But Rory said there were at least a couple of Cs at the beginning, maybe three. Who knows how fast she churns this crap out. But wouldn't it be great to have another suicide in college?'

Emilia struck too quickly for Jack this time. Her boot sole caught him at the same point of his shin as earlier in the night and twice as hard. 'That's a really horrible thing to say, Jack.' She wound up her body to slap him but Jack scooted away with his good leg. 'How can you even think such a thing let alone say it out loud?'

Jack grabbed his leg, lowered his sock and pointed to his shin. The red bud of his bruise would bloom purple tomorrow. 'Jesus,' he said. 'Look what you did to me.'

'What do you mean, another suicide?' said Mark.

'Five years ago?' said Jack. Mark shrugged. 'Christ, don't you ever read the newspapers or turn on the television, Mark, you ignoramus?'

Mark flinched. 'Sorry, guess I was too busy trying to understand the hidden nature of the entire universe,' he said.

'Well, excuse me, Dilbert Einstein,' said Jack. 'I mean, it was only the biggest news story for a month. Oxford student kills herself after bad mark. Do elite universities push too hard? Did drugs play a role in death of attractive brainbox Christina Balfour? No? She was studying Classics, failed her Mods, couldn't handle the pressure and jumped.' Mark shrugged and returned to his joint. 'I'm just saying,' Jack continued, 'we get friendly with some wrist-slitting type, and if we can just keep them alive until a week before Finals, I bet we'd all get granted sympathy firsts.'

Emilia jumped to her feet.

'Emilia, Emilia,' said Jolyon, 'come on. We all know Jack is a terrible, terrible human being. But if you use physical violence against him, you're only giving him the attention he craves. And there's also a very real danger that he might one day mistake attention for affection.' Emilia sat back down. She crossed her arms and made a face as if she had tasted something sour. 'Now then, Em,' said Jolyon, 'you live next door to Dee so maybe you know more about her than whether she likes to wear wedding dresses. Now this is important. Are her parents rich?'

'No,' said Emilia. 'Or if they are, or were, she wouldn't have the faintest idea. Her mum died when she was three or some-thing and God only knows who her dad was. She was taken into care. And then as a teenager she went through a series of foster-parents but they could never handle her for more than a year. So you bloody well deserved that kick Jack *effin* Thomson.'

'All right, all right,' said Jack, 'So she's Little Orphan Annie then. I'm truly and genuinely sorry, I didn't know.'

'Ladies and gentlemen,' said Jolyon. 'I think we might have our sixth player.' He waved his piece of paper like a flag, lowered it onto his thigh and underlined *Dee/Havisham*. And then he underlined it again.

███

XIX(i) The air feels fresh and my mind temperate today. Reading back through my words reminds me of several incidents from the past few days. Although I will admit to a few black holes, some lines I do not wholly recall writing. I discover a note to myself and immediately institute its suggestion. I place a matchstick in a coffee cup and the coffee cup on my morning plate. Yes, breakfast al fresco.

Which also prompts me to think –

Note to self: Remember to place your shoes on the bed. And when you come across them at night, find for them a place in the daily routine, beneath the second plate perhaps. Post-lunchtime walks every day would do you a power of good. Routine is vital.

XIX(ii) I remember that the outside world is my medicine now and so after my lunchtime routine I pull on my shoes and stand near my front door, by my apartment's rear window. While taking some deep breaths I look out through the glass, gazing at the rear windows of other apartments. I see a man who waves his TV remote like a magic wand, a woman forking out food for her fat ginger tom. Lower down I see dark yards, metal ducts, chain-link fences.

But then something more interesting catches my eye, a rooftop standing directly across from my own and fringed with a white picket fence. A roof garden with large blue-glazed tubs holding sapling trees, terracotta troughs full of flowers, tables and chairs. It reminds me of Blair, our own building's roof garden on the Upper East Side. Sipping rosé on cool evenings with neighbours, a life littered with surface pleasures. Everything I have lost.

XIX(iii) Down on the street I turn left and soon reach the shade of the park. I sit on a bench near the entrance, across from the stone chess tables clustered at the park's corner like mushrooms in a forest glade. There are only two chess games in progress but the seats at the other tables are full. I feel the old itch as I look at the games in progress. I get up and make my way along paths that curl and sweep around the park. I pass the dog run, lively with little dogs pedalling and scrabbling. Larger ones hooping its dusty length.

Despite my itchiness this has been a good start. Perhaps this was all I ever should have looked for from life, the pleasure of watching the world turn.

Leaving Pitt after less than a year, and never earning a degree, my dream of becoming a barrister was shattered. My snowballing nerves would not have made for a good courtroom orator in any case. So that was that. My life's ambition – crusader for justice, defender of the innocent – destroyed.

After my premature departure from university, I spent almost a year standing mournfully by a conveyor belt in a factory, returning each night to my small bedroom in my mother's house. And then out of the blue there came a surprise, a helping hand from the warden of Pitt. I moved to London to work for a legal newspaper, my first job in the world of journalism. I could write well enough and so it seemed I had finally found something at which I might excel. The theory was good but in practice the scheme proved unsound. I was a mediocre journalist. The timid creature I had become struggled to ask the pertinent questions. I wrote fine words about nothing. In every interview I felt wary of causing offence, I became someone who wished not to pry. People would tell me things when I was young, I had an interested nature, I looked out at the world with an appealing thirst. But I started to become a very different person in my twenties. Someone who looked only within and found shadows. The world clammed up.

I lived a solitary life outside of work. But eventually the skin of my guilt and grief began to split. I nudged out tentatively into the world. I even made a few friends. And then I met Blair, beautiful Blair, who thought she could fix me, who actually wanted to fix me. There is something that has always drawn me to Americans abroad. She was a Bostonian in London studying at the LSE for a year. The time limit made rapid action a necessity and I proposed to Blair before her course ended. We married in Fulham. We were happy, we were in love. But already back then I was thinking ahead to my thirty-fourth birthday. And escaping abroad made a good deal of sense for several reasons.

So we moved here to the States where I received my second leg-up in journalism, Blair's father pulling some strings at a newspaper. But of course I remained twitchy and timid. I was quickly pushed into rewrites, cut-and-paste jobs or sprucing up the words of bolder journalists at the paper, those with some people skills, some get-up-and-go.

And all the while Blair tried to fix me. Tried and failed. But in reality the failure was all mine. Next came the divorce and Papa Blair rushed back to his strings. This time he did more than pull, he tugged and tugged with all his might. The newspaper fired me within days.

And so, you see, the Game has taken everything from me. My education, the career I craved, the career I had, my wife, my happiness . . .

And now if I want any contentment in life, there is only one thing to do. The only way out is to win. Death aside, I can see no other way out of this trap.

But before I return to my training, I must place in front of you a question. Because there are two opposites to consider and before my story is told you must judge me.

What am I? Murderer? Or innocent?

XX She wore black. Jack looked disappointed. Although the dress did at least have some lace and frills. He leaned over to light her cigarette and asked her, 'So what happened to the wedding dress, Cassie?'

Cassie looked at him blankly. 'This is the wedding dress,' she said. She drew on the turquoise cigarette that had come from a tin of cigarettes in various bright pastel shades. 'But I had to dye it black.'

'Interesting,' said Jack. 'Why's that?'

Chad was sitting beside Jolyon on Jolyon's bed. He looked at the black dress again and now he could just about see it had once been a wedding dress. Then he looked at her hair. It matched the dress, black and sleek as vinyl records. Last time he saw her, her hair had been brown.

She blew smoke from the corner of her mouth. 'Well, I dyed the dress black because I'm no longer a virgin, Jack.' Cassie batted her eyelids sarcastically. 'So white isn't appropriate any more.'

Jack swallowed hard, his Adam's apple jumping in his neck.

'You should see the look on your face, Jack,' said Cassie. And then she turned to Emilia. 'He's much prettier when he's embarrassed, don't you agree?'

Emilia shrugged, enjoying the spectacle.

'I'm not embarrassed,' said Jack. He leaned back in his chair. 'So going back to your loss of cherry. What form did it take? Girl on top? Oral pleasure? Or a nice spot of anal perhaps?'

Cassie looked mischievous, she had a sly beauty about her. 'With less than half a boat crew, one can enjoy all three options simultaneously,' she said.

Jack laughed hard. 'OK, OK, you win,' he said, smiling at Cassie as if he was looking forward to many more battles to come.

Cassie rested her hand against her stomach and gave a bow, the gesture little more than an exaggerated nod. 'Don't worry, Jack,' she said. 'I'm not really into boaties. And I haven't been a virgin for some time. I dyed the dress black because I felt like dyeing the dress black.' She dragged on her cigarette and blew the smoke out in a thin stream. 'Why do you do the things you do, Jack? Like asking rude questions under the guise of being supposedly funny?'

'Because essentially I'm a cunt,' said Jack. 'Which is, to be fair to me, partly genetic. I come from a long line of utter cunts. And I suppose I have to admit, a little sheepishly, that I really quite enjoy being a cunt. Also it's the fault of my upbringing. Hippy bullshit parents, the sort who turn all conservative once they near forty. Whereupon they decide to dissolve the commune. All four of them.'

'You were brought up by four parents in a commune?' Cassie looked doubtful.

'It's true,' said Jack. 'Now bear in mind that with four parents there exist mathematically six possible coupling combinations. And I know for a fact that five of those combinations took place. It's complicated but if you ever want me to draw you a diagram . . .'

'Everyone fucked everyone,' Mark called out from the floor. 'He likes to make the ins and outs sound more complicated than they were, he thinks it sounds more exotic. But essentially what Jack's saying is everyone fucked everyone in every way possible, apart from his two dads. And if you get him drunk enough, he'll admit he even has his suspicions about that.' Mark tilted his drink to his mouth. 'And this is how one ends up with the emotional wrecking ball we all know and love as Jack Thomson, no P in Thomson.'

'Parents are too easy to blame,' said Cassie. 'And four parents might be called modest by some standards.' The room fell silent as Cassie, looking down, turned the tip of her cigarette slowly against the edge of the ashtray. Its ash now in a neat cone, she resumed smoking again.

Chad felt bad for Cassie but also a little jealous. He had fantasised often about being an orphan, adopted as a baby. Not the pig farmer's son but the secret child of an intellectual, a philandering writer, or a scientist who had died in an experiment gone wrong. It wasn't unknown riches that had been concealed from him in Chad's fantasies. He just wanted an explanation for why he was so different from his own family. At the very least he dreamed that one day his mother might tell him she had had an affair, the pig farmer wasn't really his father, their obvious physical resemblance was nothing but wild coincidence. Anything but *that* man's son.

Everyone else in the room was the product of divorced parents and Chad felt envious even of this. The exoticism of their broken homes, their splintered pasts. They had reasons to be interesting while he had excuses to be dull.

And then Cassie lifted her eyes, a cunning look spreading over her face. 'They say if you blow smoke in a man's face it means you fancy him,' she said. She sucked on the turquoise cigarette and sent its smoke in a line of quick quivering rings toward Jack's face. 'Do you think that's true, Jackie-oh?' she said.

Jack affected a cough and waved his hand to break up the smoke. 'Then if you shit in his hair it must be true love,' he said. 'So anyway, how's the latest grand opus of Pitt's most bohemian poetess coming along?'

'Like pistons,' said Cassie. 'Fast as wild rutting stallions.'

'And how many little verses are you up to now?'

'Who's counting?'

Jack now played his startled look. 'Well, you are apparently, Cassie. Or so I've been reliably informed. Unless you've been telling lies to make yourself sound more interesting?'

Cassie wrinkled her nose, a thin nose and freckled. 'I'm not interested in interesting,' she said.

'So is it true,' said Jack, 'that when you've written five hundred poems, you're going to kill yourself?'

'If I said yes, would it give you a big old hard-on?'

'I'm just trying to separate the truth from the student bullshit. There's so much of it round here you have to watch where you step. But then you are studying English Lit, so it pretty much goes with the territory.' Jack waited to be challenged on this point but no challenge was issued. 'So about this suicide pact with the Muses . . .'

'Just go right ahead and erect yourself, Jackie-oh,' said Cassie.

She tried to sound indifferent but there was a trace of defeat in her voice.

'I'll take that as a yes then. And taking the Roman numerals into consideration, we came up a special nickname for you. We're going to call you Dee. Dee for five hundred, Dee for death.'

Chad shrank inside. He didn't want this girl to think he had been part of a group talking in secret about her, discussing rumours, concocting names.

'I love it,' said Dee, clapping. 'Yes, Dee it is, you have my absolute approval. And meanwhile I'm going to call you Jackie-oh, Jackie-oh. Like Jackie Onassis. You've got her far-apart eyes and also that whiff of bringing tragedy to all those round you. And when I get back to my room I'm going to write a poem all about you, Jackie-oh, my first ever limerick.'

Jack stared at the ceiling. 'Nothing rhymes with Jackie-oh,' he said.

'Ralph Macchio,' Mark called out from the floor. 'The kid from *Karate Kid*.'

'No, no,' said Dee. She twisted her fingers creatively in front of her. 'The first line would read something like . . . *A boy who was surly and blunt.*'

Jolyon rapped his knuckles on his bedside table. 'Well, I for one could listen to this all night long. And I know Jack could keep going possibly forever. But right now we need to talk about the Game,' he said.

———

XXI Early on in my morning routine I find a cup on my breakfast plate and a matchstick inside the cup. It takes me a few minutes but then I decipher the new mnemonic.

Cup: tea. Matchstick: fire: fire escape!

And so in the morning I eat breakfast perched on the giddying slats of my fire escape. I feel like a tourist enjoying a fine vacation breakfast, a rare meal eaten with a warm sigh and unhurried eagerness for the day.

My neighbour across the street is also breakfasting on his fire escape. He has a sunlounger in which he sits, sockless, filling in the crossword and dabbing his finger to pick up the crumbs of his croissant. And then it comes back to me – this was part of my routine three years ago, before I shut my curtains and blinds. We used to acknowledge each other whenever we were outside at the same time. He notices me looking across and tilts his head as if pleasantly surprised to see me. And then he raises his cup.

I return the gesture, smiling, and my neighbour goes back to his crossword. I feel a new kind of strength flowing into my chest.

And then my mood changes. While sitting there it comes to me that last night I dreamed of the six of us. I don't think I have dreamed of us together for many years now.

Dreams can be so crude and unforgiving, they blur the subtleties of why and wherefore, the complexities of cause and effect. In last night's dream everything becomes entirely my fault. Blame points its finger squarely at me in the form of a single blunt metaphor. In the dream I have a gun, I am defending myself, I pull the trigger. Game over.

And I wake up, as I do every morning of every day, seeing their faces again.

Victim. Victim's mother.

I feel her arms around me. I see the tears running down her face as she thanks me, as she tells me what a good friend I have been. And I accept her gratitude, I keep the truth to myself.

And the guilt overwhelms me. It tightens its grip. The guilt is a knot that will never come undone.

———

XXII(i) At the end of their discussion of the Game Soc proposal, Emilia wondered whether it would be better to wait a while before beginning to play. Chad disagreed but tried to keep from his voice any resentment, although he felt like a child on Christmas morning told he had to wait until lunchtime for the opening of gifts. He was only at Pitt for a year, he explained, so they should begin right away. But it was their first term in Oxford, Emilia countered, and she wanted a chance to enjoy everything university life had to offer. So they called for a show of hands. And although Jolyon sided with Chad, the two of them lost the group's first ever vote.

XXII(ii) They met Tallest and Middle and Shortest in a small cafe where the breakfasts were cheap and greasy and came with good chips. Jolyon and Chad and Jack went along. Chad felt like a general parleying battle terms.

They ate as they negotiated, Jolyon and Tallest doing most of the talking.

Tallest began by apologising. Game Soc had one further condition, it was remiss of him not to have mentioned it earlier. They required control over one consequence, Game Soc would choose the penalty for losing on a single occasion. But they would announce it later on, at the appropriate moment. Tallest assured them this required nothing illegal of them and it was nothing beyond the rules or spirit of their game.

Jolyon turned to his partners. Jack shrugged and Chad nodded.

Otherwise, there was little that proved controversial. Tallest was happy with the examples of consequences they had presented him, most of the darker ones having been suggested by Jack. And he accepted that not all them could be drawn up in advance, only those who survived would devise the later tests. The fittest or luckiest, bravest or most skilful, were those who should make the Game tougher with each passing round.

Once Jolyon could see Game Soc were happy with their proposal he mentioned, almost in passing, that they would begin playing at the start of second term. There followed a moment's silence and Middle looked as if he was about to say something but winced suddenly in pain, looking down at his leg on the side Shortest was sitting. Then Middle folded his arms tight and kept quiet. Tallest was smiling as if unaware of anything happening next to him. The timing was not ideal, he suggested, was there any possibility of beginning as soon as possible? But Jolyon stood firm, a vote had been taken, there was nothing more could be done. Democracy had spoken. Tallest raised his eyebrows but gestured for Jolyon to continue.

They would play every Sunday and expected to finish maybe by the end of second term. Or almost certainly by the end of third. Not that there would be any limit to the end of the Game. It was last man standing.

No one back then could have imagined how much longer it would take.

XXII(iii) While Game Soc had grudgingly accepted a delay to the beginning of the Game, they had however insisted that deposits be handed over a week to the day after the breakfast meeting.

A thousand pounds was only a little less than each of them, apart from Chad, received each term in student grants. And they had already paid battels to Pitt, which accounted for a large proportion of their available funds.

It was Jolyon who came up with the solution. He had noticed that the local banks were eager for Oxford students to open accounts with them. Some of them offered financial rewards and all of them offered overdraft facilities. So around the city each of them traipsed opening new accounts anywhere they could. And then around they went again, withdrawing the daily limit from various cashpoints in the city, an overdraft carousel.

Chad, meanwhile, had some money saved he could use. He

had worked the whole summer long, a tedious data entry job for Susan Leonard's alumni database. He thought that he would use his savings to travel around Europe during spring break and then perhaps in the summer before returning to the States. Although in the end, of course, he never made it as far as the summer at Pitt.

Tallest arrived at Jolyon's room at the prearranged time. He had with him a brown leather briefcase. A small piece of blue tape was stuck above its brass buckle.

'Minor repair required,' he responded, when Jolyon questioned him about it.

'Or maybe you don't want us to know your initials,' said Jolyon, to which Tallest replied with a respectful nod.

'Since the topic has been raised,' said Tallest, 'please allow me to suggest that none of you try surreptitiously to find out anything about us, about Game Soc. We've already laid down the rules, so maybe it's too late to insist, but perhaps you could consider this friendly advice. Let's just say it's a matter of etiquette. You're all intelligent and inquisitive people. But curiosity and cats and so on.' Tallest shrugged as if to say that none of this really needed saying. 'Anyway, let's move swiftly on to the important stuff, the real reason we're here,' he continued, patting his briefcase. 'Money.'

'But first we want some assurances,' said Chad. 'How do we know this isn't some kind of scam? What if you disappear with our cash?'

'I can give no such assurances,' said Tallest. 'It's a matter of take it or leave it, I'm afraid. All I can offer you is this . . .' He opened the briefcase, lifted it head high and then flipped it quickly upside down. Down onto the floorboards there fell ten bundles of money tied up with red ribbon. 'I opted for five-pound notes,' said Tallest. 'I thought it might drive home the point rather better.'

No one said anything, they only stared at the money.

'Your turn now,' said Tallest, holding out his hand.

Jack started to roll up the sleeves of his shirt. 'You hold him down, Chad, and I'll do him in with the ashtray.'

'Yes, but then you'd all have to share,' said Tallest. 'And that wouldn't be half as much fun.' He bent down and threw one of the bundles to each of them in turn. 'Just so you can ascertain whether it's real or not,' he said.

They each held the money for a moment as if it were something fragile. Jack riffled his bundle and whistled. And then quickly, but Jolyon first of all, they dropped the money limply into their laps as if it held no particular interest to them.

Jolyon lit a cigarette, everyone seemed to be waiting for him. And then he tossed the money nonchalantly back, reached into his pocket and removed an envelope. Crossing the room, he handed it to Tallest who, without opening or inspecting it, dropped the envelope into his briefcase. 'Good. One down, five to go,' he said.

One by one they approached him, each returning Tallest's money and then handing him their own thousand pounds. Jack had folded his money tightly into an empty cigarette pack. 'Careful, this stuff will kill you,' he said.

'Most amusing,' said Tallest. 'You know, all of my favourite tragedies feature the character of a good fool.' He removed the roll of twenties and sniffed at it disapprovingly before dropping it into his briefcase.

Dee's stack of notes was tied with black ribbon. 'Oh dear, we had the same idea,' she said to Tallest, pretending to be mortified.

'But your choice of colour was so much more apt, Cassandra,' he replied.

When he had received everyone's deposit and gathered up the money from the floor, Tallest snapped shut the briefcase and held it to his chest. He made the sign of the cross against the leather but paused as he finished. 'Please do excuse my dark sense of humour,' he said, his mouth squeezing out a sarcastic pout. 'Tragedies, ominous ribbons, blessings? Really, I'm just trying to have some fun with you all, no need to look so serious. Don't worry, I promise you, it'll be fun.' Tallest turned and started to leave, lightly swinging his briefcase as he went. 'See you next term then,' he said, pulling the door closed behind him.

And then Chad imagined Tallest lingering outside the door for a moment to listen in on what he had left behind. And had he done so, what he would have heard would have pleased Tallest very much. Nothing but silence. Ten seconds, twenty.

Chad pictured him turning and bounding down the stairs two at a time.

XXII(iv) It was an epochal period for Chad, those first months at Pitt. One term, eight weeks, the very best days of his life. And his resentment toward Emilia for her delay of the Game quickly subsided because it was true there was much to see in and around the city. And although the Game was the next adventure Chad had in mind, Emilia's adventures were not without their charms. For one or two days each week she became the group's ringleader, insisting on trips to quaint Oxfordshire villages or arranging walks through the meadows, an afternoon in the Botanic Garden. The others sometimes made sour faces at the idea of watching rugby in the University Parks or enjoying an autumnal stroll through the woods. But Emilia knew how to sell her ideas to them. It wasn't so much about the rugby as standing on the sidelines sharing hot toddies from a Thermos. The woods were next to a seventeenth-century riverside pub. And although Chad made his face sour as well, inside he was thrilled every time Emilia pulled them away from Pitt on another expedition.

They attended lectures in the mornings and convened as a group at some point every afternoon or evening. There were no formal arrangements for such gatherings. They would flock one by one at certain likely spots. Jolyon's room, the college bar, dinner in the refectory. A patch of grass by the ancient tree in the gardens where Dee would sit and read until winter swept in hard toward the end of Michaelmas. At night they went everywhere together, a troupe of travelling actors enlivening every scene they slipped themselves into. The parties, the bars and concerts. The strange college discos that were referred to, in the university vernacular, as 'bops'.

It was a term full of rapturous pleasures. And Chad believed he had stumbled by chance upon the very best people in the world. They all did. They were all so young.

XXII(v) 'So what are you doing for Christmas, Chad?' said Jolyon, clearing their plates away, pouring more tea. Jolyon made eggs for the two of them every Saturday morning. And then they would browse through the newspapers until lunchtime, reading out their favourite stories to one another.

'I'm supposed to be going home,' said Chad, picking up a newspaper, feigning an air of nonchalance as he opened it in his lap. 'But with the deposit for the Game, I don't think I can afford to. The other Americans are all flying back, so at least I'll have the house to myself.' He sipped the strong tea. It was becoming almost palatable. 'Mom'll be upset though. It's bad enough I won't be home for Thanksgiving this week.'

'Why don't you come home with me?' said Jolyon. 'If your house is empty we can hang out in the city a while. We only have to stay a week with my mother for Christmas, or longer if you want. I'll show you how we do it over here.'

Chad loosened his grip on the newspaper, he could feel it almost beginning to tear. 'I don't want to impose, Jolyon,' he said. 'What would your mom think about this?'

'I've asked her already,' said Jolyon. 'She can't wait to meet you.'

XXII(vi) The eighth and final week of term became a time of celebration. The horse-chestnut leaves had fallen and Christmas was coming. They lived in a world of friendships and foggy mornings. Their days were cool and reeled along slowly. Nights buzzed by fast, warm with companionship and the air full of laughter.

Margaret Thatcher had resigned as prime minister midway through seventh week and Chad delighted his friends by pointing out that it was the day of Thanksgiving. He skipped the turkey meal with his housemates and they all partied in the bar, proclaiming a new age and toasting a thousand toasts. Most of Pitt had turned out for the occasion and there was even champagne, or something that sparkled at least. At the end of the night, Chad stood on a stool and shouted, 'Happy Thanksgiving, happy Thanksgiving, everybody.' Someone put Frank Sinatra's 'New York, New York' on the jukebox and they hoisted Chad onto their shoulders. Everyone sang and everyone lifted their glasses to him as he was paraded around, kicking his legs to the beat.

Margaret Thatcher – whom Emilia would only ever refer to as Mrs Satan – would remain in office for nearly another week. And then on the Wednesday of the last week of term she officially departed and Jolyon threw a second party, this one in his room. Twenty people, maybe thirty, in a space no larger than a boxing ring. They drank tequila from the bottle and this soon became a contest until Chad, the last to fall, disgorged the contents of his stomach from Jolyon's window, staining the ancient sandstone beneath. Dee brought to the party her record player and the soundtrack from *The Wizard of Oz* in an old corner-creased sleeve. The whole night long they played the same track over and over – 'Ding Dong! The Witch Is Dead' – and everyone sang along feverishly.

When the party was almost over and the wicked witch had died for the final time, Chad hung his chin from the window. There were only six of them left in the room now, the six who mattered most to each other. The sound of deep voices rose up from the narrow street beneath, heads and shoulders making snaky paths along the pavement. Chad's mouth felt as though it were wadded with something like muslin.

But in contrast to his stomach, his sense of well-being was immense. His Michaelmas Epoch. There would be no turning back. At last Chad was beginning to kick free of that half of himself from which he had always longed to escape. For better or worse

———

XXIII(i) When I read over the last few chapters, I discover a note I must have left for myself. And when I come across this note, I look for and find my sneakers. On the white toe of one shoe in Magic Marker I write the word WALK. On the other toe I write NOON. As physical mnemonics go, this one should prove simple enough to decode. I place the sneakers beneath my lunchtime plate and think about my progress.

Everything is going so well. This morning while eating my breakfast I waved to my neighbour across the way. I even *initiated* the greeting. You see the strides I am making? My walks, my waves, this story gushing out from me freely.

And now my morning routine is complete, another chapter finished and I have drunk two of today's four glasses of water.

XXIII(ii) Note to self: Must drink more whisky. Water is fine but a life-affirming slug of whisky always soothes the soul.

———

XXIV(i) They entered the room in order, Tallest first, then Middle, then Shortest.

Usually they would attend the Game only one at a time. But on that first day, the first Sunday of Hilary term, all three of them made themselves present as if dignitaries at the opening ceremony of some international spectacular.

Tallest took the desk chair with wheels. Middle and Shortest stood stiffly against the wall like two scratches. Middle, from time to time, took a few notes but never seemingly at moments of great significance.

Dee had insisted on making a mixtape for the event – all the songs were humorously appropriate, she promised. The first track was 'Every Day Is Like Sunday', although Chad couldn't see what it had to do with their game but for the fact they had decided to play on Sundays.

And so while Morrissey crooned away softly in the background about Armageddon, Jolyon opened the proceedings with something like a speech, a brief greeting and a hope for much enjoyment to follow. He made a small joke about their mysterious benefactors but thanked them as well. And then the Game began.

XXIV(ii) After the best weeks of Chad's life, he and Jolyon had returned to the city soon after New Year's Eve. Jolyon's friends in Sussex all adored Jolyon. And as he was a close friend of Jolyon they all seemed to adore Chad as well. Everyone was interested in his opinions – as if, to have been chosen by Jolyon as a friend, you clearly had some of the most fascinating thoughts on earth. They ate most nights with Jolyon's mother at a dinner table that never dimmed in its chatter, they went often to Brighton to buy second-hand books and see the Christmas lights on its pier, they drank whisky with Jolyon's father, listened to carollers, read their books by the hearths of ancient inns, popped champagne at the end of the year . . .

The others had come back to Pitt a week before the start of term and they had all met every day in Jolyon's room to agree upon the mechanics. It had to be a game never before played so that no one could gain an unfair advantage, they would have to learn and develop tactics on the fly. They could change the rules if they encountered problems, or if they simply wished to change them, but only if the majority voted through the changes.

They chose cards to represent skill and dice to represent luck. It was a hotchpotch of many of the games they had played growing up. Some rummy, some bridge, a little poker. Mark admitted sheepishly that in his earlier youth he had dabbled with Dungeons & Dragons and they based some of the dice-play on the rules from that game. Risk further influenced their thinking on dice, particularly the number of dice to be rolled, sometimes several. The Game also bore undertones of Monopoly and shades of Diplomacy and perhaps more games besides. It was the game of all games – this was how Jack had described the Game, largely sarcastically, but Jolyon had agreed enthusiastically.

Picture cards were strong and aces strongest. High dice rolls were useful to a player involved in a challenge with an opponent but not desirable when consequences were being rolled for.

They ran trials and made small adjustments and finally everyone felt happy. The Game was intended to be a contest for individuals, although eventually it would become apparent that the structure allowed numerous opportunities for both cooperation and backstabbing. In fact it seemed almost as if some of the rules had been designed to encourage such behaviours.

None of them flinched at any of this. The Game was going to be fun, sometimes challenging, but mostly fun. And the prize money was a goodly amount but they told themselves earnestly that the money came second to the challenge, money was merely the cherry on top of the cake.

Of course, in the end, the mechanics of the Game proved irrelevant. What mattered most of all was the players. And with regard to the consequences, they had formulated absolutely no rules at all. They were young and idealistic and they all believed in trust and honour and each other's inherent decency.

In retrospect, their naivety was staggering. Like newborns gurgling with pleasure as they crawled into the lions' den.

XXIV(iii) As cards were fanned and played and picked, and dice were rolled, the conversation remained guarded and slight. Tallest, observing this fact, said, 'Just carry on as if we're not here.'

'Who are you people anyway?' said Jack.

Shortest moved forward from the wall. 'You do not speak to us,' he said. 'Under no circumstances is this permitted. Not unless we specifically invite you to do so. Is that understood?'

Tallest raised his hand. 'It's all right,' he said, 'I don't mind fielding that one. But my colleague is right. We come here as observers, not participants. I'd be most grateful for your cooperation. As to your question, Mr Thomson, regarding our identity, we will in fact be revealing that information at a later date. Once the Game has concluded.' Tallest removed his glasses and started to clean them. 'But to one individual only,' he said. He fogged his lenses with a hot breath. 'And I doubt very much that the individual concerned will feel inclined to share such information with the rest of you.'

'And why's that?' said Jack. 'Because you're so powerful and secret and scarily important?'

'No, not at all,' said Tallest, returning the glasses to the tip of his nose. 'Because I doubt any of you will be on speaking terms by that point.'

'That's so wrong!' Chad shouted. His anger came quickly and his face was inflamed. 'You have just . . . you have no idea just how wrong you are.'

Tallest pushed back his glasses. 'Of course, Mr Mason,' he said. 'Whatever you say, I'm sure you're right. This is, after all, *your* game, is it not?'

'It's everyone's game,' said Jolyon. 'It belongs to the group. We arrive at our decisions democratically.'

'Yes, that's right,' said Tallest, 'quite the collective.' He sniffed cheerfully. 'As I was saying, it's as if we're not here.'

XXIV(iv) The first session of the Game finished with neither clear winners nor losers but Chad could perhaps claim to be happiest with his position. He would have to perform only one consequence, to be drawn from the first pot, the one containing the lightest and least daring of challenges. There were three pots in total, each one containing small cards on which the consequences were printed. They had agreed that whenever a card was chosen, the other players would hold on to it and return it only once the dare had been completed. And then the successful performer could ceremonially tear the thing up in front of them.

To complete his single consequence, Chad had to wear a Pitt College scarf for a week. He hadn't even understood why this was any sort of consequence at all when the scarf had first been suggested. Jolyon had explained that, in most cases, it was the privately educated students who gadded about town wearing college colours. And therefore those students from state school who wore college scarves were acting as if they were ashamed of their backgrounds, or were behaving pretentiously. Everyone else had agreed, none of them would choose to wear the college scarf. 'But I suppose Americans aren't like that,' Jolyon had said. 'You mean we dare to show pride in our achievements?' Chad had said. Jolyon had shaken his head, frustrated that he couldn't make Chad understand. 'I suppose it's more than just a common language that separates our countries.'

And so for Chad the scarf-wearing proved the simplest of tasks. Not that any of the challenges were particularly severe at the end of round one. They would of course escalate as the Game evolved.

Mark had perhaps fared the worst in the first round. He had to face two challenges from the more serious end of the scale, both cards coming from the third pot. The first was entitled

'Beggar-man Rich'. To perform this consequence he had to sit for half a day on the pavement outside the university library's most ancient buildings, wearing the apparel in which the university insisted its undergraduates should dress for all important events. Black suit with white shirt and white bow tie, black gown and mortar board. In front of him Mark had to hold a sign reading, 'Student requires donations to fund beer consumption. All contributions gratefully imbibed!' The card further stipulated that the receptacle for donations should be an ornate and silvery soup tureen.

Mark completed the challenge while Shortest observed on behalf of Game Soc. The other players took turns to mill around him for an hour each, both for their own amusement and also to protect him in case the public vitriol became physical.

In the bar that evening Mark remained entirely phlegmatic as he tore up the card and dropped its pieces into an ashtray. 'It wasn't so bad,' he said, yawning and spreading his arms. 'I'll admit, though, I haven't ever been called a cunt quite so many times in a day.' He waited for the knowing nods of his friends and then added, 'Who'd have guessed so many of the old ladies even knew the word.'

For his second challenge, 'Academic Polemic', Mark had to submit an article to Pitt's weekly newsletter. The piece had to argue that British students did not deserve to receive government grants and the American model of higher education was greatly preferable. Tallest insisted upon the power of approval before the article was submitted to the *Pitt Pendulum*, concerned that Mark might employ a satirical tone, like Swift proposing the eating of babies in famine-stricken Ireland. But in the end he changed not a single word. Mark had hoped the *Pendulum* would never publish such a piece. But in fact it did, as its topmost story and beneath the headline, 'Pitt Turkey Votes For Xmas'.

Mark seemed to suffer the barbs that came his way after

publication with a laid-back air. He never lost his temper with his assailants, who would stop him in front quad or corner him in the bar. Instead he argued the case as if he genuinely believed his words. Only once did Chad think he detected a twitch. The Student Union president, a little drunk, started to shout across the bar. Mark was stupid, he was ignorant, an idiot. Mark raised his glass as if he found the name-calling mildly amusing. But after he put down the glass he gulped hard and when he saw Chad's eyes on him, Mark looked quickly away.

Emilia's solitary consequence came from the second pot. She was mandated to raise her hand during a lecture and ask for permission to visit the toilet. The words on the card went on to speculate, correctly as it transpired, that the lecturer would then point out that permission to visit the men's or ladies' room was not required. And so, upon this actually coming to pass, Emilia responded, just as the card instructed her, 'What, not even for number twos?'

It was a dare that perhaps Jack could have pulled off without suffering any humiliation. But Emilia had none of Jack's comic powers and could not convey in her voice or bearing that she was in on any sort of joke. Yes, there was laughter in the lecture hall but the amusement didn't embrace Emilia as she skulked from the room. The laughter pitied her, the room felt embarrassed on her behalf.

Emilia drank more that evening than she was accustomed to drinking. But still she felt the heat in her face and a breathless pinching in the paths of her chest. The shame flowed through her the whole night long and when she awoke the next morning, she became convinced she could sense an approaching sickness in the back of her throat. For the benefit of her fellow students, whom she did not wish to infect, she decided to skip the day's lectures. By the following morning the sickness had been successfully repelled and a flushed Emilia returned to her lecture-mates.

Dee had earned a single consequence from the second pot, the wearing of a touristy Oxford T-shirt for a week rather than her more usual melodramas. It discomfited her more than she allowed anyone to see. Meanwhile Jolyon and Jack both fared almost as well as Chad, each with only one of the lesser consequences. Although unlike Chad they did at least comprehend the supposed embarrassment the dares were intended to provoke. But the challenges were neither severe nor of the sort that would prey upon their unique sensitivities.

A week on from the end of round one, feelings of embarrassment and shame were only residual. The six of them joked about the dares and mocked each other and everyone was smiling again. They gathered for the second round in Jolyon's room, all of them ready and willing. They had democratically agreed upon the next set of consequences and Tallest had passed the list with only a small number of mostly technical changes. Snow was falling outside and shelving the panes of the window. And then, several minutes late, Middle arrived on his own to observe.

━━

XXV(i) For today's walk I decide to wander south. I pass a girl who smells of peaches and realise how much I miss the company of women. Soon I find myself beside a schoolyard, the air shrill with the bright screams of children, young lungs challenging the world.

A boy hooks his fingers through the diamonds of the schoolyard fence and says, Hey, Mister Beard. I like your beard. Another boy hooks on alongside him and says, Hey, Mister Weird. What you got written on your sneakers? You look like a *looo-zurr.*

I turn around, they shout some more. I plug my ears and run back toward the park.

XXV(ii) Around the corner, I bend down and try to erase the words WALK NOON from my sneakers with spittle and a fore-finger. But the words barely fade and quickly I check myself. No, the fighter doesn't hide his scars. And the hermit doesn't meddle with routines. But the encounter with the children prompts me to buy a small mirror. Yes, the beard is immense and unkempt, I can't remember the last time I trimmed it. I head home, there must be some scissors and a razor somewhere in my apartment.

XXV(iii) Before I open the front door I can hear that the phone is ringing. If it is Chad calling I will not be so pliable this time around. I should have made some demands, I should at least have left my own mark on some of our arrangements.

I answer with a strong sense of resolve. Hello, I say. What do you want?

Jolly?

Oh, I swallow hard, I wasn't expecting you, I say.

You called me last night, Jolly. You left a message.

I'm sorry, Blair, I say, heading toward the kitchen, trying to remember. What did I say?

You said you wanted to talk. Has something happened?

No, I say. When I reach the kitchen I see my whisky glass on the counter. The black line that tells me how much to pour indicates more than a nip, a quarter-glass. Perhaps I have been drinking a little more of late, or maybe this is just one of my everyday lapses. I'm sorry, Blair, I say, I really shouldn't bother you like that.

It's no bother, Jolly, I still care, you know. And I'm sorry I haven't called in a while, I suppose –

Don't apologise, Blair. Thank you for caring. Thank you for calling me back.

Are you working yet?

Yes, I say, I'm writing.

Oh, Jolly, I'm so happy. You know, I still haven't forgiven Papa. Who are you working for now?

Myself, I say. I'm writing a story.

The line crackles as Blair breathes out hard.

It's all right, Blair, I say. Don't worry, I have to do this. This is something I just have to do, please understand.

OK, then, Jolly. I understand.

Thank you, Blair, I say. Blair, I miss you.

I have to go, she replies. Trip's on his way back from the restroom.

How is Trip?

Trip is well, Jolly. Look, I have to go. We're having lunch, I'm sorry.

Lunch? On a Wednesday? Special occasion?

It's my birthday, Jolly. I thought maybe that was why you called last night. I have to go, sorry . . . Just one second, Trip, darling . . . Good luck with your writing, Jolyon. Oh, and it's Friday, by the way.

She hangs up.

XXV(iv) I am still holding the mirror. I look at my guilty reflection, my long straggled hair and wild bristles of my beard. There must be some scissors, a razor. Somewhere, please.

Nothing in the kitchen drawers, not even a sharp knife.

The beard itches and I scratch, I want to tear it from its roots. I taunt myself with my reflection again and then slam the small mirror down on the counter.

I think I once had a kissable face. Blair liked to hold it in her hands, her lips brushing my cheekbones. And then she would slide slowly inward until her lips were nuzzling the foothills of my nose. There are so many things I miss about Blair.

We lived on the Upper East Side, not far from the best of the big money. We went often to the Met and dined at the Met and then wept at the Met after the deaths of Butterfly or Carmen or Violetta. We knew gallery owners and would-be heiresses and we summered with them in the Hamptons each year. We had started to receive invitations to the most important charity events, gala balls, auctions. Blair's father was good to us and I was bad to her. Not outright bad or bad because I chose to be. But bad not far beneath the surface, apt to vanish into one of my black holes for weeks at a time.

Eventually Blair was unable to summon up her epic bedside patience any longer. So when she said divorce I said sure and that I understood completely. I tried to hide from her how much it would hurt me to lose her, to walk out into the wilderness alone. Blair did not deserve to feel any guilt for what my life would become without her. I was good to her throughout the break-up. I was the best I had been to her for years.

I emerged from our divorce with a small lump sum and a suitcase full of board games. And then, four years ago, I moved down here to the East Village where space is cheaper, where I hoped no one would find me. And within a year of losing Blair I was driven down into a hole by my loneliness and fear of what now awaits me, the end of the Game. Soon my apartment had become my prison. But that was fine, imprisonment is tolerable. Because punishment is all I deserve.

XXV(v) No scissors, no razors, no kitchen knives. Nothing.

What exactly did I think I would do if I had anything sharp in my home?

——

XXVI(i) Chad discovered something not far from enjoyment in the performance of his early-Game consequences. There was, for example, the time he had to wear a single glove like Michael Jackson for a week. The task became easier day by day and not everyone, Chad noticed, looked at him with outright disdain. He even thought he could sense approval from certain quarters, not approval of his exact choice of fashion statement but approval that at least some statement was being made. Another time he had to refer to himself in the third person for three days running. Can Chad get the chicken salad, please? Chad's here on a year-long study abroad programme. Chad's so sorry to hear about your mother, Dorian. And yes, Chad found some of these moments enormously humiliating. But he survived every one. And with each survival Chad learned more and more how to live with the clench of social discomfort. Gradually he was growing stronger.

Jack meanwhile performed each of his consequences with great elan. The highlight came when he had to practise break-dancing on the lawn of back quad. And although he had to appear very serious as he whirled and popped and rippled, although he had to wear large protective pads on his elbows and knees, the audience that gathered soon began to applaud his earnest but dismal performance. Jack left without a nod or bow to the crowd, he was not allowed to indicate his performance had been anything but the sincere pursuit of a hobby, and hands slapped his back heartily as he slipped away. That night in the bar, a female admirer bought him a pint.

Jolyon also continued to land dares that didn't seem troubling to him. One time he had to give an impromptu speech in the street while standing on an upturned milk crate. The others kept the topic hidden from him until the last minute so that Jolyon would have no time to prepare. But his speech on 'A History of the City of Oxford' proved a great success. Tourists flocked around him. And although Jolyon had to make up nine-tenths of the facts he delivered to the growing crowd, he stated them with such conviction that no one doubted a single word. Some of the

American tourists even pressed money into Jolyon's hand at the end. He made forty or fifty pounds.

Another time, he had to crash the funeral of a stranger. And he made so great an impression on the mourners they invited him to the buffet and drinks following the burial, even though he admitted to not knowing the deceased. He stayed for several hours, returning with numerous tales and a bellyful of Scotch.

The closest Dee came to feeling any shame was when she had to audition for a spot in the Pitt tiddlywinks team. It wasn't so much the tiddlywinks itself that embarrassed her but more the sense that she might want to spend time with the sort of people who played in the tiddlywinks team. Mathematicians, engineers, Christians. People who wore navy-blue V-necks over stiff white shirts, or sensible skirts coupled with blouses.

Emilia, meanwhile, was just about getting by. While random consequences only occasionally found their best target among the other five, Emilia seemed to possess a dearth of such luck. Everything seemed designed to attack her sense of decency, even though most of the consequences were supposed to be humorous. One dare that especially shamed her had been dreamt up by Jack, a creature that had to be scrawled on the walls as graffiti, a creature to which Jack gave the name *Cocktopus*. Cocktopus had the body of an octopus but each of its eight tentacles took the form of a penis. This consequence required Emilia to be caught on three occasions graffitiing cocktopi in public. One night several girls saw her as she drew her numerous phalli in pink Magic Marker over the washbasins in the toilets nearest the bar. Dee was the only person able to observe and verify on this occasion and she did so through a crack in the door of one of the stalls. Emilia was next seen by male and female students alike when she scratched a large cocktopus into the plaster by the payphone near the junior common room and then by an old lady as she spray-painted her third cocktopus onto the side of a bus shelter. On the final occasion Emilia fled the scene while the old lady shouted out for the police. She ran all the way back to Pitt, gripped by her sense of shame and fear of arrest. And although the other players assured her the police didn't use sketch artists or issue wanted posters in the case of reported graffiti, for some time Emilia wore a hat and a scarf wrapped all the way up to her nose whenever she left the safe confines of Pitt.

Mark was trying hard to hold on to his sense of calm but something was building inside him. Every week he finished with at least a single consequence, sometimes two or three. The rolls of the dice were against him, the cards in his hand often weak. Frequently the other players would look on as he strove to appear untroubled at the end of another dare. Asking questions at the end of lectures that implied a stunning level of ignorance. Eating his dinner in the refectory with a pair of fine lacquered chopsticks for a week (one night it was soup). Cheering on Pitt's rugby team dressed in the same kit as the players, star-jumping on the side-lines as if he thought he might be called up in an emergency. (Mark weighed one hundred and forty pounds and possessed the sporting prowess of the average physicist.) Having to be seen in public with a pink G-string peeking over the top of his jeans . . .

But yes, it was fun. And none of them seemed for even a moment to consider that, for the Game to end, they would have to subject one another to greater and greater humiliations. It couldn't remain light-hearted forever.

Because, ultimately, what would be the point in a game without losers?

XXVI(ii) They were thigh to thigh on the panelled seats, halfway through Hilary term. The bar was crowded and the smoke looped slowly where it bathed in the uplights.

Dee had recently abandoned her coloured cigarettes and instead contributed to the bar-room fug with an antique corncob pipe.

Her dark hair was drawn back and tied with old lace, her tobacco scented with cherries. She looked like Olive Oyl stolen away for the night with Popeye's pipe. 'Jack is back,' she said, with a sarcastic sense of drama.

Jack and Mark had only just arrived, followed not far behind by two boys carrying beers and with cigarettes pinched at the corners of their mouths. Jamie and Nick. Smoke was billowing into their faces as they approached and they had to toss their heads this way and that to prevent their eyes from tearing.

'Jolyon, mate,' said Jamie. He slapped Jolyon enthusiastically on the back.

'Did you check it out as I suggested?' said Jolyon.

'I did, mate. And you were only right on the button.'

'What did I tell you?'

'Seriously, mate,' said Jamie. He winked and pulled his cigarette far from his mouth, deep in the V of his fingers. 'I owe you one.'

'And Mr Nick,' said Jolyon. He half turned and reached over his shoulder to shake hands with the second boy. 'I have that book for you, remember? Just come to my room and if I'm not there let yourself in. I usually leave the door unlocked. Third shelf down.'

'You're a gentleman, sir,' said Nick.

'Listen, mate,' said Jamie. 'Little dicky bird tells me there's some kind of a game being organised and you might be the man to ask. And Nick and me just wanted to say count us in if at all poss.'

'And which little dicky bird told you this?' said Jolyon.

'Steady on,' said Jamie, sucking hard on his cigarette and whipping it away in his V. 'Grapevine, mate, nudge nudge. Man has to protect his sources and so on et cetera.'

'It's odd, that's all. You're the second person to ask me and I have no idea where this came from. But if you ever want to come round for some poker, I'd love to host.'

'Superb,' said Jamie. He sucked and whipped and blew. And then he patted Jolyon on the shoulder. 'Must dash,' he said, indicating a blonde girl with a motion of his head.

Jolyon waited for Jamie and Nick to filter away through the crowd, watching them depart over his shoulder. And then he turned quickly to the table. 'What the fuck's going on?' he said. 'And Jamie wasn't the second person to ask me, he was the fourth fucking person.'

Around the table there were shrugs and lips turned in and brows furrowed and the itch of discomfort. And also there was fear, or something not far from fear.

'No idea,' said Jack, who then felt it a grave mistake to have spoken first.

Jolyon prodded his finger at Jack. 'Secrecy is the whole fucking point. Anyone here doesn't understand that, they should walk away now. Jamie and earlier Rory and yesterday two second-year rugger-buggers who I've never even laid eyes on before. And when I find out who the fuck –'

'Don't blame me,' said Jack. 'Why are you pointing at me? I didn't do anything.'

'And the *Pitt Pendulum* a few days ago ran that ridiculous bullshit in *Rumourist* about us all being a sect and me being some kind of Jim Jones figure.'

'That was just supposed to be a joke, Jolyon,' said Emilia.

Jolyon ran his hands through his hair and locked his fingers on top of his head. His body rocked back and forth with disappointment.

Chad leaned forward and looked at each of them in turn. 'The Game is closed to outsiders,' he said. 'Maybe we didn't discuss this forcefully enough but we're all agreed, right? The Game becomes public knowledge and there is no game.'

Everyone but Jolyon nodded in agreement. Jolyon had slumped back in his seat and his face was turned to the ceiling.

Chad stood up and clapped his friend on the back. 'I'm going to the bar,' he said. 'You ready for another drink, Jolyon?'

'All right,' said Jolyon, sucking his lips to his teeth. 'But it's not your round. It's fucking Jack's fucking round.'

'I'm getting these,' said Chad.

XXVI(iii) Gradually the sense of deceit in the midst of them subsided. Jolyon's cloud dissipated and he drifted back into the conversation when it moved on to politics. He told them about the famous politician who'd had a Nazi swastika tattoo quietly removed a few years earlier. It was one of those well-known secrets, Jolyon told them, although nobody else at the table seemed to have heard the rumour before. Jolyon said he had a friend who worked at one of the tabloids. The friend had told him the newspapers were sitting on the story, hoping the politician would make a run for leadership. And if so, all would be revealed.

Then Jack told a story about a boy at his school who had tattooed himself while locked up in borstal. He had wanted the tattoo to honour his girlfriend Nadia and had done it himself with a pin, a pot of ink and a mirror. The mirror had been the root of the later problem. Now on his forearm, inside a big red heart, there was inked not the name *Nadia* but *Aidan*.

They laughed and drank and Dee said she didn't believe a word of it, Jackie-oh, but it was a good enough story in any case.

Emilia stretched her arms and yawned.

'Oh no, it's infectious,' said Jack. 'You've caught his disease, Markolepsy,' he said pointing. 'This is serious, Emilia, you're turning into a Markoleptic.'

Emilia tried hard not to smile. 'No, I'm just bored,' she said. 'Oh, only a little,' she added, 'nothing to do with any of you. I just feel a bit trapped here.'

'Then let's finish these and go to my room,' said Jolyon.

'It's not the bar,' said Emilia. 'We don't *do* anything any more, just the stupid game all the time.'

Chad was about to protest but then Mark blinked hard and rapped his knuckles on the side of his head. 'I've just had a brilliant idea,' he said. 'You want a change of scene, Emilia? Then you all have to come down to London Friday night for my birthday. I don't know why I was planning on spending it in this place. We can stay the whole weekend at my mother's house. I can't believe I only just thought of it. Look, my sister's living with my dad for a bit, small family falling-out, so her bedroom's free. And then there's the study, which you can take, Dee. You'll love my mother's study, it's full of old books by dead people. And I'll find sleeping bags for you two.' Mark pointed at Jack and Chad. 'There's plenty of room in my bedroom.'

'Then what about Emilia and Jolyon?' said Jack.

'I just told you,' said Mark, speaking slowly in a monotone as if to the village idiot. 'My . . . sister's . . . away.' It sounded to Chad like the slow toll of church bells at a funeral. 'Her . . . bedroom's . . . free.' Mark picked up the pace again. 'So Em and Jolyon can take her bed.'

Chad's head began to swarm and he felt the space between the six of them fog over, the sense of displacement thicker than the bar-room smoke.

Jack was squealing, demanding to know why he hadn't been told about this new relationship, his outraged pitch carrying vaguely over the haze.

Chad looked at Jolyon's face. Their eyes met. Jolyon's eyes fell.

Jack's fist began to pound the table with mock fury, the fullest pints overrunning their lips.

Emilia's face, Dee's face, Jack's face . . . All eyes on Chad now. And then Mark's fingers were clicking in front of his eyes, snap snap snap.

'Snap out of it, Chad.'

'I said you must have known about this, Chad,' said Jack.

A trickle of beer ran over the table's edge and splashed near his toes. 'No, no, I didn't,' said Chad. He swallowed, trying to hold his stomach down, trying to loosen the knot in his gut. They were all looking at him, so he pretended to appear amused or happy and maybe it worked. Soon everyone was looking at Jolyon and Emilia.

They locked fingers, their hands resting between them on the seat of the bench.

XXVI(iv) When Chad walked back home to the house beneath the river that night he tried to hide his tears from passers-by. He had a Mets cap he kept in his pocket for rain emergencies. He didn't like to look too American in this city but he wore the cap now, its peak pulled down low.

His thoughts were like a moth trapped in a lampshade, a furious beating and burning of wings, the singed creature finally falling away exhausted. And then, after a moment's calm away from the blaze, another bout of furious activity. And then another and another, each more feeble and futile than the last.

He cleared his eyes and his thoughts for long enough to ask himself a question. What would have been worse, rejection or this?

What would have been worse, rejection or this?

The house was empty. When he closed the door to his room he picked up the chair by his desk and smashed it against the wall. He grabbed objects from his desk one by one – the ring binders, the desk tidy, the coffee cup with its pool of dark dregs – and pitched them at the framed print of an English rural idyll hanging on the wall. The glass over the picture smashed spectacularly.

It seemed a good time to stop.

What would have been worse, rejection or this?

What would have been worse, rejection or this?

Chad pulled out the drawers beneath his wardrobe and threw them to the floor so they would land upside down. He stamped and stamped and the wood split and then splintered. And when he finished, he looked around quickly for something else to destroy.

XXVI(v) He was awoken by a pressing of fingers against his shoulder, the sound of his name. When Chad opened his eyes, Jolyon took several steps back from the bed. 'One of your house-mates let me in,' he said.

'Which one?' said Chad.

'She had way too much energy.'

'Mitzy,' said Chad.

'Brunette,' said Jolyon.

'No, that's Jenna. You think that's energy you should meet Mitzy.'

Jolyon looked around the room. 'What happened in here?'

'You ever hear of a twister?'

'Like in *The Wizard of Oz*? I thought they only occurred outdoors.'

'Shows you how much you understand about extreme weather conditions in this *frickin* country then.'

Jolyon looked down at his feet and then quickly back at Chad. 'That's actually really unfair of you,' he said. 'It once rained for nearly two whole days in Tunbridge Wells.'

Chad snorted and Jolyon smiled. It was enough.

'I meant to tell you first, Chad.'

'Sure you did.'

'Mark only knew . . . Usually Emilia would remember to lock the door whenever we were alone. But then one time . . . So Mark walked into the room and . . . That's the only reason he found out before anyone else. Before you I mean.'

'Why so secretive? Everyone's blissfully happy for you.'

'You are?'

'Sure I am.'

Jolyon was looking down at his feet again. 'Emilia thought that you . . . She said sometimes she sees you and . . . I don't know.'

'Then Emilia's crazy, all right?'

'You're right,' said Jolyon, 'she is.' He nodded. 'Come on then, we're going for a pint. We'll head off to London tomorrow – I'm sure the others can amuse themselves for a day. Get your clothes on, I'm buying.'

Chad lifted the covers high enough to peer at himself underneath. 'I seem to have all my clothes . . .'

XXVI(vi) I'm sorry, I don't want to do this, I don't want to interrupt the past with the present. But I had to stop writing. I had to get up from my work. Rewind.

XXVI(vii) The intercom lets out a long, sour buzz. Someone outside at the door to the building.

I decide to ignore them. Probably just a neighbour who has forgotten their keys, it happens all the time. But I am writing and the scene is important, my old diary is hazy on the exact words we exchanged that morning. And then frustratingly another buzz and another. I try to ignore the fat-fly sound. I close my eyes to recall how things ended in Chad's room, whether we said anything more that might be important. I feel tantalisingly close to the end of the chapter. And then another buzz and another and again and again.

I slam my diary shut and jump to my feet. I can't work like this. I go to the intercom.

What is it? I shout.

Help me, please help me. A woman's voice.

My anger vanishes. The chill wind of panic blows through me. What's wrong? I say.

Quickly, please, he's going to . . . And then a scream.

I'm coming, I say. Just hold on.

I feel frantic. I look at my bare feet, think about shoes, wipe my hands at the hips of my pants.

I run out the front door. A neighbour stands at the entrance to his apartment along the corridor fumbling for keys, patting his pockets. I think about asking for help.

No time to explain. My bare feet slap against the stone as I run down the stairs two and three at a time.

I am running too fast, I might break my neck at this speed.

I slow down. And then I slow down some more.

Halfway down and I stop. I lean against the balustrade, clenching my fists to the rail.

And then something terrible happens . . . I'm so sorry, if only I were all the way fixed, if only my recovery were complete, if I felt stronger then perhaps I could . . . I turn and walk back up the stairs, neighbour still fumbling for keys, swearing now as he pats every pocket again.

I close my door and fall to the floor, breathing heavily. And then a minute later I get to my feet and rush to find the ice-cube tray. I snatch up my evening dose of pills and swallow them desperately. The guilt is awful, the guilt makes me

and now somebody somewhere is tapping and tapping and tapping and

think that the world doesn't want me to *tap tap tap* that sound like a bad memory makes me feel so sick and Jesus will you please just let me finish this chap

or knocking perhaps

maybe someone is knocking on my

———

XXVII(i) It has been at least a week since I last wrote anything. Ten days perhaps.

It starts with a headache. I wake up with a start as if woken by a great roaring, as if the earth is splintering outside my window. And then I feel the pain in my head, such a sore head that I don't move from my bed for a day. (Note to self: The pills are part of your routine. The pills are there to take away the pain. More pills, less pain.)

I lie there trying to recall a peculiar dream. Was it the dream that woke me? Not the six of us this time. I am with a woman, somewhere crowded, words tumbling uncontrollably out of my mouth. Emilia or Dee? The woman in my dream seems to be sometimes one and then the other, or at other moments instead of a dream it feels like a memory of sleepwalking – trudging along in a trance to a bar, talking about the Game and drinking whisky, shot after shot. The whole thing starts to take on the feeling of a hologram, fuzzy at its edges and yet somehow real as if I could reach out and touch my memories. I feel sick, lying there in my bed, as if I have been drinking heavily. But I was drinking only in the dream, wasn't I? And how can a dream cause this physical pain in my head?

Even the next day the pain is still there, lessened but present, and I can't write. Is the headache a symptom of my writer's block, or is it the cause? Or has this listless state been induced by a fear of writing the rest of my story?

I could delay the inevitable, put off the decline. My story could linger wistfully on our trip together to London for Mark's birthday. But what would such a chapter tell you? That we had a wonderful time and everyone was happy. We revelled in our youth and the discovery of a new group of people we thought truly unique.

No, the words will not flow. This is a hitch in my recovery and yet I do my best to fight back. I force myself to answer the call of my sneakers each day. And I travel further than on my earliest walks. I wander as far as Times Square. Bold and brash, dumb and beautiful. I move through Chinatown, fresh with the arcs of live fish and tubs brimful with alien fungi. I make it across to DUMBO via the Manhattan Bridge, walking high above the grey hide of the East River. I stroll Wall Street with its towers leaning in above my head like the trees that line French avenues. I move through the old ironwork and new glass of SoHo. I do the two bays, Kips and Turtle. I round Ground Zero.

And then something happens, a shock to the system. And as you can see, I begin to write again.

This is what happened –

XXVII(ii) I pull on my WALK NOON sneakers at 11.59, leave my apartment and shuffle out onto the street. I have Central Park in mind, an ambitious distance, but I need to shake off this listlessness. And then I notice my breakfasting neighbour coming out of his own front door across the street from me. He looks over at me and waves, just as he does when we see each other on our fire escapes. But neither of us has any breakfast and he pauses hesitantly. (Record this moment, the fighter makes a breakthrough in his training.) I take a deep breath and hold up a finger. My neighbour smiles. A taxi rolls by and I cross the street.

XXVII(iii) I greet him awkwardly but successfully negotiate the exchanging of names. Although please forgive me for having forgotten his name in the unsettling rush of what happened next. My neighbour asks me where I have been for the last three years and I make something up about a sick mother in England. And then my neighbour says to me, Is that where you got married, back in England?

I give him a confused look.

Sorry, he says, just a girlfriend then? It's just, I never see the two of you together, so I thought to myself, hey, then she must be his wife. My neighbour laughs awkwardly. Sorry, dumb joke, he says.

I have no wife, I say, I'm divorced. No girlfriend either.

My neighbour swallows. Right, right, he says. Of course, just the maid. He slaps his forehead. Hey, maybe you could let me have her number, he says. I guess I'm pretty neat but I could get dirty for a hot maid like that.

He laughs and punches my shoulder playfully. But something about the way I force out a laugh causes him to fall quickly silent.

Are you saying that you've seen a woman in my apartment? I ask my neighbour.

The question startles him. Uh, yeah, he says, his *yeah* like a *duh*.

I lower my head to think this through as quickly as I can. And then, looking at the smudged words on my sneakers, I say to my neighbour, Do you see her at the same hour each day? Always at noon?

Twelve o'clock? Sure, now you mention it.

I place my hand on my neighbour's shoulder. He looks down slowly as if there might be a large poisonous spider climbing its way up his body.

I have to go, I say, turning and starting to run.

XXVII(iv) I am quiet with my key and light on tiptoes. Soon I have looked everywhere except for one place.

Something about the sight of the closet makes me feel sick and afraid. What do I keep in this closet?

I beat my fist against its surface. Come out, I say, come out, I know you're in there. I have a gun, I say, and if you don't come out I'm going to start shooting.

I wonder if I should get a knife from the kitchen. And then a vague memory washes through me. I own only butter knives.

This is your final warning, I yell.

When was the last time I opened this closet? Perhaps not opening this closet has become part of my routine. But wouldn't I have left myself something to remind me of this, something that would seem out of place there? Electric cables looped around the brass knob? Something kitchen-related wedged in the crack of the door?

I press my ear to the closet and listen hard. And then I throw open the door in a breathless rush of adrenalin. I let out a guttural roar and raise my fists.

Nothing, the closet is empty. Mostly empty. Then I notice that, lying on the floor, there is a very small, green plastic house.

I turn the little house over and over curiously in my fingers. It takes me a minute or so before I remember Monopoly and then the other board games. I drop the house in the garbage. This is not one of those important memories I need to retain.

XXVII(v) I perform my afternoon routine quickly and then hurry back to my story. I want to read everything I have written so far with great attention to detail, right from the very first word.

And now, as sleep begins its pull on the cords of my eyelids, I have something to report.

XXVII(vi) First let me say that my mind is not what it used to be. And even in the past it was not exactly free from hairline cracks, or the odd crevice or two, so please read the following statement with some degree of caution.

I cannot say with utter certainty that all of the words in this story have been written by me. It seems that some of them may not have been my own.

——

XXVIII(i) Mark's birthday was a loose affair, a gathering of friends old and new in a Thames-side pub. A bewildering number of friends, thought Chad, and all of them like characters from a book that once would have made him feel callow and small yet eager to climb into a world way above.

When the pub closed they fell out of its doorway straight into the home of one of Mark's friends whose parents were away for a month, business and pleasure in Cape Town. And the party began anew, its vigour refreshed.

When at last they headed back to Mark's mother's house, the new day was at their backs, raising itself over Victorian rooftops. And in the half-light, drunk and in a whirl of other hazes, Chad felt almost like one of Mark's London friends. As if overnight he had been lightly sketched in by the brush of the city.

XXVIII(ii) When he awoke his head hurt and there was a note next to him on the floor. They had tried unsuccessfully to rouse him. '*Hair of the dog, the Starling,*' the note concluded.

Oh shoot, Chad groaned. And then he remembered himself, rose, showered and dressed. But none of it made his head feel any better.

The pub stood at the far corner of the square. A residents' key was required to access the private garden and beyond its black railings were trim lawns and gravel paths as yellow as a beach. Chad ran his finger along the tips of the railing spikes as he walked, as he promised himself that one day he would live somewhere like this. It was the sort of thought he could only allow himself to enjoy without Jolyon present.

He found them lounging in the pub, near to the fireplace. Jolyon, his arm around Emilia, had a chair and a beer ready for him.

Emilia saw him approaching first. 'Oh good,' she said. 'How are you, Chad? I was so worried about you this morning.'

Instead of replying, Chad dropped heavily into his seat and let his head fall to the table.

'See, I told you. He's the silent type, Emilia,' said Mark. 'Or maybe that's just his game-playing tactic. They say it's the quiet ones you have to look out for.'

'I know,' said Emilia, 'but I can't work out which type of silent type Chad is.'

Chad peeped up at Emilia. Of all her sweet faces, perplexed was perhaps his favourite.

'Is he the strong silent type or another type of silent?' she said. 'Are there any other names for any other silent types? There should be. There should definitely be *the stupid silent type.*' And then Emilia looked alarmed. 'Oh, I'm not saying that's you, Chad. Sorry, just thinking out loud.' She hmmed and bit her lip. 'The shy silent type, the weak silent type. The psychopathic killer silent type. Come on, what type of silent type are you, Chad?'

Chad pushed himself up and back into his seat. He stared at Emilia, not blinking. He stared and stared.

'I'm sorry, Chad,' said Emilia, her fingers dancing at her neckline. 'I really didn't mean to offend you.'

Chad laughed. 'No, I was answering your question,' he said. 'I'm the silent silent type.' Emilia laughed too but it came out rather forced.

Jack stepped in – there could be no humour in Jack's presence without Jack's approval and involvement. 'No, he's the last one, psychopathic. Silent but violent. Like a fart,' he said.

Dee looked disgusted.

'What?' Jack complained. 'Surely you did that at school. I thought everyone did.'

'Being at school with you must have felt like one long trip to the circus, Jackie-oh,' said Dee.

'You tell me, Dee. What was it, a hundred schools you went to? Two hundred? You must have passed through my hood at some point.'

'Oh, it's *let's make fun of the orphan time*, hooray,' said Dee. 'I do so love our quality time, Jack. I only wish there'd been more tragedy in my life for you to mine with your cute little funnies.'

'What? I'd have loved being an orphan. You think four parents are better than none? I'd have killed to have no parents.'

'There's still time for that,' said Chad. 'We could make matricide and/or patricide one of the later consequences.'

'See, I told you,' said Jack triumphantly. 'Silent but violent.' Jack shaped his hands as if around a crystal ball and gazed into the imaginary globe before him. 'Chad, yes, I see you now. Leg chains and handcuffs and a prison boiler suit. But which one of us did he kill?' Jack's eyes widened and he let out a scream, oblivious to the silence it provoked in the crowded pub. 'Let me put out my eyes.' He mimed driving a pair of spikes into his face. 'The horror, the horror.'

Dee applauded sarcastically. 'Bozo the clown brings the house down again,' she said. 'You're quite the prognosticator, aren't you, Jack.'

'If whatever you just said means psychic, then yes,' said Jack. 'I mean, come on, it's not like any of our futures are that hard to predict.'

'Oh really?' said Emilia. 'Why don't you try us then, Jack?' She now wore her serious face. Almost as sweet as perplexed.

Jack returned to his imaginary globe. 'Emilia, the pretty one who pretends to have no hate,' he said, affecting a soothsayer's croak. 'Emilia will marry first of everyone gathered here today, for she cannot bear to be alone. She will marry a country veterinarian named Giles. His family own a stud farm on great England's southern coast.'

'Crap,' said Emilia. She folded her arms disagreeably. 'I'd never marry a posh Tory type,' she said. 'My dad would never speak to me again.'

Jack raised his finger to silence the interruption. 'She does not like the truth but truth must out,' he said. 'Giles has red hair and freckles and they have children four, all ginger sons. Giles in his spare time is a Mick Jagger impersonator and his band is named the Rolling Clones. And what a merry band they are, the most in-demand Rolling Stones impersonators at all the weddings taking place within a thirty-five-mile radius of the city of Winchester. For three years running.' Everyone was laughing except for Emilia, her folded arms stiffening. 'At forty years of age,' said Jack, 'Emilia wonders why she never made use of her psychology degree. She volunteers as a prison visitor and develops a dubious rapport with one prisoner in particular. Inside of jail he is known by a single moniker. Gash. *Aargh*, put out my eyes again, for Gash is none other than Chad.' Jack closed his eyes and then opened them again. 'The vapours have passed now,' he said.

'You're such an arsehole, Jack.'

'What? It's a way better future than mine,' said Jack, and then his eyes drifted back to his globe. 'Yes, it is Jack I now see before me, the handsome funny one. Forty years of age and still with youthful hair and striking bones of cheek. Yes, Majestic Jack, such a success in whatever his chosen career happens to be. Film scripts probably, insightful comedies. Oscars two or three I see. And everything else he ever wanted from life. Money, a beautiful wife, the perfect family. But most importantly of all, the intellectual self-esteem that comes from being a far greater success in life than all of his friends.

'But what is this I see now? A catch. Oh no, Jack, no. He has everything he ever desired and yet life still presses heavily upon him. Yes, Majestic Jack soon discovers that his cynicism for every last shit-scrap of the world stemmed not from any material lack in his life. No, instead Jack's cynicism stemmed from one thing alone. A singular inability to be happy. Poor Jack, for he discovers that he has a heart yet cannot feel, he is the Tin Man in reverse,' he wailed. 'Storm clouds gather. I see Majestic Jack slide headlong into the kind of sordid midlife crisis for which he once despised so many dismal middle-aged men, not least his fathers, two.'

Dee wiped fake tears from her eyes. 'Oh, stop it, Jack,' she said, 'you're breaking my heart here.'

Jack continued, his croak filling with sadness, his words slowing down. 'Success brings to Majestic Jack nothing more than misery and the cruellest loathing of self.'

'No, Jack, no,' cried Dee. 'I'll be nice to you, I promise. I'll laugh at all your jokes. I'll write you happy stories and teach the mockingbird to sing your name.'

'The vapours have passed,' said Jack. He looked intensely proud of himself. 'So you see, Emilia, you get off lightly in the long turning of life's bitter wheel.'

'Well, I disagree with everything you've said so far,' Emilia snorted. 'I think we're all going to be happy and successful and go wherever we want in life. We're young and we're smart and I think everyone here is just great. Even you, Jack. Just occasionally.'

'Maybe you're right, Em,' said Jack. 'What the fuck do I know, right?'

And then there fell a brief silence. Chad looked at Jolyon and wondered if he too was thinking this had been a mistake, the revealing of a weakness to his opponents. Jolyon returned the look with a small shrug.

'Come on then, Jack,' said Dee. 'You know you want to.'

'Want to what?' said Jack, acting confused.

'Want to perform your little trick on me. Let's just get this over with.'

'No, you're too easy, Dee. You've already written your own future. After completing your five hundredth poem you're going to commit suicide, aren't you?'

'So you keep reminding me, Jackie-oh.'

'Please address the oracle by her birth name,' said Jack. 'Her cognomen is Psychic Fucking Sue.' Jack lowered his eyes. 'I do not know this Jackie-oh,' he said. 'Though I see you speak of him with tones of hate deployed to hide your sexual love.'

Dee sighed and mimed a swoon. 'Will no one rid me of this turbulent Jack?'

Jack gave Dee a piercing look and the act began anew. 'And now I see before me a female who goes by the name of Dee, the artsy histrionic one. A twist, I see, for Dee survives her time at Pitt. She had been beaten to the suicide punch, Christina Balfour got there first. They say no one ever remembers who comes second and so Dee was forced to bide her time. And now five hundred poems I see at Dee's feet, unpublished, for the poems are almost certainly derivative teenage shit. And lots of haikus, no doubt. Yet on she goes unscathed, six hundred, seven. To London she moves and for the BBC doth work. And meanwhile bides her time and thinks about which branch of the arts to favour with her creative brilliance. Time passes. Ten turns round the sun and Dee festers on where we left her, the arts still devoid of her benefaction. Yet then she leaves her job. Yea she leaves and doth marry a lawyer who can support her latest life choice. To write a series of beautiful, groundbreaking and utterly unpublishable novels.'

'Oh, I do so look forward to that.'

'Time passes. Ten more turns round the sun and Dee remains very much unpublished. When suddenly at forty Dee changes forever her life's meagre course. For so many years nothing but rejection until at last she relents and writes a tale about a downtrodden girl working a lowly media job who overcomes the male hegemony, takes over the company, and finds love in the most unlikely of places.' Jack flung up his hands like fireworks bursting in the sky. 'Success at last. The novel becomes a best-seller and in record time reaches UK sales of five hundred thousand copies . . . And then, and only then at last, Dee fills up her pockets with stones, walks to the end of her garden path and finally out into the river.' Jack flung out three final fireworks in front of his eyes. 'The vapours pass,' he said.

'Oh, Jack,' said Dee, 'you know me better than I know myself. It's extraordinary. And I love your use of the five hundred theme, how it comes back to haunt me when at last I sell my soul to the devil of the mainstream. And a suicide just like Virginia Woolf. How did you know that's how I was planning to go?'

'Never doubt the powers of Psychic Fucking Sue.'

'Oh, how I love Psychic Sue. Please, we need more.'

'Well, I did Chad already.' said Jack. 'Life imprisonment for gruesome murder. The victim was obviously Jolyon by the way. A fight broke out between the two of them following a rule dispute during a hard-fought game of snap. Jolyon was –'

'Don't even think about doing me, Jack, I'm warning you,' said Jolyon, laughing.

Jack acquiesced quickly. 'OK, Jolyon,' he said, 'I truly wasn't planning to predict how, in an ironic twist, Pitt's most popular student ends up sad and all alone. So just don't go chucking one of your spanners at me, all right?'

'There's only Mark left now,' said Chad, while Jolyon threw Jack a playfully threatening look.

'Oh, Mark's the easiest,' said Jack.

Mark's eyes had closed but he opened one of them to peer at Jack suspiciously. 'Go on then, if you really must,' he said.

'Mark, the one who hides his ruthless streak behind sleepy eyes. I see the managing director of the world's largest and fastest-ever-growing company,' he said, 'which Mark started from scratch with only twenty pounds. He worked and worked for twenty-five hours a day zealously back-stabbing his way to the top. His employees call him, among other less complimentary names,

Marcus Brutus.' Jack stroked his globe one last time and finally sat back with his drink.

Mark yawned and closed his eyes again. 'Yep, you've got me pegged,' he said.

——

XXIX(i) I scribbled some notes late last night during the whisky hours of the night-time that I'd like to share with you now.

I have a number of points I would like to make regarding the narration of this story. And also some questions and thoughts. But first of all let me make one thing clear – when I leave at noon today, I plan to buy for myself a pair of powerful binoculars.

So on to point one. It seems I now have two audiences. The first, my reader. The second, my visitor.

Point two (for my visitor). You should know right away that I have no interest in trapping you in my apartment, I will allow you some time here. I will not return until two o'clock, you have until then. But in exchange for this kindness I expect some answers.

Point three (also for my visitor). Furthermore you may by now have deduced why I intend to buy for myself a pair of binoculars. You may as well come to the rear window right now. Look for a rooftop with a white picket fence. You might also wave to me. Let's start out on polite terms.

Point four. Breaking into a gentleman's home is generally considered rather impolite.

Thought one. These walks of mine, I'm sure they were my idea. They must have been, yes? But when I read my words again I wonder if I have really been so insistent about them. Because the following (point five) has occurred to me – while I have been out walking, my visitor has been in here with her eyes on my story, her fingers on my keyboard. (Thought two. But I remember wanting to build the walks into my routine. I do remember that, don't I?)

Thought three. I'm not saying dishonesty worms its way through this tale. Even if the words are not all my own, I have read and reread this story and everything rings true. But I am left with some questions.

Have I filled in the gaps myself for the sake of the story, or has someone else done this for me?

Who are you and what do you want?

And finally, what have you done to my story?

XXIX(ii) I am out of breath. My purchase swings in its plastic bag – I have been casting off its packaging as I run to my neighbouring block. Earlier I took note of the height and colour of the building and I find it soon after passing the tattoo parlour whose sign reads Cappuccino & Tattoo. I don't even pause to take a deep breath, I slide my hand *glissando* down the intercom's buttons. An impatient voice answers, 'Whaddya want?' Before I even offer an excuse, someone else has buzzed me in. I run up the stairs, fingers crossed, and pause in silent prayer before pushing the door at the top. And it opens.

The sun is fierce and no one is up here. I run across to the white picket fence and impatiently pull the binoculars out of the bag. I lift them to my eyes and start fumbling with the focus.

My breakfasting neighbour didn't appear on his fire escape today. I wanted to shout across the street, My visitor, does she have blonde hair or dark hair?

And now, the image sharp enough, I try to peer into every corner of my apartment. I can see no one. I am thinking about my dream, the one I had the night before my writer's block began. A woman somewhere crowded, Emilia or Dee?

Sweat drips from my brow, stings my eyes. I lower the binoculars, dry my face with my shirt. Blonde hair or dark?

And then, when I look up again, the door to my apartment, distant and made ghostly by the dark reflections in the window, opens slowly.

——

XXX Jack cast off his shroud of doom with a great flourish and the others sat back in their seats. They cradled their drinks and began to laugh about other things.

Chad was quiet, only half listening to the words spinning around him. His hangover had deadened any will to speak but his mind was wandering, at first drifting in one direction and then taking a sharp turn in another.

Dee was saying something about Jack keeping his filthy hands off her soul.

And then Jack was laughing about the cartoon that had recently appeared in the *Pitt Pendulum*. Jack said you could tell from the way they had drawn the hair that it had to be Mark. It was called 'Home on Derange'. He'd heard there were more in the pipeline.

Chad closed his eyes. His thoughts were strange distortions as if he were seeing them through Jack's crystal ball, the light bending and everything stretching then shrinking away.

When he opened his eyes he saw a television parading silent pictures above the bar. The stern faces of generals, a lurching camera chasing flashes in the dark of a distant night. Weapons from the skies in the Persian Gulf, Baghdad being bombed by the Coalition.

And that's when, very suddenly, Chad's mind lit up with an idea. Yes, it was time for a change. It was time for the Game to become less random, for the consequences to become more personal. If you could take careful aim at another player's weaknesses, his or her innermost fears, then this would bring a whole new dimension to the Game.

He was about to excitedly reveal the idea, it felt very important, but Jolyon had shushed everyone and was pointing to the silent television. There was a headline displayed at the bottom of the screen. The United States had issued a twenty-four-hour ultimatum for Iraq to begin withdrawals from Kuwait. In the absence of any such withdrawal, war would begin on the ground.

Jolyon's chair screeched as he pushed himself back from the table. 'When was it the Berlin Wall fell?' he said, squinting as he performed a calculation in his head. 'Well, we had something close to peace for just over a year,' he said, and then he took a long drink from his glass.

And now it felt wrong for Chad to say anything about the Game. Anyway, perhaps it would be better to keep the idea to himself for now, he thought. And better still, perhaps he should speak to Jolyon first. Jolyon would know how to talk everyone around.

And then, next time they played, they could call for a vote. An exciting change. An interesting new chapter.

XXXI(i) Her head moves slowly into my hermit's hole. After a moment her body follows. She pauses again, her back to the window.

I lift the binoculars to my eyes. The lenses find the top frame of my window and carefully I tilt the binoculars down. And there she is, *blonde*. Hair light and straight and cut in a short bob that lips in toward her neck. My eyes slide down. She wears a nondescript top, a white patternless garment with short sleeves. And she has on tan shorts that reach down to the crease at the back of her knees. The window frame cuts her off at the calves.

My hands shake, I find it hard to keep the image of her steady.

I lower the binoculars and let them hang by the thong at my chest. Turn this way, I whisper, as if my visitor might hear me.

She does not obey.

She bends and when she straightens a pair of sandals are in her hand. She holds them by their thin straps. And then, barefoot, she begins to creep forward through my kitchen.

I have deliberately placed my laptop on the bedside table so I can see it from here. She takes the computer and moves on to the living room where she turns left and is lost to my eyes.

XXXI(ii) I presume from what comes next that my visitor reads the message I left her. She comes to the window fifteen minutes after she entered.

She stands for a moment in the doorway between my living room and bedroom. And then she moves forward like a model, as if along a thin painted line, her hips feline as she sways. She wears sunglasses of a style I have observed to be very much in vogue since my return to the world, panes as large as children's palms, they make her nose seem small against her face. Black lenses and red lipstick. The lips are clenched – uncertain or sullen, I can't decide which.

When she reaches the kitchen window she puts her left hand on her left hip and stands there, weight mostly to her right. She holds the pose and lifts her chin toward me.

And then she waves.

I wave back. My visitor reaches for the string that hangs at the side of my window. And she lowers the blind.

——

XXXII(i) 'If we're supposed to act like they're not here,' said Jack, 'then I feel I should say that of the three, I think this one is quite the least arseholey.'

They had sent Middle and he sat impassively against the wall.

'I agree with Jack,' said Dee. 'And the best-looking as well.'

Chad shuffled the cards. 'Have you noticed,' he said, 'they do everything in height order?'

'Absolutely,' said Dee. 'Tallest, Middle and Shortest. That's what I call them.'

'When?' said Jack. 'Don't tell me you've written a poem.'

'Now, now, don't go getting all jealous, Jackie-oh. You know that you're the only living object adored in my odes. It's just how I've been thinking of them.'

'Tallest is clearly the leader,' said Jolyon. 'Shortest is the Goebbels. But I'm not sure which role this one plays.'

'I think he looks lost and scared,' said Emilia. 'A poor little lamb trapped in the gorse.'

Middle folded his arms. His hair there was dense and dark as if plastered on, fished from the drains of several showers. 'I know precisely what you're trying to do,' he said. 'And I can assure you that your silly little mind games won't work with me.'

'The Einstein of the operation as well,' said Mark.

Middle rubbed his face. 'Can we begin now?' he said sharply. 'Because then you can get back to screwing each other up. None of you seem to have realised that's where this thing is headed but I can assure you it is. And, off the record, when you discover I'm right, it just so happens it will give me absolutely no pleasure at all.'

Jack started to laugh and then, seeing Emilia giving him a hard look, said, 'What? It's funny because it's true.'

'Let's just get started, shall we?' said Emilia.

'Just a second,' said Chad, 'Jolyon has an announcement to make, don't you, Jolyon?'

'That's right,' said Jolyon. 'Listen up.'

XXXII(ii) Emilia spoke first, she was absolutely against the idea, and Mark quickly agreed with her.

'Well, of course you're against it, Mark,' said Jolyon, 'you lose more than anyone else, don't you?'

'Fuck you, Jolyon,' said Mark. 'It's just a game of dumb luck.'

'Look, Mark,' said Jolyon, 'no one can be good at everything. Maybe you just don't have it when it comes to this particular game.'

'Now really fuck you,' said Mark. He glared at Jolyon and Dee spoke up to come between them.

'I'm in favour,' she said. 'It's been a lot of fun but we need some movement here.'

'Dee's right,' said Chad. 'Look, I'm only here for a year. We've got a term and a half remaining and we need to narrow the field at some point.'

'That's three votes to two then,' said Jolyon, looking away from Mark. 'Which means it's all down to you, Jack. You say no, it's a draw, status quo. You say yes, we change.'

Jack looked unusually serious. 'Here's my concern,' he said. 'What's to stop you all from ganging up on me? I mean anyone,' he added quickly. 'You could all agree a list of consequences I'd rather gnaw my own foot off than perform. And maybe you all do a little deal to go easy on each other. At least when it's random anyone could get any consequence.'

'Worried we'd gang up on you specifically, Jack?' said Chad.

'No,' said Jack. 'It's not me I'm worried about, you've got nothing on me. But look, Jolyon and Emilia are fucking each other.' He was too far across the table for Emilia to kick but instinctively he shrank back anyway. 'I'm sorry, I mean Jolyon and Emilia are making sweet beautiful love every night. So there's one potential little vote bloc.'

'That's right,' said Emilia. 'So just vote no, Jack. And stop being such an arsehole.'

'What do you say, Jack?' said Chad. 'Are you going to try not being an asshole like Emilia says?' Emilia gave Chad a look. A look as if he and not Jolyon were her lover, Chad thought. As if he were her lover and had just admitted to sharing their bed with another. How dare she give him such a look, how dare she. 'And as you say, Jack,' he added, 'we've got nothing at all on you.'

Jack bit his nails. And then after thinking it through for a few more seconds, he said, 'OK, OK. Ladies and gentlemen, let's go ahead and make this game a whole lot more interesting.'

XXXII(iii) They agreed on the following system. Three pots for each player – easy, medium and hard – with three bespoke consequences in each. To decide upon each player's set of personal challenges, the other five would gather in the bar to negotiate and agree a list. They would take it in turns to sit out the discussion, wondering what the others were brewing up for them.

Emilia queried how any of them could be sure that, while absent from the discussion, the others were playing fair with them. And Jolyon gave a heartfelt speech about friendship and the honour system, and how even regardless of their innate sense of fair play, it wouldn't be in anyone's interest to propose ganging up on another. Were any player to suggest such a thing, no doubt the others would turn on him or her. Cheats never prosper. What goes around comes around.

A generous observer of Jolyon's speech might have suggested only that he hadn't thought everything through to its logical conclusion.

────

XXXIII(i) When I get back to my apartment, shortly after two o'clock, I find a message from my visitor. She left me a note at the foot of my story.

XXXIII(ii) Oh, Jolyon, I feel terribly upset by the hurtful allegation of trespass. I realise you were gruesomely drunk when you handed me your spare key, but have you really forgotten everything? Have you forgotten what you said to me? Did it matter so very little to you?

You call me 'my visitor'. MY VISITOR? You don't even remember who I am? Oh, that hurts me so deeply, Jolyon. Because, foolish me, I believed you. I believed every last word you whispered that night.

And I have done only what you asked of me. Nothing more. You wanted me to read your story and I am reading your story. All I asked in return was a little peace and quiet. You think this is easy for me to do? To read about the worst year of my life? Snooping and accusations, you think this is fair?

And there was I thinking perhaps we might . . . but never mind. And now this.

Now. This.

I don't know if I can continue now, Jolyon. I'm sorry, I'm so deeply and sorely upset.

Goodbye, Jolyon. Goodbye and good luck.

XXXIII(iii) I delay the whisky and pills portion of the afternoon routine, hoping a clear head will help me. And when this fails to work I take my whisky. She said I was drunk when we met, so I fill the glass high above the black line and then I fill it again. Quickly I overindulge as I hope to recreate conditions, to stir the memory into action. And when this doesn't work I swallow down my pills and still fail to remember. So I double the dose, pour more whisky . . .

Eventually I puke so hard I strain my back.

And now I am flat out on my sore back with aching head and voided stomach. I am here all alone and pondering the following question.

Is my visitor playing games with me?

I don't know, I just don't know.

But I think it is clear I must proceed with some caution.

———

XXXIV Jack played two cards, both queens. On top of Jolyon's pair of threes it was a strong move. He picked up the blue cup, covered its mouth with his hand and shook. He felt the dice jumping against his palm and then rolled them out on the table. Six and four, high enough. Probably. Jack clenched his fists and breathed out hard. 'Jack attack,' he said.

Mark leaned back and swore. He played a run of cards from his hand, three four five, and then shrugged. He picked up the cup and rolled the dice after barely a shake, a one and a two, the margin of loss to Jack large enough to earn him a second consequence. No one else had earned even one. He let his head fall back and dangled his arms limp as ropes. Then he swore loudly again and shouted, 'Christ, that's unlucky. Twice! Both fucking times.'

Emilia reached across the small table and stroked his arm. 'But at least they're only from the second-worst pot,' she said. 'Don't worry, Mark. Things have a habit of levelling out in the long run.'

Jack relaxed back into his chair. 'Has anyone spoken to Camp David in the last few days?' he said.

'Stop calling him that,' said Emilia.

'What?' I'm not judging him, Emilia. It's just undeniable that the man happens to be very camp. And with his Christian name being what it is, what else should I call him?'

'How about . . . *David*?'

Dee started to sing, 'David and Jackie-oh sitting in a tree, K I S S I N G!'

Jack's voice lifted an octave. 'Camp David does not have a crush on me,' he squealed.

'No,' said Mark bitterly, 'and a north pole doesn't have a crush on electrons.'

'What?' said Jack. He shrank back and eyed Mark up as if he had suddenly produced something shocking from beneath the table.

Mark looked hurt. 'Because electrons are attracted to . . .' Jack began to blink rapidly as if he were about to have a fit. 'What?' said Mark.

Emilia reached over and rubbed his arm again. 'Please don't ever let anyone try to make you any less strange, Mark. You just wouldn't be you any more.'

Mark looked confused but before he could say anything more, Jack returned to his story. 'Anyway,' he said, half a wary eye still on Mark, 'David's becoming suspicious of our gatherings. He wants to know what goes on when we all disappear into this room. He asked me who the tall stranger is. And there was a definite glint in his eye.' Jack turned to Middle and continued, 'So if your leader is into wannabe Oscar Wildes with enormous beards but without the slightest hint of humour . . .'

Jolyon started to rub at his forehead, his knitted brow. The ominous sense of his anger mingled with the smoke in the air. 'Who the fuck has been talking again?' he shouted. 'We already had this conversation about how vital – Jack, did you fucking say something?'

Jack recoiled. 'Why would I tell you the story in the first place if I'd been blabbing to people?' he said. 'Don't make out I'm some kind of idiot here.'

'Mark?' said Jolyon. His eyes were emptying of their light as if he could focus only on the rage building inside.

'Why do I get suspected next?' said Mark. 'Why not your best friend, the toy poodle over there? Or your trophy girlfriend? Or the one you look at all the time like you really want to fuck her as well?'

'Whoa,' said Emilia, throwing her hands in the air, 'I think that's enough from everyone.' She took a deep breath. Jolyon appeared to be on the verge of shaking. 'Jolyon, listen, no one has said anything to anyone.' She stood up and moved behind him. She started to knead his shoulders and a calmness slowly worked its way down through his tensed body.

The room was quiet as Jolyon came down from his rage. And then eventually he spoke. 'OK, OK,' he said. He rubbed at his forehead as if removing some smudge from his brow. 'I'm sorry.'

'David's just very observant, that's all,' said Emilia.

'He's just nosy,' said Chad.

'He's hoping it's some sort of orgy,' said Jack. 'And he's worked out that with five boys and two girls in a room, there might be a spare man for him.'

'That's enough now, Jack,' said Emilia.

Jack looked exhausted. 'What have I done?' he said. 'The man's gay, Emilia. It's a simple fact.'

'You don't have to take such salacious pleasure in bringing it up all the time.'

The dismay loitered on Jack's face and Dee gave him a curious look, her eyes narrowing like an archer taking aim. 'Ah, Jackie-oh, eureka,' she said.

'Eureka what, Suicide Girl?' said Jack.

'Oh, nothing. I just realised how intensely fascinating I find you, that's all.'

'Look, everyone,' said Emilia, 'I really think we've played as much as we can today. It's lunch in five minutes, so why don't we all go down early for once?'

Chad threw down his cards. 'That's fine,' he said. 'But first things first, Mark has to pick his consequence from the pot.'

'No, Chad,' said Emilia, sounding unnaturally stern. 'That can wait for later. We're all going for lunch, we're going to sit down together and we're going to talk about anything but the Game for at least an hour. Right now. You understand?

———

XXXV(i) Was I to blame when everything fell apart? When everything went wrong with the Game, was it because of mistakes made by me? I don't think so. Maybe we should all share the blame. The right cocktail of people, the perfect blend for calamity. Every one of us secret competitors who kept our desires carefully hidden at school, where aspiring to be the best is acceptable only in sport or fashion or dating. So you keep your secret inside, your ambition to be the cleverest, the most successful. You shrug and pretend that good luck is behind your high marks. So many years suppressing a secret, the strength of it building and building inside. Then you arrive somewhere like Pitt and something dark and dangerous becomes unleashed.

Although I don't think you can blame anything on Emilia. The sea change may have started before she left us but it was only afterwards that life in the Game began to deteriorate rapidly.

XXXV(ii) There now reside in my apartment two items I do not necessarily remember being here before. On the kitchen counter sits a beer coaster printed with a large and intricate B like a sailor's knot. It is a white B set on a green disc. Brooklyn Brewery, the coaster reads at its edges. I also find, inside a cup on the same counter, a book of matches bearing the name of a bar – ACE bar – a place I have seen on my walks, several blocks from here. About a third of the matches poke out from the matchbook, curled and burned. Years ago, when I was a smoker, I never tore the paper matches from their books. I bent them out against the strike strip and flicked them with my thumb to light them. To extinguish the flame I always gave the matchbook an insouciant wave, leaving the match in place. I used to have such an easy manner, a certain cool lack of urgency.

But as far as I remember it has been maybe a decade since I last smoked a cigarette.

I picture the bar, its three neon letters red and glowing in the night. ACE. Fate plays mischievous games – it had to be *that* playing card! I imagine myself standing out front and lighting a cigarette for someone else.

But for whom?

Nothing comes to me. The entire set-up feels false in my mind. Right now, life feels like one long series of stabs in the dark. And I am locked inside a room that I never saw lit from the start.

This entire search is futile. One simple truth.

I don't remember her.

XXXV(iii) It is nearly noon. Soon I will put on my shoes and leave, will keep my fingers crossed as I make my way around the block.

If my visitor comes back, I ask of her only one thing. Please forgive me.

Please. This here and now is not the whole man. Give me just a few weeks.

XXXV(iv) She didn't come.

I can hardly bear to type another word. She didn't come. Of course she didn't come.

———

XXXVI(i) The Churchill Arms felt sleepy after lunch, its air draped across the lounge bar. Mark lit a cigarette and soon his smoke filled the wall of sunlight dividing the space from corner to corner. The quiz machine flickered festively across from them.

Dorian, a fellow freshman, played the Churchill Arms quiz machine several times a day. Whenever it was ready to be milked, as Dorian described it. Ready to be milked meant the machine was full of tourist money and therefore the questions were easier and you had to answer fewer of them to win the grand prize. Twenty pounds.

Dorian made notes of the questions he answered incorrectly and went to the library most evenings to research. He kept a red folder full of information and spent an hour each day memorising new facts. Jolyon had told all of this to Chad some months ago and Chad held on to everything Jolyon told him. This had been Chad's idea.

When Dorian entered the pub he moved purposefully toward the machine but glanced around long enough for Jolyon to catch his attention and beckon him over. If you looked closely at Dorian you could see the haemorrhoidal outline of the pound coins bunching in his front trouser pocket.

Jolyon greeted him and they shook hands. Dorian nodded hello to the others, Chad and Mark and Jack.

'How much are you taking from it these days?' said Jolyon.

'Single digits on bad days. Twenty, sometimes thirty, when the going's good.'

Jolyon smiled approvingly and Dorian shifted to and fro on his feet, not nervous but itching to be some place else.

'Mind if we join you?' said Jolyon.

'Erm . . .' said Dorian. He couldn't say no to Jolyon, not many people could. At best he could indicate his reluctance, shifting his weight back and forth, hoping for release. 'Well, I suppose . . .' His jiggling increased.

'Just say no if it's a problem.'

'No, no, it's not that.'

'Great,' said Jolyon. 'Look, we'll stick to one simple rule. None of us will say anything unless we're one hundred per cent sure of the answer.'

They huddled around the machine and Dorian fetched a coin from his pocket. When the coin dropped, the machine's lights flashed faster and Dorian pointed at a trail of colours that appeared on the screen. 'That's good,' he said, 'that's really good.' He gazed into the glass, lost and happy. 'You have been fed, my beauty,' he said, 'time to be milked.'

By dint of both his knowledge and his daily research, Dorian's playing of the machine impressed them all. On history, the subject he was studying at Pitt, he was always quick to hit the correct answer. And whenever instantly certain he would hammer the button with his fist like a mallet. He hesitated sometimes but only to look to the ceiling and call on his memory, to rifle fast through its index cards. He even knew the answers to questions he referred to as deliberate trip-ups, questions with obscure statistical answers. The number of UK convictions for bestiality in 1987. The average annual precipitation on Blackpool beach. The number of golf balls on the moon.

Dorian quickly progressed to potential winnings of ten pounds, and although any mistake would nullify what he had already gained, he played on without a moment's hesitation.

Up to fifteen pounds. And then –

WINNER OF THE 1932 NOBEL PRIZE IN PHYSICS, WHAT WAS THE FIRST NAME OF GERMAN SCIENTIST HEISENBERG?

A. KARL B. MAX C. NIELS D. WERNER

'Shit,' said Dorian. 'This hasn't come up before. Anyone?'

'It's Niels,' said Mark.

'One hundred per cent?' said Dorian.

'I'm studying physics.'

Dorian gave button C a tentative prod with his forefinger.

INCORRECT – YOU LOSE.

'Fuck, Mark.' Dorian, irritated, bounced up and down and the coins jingled in his pocket. 'I still had a fucking pass available.' Jingle jingle jingle. 'We said only answer if you're one hundred per cent certain.'

'I was,' said Mark. 'But now I come to think of it, the machine tricked me. Werner Heisenberg worked with Niels Bohr. I guess I got their first names muddled up in my head. Sorry, Dorian, really.'

'It's all right, it's fine, it's fine.' Dorian took a deep breath. 'The trail should still be short next time. She thinks we just got lucky. She thinks we play fast and loose. Don't worry, she'll sell herself cheap for a little while yet.'

Jack clapped Dorian on the back. 'She?' he said. 'Dorian, you spend nearly every waking hour with this machine and you call it she?' Jack paused. 'By the way, how's your sex life these days?'

Dorian didn't turn to answer, he stared into the flashing lights. 'She's always hungry for me,' he said, dropping another pound into the slot, 'and the more time we spend together the less often she tells me I'm wrong. Good luck finding an improvement on this model, Jack.'

In the next game the question that stumped Dorian arrived early on. The winner of the 1971 Epsom Derby.

'It's Nijinsky,' said Mark.

'Are you sure this time? It's not Mill Reef?'

'My dad's a horse-racing freak.'

'Mark's truly amazing on sport,' said Jolyon.

Dorian, with no great enthusiasm, pressed Nijinsky.

INCORRECT – YOU LOSE.

XXXVI(ii) Mark lost three further games for Dorian, each time with escalating promises regarding his certainty. After Mark had sworn on both his mother's and sister's eyes and again been proved wrong, Dorian ceased to listen to him entirely.

Mark then began to increase the frequency with which he offered his opinion, while providing more and more patently absurd answers to the simplest of questions. Mars was the closest planet to the sun. General Franco had been an operatic tenor. The winners of the 1970 football World Cup had been Scotland.

Dorian asked him to leave and Mark promised not to say another word. In the sixth game Mark kept to his promise. But when Dorian hesitated as he summoned up his recall of the distance in miles between New York City and Toronto, Mark leaned forward and without uttering a word pressed the button for the answer 2,698, the three other options having been 243, 343 and 443.

Dorian swung quickly around, his arm tensed and his hand bunched as if to throw a punch. 'You fucking arsehole, Mark. You fucking fucking arse.'

'Chill out, Door, it's only a game,' said Mark.

'You owe me six fucking pounds.'

'Look, Door, you have free will. We don't live in a fascist dictatorship. Nobody made you listen to me.'

'You hit the fucking button.' Dorian was incredulous.

'Once,' said Mark. 'Fine, so I owe you one pound.'

'OK then, where is it?'

'I'll give it to you later,' said Mark. He shrugged as if Dorian were being inexplicably rude.

Dorian poked him in the shoulder and held the finger there, pushing into him as Mark spread his arms and grinned.

'You're a cunt, Mark,' said Dorian. 'Don't you ever ever come near me again.' Dorian stroked the machine goodbye and rushed out from the pub, shaking his head.

Shortest had been watching and listening from the table nearest the quiz machine. He looked like a movie director, imperious and leaning back in his own special chair. One of his legs was crossed high over the other. Shortest scribbled into his notebook, then looked up and nodded at Jolyon.

Jolyon handed to Mark a small card, printed with the words 'The Picture of Dorian's Rage'. Mark tore it in four and pushed the pieces into his pocket. 'That's enough now,' he said. 'Come on, Jolyon, one consequence a week is more than enough. Surely I don't have to do another one as well.'

'Of course you do, Mark.' Jolyon's eyelids slid slowly down as he shook his head. 'It's the rules. Of course you do.'

Mark shouted, 'I've fucking had it with this.'

'Then quit,' said Jolyon calmly. 'You perform your next conse-quence and you're all square with the Game. You do that, then you quit before the next round begins, and you get your deposit back.'

'Just give me the money back now. I'll quit now if that's what you want.'

'I don't want any one thing more than another,' said Jolyon, 'apart from the observance of the rules. We have to be fair to everyone. You know we can't give you back the money until you're all square with the Game, Mark. Don't ask the impossible.'

'Come on, Jolyon. Don't be an arse about this.'

Jolyon's body snapped back. 'Why pin this on me?' he said. 'Why do I have to play sheriff? Ask them if you can just walk away and break any promises you made.' Jolyon was pointing at Chad and Jack but they weren't looking, their eyes elsewhere, lips clamped tight. 'Ask Emilia, ask Dee. And don't call me an arse.'

'OK, *fine*, Jolyon.' Mark was rubbing his face. 'Shit, but I really liked Dorian,' he said. 'I met him on my first day here and he came over when he saw I was on my own and introduced me to a whole bunch of people. I really fucking liked him.'

'Why the use of past tense, Mark?' said Chad, putting his hand on Mark's shoulder. 'You can still like Dorian. Just because he now despises every last human fibre of you doesn't mean you have to hate him in return.'

'Fuck off, Chad,' said Mark.

Chad laughed. Jack laughed too, it was his favourite type of joke. But Chad laughed harder than Jolyon had ever seen him laugh before.

XXXVI(iii) In Jolyon's room that night they smoked joints and ate salted pistachios. As they threw the half-shells into a metal wastebasket in the middle of the room, they recounted the tale of the quiz machine to Emilia and Dee.

Jack told the tale. He was the best storyteller by far with his tweaks and his colourful untruths and his timing. No one objected to Jack's fish-eyed accounts of various incidents, even when those incidents were fresh and different in their own minds. They even nodded along harder with the best of the lies, each of them sounding a much better person when Jack told the tale.

Chad, sprawled in the armchair, was considering Dee's latest outfit. She was wearing an extended pair of bicycle shorts, or cropped leggings perhaps. Whatever they were they were black and tight and they came to an end an inch beneath Dee's knees. Over these she wore a yellow tutu poufed and patterned with black polka dots. She was sitting on the floor, her back against Jolyon's bed, with her knees steepled and legs disappearing into a large pair of construction worker's boots coloured oxblood, their toes nicely scuffed.

It had taken Dee's unique eye to match to her lower half a strikingly red military jacket. The jacket was weighed down heavily with gold. Gold chevrons and braids and epaulettes. Gold buttons unfastened and the open jacket revealing glimpses of a Sex Pistols T-shirt. Her breasts made the shirt stretch wide at its middle, taut like the plastic wrap over a joint of beef.

Chad felt guilty for making the association with a piece of meat. Dee was obviously no piece of meat. Dee was funny, wild, smart as anything. But still, her breasts looked spectacular. Better than Emilia's even.

But Dee lived in a different world to Chad and he had no chance with Dee. Had she ever been normal, once upon a time? Normal as he was normal? Perhaps one day she had flicked a switch, consciously decided to change. Maybe the transformation took place while moving from one foster family to the next. A long journey, a car window and beyond the beads and runlets of rain the bleak hills of another failed life. Grey scene behind, fresh start ahead.

Now Mitzy on the other hand, Mitzy with whom Chad lived in the house of Americans, she did at least come from the same world as him. And yes, Mitzy had recently been showing signs of interest. Despite Chad's inexperience he wasn't dumb enough to miss every sign. And the more he ignored her the harder she tried, as if he had stumbled by chance on the perfect tactic. Maybe Mitzy wasn't so bad. Pretty cute to be honest. And who else did he know?

Chad tuned in again to Jack. His story was nearing its end and now even Mark was laughing along. 'I wasn't worried so much that Dorian might punch me,' he said. 'I thought he was going to burst into tears because he couldn't take losing, it would have been terrible.'

'And he takes it all so seriously,' said Jack. 'His little notes and his strategies. I felt like saying to him, Door, you do know they can train a fucking pigeon to recognise the correct button in return for a little scrap of seed. Anyone could be good at this game if they wanted to. But they don't. You understand? Nobody cares.'

Jolyon was lying on his bed smoking down most of a joint that had not made its way far around the room. Feebly he puffed out the smoke in little florets and let his spare arm dangle down to the bed skirt. While he lay there, Jolyon's fingers moved rapidly back and forth as if performing a series of intricate sleights of hand.

'Jolyon,' said Mark, 'come on, let's have some of that joint before you finish the whole thing.'

Jolyon said nothing. The fingers paused and then flurried again.

'Joe?' Mark clapped his hands. 'Hey, come on, Joe.'

Jolyon sat up, the action twitchy and sudden as if he were waking from a nightmare. 'What did you call me?' he said.

'I just asked you for some of that smoke before it's done.'

'I said, what the fuck did you call me?'

'Jolyon, forget it. You have the rest. It doesn't matter that much.'

'Did I hear you call me Joe?' Jolyon's anger pulsed and flooded the room like black paint swirling in a water jar.

'Whatever, Jolyon,' said Mark.

'No no no, Mark. Did you or did you not call me Joe? You see, I say you did. Now you have to decide whether or not you want to dispute that fact.'

Mark blinked and shrugged while Jolyon stared hard at him. 'Sure,' said Mark. 'Maybe I did.'

'Then what I want to know, *Marcus*, is who the fuck is Joe? Who the fuck ever said you could call me Joe? Did I tell you to call me Joe? Did you ask for permission to call me Joe? Joe who? Joe what? I don't even know who the fuck this Joe's supposed to be.'

'Fine, Jolyon, I get it, all right.' Mark lifted his hands and then let them fall limp to the floor.

Jolyon looked hard toward Mark but did not see him. Jolyon saw darkness, the long tunnel of his fury and its daylight end no larger than a coin. 'What matters here,' he said, 'is that if anyone ever could call me Joe, it certainly wouldn't be you, Mark. Have you got that? Understand?'

'Just chill out, Jolyon.'

'What the fuck do you mean chill out? What, chill like you, Marcus? You mean I should spend every waking hour acting like I have some form of muscle-wasting disease just so everyone will imagine how little I must work, and therefore how clever I must be? Or maybe I should try and change the rules of an entire fucking game because I'm not feeling up to the effort it demands. Is that your idea of chill, Marcus, your best version of cool?'

'No,' said Mark. 'Just take it down a notch, Jolyon. I didn't mean anything.'

'Because you know what, Marcus, just closing your eyes every five minutes doesn't make you cool. Acting like a zombie half the time isn't so exquisitely nonchalant. And sleeping sixteen hours at a stretch doesn't make you ever so chill. It just makes you lazy. You're a lazy fucking cunt, Mark. That's all you are.'

Mark stood slowly. The transition seemed to take an enormous quantity of energy and up on his feet he looked lost.

'That's right, Marcus,' said Jolyon, 'you can fuck off now.' He gestured at the door as he bridled on the bed. 'And the rest of you can fuck off as well.' Jolyon stabbed the joint into an ashtray. 'I never get this place to myself. Can I never get even one single moment to myself?'

They all began to rise. Jack nearly said something but thought better of it and left the room behind Mark. They trooped off in a line, single file, and with Chad at the rear. Emilia peeled away and moved cautiously toward the bed on which Jolyon had spread himself.

Chad hesitated at the edge of the room.

'It's fine, Chad,' said Emilia, 'I can handle this one.'

Chad smiled, stepped out of the room and closed the door behind him.

———

XXXVII(i) If I was unduly harsh on Mark then perhaps it was because his laziness extended to the observance of rules. He was a sloppy believer in right and wrong. And why did it fall to me to enforce the rules? The others wanted the rules enforced but they all kept quiet, waiting for someone else to speak first.

I used to see the same sort of behaviour all the time before I shut myself away – on buses, in bars, on the street. A man, for example, shouting at a woman. The woman cowering, shrinking back from the fist being formed. And twenty or thirty bystanders shrinking back as well, looking to each other, hoping someone else would step in and do the right thing.

And that person always used to be me. Once upon a time. But the Game snatched away several parts of me. Perhaps life would have done so in any case but the Game got there first. And Chad got there first. And Death got there first.

XXXVII(ii) This morning my neighbour failed to look up even once from his crossword. My ex-wife is married to a tax attorney named Trip. Every time I pass a bum on the street he flashes me a don't-come-hither look.

I have no other choice. There is something I must do. I can't make it alone.

My evening routine steels me for the task ahead. I fill the whisky glass to the line in black Magic Marker, a third full. Two pink pills, two yellow, two blue. And then I leave my apartment as darkness is falling, my sternest test thus far, the East Village like a carnival parade every night.

I reach Avenue A where life throngs the streets, crowds buzzing between one drink and the next. Lines of girls move arm in arm like crabs, I have to step aside as they scuttle and slide up the sidewalk. Doorways disgorge their crowds like cats gagging fur balls. On the hood of a car there crouches a man in surf shorts bellowing, using his hands like a bullhorn. Paaaar-taaaay, he yells.

I try to recall what day of the week this is. Yes, a Monday, I seem to remember.

Baby steps.

XXXVII(iii) ACE bar sucks me into its blackness.

Whisky, I say, when eventually I squeeze through the crowd. The waitress narrows her eyes almost imperceptibly. No, I say, scratch that. Make it a beer, a Brooklyn.

Two fans spin beneath the pressed tin ceiling but don't disperse the heat. The damp crowd quenches its thirst greedily. I notice there are fewer women than men, younger also. They wear early tans and tissuey dresses that hang from thin straps. My eyes settle on them one by one. But I don't recognise a single face.

I miss the intimacy of women. I miss their warmth, their snakes of orchard scents.

The noise rises and falls. The pitch and roll of the place makes me feel seasick and I hold on tight to the edge of the bar.

The barmaid brings my beer and I have to shout to make myself heard. And a Scotch as well, I say. The cheapest, no ice.

XXXVII(iv) After an hour I drink a fourth or fifth whisky, a fourth or fifth beer, and I warm to the world. I look at the crowd and take to the rhythm of its chatter, like listening to crickets while the campfire crackles. And then through the crowd's chinks I notice red numbers spinning on an LED. I stand taller at the bar. One of the displays spins zeros while a second rises, 50, 70, 170. I see a head bobbing up and down. Sometimes there follows the sound of cheers, sometimes groans. I sway from side to side and peer through the crowd. And then I see the source of every-one's amusement. A skee-ball alley. Two skee-ball alleys and only one of them occupied.

I think of my training, of shadow boxing, sparring. Yes, if I don't get back into the ring before Chad arrives, what hope do I have of beating him? I must keep climbing, keep on running those steps.

I down my whisky, stand up and push my way through the crowd. The man at the skee-ball alley throws his last ball. He has scored 480 points. His friends pat him on the back in an appreciative way.

I approach him and tap his shoulder. You want a game? I say, yelling to make myself heard.

XXXVII(v) And it is here that my memory of the night ends. I know only that I woke up alone and in my own bed, my head being hammered from inside to out.

Hangovers lend to me the most acute sense of my atomic structure. I feel the spaces in me, the lack of matter. I am particles and I hum, my whole body set in a gentle vibrato.

I lie in bed too long, until there remains barely enough time to complete my morning routine before noon arrives. I drink two of the day's three allocated glasses of water and take almost my entire allotment of pills. I pull on my sneakers.

XXXVII(vi) Oh, Jolyon. I'm so wholeheartedly happy you came. You came back to find me. And you didn't see me but that doesn't matter. You were there, you made the effort, and that means something special to me.

You seemed to be having such a ball last night. You were rather the spectacle before the doorman threw you out. Up there on the pool table, calling out my name and declaring your everlasting love. It quite made a girl blush.

The declarations of love I will take (again) as drunken hyperbole. And although I see you have forgotten the pool table incident, I hope sincerely you still remember who I am. This cannot have slipped your mind a second time. To forget once may be regarded as a misfortune; to forget twice looks like carelessness!

Can we start all over again, Jolyon? I would love for our friendship to flourish afresh. Let us begin again as friends and take it from there. Hooray in anticipation of YES.

But first, however, I do have one teeny-weeny thing to ask of you. Just a few itsy-bitsy rules, no more mad rushing in. If you want me to finish your story there are just a few things I would ask of you. To read about what we did is already enough of a discomfiting experience. And some bare bones of structure might be good for us. Every friendship requires a structure, don't you think? Even if most of the rules remain forever unseen.

So here are my rules.

(Is RULES a silly word? Perhaps, yes. OK, let's call it a framework then. Yes, FRAMEWORK sounds so much nicer, something to which our fresh shoots might be able to cling.)

(i) Jolyon will leave his apartment at 12 noon every day.
(ii) Jolyon will not then return until 2 p.m. or later.
(iii) Jolyon will ensure that the blind over the apartment's kitchen window is lowered before he leaves.
(iv) All clocks in the apartment will always tell the time accurately.
(v) The fridge will at all times remain reasonably stocked with French mineral water and Dr Pepper soda.
(vi) Jolyon will knock and then wait 30 seconds before entering his apartment at or after 2 p.m.
(vii) The temperature in the apartment will be no greater than 75° Fahrenheit at or soon after 12 noon. (You have an air conditioner, Jolyon. USE it, please!)

OK, I must scurry now, Jolyon. If you believe, as you appear to, that I will never return then you may come home any minute.

And we cannot meet again so soon. Reading your story is stirring up so many unpleasant memories, things I have tried to forget. But how could we ever forget what we did? So if you must confess – and you must, I can see that now – then confess for us all. We were all to blame for what happened.

In time, Jolyon. Please give me just a little more time. There are things I need to come to terms with on my own. Let us restore our trust, our friendship.

And then we can meet again, soon, cross my heart.

——

XXXVIII(i) When Jolyon arrived in the bar, hand in hand with Emilia, the others were at their favourite table in the corner. Dee and Jack and Mark had been explaining bitterly to Chad for the last hour why the Tories were worse than Republicans and Thatcher more evil than Reagan. They seemed to believe it their duty to educate him on such matters.

Jolyon looked fresh and unaffected. He undraped himself from Emilia and offered to buy the next round of drinks, asking each of them what they wanted, his finger settling on Mark last of all. 'And how about you then,' he said, 'you lazy fucking cunt?'

There was an elongated silence. Mark peered up at Jolyon. And then Mark laughed hard and everybody laughed and everything was absolutely fine between everyone.

XXXVIII(ii) But Mark still owed the Game another consequence. At Emilia's suggestion, they agreed the details could wait. There were five days until the next round of the Game. Mark could pick out his next consequence then, before resumption of play.

Five days later and they started at four, a grey rain descending

beyond the windows of Jolyon's room. There seemed recently to
have been some shift within Game Soc. Tallest and Shortest divided
the observance of most of the consequences between the two
of them, Middle now came to most of the rounds.

It was Middle again that day. He entered without knocking.
And then, keeping his head low and looking at no one, he wheeled
the chair from the desk to the wall, far from the play.

'The Picture of Dorian's Rage' having been performed, and
only two pieces of paper now in the pot, they had to agree upon
a replacement. Mark waited outside while they talked it through.
The discussion lasted barely two minutes.

Dee was nearest the desk so she wrote down the agreed-upon
words. Chad liked the way she held the pen, dainty and ladylike,
her gestures elaborate as she looped her Gs and crossed her Ts.
She was wearing green army surplus cargoes and a shirt in
gunmetal grey. She also had on a woollen cream scarf, long enough
to hang beneath her knees. It all seemed very restrained to Chad,
except for the addition of bright blue pumps and an azure fedora
with a tawny feather tucked into its band. He began to imagine
her writing a poem, a poem for him, the unveiling of a hidden
love. But no, secret poems were too passive for Dee. Dee was
stronger than him, Dee would act. She would come knocking on
your door late at night or she might tell you very matter-of-factly
while sitting beside you at dinner in the Great Hall.

That morning Mitzy had found him eating breakfast in the
kitchen and gabbled her way into making a tenuous link between
Chad coming from New York State and there being a band playing
at a pub called the Albany that night. And then, as if the thought
had only just struck her, she invited him along, she was going
with Jenna and Fredo. And what with Jenna and Fredo being like
totally icky all the time together, he'd be doing her a favour. Chad
had told her that, oh shoot, he really wished he could but he had
already made plans with friends. 'What, those English friends of

yours?' Mitzy had said, and then left the room with a snort when he nodded.

When Dee finished folding the consequence and dropped it into the pot, Jolyon called Mark into the room. He headed straight to the coffee table, not with any great speed but with something like a look of intent. He plunged his hand into the pot, swirled the three pieces of paper and plucked one up as if it were a prize.

The slip of paper required five or six unfoldings. Already Chad could see Dee's handiwork, the flourishes in ink. Dee's handwriting but his idea, the others having leapt at his suggestion. All except Emilia of course. Four votes to one.

Mark's cheeks paled as he read. 'That's not fair,' he said, 'I'm not doing that.' He slapped the consequence down on the coffee table.

'Don't worry, Mark,' said Emilia. 'Whichever one it is, I'm sure you can do it.'

'Well, that happens to be irrelevant because I'm using my veto. We each get one veto, OK. So I veto this and we move on.'

Dee spoke his name, long and susurrant, 'Mhhhhaaa-ark . . .'

Jolyon made his voice gentle as well. 'Mark, there aren't any vetoes. We never discussed vetoes. If you want to talk about a rule change then we can do that. But only for future rounds.'

'Fuck off, Jolyon.'

Dee snatched up the slip of paper. 'The picture of Dorian's rage, part two,' she said, displaying the consequence to the others.

'After being upbraided by Dorian you feel a great sense of injustice. You were only trying to help him win. You will stride up to him in the bar and tell him as much. You will then produce a leather glove from your back pocket with which you will strike him while challenging him to "a fist duel".' Although the essential idea had been Chad's, both the leather glove and the phrase 'fist duel' were Jack's garnishes.

'I mean, it's stupid for a start,' said Mark, his voice only a few degrees from shouting. 'Since when did students believe in fighting? No one at Pitt fights. No one's going to buy this, it's just ludicrous.'

'Then it shouldn't be so hard,' said Chad. 'Everyone will presume it's just a crazy kind of joke. Everyone already assumes you're a crazy kind of person. Did you see last week's *Pendulum?*'

'And what if he says yes?' Mark turned and stared at Chad, his eyes like flint.

Chad acted confused. 'Come on,' he said, 'you just told us no one at Pitt believes in fighting. So why would Dorian say yes?'

And then Jolyon spoke, his voice still measured and low. 'If he says yes it's up to you, Mark. You can go through with it or you can back down. Your choice.'

'Shut the fuck up, Jolyon, I didn't fucking ask you.' Mark took a long breath and then tried to restore the cold sense of certainty to his voice. 'I'll do it on back quad or in the Churchill. Just not in front of everyone in the bar.'

'What?' said Chad. 'Mark, do you even begin to get the point of this game?'

'Sorry, Mark,' said Dee, nonchalantly adjusting the feather in her hatband. 'You have to do it just how the card says.'

'Fine,' said Mark. 'Then like I told you, I'm using my veto.'

Jolyon spoke less gently now, still calm but with loose threads appearing at the edges of his voice. 'There's no veto,' he said. 'Come on, Mark, you have to know you're in the wrong here. You're easily intelligent enough to know that.'

Mark screwed up his face in disbelief at Jolyon. He turned quickly and snatched the slip of paper from Dee, rolled it up between his fingertips and fed himself the ball of paper as if the consequence were a peeled grape being lowered suggestively onto the tip of his tongue. He swallowed with an exaggerated gulp. 'How's that for intelligent, you arrogant cunt?'

Middle let out a long sigh and Chad turned to see him shaking his head, staring at a spot on the floor between his feet.

All gentleness departed from Jolyon. 'Me arrogant?' he said. 'It's not *me* who thinks I'm so special the rules don't apply to them.'

'Fuck you, Jolyon.'

Emilia tried to soothe Jolyon with a touch but he brushed her roughly from his arm. 'No, not fuck me, Mark. Because I'm not the one who's fucked. I'm not the one who's talking about avoiding a consequence. So I'm not the one who's going to forfeit his deposit.'

'Oh, here we go, Jolyon the rule master. Just who the fuck do you think you are?'

Jolyon's eyes were like metal balls drawn back in a slingshot. 'Who am I? I'm the one who plays this game properly, that's who I am, Mark. I'm the one who pays attention to which cards have been played and doesn't make stupid mistakes that earn them two consequences in a single round. And I'm just one of many people playing the Game a whole lot better than you, that's who I am. Which means the only real question here is who are you, Mark? And the only answer I can think of is this – you're the stupid one, Mark, that's who the fuck you are.'

'What did you just say to me?'

'I said. You. Are. The stupid one. And you are. You must be a bit dim. Why else do you think you've had more consequences than anyone else? It's not unlucky cards and bad rolls. It's because you're just a bit thick, Mark.'

Since the earliest days of their making friends they had all, except for Emilia, freely and liberally insulted one another. Anything was permissible, desirable even. Each night they would eat and then they would drink and then they would argue. And no one would flinch. Or Emilia might flinch just a little. And while Chad enjoyed the verbal roughhousing, he felt more comfortable tussling in his language of *fricks* and *shoots*. But all insults were acceptable, debating points that were forgotten by the next drink. And obscenities were not terms with which they could hurt or offend one another, such words meant almost nothing beyond 'I strongly disagree'. But never, not once, had any of them around that coffee table used such a word to describe another. Never had any of them called another stupid.

Mark leapt to his feet. 'Fuck you, Jolyon. I mean really fuck you.' You could see Mark's teeth when he swore as if he were tearing the obscenities clean out of the air. 'Oh, Jolyon's so masterful at cards like everything else in the world. Well, fuck you. Yes, you, Jolyon, the wannabe Renaissance man. Jolyon who knows everything, who everyone loves. But you're such a fraud. And I've seen how you play your game. You're just a con man peddling vapid ideas to people, empty little theories that sound pretty, and then you pretend to care what they think. Like with Chad. As if you give the slightest shit what Chad thinks about anything.

'There's not a single person on the whole planet you don't secretly despise for a thousand obscure reasons while at the same time you try and sell everyone this bullshit shtick about believing in human decency. And it's all one big power trip like this dumb fucking game of yours. It's pulling the wings from insects and picking on fat kids. So fuck you, really, this time.' Mark's body began to lurch back and forth as if he were hurling his words. 'You're a bully, as plain and boring as that, Jolyon. Just like the worst kids at our schools we couldn't wait to get away from. You're wrong in the head. You're a phoney. And when everyone else round this table figures this out, they're going to make you pay for it. *Joe.*'

Jolyon started to rise but Emilia caught hold of his shoulder and it was she who stood up instead. 'Enough!' she shouted. 'Stop it now, the both of you. Don't you dare say a word, Jolyon. I'm serious, not one word. And, Mark, sit down and shut up, I bloody mean it.' Mark sat down and crossed his arms. 'And now

I'm telling you what we're all going to do, OK?' said Emilia, although having said this she began to look uncertain. 'Right then, well, we're going to vote. Yes. On Mark's veto. That we all get one and only one. And if we vote in favour he can use his today if he wants to.'

Jolyon slapped his hand against the coffee table. 'You can't do that, there's no –'

'Yes, Jolyon, yes I can. I'm sorry but you're bloody well wrong. Now isn't the time for your cast-iron principles because what we have here isn't theories or justice systems in textbooks. This is friends and real life and sometimes you need to know when to turn it off. And I'm telling you, Jolyon, it's right now or I'm walking straight out this room and never coming back.'

Jolyon fought to keep the words from flying out. If his words surged too quickly then soon he would follow them and everything would soar away, out of control. 'Refusing a veto for Mark today has nothing to do with what I want,' he said. 'It's about the Game, Emilia, it's about rules and fairness to everyone.'

'Listen very carefully to me, Jolyon,' said Emilia. 'If I walk out that door then it's not just this game I'm walking away from. You understand that?'

'Fine then,' said Jolyon. 'Have your little ballot. You know my vote.'

Emilia slumped back down in her chair, an emptiness fading away, a warmth bleeding back. 'Thank you, Jolyon,' she said. 'Right. Jolyon votes against the veto and we know Mark's vote, don't we? So now it's down to everyone else.'

'I'm with Jolyon,' said Chad immediately.

'The evil twins vote as one, what a surprise,' Mark snapped. 'Little fucking lapdog.'

'Leave it, Mark,' said Emilia. 'That's two each then,' she continued, 'because I'm voting for the veto. But I want to say why. I'm voting for the veto because our friendship is what matters the most. There are things about this game we couldn't have guessed beforehand. And no one's to blame, no one at all. But I think if we'd seen more clearly how the Game would go, we'd have done things differently.'

Chad snorted. 'How does Mark's veto change anything, Emilia? He'll get another consequence and we'll be right back where we started. You're delaying the inevitable. There's kindness, and there's decency, and then there's utter pointlessness. And this veto idea doesn't have any logic to it. It doesn't do anyone any good in the long run.'

'His master's poodle barks out his latest tune,' said Mark.

'Screw you, man. If you haven't got the balls for any of this then that's your problem. Fine, I'll say it, I don't care. I'm better than you at the Game, Mark. You might understand ten dimensions but you have no idea about our game. I've had the fewest consequences of anyone but if I draw the worst I'll do it, no complaints, no tantrums. I almost wish I could vote for your dumb-ass veto just to see you screw everything up again. You're losing, Mark, so do what you're supposed to do and then you can call it quits like a man. You're not going to win, not in this lifetime.'

'Woof woof woof.' Mark snapped his hand like jaws. 'Yap yap yap.'

'Jack,' said Emilia, 'your turn to vote.'

'I know, I know. But before I vote I want to say something.' Jack looked down mournfully.

'OK, Jack,' said Emilia, 'of course you can say something.'

Jack looked quickly to the ceiling, pausing to gather his courage. And then he said, 'Am I the only one here who thinks Dee's hat makes her look like a medieval troubadour? I mean, where's your fucking lute, Sir Prancelot?'

Emilia swung her foot at Jack but he was prepared and already dodging the kick before her foot came close. 'What?' he said. 'Bad timing?'

'Just vote, Jack,' said Emilia. 'Jesus!'

Jack shrugged. 'I just thought I felt a certain chilly atmosphere in the room,' he said. 'I don't know if anyone else in here noticed. But it must be the hat, I can't think of anything else. And someone had to *fuckingwell* say something.'

Dee snorted and something in the room softened. 'Don't make the mistake of thinking that medieval fashion is passé, Jackie-oh.'

'Oh no,' said Jack, 'that's a mistake I've made once too fucking often.'

'Come on, Jack,' said Emilia, 'this is serious,' she said, but she couldn't keep a half-smile from appearing at the corner of her mouth.

'I vote veto,' said Jack. 'I'm sorry, Jolyon, Chad. In theory I'm completely with you. A hundred per cent. But in practice I have to go this way right now.' Jack swallowed and his eyes darted to Jolyon but Jolyon was looking elsewhere.

'Three votes in favour of the veto, two against,' said Emilia. 'Dee, it's all down to you, I'm afraid.'

Dee removed her hat and smoothed her hair. She seemed not to have to think very hard before giving her answer. 'I'm against the veto,' she said.

'Fuck that,' Mark shouted. 'Why? What the fuck, Dee?'

'I don't have to explain myself,' said Dee. She put the hat back on her head and then cocked it forward and slightly askew.

Emilia gave Dee a confused glance and then looked consolingly at Mark. 'I'm so sorry, Mark,' she said.

'But I didn't lose the vote,' said Mark.

'You didn't win it, mate,' said Jack.

'But I didn't lose the vote. I didn't *lose* the fucking vote. So fine. I'm out of this horror show and you can keep your stupid childish little game. And I get back my deposit. Because the vote was inconclusive.'

Jolyon and Chad had visibly been making an effort to remain detached from the conversation. But before Chad could think of what he wanted to say, Jolyon was shouting. 'No you don't, Mark, no way. That's not in the rules. A player performs all consequences drawn before leaving the Game or the Game keeps that player's deposit and adds it to the prize fund. We were always explicitly clear about that.'

'Fuck you, Jolyon.' Mark's anger flared again but its energy was sapped. He had to stir himself for the fight this time.

'Oh, not this again,' said Jolyon. 'It's becoming tiresome, Mark. Fuck me? OK, fine. That's me fucked then. And now we'll have another vote if you like. I say no deposit, so that's one. Dee?' Dee shook her head. 'Chad?' Chad did the same.

'Fuck the three of you,' said Mark. 'But you, Jolyon, you listen to me. I'm getting my deposit back and I'm holding you personally liable. You, Jolyon, *you*. This doesn't end until you place that money in my hand. Personally. You don't sleep, you don't get to read quietly in the refectory on your own, you don't get to walk down the street without . . . without something . . . You'll see. You just wait. Until this injustice . . . Until then.'

Snap. And it was Jolyon's teeth now. He was untethered, the last cable severed. Throat and gut and spleen, words were not sounds any more, were no longer vowels or consonants. Words were feelings and the feelings were good. His words were soaring, Jolyon was flying.

And then Mark was on him, his flesh but even more his bones. Knucklebones, kneebones. And then a crush as other bodies piled above him, above them both. Jolyon felt a panic, the lack of a breath, two breaths, three.

Then at last the relief of fresh air, the hard suck and swallow of life returning. And Mark receding. Jack and Chad receding. Mark shouting again. 'I'm telling everyone, I'm telling everyone about your stupid game.'

Suddenly Middle jumped to his feet. 'No,' he cried out, 'no you can't.'

'Everyone,' Mark shouted back at him.

And Middle moved toward him but not with any sense of threat. Placing a hand on Mark's shoulder, he glanced at the door and then spoke in a low voice as if afraid that someone might be listening. 'Please,' said Middle, 'you don't want to do that, Mark. *Please.*'

And everyone in the room became quiet as they were surrounded by the gently echoing sincerity of that final word.

Jack and Chad were not holding him tightly now and Mark's body slackened. He looked confused and uncertain.

Chad opened the door. Three bodies departed. The door closed.

———

XXXIX I am overcome with joy.

This happens to be true. I'm not saying this solely to please my visitor.

Yes yes yes. I agree to all rules, guidelines, frameworks . . .

And I mean this as well, absolutely I do. But my feelings of joy at seeing that my visitor had left me a note were soon transformed into a sense of breathless panic. Because, you see, I don't remember the pool table or being thrown out. I don't remember my drunken declarations of love. And therefore I have no idea whose name I called out. And if I reveal this to my visitor now, if I admit to forgetting her a second time . . .

Yet neither name seems any more likely than the other.

Emilia, Dee.

Dee, Emilia.

I loved them both. If things had only turned out differently . . .

And so now there is something important I must do with my story, something I need to tell you about. Henceforth, when I type in italics, these passages will be strictly for your eyes only. For you and only you, my reader. Which means there now exist two versions of my story. Not that I will be writing an entirely different account. Both versions will be the same file copied and recopied to keep them identical. The only difference will be the italicised passages, these italicised passages, which my visitor simply must not read.

This italicised version will lay hidden, buried like pirate gold, nestling inside a folder inside a folder inside a folder . . . the last in a series of Russian dolls, folders with names like Utilities, Dialogues, Cookies, Mnemonics and Preferences. I have created blind alleys and false leads like the wrong turns in a maze. At certain dead ends I have thrown in older versions of this story, or articles I worked on years ago for the paper. There is no way that my visitor can find the hidden treasure of this second version.

Because I want to be honest with you, my intended reader. I want to be honest with the world. But my visitor will expect me to start using her name, hence my panic. And I don't want to lose her again. I don't want to lose her for good.

*

I pace around my apartment in a state of high anxiety. Emilia or Dee? Dee or Emilia? I lie on my bed, sit at my table, stand by my window. Nothing comes to me. I pull on my sneakers.

*

I start to walk aimlessly, my mind whirling pointlessly without anything physical that might nudge me toward remembering her. Emilia or Dee? Dee or Emilia? My system has failed me. Or maybe I have failed my system. I loiter in a drugstore staring at its shelves of cigarettes. I go into a liquor store to pore over its bottles of whisky. And then I stand outside a women's clothes store blinking at the window display, its crowd of draped mannequins. But nothing comes back to me.

Evening has arrived when I find myself in the park.

And that's when it happens.

*

I hear a voice calling out, Hey! Hey, you! The voice is getting louder. Looking up, I see a young man staring angrily at me, striding closer and closer. When he is in front of me, he pushes my shoulder and yells, I said, asshole, you owe me twenty bucks.

I look at my shoulder and then the young man. I have no idea who you are, I say.

Bullshit, motherfucker. Twenty bucks now. He pushes my shoulder again, harder this time.

And I try to push him back. Get off me, I say. But, the final word is swallowed as I feel a sudden pain in the left side of my face. I stumble forward, something catches my shin and I fall, my head hits the ground with a hollow thud.

I roll over and the young man is above me. He has my lapels in his fists. Twenty bucks now, he says. His face is dark against the sky bright above. The pain rings out in my head. And that's when it comes back to me with a jolt. I let out a laugh of childish delight. Yes, I say, yes, I do owe you twenty dollars.

So where is it?

Let me get up, I say.

The young man keeps a hold of one of my lapels as we get to our feet.

I reach into my back pocket and find a twenty-dollar bill. I laugh again as I hand it to the young man. There we go, twenty dollars, I say. And thank you, so much.

The young man looks nervous now, confused as he takes the money, pushing me away as he lets go of my shirt. Dude, you're on some serious crack, he says.

You're right, I say, tapping my head as if my finger is the needle of a sewing machine. You're absolutely right, I say.

The young man examines the bill in his hand and starts to back away from me. When he turns, he puts a little more speed in his step.

And now I know. It came to me quickly, behind the pain. The whole scene played itself out in my mind in the space of less than a second.

*

How about we make it interesting? I say. Twenty bucks a game?

Sure, the young man replies. Whatever, dude. One of his friends begins to massage his shoulders.

We put our money in the slots. The young man's friend starts to chant. Skee ball, skee ball, skee ball.

Nine balls later – nine awful, drunken arm jerks later – I look up at the score.

I have ninety points. My opponent has trounced me. My opponent has five hundred points.

Five hundred.

Moments later I am on the pool table. I am calling out her name, drunken declarations of love.

*

Yes yes yes. I accept your terms, Dee. Anything and everything. Unequivocally and overwhelmingly yes.

———

XL(i) Now they were five.

Monday lunchtime and the bar was empty but even so they all leaned in, elbows on table, so as not to be heard.

'You mean he followed you?'

'No,' said Jolyon, 'he didn't follow me. You couldn't call it following. He walked beside me as if we're still friends.'

'Mark still *is* your friend,' said Emilia.

Jolyon didn't acknowledge her words. 'I went to a lecture this morning,' he said, 'and he sat right next to me.'

'Mark got up early to go to a lecture?' said Jack. 'Then he's definitely lost it.'

'What did you do?' said Chad.

'Nothing,' said Jolyon. 'I didn't acknowledge him but I didn't ignore him. I don't want him to think he can affect me. He can't affect me.'

'And what happened when you left the lecture?' said Emilia

'The same as before, walking beside me. I went into a shop for cigarettes and he waited outside like a dog tied to a lamp post. When I came out, he picked up where he left off, at my shoulder as if we might start discussing the finer points of the eggshell skull rule or Lord Denning's greatest judgments.'

'But he never said a word?' said Dee.

'Not until I went back to my room. And he didn't follow me up, he just held the door for me. And then he said, as if the thought had only just occurred to him, oh, and Jolyon, don't forget about that thousand pounds you owe me.'

'What did you do?' said Dee.

'I told him very politely that it wasn't going to happen.'

'And what did he say?'

'He said, see you tomorrow.'

'That's so creepy,' said Chad.

'But that was the odd thing,' said Jolyon. 'It wasn't creepy. I mean it was, it was creepy as hell. But only because he seemed so unthreatening. He acted just as if yesterday never happened.'

'Where is he now then?' said Jack. 'He didn't follow you to lunch.'

'But it's not the rest of you he's after,' said Jolyon, 'it's me.' He lifted his beer to his lips, drank and leaned back.

Chad looked at his friend and admired him once more. Jolyon looked incredibly dignified, regal almost, proud of being the chosen one.

Emilia raised her hand as if she were sitting in class. 'I have a question for everyone,' she said. 'What do we all think about Middle? The way he said *please* yesterday, it gave me the creeps.'

'Well, that was the point,' said Chad. 'He was acting, he worked out the quickest way to get Mark to shut up and he did a good job.'

'It's not like Middle could have outright scared him into submission,' said Jack. 'Not like that troll Shortest, he's got some psychopathic Ewok thing going on.'

'Really?' said Dee. 'I always thought of Tallest as the creepiest. For some reason he makes me think of undertakers, quiet and pale and you wonder what's really going on beneath all that surface dignity.'

'Don't worry, Emilia,' said Jolyon, 'they're all harmless enough.'

'So, Chad,' said Jack, 'did you meet up with the liaison officer?'

'I did,' said Chad, 'it's all arranged, just waiting on a couple of OKs. Friday at two.'

'That was fast.'

'The power of the almighty dollar.'

'So you're not going to pull a Mark on us then?' said Jack.

Emilia sighed and placed her hands in her lap one atop the other. She looked like a priest's wife left alone in a brothel, her husband busy absolving upstairs.

'I can do it,' said Chad.

'Sure you can do it,' said Jack. 'Anyone could literally do it. But it's not just about doing it, is it?'

Dee took her pipe from her mouth and used its end to prod at Chad like an accusing finger. 'Forgive me for saying this, Chad,' she said, 'but you're not the most self-confident person I've ever met. I mean, Jack could do it and probably feel nothing. Yes, you can do it but how are you going to feel the next day?'

Chad leaned back and stretched his arms along the top of the bench. 'Well, I guess I'm about to find out what I'm made of,' he said.

XL(ii) After lunch Chad went for a walk to think everything through. Past the old city wall and its vines, the ivy-clad towers. Past the spires and domes and cool stone porches.

After Mark's exit the day before, they had played on, Jolyon had insisted. No one wanted to provoke Jolyon and so everyone seemed to go easy on him. Perhaps this was why Chad, sitting to Jolyon's left, had lost badly.

But so far he had played the Game well. This was his first serious consequence and that was down to misfortune, a bad situation, an unlikely roll. But the Game was still in its early stages and he doubted it would come down to cards and dice now the consequences were becoming stiffer. Survival would come down to mettle and spirit and perhaps down to nature as well, some part of themselves they didn't yet know. He wondered how many of them realised this.

He passed Bethlehem College and then St Christopher's where a famous English poet had kept a bear in his room after the college had banned the keeping of dogs. Chad had taken the open-top bus tour in his first week in the city, a fact he had not told his friends, who would have despised such behaviour.

He took the scenic route home along the river and as he wandered opposite the slipways and boathouses he thought about the consequences awaiting the others. What lurked in each pot remained a secret from each of them. And in many ways the threat of the unknown was a good element of the Game. But surely if some of them knew what might befall them, the play might progress a little faster. And Emilia in particular, if Emilia . . . And then, feeling guilty, Chad snapped away from his thoughts. Instead he stared at an eight on the river, their pairs of oars folding and straightening, the ephemeral fog of their breaths.

But the thought wouldn't go away. Because it was undoubtedly true that if Emilia knew what they had planned for her, she might run from the Game. And in all honesty, forewarning would be an act of kindness, much better for her to know in advance than to have to go through with it. Why should he feel guilty for the simple recognition of a clever strategy?

But first of all there was Friday to get through. He would worry about everything else after that.

When he got back to the house below the river, Mitzy was in the kitchen, perched cross-legged on a dining chair. Although it was nearly five o'clock she was eating Honey Nut Cheerios from a large bowl cradled between her thighs. She had on a pair of red terrycloth shorts and a grey T-shirt, Notre Dame, where her brother played football. Somehow, despite the sludgy weather in Britain, she had maintained her deep tan, her legs the colour of the strong tea Chad was trying to acquire a taste for.

When she saw Chad she became excitable. Bouncing on crossed legs she told him she had just taken a phone call from the liaison officer about Friday's event. She relayed the message, everything had been OK'd and arranged. 'So then, Mr Mysterious, do I get an invite?'

'Of course,' said Chad, resisting the urge to tag on the observation that it was a public event in any case.

'Awesome, Chad. Friday's gonna be awesome. I'm so proud of you.'

'Thanks, Mitzy,' said Chad. The word *proud* seemed inappropriate between them. But never mind, it was sweet of her. Mitzy *was* sweet, the sort of girl he should love, a simple sort of love for his first.

'Hey, how about when it's over, like to show you how awesome you've been, I mean only if you haven't already arranged something with your English friends, because I like totally understand if you have, how about I take you out to dinner? Just you and me, Chad. To celebrate. What do you think?'

'I think definitely, Mitzy,' said Chad. 'That really would be great.'

Mitzy clapped her hands, a small fluttering motion. And then she sang out the word awesome, pitching it at the highest note she could reach. Chad noticed the milk from her spoon dripping as she held it like a microphone, dripping and splashing and running down her thighs.

———

XLI(i) I leave a bunch of gerberas and a short note for Dee before I head out of my apartment at noon. My beard has been itching hideously for days. I think it might be time for a shave. A haircut as well.

OK, between you and me, dear reader, the truth. I would like to look good for Dee. But please keep this to yourself. All I can think of is Dee. Dee Dee Dee.

Chop chop chop and enough hair on the barbershop floor to stuff a large cushion. Next the beard – first a buzz cut with clippers, then the scrape of the blade. And now I look better than I have done in years. Not that I have spent much time admiring myself in the mirror. Because when I get home I find Dee's letter.

XLI(ii) Oh, Jolyon, thank you for the flowers and the very dear note. You are utterly sweet and I feel truly blessed having you back in my life. And thank you for agreeing to the rules. I'm sorry, the FRAMEWORK.

This is now my third version of this letter. The first two were terribly coy and they just didn't work. This time I have decided to tell you the truth, the whole truth and nothing but the truth, because I'm sure you're wondering why I'm here in New York.

Deep breath.

For the past fourteen years, sometimes for as many seconds as any day has to offer, I have been writing. Writing and rewriting, ripping everything up, starting all over again. Tormenting myself, tormenting those around me. Fourteen long, barren years.

And what else could I do with my life but try to write? I was raised by books, Jolyon, a pack of writers weaned me, like Mowgli brought up by his wolves. And without bewailing too much my Little Orphan Annie story, perhaps I should explain.

As a child, aged twelve perhaps, I began to regard Jane Austen as my mother and Charles Dickens as my father. These were the only two constants in my life, the only two people to whom I gave my unconditional love. Austen and Dickens whispered bedtime stories to me, made me laugh, taught me all about life. And soon came three sisters: Anne, Charlotte and Emily. This was my family and between them they couldn't do anything wrong. I loved them for their words as others love, without question, for blood or lust or family ties. As I got older I unearthed thrilling aunts and uncles. Greene, Nabokov, Woolf, Updike. Each would come to visit with fascinating tales from worlds a million miles away. And they too earned my love, my adoration. Here was a family I could choose, not the other way round. I read and I read and I loved.

So perhaps I write because I want to earn the sort of love I felt for others as a child: that utter and unconditional sense of devotion to another human being. And what else could I write about but the Game? Just like you, Jolyon. What else is there for us to say?

I tried telling it straight, then skew-whiff, back-to-front and oblique. I tried to be Dickens then Austen. I tried Greene then Nabokov. I even tried to be myself. Then I tried you. And then Chad.

But every time I failed. And why? I think the reason is because I never truly worked out what our story was about. This story wasn't about jealousy, malice and spite. No, it transpires that our story wasn't a tale about hatred at all, it was always a story about love. Yes, there are some satellite love stories circling the tale. And of course *all* of us loved each other in some way. But at its centre, at the heart of it, ours was a singular tale of love. The love story of Jolyon and Chad. And this is the thing I could never understand. The curious, complex, ill-explored, secretive, unspoken and venomous love between men.

Mark was so utterly wrong. Of course you cared what Chad thought. You cared too much. (I'm sorry, Jolyon, I'm not here in New York to accuse.)

So, writing and writing and failing. And how have I supported myself throughout these fruitless years? Well, there have been men. There were always men. Not artists or authors, but bankers and businessmen, barristers and bean counters. (B for bed and board, B for bread and bored.) And I even loved one of them, the only one who left me, a bookkeeper with the soul of a poet.

I gave myself to them, my body in exchange for my mind. And they took care of me, looked after the minutiae of life, everything in the world that is not the blank page.

Writing and writing and failing. But I could never give in. Oh, I made friends, joined writers' groups, people liked me. I could have written fluff for magazines, collaborated on children's books, read slush piles of chick lit. But no, I could never sell out. And why?

Well, for two reasons, one surface and one underlying (bu' both the same, it transpires). I feel slightly ashamed to ' this, but I think the surface reason for not giving in w' had I done so, it would have proved Jack righ' Jack would have won. I denied myself all ' of work because of the memory of a pub joke. Just another one of Jack's skits. Except to me it wasn't just another joke, Jack's Psychic Sue was the only dagger he thrust that ever stabbed close to my heart.

Write seriously and fail. Write commercially and succeed.

Jack had a way of getting under your skin with his jokes, an intuition for raw nerves.

And here is my raw nerve: the reason why I had to write seriously, why I could never give in, is because unconditional love can only be earned through the most serious and heartfelt work. The love I feel for Dickens, Austen, Greene . . . this is not a love that has ever been earned by any commercial writer. People might LIKE populist books very much, but they don't ADORE them, they don't suck them down into their souls. There is a difference between success and love, and so it seems that the reason why I could never give up writing seriously is this: I write not because I want to sell but because I want to be loved. I want to be wholly adored.

Now have your way with Little Orphan Annie, Mr Freud.

So this is why I came to New York, it has nothing to do with Chad, I had no idea. I came here only to write, Jolyon. One of my Bs, a businessman with whom I managed to remain friends after our break-up, lent me his New York apartment. He knows all about my struggles and thought a change of scene might do me some good.

And, quite by chance, how right he was. Only my third night here and I was struggling to sleep. I could see the bar from the bedroom window. I went in and, two drinks down, took a cigarette break. And there you were, walking along the pavement towards me. I swear I nearly died of shock.

Do you believe that the universe brings people together, Jolyon, ople who need each other? Well, I do, because I know for a fact nd what did I need in my life but a saviour? The universe threw us together before and we failed to stick. It had to intervene one more time.

I am broken, Jolyon, broken like you. But this is our chance. We can mend each other. Sticky tape, stitches and storybooks. Not all the king's horses or all the king's men, just you and me, Jolyon, the two of us.

Another thing of which I'm certain is that the universe sent me also to make sure you finish your book. You must, Jolyon, you have to. I am enjoying it hugely. You tell it so truthfully, I wouldn't debate a single word. (Please please please, treat me not too unkindly when it comes to it.)

And then, when you finish, I will be free of having to tell the story of the Game. I will be free to write about love, beauty, silken catkins afloat on dark mountain lakes. I will be free to live my life.

Oh, and on the subject of freedom, there is a small something you can do for me. Yes, we will meet, we absolutely must. But first I have to ask you a favour. Will you promise me something, Jolyon? There is something, a very small something, I wish to ask of you.

Kisses,

Dee xxx

XLI(iii) Dearest Dee, ask away. For you, Dee, anything.

Of course it was the universe that brought us together, I don't doubt it for even one second. We are entangled. I'm sure if we understood half the laws of physics it wouldn't seem the slightest bit strange we've been thrown back together.

Anything you did to me all those years ago . . . Well, you thought I had betrayed you, I understand now how it looked. Of course I won't treat you unkindly.

I'm so sorry to hear of your unhappiness. Broken pieces of something once beautiful. But we can do it, you and me, Dee. And one day nobody will be able to see our cracks, or will think it is only the charm of old glaze.

Ask me ask me ask me. Anything, Dee, I promise.

Jolyon

XLI(iv) I'm so happy to have Dee back in my life that I write and I write and I write. But when I am done, I feel thirsty and strangely sickened by my evening pills. So many to swallow. Three pink pills, two yellow, three blue. They make me feel so muddy these days, not the way they once made me feel.

But must trust my routine. Must trust Dee. I'd do anything, for you, Dee, anything.

And how hard the whisky is to swallow tonight. Half a large glass, all the way up to the line, and it feels like such toil.

Suddenly my mouth fills with sweetness. I run and vomit in the toilet bowl, forewarned just enough by a surge of saliva. I once read that this is how our bodies save our teeth from the corrosive burn of our guts. To keep us away from the dentist. And have you noticed how the dentist always arranges the most painful procedures to take place at two thirty? Ha, *tooth hurty*! Starts drilling at tooth hurty two. Where is my lucky tooth? Need some strength, need Dee. Oh, I'd Dee anything, dee dee dee anything. What's the time anyway? Tooth hurty heaven?

What's the time, Mr Wolf?

What's the time, Mr Wolf?

What's the time, Mr Wolf?

Dinner time.

XLII(i) 'Wake up,' said Emilia. 'Chad, wake up.'

In Jolyon's room the afternoon sun had lifted above the dormered roof of Pitt's neighbouring college. Daylight cast itself in abstract wedges against the pinched corners of the rooms. It lit the coffee table amber and danced in a marble swirl where it shone through a bottle of whisky.

'How many has he had?' Emilia held her hand to Chad's forehead.

'That many,' said Jack, pointing to the bottle, two-thirds full. 'I don't know. Six, maybe seven shots' worth.'

'That's plenty,' said Emilia. 'Stop now. How can he –'

'I've seen him put at least twice that much away,' said Jolyon. 'This is what might be termed a tactical pass-out.'

Chad opened one eye and laughed. 'You can't blame a guy for trying,' he said, his words scuffed at their edges.

Jolyon poured him another glass and Chad started to work his way through it.

Tallest was in the room, he had finished reading two magazines and they lay at his feet, the *London Review of Books* and *Literary Review*. Next he opened an old book with no dust jacket and Jack showed enormous interest in its title. When Tallest wearily displayed its cover, *The Prince*, Machiavelli, Jack declared it Tallest's greatest ever joke.

Dee tamped her pipe tobacco and brushed its chaff from her trousers, tartan and held up with bright red braces 'It feels weird for one of us to be drinking and the others not,' she said. 'Like a funeral in reverse.' She struck a match and held it to her pipe. Chad watched the jump of the flame as he finished what was left in his glass.

Jolyon looked at the clock and began to perform calculations in his head. 'Another quarter-bottle in the next hour,' he said, 'and then a final quarter just before you're due to start, Chad.'

Each of Chad's eyes seemed to be trying to focus on a different object. But then a thought gripped him and held him rigid for a moment. 'Hey, Jolyon, what's happening with Mark?' he said. 'Is the guy still following you?'

'He is,' said Jolyon, 'but yesterday brought an exciting new development.'

'Really?' said Jack, with a burst of enthusiasm. 'What did he do?'

'He tidied my room.'

'He did what?' said Chad.

Jolyon looked only perplexed, not overly concerned. 'Yesterday afternoon I went out to buy some cigarettes. And while I was out, I decided I might as well go to the bookshop. And then when I got back, my room had been tidied.'

'He broke in and tidied your room?' said Dee. She looked around. It was certainly neater than usual.

Jolyon shrugged. 'Maybe I should start thinking about locking my door. But I was only going to be two minutes getting cigarettes.'

'Did he take anything?' said Emilia.

'No. Nothing.'

'Just tidied up?'

'That's right.'

Chad let out a boozy bar-room snort. 'Did he do a good job?' he said.

'Superb,' said Jolyon.

'Man, that does it for me,' said Chad. 'That guy is a freak.'

XLII(ii) Jack and Jolyon stood either side of Chad as they walked him.

In Jolyon's room, Chad had finished the drink in a single gulp. Now he looked up at the latticed windows surrounding back quad and smiled as their diamonds of lead softened and the glass shifted woozily as if in a heat haze. The flags at the side of the tower were still and the rosettes of the college crest took on the appearance of eyes above a beaming chevron mouth. They walked through the passageway beneath Loser's Leap and the chill of old stone soothed him. The world was cushioned and soft, he felt a sense of velvet, of feather-down and candlelight. He thought about his date later, remembering the milk running down Mitzy's honey-nut legs, cute enough. This feeling had been mounting for days, Mitzy becoming sweeter the more he reasoned it through.

They walked back into the light and Chad felt Jolyon steady him gently at the elbow. The liaison officer had been insistent on the subject of dress code. Only subfusc was appropriate and the borrowed suit was snug to Chad's body while the black gown above it flapped loosely as they walked. The white bow tie pinched the white shirt to his neck but it felt less uncomfortable now. The grass of the lawn was vivid in the late-winter sun and the heels of Chad's dress shoes rang out in the stone theatre of front quad.

The liaison officer was waiting halfway up the steps. 'Good show, good show,' he said. 'Brought some friends for moral support. Excellent, excellent. More the merrier.' With a sweeping gesture he indicated the door to the Great Hall. 'Shall we?'

As the liaison officer led the way, Jolyon removed something from his pocket and handed it to Chad. 'Technically I'm not supposed to give this to you until after,' he said. 'But I thought it might bring you luck,' he said.

Chad turned over the small piece of paper he had pulled from the pot five days earlier. 'LUCKY JIM' it said in large letters. 'Thanks, Jolyon,' he said, putting it in his pocket.

'You're going to do great, Chad,' said Jolyon, 'don't worry about a thing. And if anything happens, I'll be there, OK?'

Chad nodded gratefully.

'Come on then,' said the liaison officer, beckoning. 'The rest of you should go in now. The warden's ready to begin introductions. I'll take care of Mr Mason here in the vestibule.' He closed the ornate door and then he and Chad were alone amid the tawny panels and gold-framed oils. 'Any jitters, Mr Mason?' he said.

'No way, José,' said Chad.

The liaison officer flinched at the odd choice of words. But Susan Leonard really was a hugely well-endowed institution. And if one of their presumptuous Americans truly desired to give a speech in the Great Hall, then he supposed everyone was just bloody well going to have to fall into line.

XLII(iii) The Great Hall was far from crowded. There were three of Chad's tutors, one of whom he was yet to meet, and the warden. There were the Americans, Mitzy and Jenna and Fredo. There were the four other players and Tallest and a handful of students whom Jolyon had talked into attending. The hall could have accommodated two hundred and there were maybe twenty or thirty, all of them bunched toward the far end where next to high table a lectern had been erected. As Chad walked the length of the hall a few heads turned. Mitzy beamed.

There was a video camera on a tripod. 'Don't worry about that thing,' the liaison officer said. 'I thought the benevolent Ms Leonard might be interested in a recording.'

There was a flutter of polite applause as they neared high table.

His charge delivered, the liaison officer waved to the warden who rose and said a few words concerning vitality and transatlantic cooperation and intellectual stimuli. He then expressed his huge disappointment that he was unable to stay and his shoes chimed his exit as he left, headed no doubt to the considerably greater enjoyment of a pipe in his quarters that lay in the opposite corner of front quad.

And there he was, Theodore Chadwick Mason, the boy from the swine-stead, game player, mouse, innocent, survivor, standing at a lectern in one of the world's foremost centres of academia, nine parts drunk.

Chad looked down at the notes resting on the ledge. They had been typed up under more sober circumstances and he could read the title clearly because it was in a bold font and a large point size. 'The United States, Britain and the Special Relationship: A Personal Perspective'. However, the text beneath it was lighter and smaller. And also moving erratically. In fact the text appeared to be behaving in a deliberately contrary manner. If Chad chased it to the left, it would skip to the right. If he moved his nose closer, the words would dissolve. Nose further back and the letters reassembled but then dropped away as if peered at through the wrong end of a pair of binoculars.

But this was precisely why Chad had memorised the speech.

'Hi,' he said, 'I'm Chad. How's it going?' And then he laughed at himself for using such informality in so grand a place. His audience laughed along, even the three tutors. It was a good enough start.

'The United States, Britain and the Special Relationship: A Personal Perspective,' he said.

The drink seemed to be gathering at the top of Chad's head in a layer about two fingers thick. But this left enough of his mind to recall his words and transfer them into speech. Although for some reason he appeared to be pronouncing certain sentences in a strange English accent.

The timbers of the hammerbeam roof were as dramatic as a thunderous sky, great arches and braces and posts and a tremendous sense of mass, of something unsustainable so high and so old. The glowering weight, the dim brooding of the dark timber, made Chad feel uneasy. And though he knew it unlikely that a roof that had been there for many centuries was about to collapse, he began to feel exposed and vulnerable. He shifted his focus to the ornate screen at the hall's far end, as intricate as lace doilies, and continued to gather more lines from his memory.

'And so for those first few weeks in a new country, you notice a thousand small and new and exciting differences that a month later must still be all around you but to which you have now acquired a spined blot.'

Chad stopped. He had just said 'blind spot', hadn't he? He let his eyes unfocus and his inner ear loop back through his last sentence. No, in fact it seemed he had actually said 'spined blot'.

Jenna and Mitzy and Fredo were laughing. They were good people trying to make everyone else in the crowd believe this had been a deliberate joke. But the three tutors weren't laughing, they were shifting in their seats. One of them had crossed his arms, the second was pinching his brow, the head of the third was turned away completely.

Chad decided not to look at his crowd but instead to address his words to the side of the hall, the walls lined with paintings. Portraits of college founders and bygone luminaries, bewigged men of centuries long past. Chad had the vague sense of breaking off from what he was saying to point out a Pilgrim-style hat. And then he seemed to be imitating Emilia's northern accent, although he couldn't piece together the sound of her voice in his head any more. He sounded Canadian, or maybe Indian, or like a man impersonating the way a cow might talk.

XLII(iv) Now he was standing very still, silently, before them. It was as if he were in a dream and unable to move. Thoughts were running through his head. Very secret thoughts and yet somehow in his dream everyone in the crowd knew what he was thinking. You could tell from the looks on their faces. The shock, the confusion. It was as if he were standing naked in a room full of mind-readers.

Chad sensed that in this dream he was standing in the Great Hall in order to talk about relationships. It then ran through his mind that he was entirely unqualified to talk about relationships, what with him being a virgin. The mind-readers all reacted with shock to this thought, as if he had spoken it aloud. This was a horrible dream.

The liaison officer got to his feet and began to gesticulate but Tallest slid quickly from his bench, placed a hand on the shoulder of the old man and whispered something. The liaison officer looked surprised and uneasy and then sat down again.

Chad wanted this nightmare to end. But as with all bad dreams he was powerless.

The main person Chad did want to sleep with was Emilia. Oh, Emilia. But Emilia was taken. Taken by his best friend. And now Chad secretly wanted his best friend, his only ever real friend, to go and screw the whole thing up.

The practice of mind-reading took an immense amount of effort. This much was clear to Chad from the way that many of the people in his dream, including Emilia, were now holding their heads and rubbing their faces.

Chad felt so guilty having such awful feelings. And another thing he felt guilty about was lying, letting everyone believe he was from New York City when really he grew up on a pig farm upstate. And on the topic of guilt, what he most felt guilty about in life was self-abuse, so guilty that he imposed a limit on himself, only once a month and even then only as a reward for good grades. Also, he had been terrified for years that it was masturbation that was causing his acne but the limit didn't seem to help.

His thoughts continued to spin but Chad couldn't hear them any more. Where was Mitzy? The hall was turning dark and people were moving toward him. Coming faster, then tilting, then slipping away.

XLII(v) 'You really don't remember anything?' said Emilia.

'Spined blot. Something about a hat? But after that, nothing.' Chad pushed the damp cloth harder against his head. 'OK, Jack. You can tell me one thing. I get why my head feels like this but what about the pain all down my right arm?'

'Oh, that was the grand finale,' said Jack. 'The blackout. It was like timber going down in a forest.'

'Yeah, I guessed it was something like that. I just hoped it had happened away from the crowd.'

'No, in front of everyone.' said Jack. 'And on camera. The money shot.'

'And why didn't anyone stop me?'

'Tallest whispered to the old guy you were recently diagnosed with multiple sclerosis. Smart move because then the old guy signalled to the tutors that everything was in hand and he'd explain later. They wanted to call an ambulance when you went down but Jolyon smoothed the whole thing over.'

'Wait,' said Chad, sitting up, looking unsettled, 'how long have I been passed out?'

'A good four hours,' said Dee. 'It's six thirty now.'

'Oh shoot,' said Chad. He tried to get up quickly from the bed but the pain was too severe. 'Jeez, I really have to go.'

'Go where?' said Dee.

'I have a date at seven with Mitzy.'

Jack started to laugh but quickly covered his mouth. 'Sorry,' he said, 'I don't mean to . . . Mitzy? You mean one of those Americans who came to offer you moral support? Blonde hair? California tan?'

'What's wrong?' said Chad.

XLII(vi) It was a French bistro. The pain was a dark blot at the rearmost crook of Chad's skull and the bruises showed when he rolled up a sleeve, so quickly he turned it down. He sat at his reserved table. He was certain Mitzy wouldn't arrive but Chad knew he had to sit there anyway.

An hour alone at a table in a crowded restaurant, Friday night. But this was a punishment Chad felt he deserved. After the manager told him that regretfully he had to ask him to order or leave, Chad stood up and walked out through the whispers, past the eyebrows, beyond the over-shoulder glances.

He made it up to his room without seeing anyone. But just as he had known that sitting and waiting in the restaurant was the right thing to do, Chad was also certain what he had to do next.

He saw a light beneath her door and knocked lightly. Because perhaps if she were in, she might be listening to music and wouldn't hear the lightest of knocks. And then he could return upstairs feeling that at least he had made the effort to do the right thing.

But she opened her door.

Chad dropped his head. 'Mitzy, I'm so sorry,' he said. She didn't let him say anything more.

'Just shut the hell up, Chad,' Mitzy shouted. 'You know, we just had a house meeting and everyone agreed that *noooh one* is going to talk to you.' Chad hadn't noticed until this moment how shapely Mitzy's eyebrows were, neat arches made perfect by her rage. '*Good enough for your first time?* Who in the hell do you think you are? I'm awesome, Chad. I am *waaay* better than any of the skanks who'll ever go near you with their filthy diseases. There's a word for people like you, Chad. Tragic . . . virgin . . . *loser.* I was only nice to you because I felt sorry for you. Everyone agreed in the meeting, you come anywhere near me or try to talk to me ever again, the whole house will back me. We'll all say whatever it takes to get you kicked out of college.' She sniffed before delivering her final line. 'So just go back to your room, Chad, do everyone a favour, and kill yourself.' And then Mitzy slammed the door on him, just as he had imagined she would.

Chad climbed back up the stairs. And then in his room, leaning against his door, he had a terrible thought. If no one in the house were ever to talk to him again, then perhaps humiliating Mitzy had been a wonderful thing to do. No, he chided himself, that really was a terrible thought.

Chad curled up on his bed holding one of his pillows tight to his sick-feeling belly. A minute later the thought came to him again. Really, that's hilarious, they call *that* a punishment?

———

XLIII(i) When I awake I soon detect the symptoms of a hangover. Drink keeps the demons at bay in the night but invites them to breakfast next morning.

Almost noon and this is all I can manage. I don't think I can walk today. I want only to lie in the park.

XLIII(ii) Oh, Jolyon, I'm so happy.

I won't delay revealing what I wish to ask you. It's something so silly really. My book of poems, I've reached four hundred and ninety-eight. Did I ever mean to kill myself if I reached five hundred? Maybe once, maybe some part of me believed what I told myself. But the whole thing does feel rather childish now.

However, I still keep my book close to me, my poems remain a part of me. Anyway, this is my favour – will you look after my book? Oh, I was going to make up some silly excuse – the lock on my apartment door is weak, the flat below was burgled last week – but I think I should tell you the truth. Coyness be damned, Dee, just come out and say it. Here goes:

I would like you to read my poems, Jolyon, that's the truth of it. Writing and writing and failing. It would be nice to have one reader in the world. And I am greedily devouring your words, it seems like a fair trade.

I suggest you start at the end and work your way back. (You may wish to stop when you reach the dark centre of my teenage-hood.) But you should read my book however you wish. And then when you are done telling your story, you can return it to me.

We were together for only a few days all those years ago, but now I look back, I realise that I was so wrong and I'm sorry. I should have trusted you, Jolyon. And now I hope to make amends. I am handing my heart to you.

We will find our way back into the world together, Jolyon, pearls before swine. We will read each other's words and keep them safe.

Friends once more. Fresh words in our story. And let the past fade away.

Kisses,

Dee xxx

XLIII(iii) Dearest Dee, I am a man of my word. Of course I will hold on to your book. I will treasure it, I will read every word. And I feel deeply honoured.

Please, no more apologies for what happened in the past between us. What happened was the result of misfortune. Misfortune and Chad. Let us look only to the future.

And I have a request of my own. Surely now we can meet. You will read this at noon. Perhaps we can see each other in the evening.

I know the perfect place. Tompkins Square Park at the end of this block. Toward the middle of the park there is a grassy knoll where the sunbathers tan themselves until the light shrinks away. Near the grassy knoll is a tall evergreen that looks like a Christmas tree. They string frost-coloured lights all around it each year and, lit up, it looks just like the Chrysler Building. If you say yes, we could meet beside the Christmas tree at six. What do you think?

Jolyon

*

While I am reading Dee's letter over and over, I realise there is something very important I have to do.

Occasionally, out from the gloom of a hangover, enlightenment shines. Ideas are shaken, disparate thoughts come together, linear turns lateral. And when I read Dee's words for a third time – pearls before swine – epiphany strikes.

I hurry downstairs to my building's lobby where the lazier leafleters drop delivery menus or wedge cards into the cracks of the mailboxes. I find what I need, return to my apartment and dial the number.

And now everything is arranged. Early tomorrow. The car will pick me up at six in the morning.

XLIV(i) Someone had pushed a note under Chad's bedroom door, a message from the liaison officer, a summons to an urgent meeting early the next day.

When Chad emerged from his dressing-down, he felt the usual sense of shame. The heat in his cheeks and his forearms itching. The liaison officer had shouted at him for some time, his voice straining like the wail of an old gramophone record. He claimed Chad had let everyone down. Yet the punishment was hardly severe, a housing probation. 'Another offence and your place in that house will be curtains!' But nothing would be marked down on Chad's record. 'You're an exceedingly lucky young man – I strongly considered a large fine. Fortunately for you no formal complaints have been brought.'

Lucky for me *and* lucky for you, thought Chad, as he climbed down the staircase out into front quad.

As the shame subsided, Chad began to detect another sensation, some small sense of warmth. Maybe even inflation. Was this the worst shame could do to him? Today really was another day. And yes, it truly did all seem better in the morning. For the first time in his life those clichéd words made sense to him.

Front quad was glistening with morning dew.

Perhaps it was like exercising a muscle, you had to work that muscle so hard that you damaged its cells. And then, as it repaired itself, the muscle would grow. The muscle would come back larger and stronger, ready for heavier lifting.

XLIV(ii) Dee approached Chad from behind, unannounced but gently, as he rounded a corner of front quad. She took up his arm and held it in hers as if clinging to a mast.

'Hey, Dee,' said Chad.

'How was your date?'

'You English would probably say something like, *slightly disappointing.*'

'Oh dear. That bad?'

'She didn't show. No one in the house is speaking to me. And I just spent fifteen minutes being bawled out by Lord Greyskull. Oh, and if I put another foot wrong . . .'

'Oops. Maybe not ideal to be playing a game of wrong feet then.'

'I'll just have to get smart. Hey, maybe you and I should form an alliance.'

Dee laughed. 'Oh,' she said, 'I'll consider your offer very carefully, Chad.'

And then a silence fell between them as Dee rested her head on Chad's shoulder. Her hair smelled of woodland and vanilla and they walked on slowly through the cold stone passage out onto back quad where the vast tree was now pimpled with green buds and the flags were swaying like fishtails. Then, with a squeeze of his arm, Dee said, 'You know you have absolutely no reason to be embarrassed, Chad.'

'Really? Because I have this weird little itch that tells me you're wrong,' he said. 'It's funny though, there's also a small part of me that doesn't care any more.'

'Good,' Dee said, and she squeezed him again. 'But all the stuff you said in the Great Hall yesterday – don't worry, I'm not planning to remind you of everything – but there's just one thing, Chad, one question I have to ask you.' She tilted her head to look up at him. 'Why didn't you just tell us you grew up on a pig farm?'

'The others knew,' said Chad. 'I guess it must have come up before I met you, Dee.'

'No,' said Dee, 'I asked everyone. And Jolyon knew. But of course Jolyon knew. The others thought you were brought up in New York City.'

'Dee for detective,' Chad smiled. And then he paused, he felt the press of the new feeling in his chest. 'I don't know, Dee,' he said, 'I'm ashamed of a whole bunch of things. I guess that once it has a hold of you it's like shame has the freedom to roam. If I think it through logically, I can't think of any good reason I wouldn't tell my best friends I grew up on a pig farm.' He paused and tried to work it out again for the thousandth time. 'The thing is, it's as if there's another creature inside here who refuses to explain anything he does. Does that even make any sense?'

Dee pushed her head further into the crook between Chad's shoulder and neck. 'Of course it does, Chad,' she said. She let out her breath with another expansive huff and clinging tighter now to Chad, she said, 'We're all ashamed of too many silly little things. I used to be ashamed I didn't have a father. I knew my mother had died when I was three. But my father? Who knows? Maybe he was dead too, or maybe he was alive but just didn't want me. Maybe there was something wrong with me that made him leave.

'When I was little, when I was scared of the dark in my bedroom at night, sometimes I would count up to a hundred. And if nothing bad happened before I got all the way there, I'd tell myself everything was OK, I was safe from the monsters. But to make this work, I had to offer something in return, like a sacrifice. Very *small* sacrifices. If I didn't get told off at school or hit by a foster-parent, I had to cut my hand with a penknife or stab my arm with a compass. And then, when I was eleven, I thought up this way bigger deal than anything I'd come up with before. I decided I'd write five hundred poems, I was always good at poetry at school when I was little. So this deal was with God, I was daring Him to exist, daring Him to let me go through with it. Anyway, I made a wish that, before I got to the five-hundredth poem, my father would find me. But I had to put something on the line. So I made this threat . . . Well, you know what that was, I don't need to say it out loud.' Dee was quiet for a while and then quickly she rubbed Chad's forearm as if it needed warming. 'So there you go,' she said, 'that's one of my very best secrets. And I think you deserve to hold on to it in return for so many of yours.'

Chad tilted his head so his temple was resting on the top of Dee's skull. 'Did you ever try finding him, isn't there anything you can do?'

'Oh yes, we orphans have rights these days, not like poor Oliver,' said Dee. 'Apparently my mother refused to say anything. No one knew if she was seeing anyone at the time she got pregnant. All I can do now is wait.'

Staircase six was just a short way across a cobbled rise. They felt the press of the stones through the soles of their shoes. Dee's head rocked on Chad's shoulder and a loose hair made him want to sneeze but he didn't brush it away.

He opened the door and gestured, after you. Dee went in and they climbed up through the creaks to the room at the top.

———

XLV(i) *Four hours on the road and we find the place without taking any wrong turns. My driver pulls onto the unpaved drive.*

It is not a long driveway and the house is modest. Especially modest when you consider the acres of land all around. Two floors, gable-fronted, fifteen yards of porch. The wooden siding is cedar clapboard painted grey with no trim.

Soon after we pull up, before I have a chance to get out of the car, the front doors open. Wooden door, screen door. The screen clatters shut on its springs.

The man who comes out of the house is in overalls and an old flannel shirt. He wears a frayed cap that displays on its brow the Ford logo, florid swan, blue pond. And he carries a shotgun. But the way he handles it, knuckles pink and loose, the gun is not threatening but simply a presence, a yard of potential. He stops and stands on the wooden steps that descend from the porch. And then he spits.

This is perfect, this is just how I imagined it. I want to clap my hands with glee but decide against any sudden movements.

I open the passenger door and step out slowly. The sunlight gently stirs the pig-shit in the air. Palms showing, I raise my hands to my chest the way Jack used to do a hundred times a day. And then the brightness makes me shield my eyes.

Are you Mr Mason?

Who wants to know? the farmer replies.

A friend of your son, I say.

You English? the farmer says.

That's right, I say. We went to college together.

And your friend in the car there? the farmer says. He go to Pitt too?

No, I say, he's just a driver. I don't own a car.

This last piece of information appears to amuse the farmer greatly. I suppose you want to come in, he says. I can't give you much time. There's work won't be doing itself.

He turns and steps inside. The screen door clatters behind him.

XLV(ii) *Chad's mom has given me freshly baked cookies for the ride home, warm pucks cloudy in their wax paper bag.*

She comes outside to wish me farewell. The farmer has been feeding his animals. I see him emerge from the large shed behind the farmhouse.

The driver turns off his music as I climb into the car. I wind down a window to wave to Chad's mother as we crunch down the drive.

Did you get what you came for? the driver asks me.

Yes, I tell him, I think so.

————

XLVI(i) Emilia was becoming tired of Jolyon's room. The year's first bright days called out to her from beyond his windowpanes, fields beyond the towers and the spires of the city. It was predicted to be unseasonably warm the following day, so she proposed they should play the next round of the Game somewhere with grass. They could pack a picnic blanket, there would be fruit and sandwiches.

The others acquiesced although Jack took great pleasure in bemoaning the effort required. He also voiced bemusement over the fact that Emilia not only owned a picnic blanket but had brought it with her to Pitt.

Emilia was also the only owner of a bike among the remaining five. The others had to borrow, Jolyon's requests quickly rustling up another four bikes, fellow students jumping to the task like footmen.

Away they pedalled, Emilia in front, her bare legs turning in the sunshine. She wore a silk scarf dotted with spirals and daisies and her hair was tied back. Chad had to pedal hard to keep up with her, those buttermilk legs going around and around. After the incident in Great Hall, however, he felt awkward enough to stay several bike lengths back.

Jolyon, Jack and Dee formed the peloton far behind. They

motivated each other with talk of how good the cigarette would taste at the end of the journey, the wine in the sunlight.

Emilia was a natural leader of expeditions, every half-mile or so she would coast, standing tall on her pedals and glancing back at the others while shielding her eyes from the sun. It looked as though she were saluting the stragglers, proud of her brave troops. While she and Chad waited, she would busily consult a map for which there appeared to be designed in her rucksack a specific map pocket. When finally the cursing peloton arrived she would exhort them to continue with lines like 'Come on now, the wine won't stay chilled forever' or 'Last one there gets the funny-shaped strawberries'.

Seven or eight miles beyond the city they reached a large ornamental gate, the entrance to a grand old palace. And then after the cigarettes were lit, Jack found something further to bemoan. A sign listing entrance fees.

'I'm not paying to support the upkeep of a fetid symbol of the fucking aristocracy.'

'Jack, it's one of the most beautiful houses in Britain,' said Emilia.

'Not to me it's not. A tower block full of working-class families, that's beautiful. Not this overwrought wedding cake.'

Emilia looked to Jolyon for some help, the sway he had over Jack, but Jolyon only shrugged.

'I don't mind paying,' said Chad. 'I'll pay for you, Jack.'

'Of course the American doesn't mind,' said Jack. 'It's not your utter corruption of a democracy, is it? No, Americans are always pleased to swan over here then pour their dollars into this kind of shit. The quaint symbols of an institution they themselves rejected more than two centuries ago.'

Emilia became businesslike. 'Middle is meeting us here,' she said. 'Up by the house.' She consulted her watch. 'And we're late because . . . well, we're late and he'll be there already.'

'I signed up for a field and some wine, that's all,' said Jack.

'Not to spit on the graves of the working class. Look at this village.' He pointed to the cottages and inns and terraces behind them. 'Now look at the grounds of this fucking monstrosity. It must be ten times the size of the entire village. All for one family. And I bet they only built the village to house the staff they needed to run that place.'

'Come on, Jack,' said Dee. 'You're right, but come on. Look,' she pointed to the admission sign, 'it costs less to go into the grounds only, we don't have to do the whole house tour thing. Chad can pay for your ticket and you can buy him a pint later on.'

Jolyon lay his arm across Jack's shoulder and led him slowly toward the gate. 'It's a good compromise, Jack,' he said. 'And we can piss in their lake when we're done.'

As they walked toward the entrance, Emilia in front and Chad nearby, the peloton formed again. The brooding young turks, their smoke around them like dust.

Chad handed over his money, two for grounds only, and waited for Jack. He would have liked to have gone into the house. Chad had never been inside a palace before.

XLVI(ii) Emilia and Chad crossed an arched stone bridge over a lake that Jack had chosen as his line in the sand. He and Jolyon and Dee lay on the picnic blanket by the water's edge, into the wine already.

Emilia told Chad some of the history of the place as they walked, the rush of her voice outpacing any awkwardness there might have been. A rapid history repeating. Dukes and scandals and heroes, scandals and heroes and dukes.

Atop a gentle rise sat the vast palace, an ornamented pile unsure if it was castle or palace or Roman temple. Gilded and pillared and with towers and balustrades.

Emilia's tale was hovering on the brink of the twentieth century, a loveless marriage, the fortune returned to the bankrupt family. And it was then that she began to cry. Chad turned and she snuffled back tears, wiped her cheeks and apologised.

'There's nothing to be sorry about,' said Chad.

'I just wanted us to do something fun together,' said Emilia. 'We used to have fun, didn't we?'

'We still do.'

'You might be in love with this game, Chad, but I'm not. I hate it.'

'Then why don't you just leave?'

'And when would I see everyone? We've lost Mark already. You'd all be off in secret, no visitors allowed.'

'You mean when would you see Jolyon,' said Chad.

'No, Chad, I don't mean just Jolyon. I mean all of you. Even Jack. Though I could quite happily punch him in the bloody face today.'

They could see Middle now, he was sitting on a bench staring vaguely toward them. Emilia waved but Middle didn't respond.

'Don't tell the others I cried,' said Emilia. 'Specially not Jack.'

'Of course not,' said Chad.

They continued in silence. Middle seemed not to notice them until they were close enough to startle him and his stare dissolved upon them with a twitch. 'Right then,' he said, 'well, I only came along because there's something very important I need to say to you.' Middle stood up and straightened his jacket, as if Emilia and Chad were a large crowd and he had to give a speech. 'Here's the thing then,' he said. 'I'm quitting, so, yes, I'm leaving right now.' Middle closed his eyes as if he might be imagining palm trees and the purest blue skies. 'I'll let them know myself, Tallest and Shortest, don't worry. Long-distance phone call,' he smiled. 'They can try to do whatever they like with me. But that's it as far as I'm concerned.'

'Right,' said Chad, looking at Emilia uncertainly.

'I wanted to tell you in person,' said Middle, and then he

snorted. 'Well, actually, I always wanted to take a tour of the house,' he said. 'It has quite the history, you know.'

'Emilia was just telling me the same thing,' said Chad.

Middle beamed generously at Emilia. 'Well, this is goodbye then,' he said. He started to head toward the house but then, hesitating, turned back to face them. 'Actually, there was something else I came here to say.' He looked around suspiciously. 'I know you wonder who we are – Game Soc, I mean. But that's really missing the point. The point, the thing that actually matters, is what we represent. And I don't have an answer for that.'

'Very enlightening,' said Chad, 'thanks for the riddle.'

Middle's head twitched like a bird of prey. 'All right then,' he said, 'so it's possible that you might be told certain things. And I don't mean things about Game Soc but something larger than that. Much larger. But I don't know if it's all just ghost stories. So what am I supposed to do? Perhaps it's just meant to scare me into carrying on.'

Middle swallowed hard and looked off to the side. 'It's a little like Pascal's Wager, I think. Blaise Pascal suggested that, when it comes to the existence of God, the only rational way to behave is to believe in His existence. He said we are all playing a game, a coin is being thrown and will land heads or tails, existence or non-existence of God, and we have no choice but to play. We must place a wager because we're engaged in the game whether we like it or not. And the rational choice has to be belief. Because if you win, you win everything. Heaven, eternal life, infinite happiness. And if you lose, you lose nothing, you are the same quality of dead as the atheist.' Middle began to look tired, as if this speech were an essay he had been writing all night. 'And the thing is, you could frame the argument just the same way for belief in Hell of course.'

Middle put his hands in his pockets and hugged his elbows to his side. 'If one of them comes to you,' he said, 'if one of them tells you certain things, you might decide the only rational behaviour is to believe them. Because to act any other way is too great a risk.' And then he became almost enthusiastic. 'But here's my take on Pascal's Wager.' Yes, it's a wager. But the thing with wagers is that the true gambler, the purest player of the game, isn't playing to win. The true gambler plays for the thrill, the sheer ecstasy of taking part. And the purest thrill comes not from the idea of winning but from the fear of defeat, from there being something real and valuable on the line. If there's nothing to lose, then where's the thrill? The true gambler does the opposite.' Middle was gesturing with his fingers, letting them flutter here and there. 'Yes, the purest lover of the game bets the other way, he goes entirely against the grain. Doesn't he, Chad?'

Chad gave Emilia a confused look. 'OK, well, that was fascinating, Middle,' he said, turning. 'I'm now feeling highly educated. And we're both so pleased you came.' He tried to sound sarcastic but felt as if he were caught suddenly in a spotlight.

Middle looked thrilled now. 'Chad, you understand every word I just said. But Emilia . . . oh, Emilia, you're too good for this game. Listen, the only one of you who is safe right now is Mark because he's out. Get out clean, get out early, because the longer you stay in the more dangerous things become. Run away just as soon as you can. Unless you're a true gambler that is, unless you actually thrill for the rough stuff.'

'So what about you?' said Chad. 'Are you getting out early enough?'

'I don't know,' said Middle. 'Like I say, it depends where the truth lies. Maybe not. But I just don't have the stomach for this any more. Good luck,' he said. And then Middle turned and started to make his way toward the house. He looked to Chad very much like an old man from behind. The abundance of wool in his jacket and pants, the hunching of his shoulders, heavy press of the years.

Chad looked at Emilia, the sweet confusion on her face, a look that was not so very far from fear. And that's when Chad realised he had been right. And Middle was right. Emilia didn't belong in this game. And now it was time for Chad to perform his act of kindness.

XLVI(iii) 'What was that all about, Chad? Did you really understand what he was saying?'

'The guy's a freak, Emilia, I honestly have no idea.'

'Do you think we should tell the others?'

'Tell them what? The riddle of the sphinx? I say we just ignore the whole thing.'

Chad turned and Emilia followed. They started to make their way back toward the bridge. 'Let's just talk about something else,' said Chad.

'Like what?' said Emilia.

'I don't know. Riddles. More things the American just doesn't *get?*'

'Shouldn't we slow down then, Chad? We've only got a couple of minutes before we make it back to the lake.'

'That's funny, Emilia. No, honestly, you're a seriously hilarious person.'

'Oh my God, Chad, you've learned sarcasm from Jack. It's the beginning of the end. Come on then, hit me, something you don't understand. Although why you'd ask me rather than Jolyon . . .'

Chad's hands were in his pockets, his shoulders angling forward like a nervous teenager about to ask a girl on a date. But Emilia didn't notice, she moved breezily as they walked together toward the lake.

'Actually, Emilia, there's something about *you* I don't understand,' said Chad. 'The thing with your dad. The whole miners' strike thing, why it gets you so angry. I don't understand it at all.'

'Why should you, Chad? I doubt it made very big news in the States. Most people in this country have already forgotten.'

'So tell me what happened.'

Emilia sucked her lips. 'I don't think I can give you an especially balanced account,' she said.

'But I don't want a balanced account,' Chad said. 'I want your version, Em.'

'OK then, Chad.' Emilia suddenly had a severe look to her but there was nothing she could do that didn't spur the pounding of Chad's chest. 'Well, first of all,' she said, 'you need to understand that in this country the mining industry was nationalised. And it was subsidised as well, it wasn't profitable. So plenty of people would argue something had to be done about it and maybe that's even true. But what makes me angry is how they went about it, how Thatcher and her Tories wanted blood. Because they had this plan of theirs, to crush the unions, right from the very start. They engineered the whole thing.

'The miners' strike began in 1984. But ten years earlier, 1974, another miners' strike had taken down the Tory government. So they cooked up a report right away, how they'd defeat them next time round, get their revenge. It's all out there, meant to be secret but the whole thing got leaked, their plan of attack. You take a look and you'll find they stuck to it pretty well.

'First step, they secretly built up their coal reserves at the power stations so any strike would be ineffective. Next they announce they're closing down twenty pits, with twenty thousand job losses, and they know the unions have got to respond, no choice. So it starts out like most strikes. Only this one was different for the Tories, this was how they were going to stamp out the unions, make their mark on the country. And they weren't going to fight fair. So they used MI5, our own secret services, against us, they knew every move the unions would make. And then Thatcher gave a speech comparing the miners to Argentine soldiers in the Falklands War, the Argentines were the enemy without, she said, and now she was telling the country the miners were the enemy within. Because that's what she wanted, another war.

'Half the working men in my village were miners. And the next village and the one after that. Unemployment was sky-high and they were all lucky to have jobs as it was. How do you do that, take away their livelihoods, the livelihoods of their sons, their daughters' husbands, and expect them to do nothing? So the miners went on strike, formed pickets, and the government brought in police from other parts of the country because they were worried a local police force wouldn't have the stomach to attack its own. Because that's what they had planned, an attack, a fight. Police horses and baton charges, kicking picketers to the ground, beating men in the back of the head with truncheons as they ran away.

'It was winter and they made sure no one could get any benefits, not the strikers, not even their families. Two brothers, teenage boys in a village near mine, died scavenging coal from a waste heap. The embankment collapsed and buried them alive. Those boys died trying to keep their family warm when their dad had no money to pay the bills.

'Our own government, Chad. Spied on us, vilified us, attacked us and finally starved us until we had to surrender. Just as they planned it all along, ten years in the making, their revenge. Thatcher won, Chad, she gave us a bloody good kicking and she enjoyed every minute.'

'Jeez, Emilia, I'm sorry, I didn't realise,' said Chad. 'If I'd known all that, I don't think I would have . . .' And there it was, in his pause, Chad's gift to Emilia.

'Wouldn't have what, Chad?' Already Emilia was becoming agitated, sensing the enormity in the words left unsaid.

'Emilia, I'm sorry. I shouldn't have . . . I didn't mean to . . .' Each of his pauses a gift to her. Gold, frankincense, myrrh.

XLVI(iv) 'Whose idea was it?' Emilia was fifty yards from them, striding, screaming, her silk scarf fluttering discordantly. 'Was it you, Jack? I bet it was. Bastard.'

Jolyon, Jack and Dee were motionless on the picnic blanket, Jack not even raising his palms. They held the pose, their shock, as Emilia continued to advance. 'Come on then, who was it? Which one of you?'

'Emilia, what's wrong?' said Jolyon.

Chad was scampering behind the marching Emilia, hands locked behind his head. 'Guys, I'm sorry, it just slipped out. She was talking to me all about her dad. I swear I didn't tell her. She saw my face and kinda guessed and then I had to say something.'

Emilia was at the border of the picnic blanket now. She stood there, hands on hips. 'Oh, but won't that be a funny one, that'll make a good consequence,' she shouted down at the others. 'Just imagine Emilia standing up in front of a crowd giving a speech about how Thatcher's defeat of the miners was the most important single step in Britain's economic recovery. A personal heroine. Just imagine. Funny as *fook*. Well, I hope this is a bloody good joke for you all. I hope you all laugh yourselves to sleep tonight. Come on then, one of you do the decent thing and tell me whose stupid idea it was. Jack?'

'Why do I get the blame for everything? It wasn't my idea,' Jack yelped insistently. 'It wasn't me, OK?'

Chad was scratching the back of his head. 'Jack,' he said, 'if it wasn't your idea then who else said it first?'

'Whoa whoa whoa,' said Jack, 'it was *literally* my idea. But that doesn't make it *actually* my idea. If I said it then it was *way* before I had any clue about Emilia's dad.'

'Oh, then never mind, Jack. So you just went long for the ride, did you? Hah-de-hah, there's no way she'll do that, not in a million years, so she'll lose her thousand pounds and we'll all have a good chuckle about it in the bar later on. Or maybe you thought I'd be forced to do it, poor little miner's daughter can't afford to throw away that sort of cash. So which one of you was going to phone up my dad, "Hello, your daughter's a bit shy about it and she won't tell you herself, but she's giving this speech and I think she'd really love you to be there"? Pathetic, the lot of you. You know, Jolyon, you're not the only one of us who's allowed to have principles. And I will never, ever show any disloyalty to the memory of what my dad went through, you understand? So this is all just a game, is it? Irony trumps love or values or loyalty every time. Just a game, a bit of a laugh to pass the time. Well, that means everything's all right then.' Emilia looked around. Only Chad looked back at her, at least you could say that much for Chad. 'I've had enough of you all. It's like we're not even friends any more because of this game. Why would I want anything to do with something like that? The only losers in this stupid game are the ones still playing.'

They sat on the blanket feeling sick. Sick and ashamed.

But Jolyon decided that someone had to speak. 'What do you want us to do, Emilia?'

'Take it out,' she said. 'And I want us all to promise we'll never put anything in as bad as that one. Not for anyone.'

Jolyon shifted uncomfortably. 'That does sort of miss the point of the Game, Emilia. Look, Chad's only here for a year. We have to finish at some point.'

'Then let's all just stop it right now. Why shouldn't we? We can all agree it ends now before someone gets hurt. Come on, who's with me?' The others swallowed and looked down at the blanket.

'Look, Emilia,' said Jolyon, 'you never really had the stomach for this game. You found out something you shouldn't and maybe it's for the best. You don't owe the Game anything. Maybe you just pull out and we give you your money back. You walk away with your thousand pounds, no damage done, and everyone's happy.'

'Right, I see,' said Emilia, 'and that's how you all feel, is it?'

No one said anything.

'OK then,' said Emilia, and then the anger seemed to drop away and was replaced by efficiency. She picked up her rucksack and slowly threaded her arms through its loops, each motion very deliberate. And then she began to walk across the grass, heading straight for the gate. There was no urgency to her step, perhaps she thought someone would follow. Very soon they all could see that her shoulders were shaking, shuddering to the rhythm of her tears.

'Do you think I should go after her?' said Jolyon, turning to Dee.

'You should wait till tomorrow.'

While Chad sat down, Jolyon picked up the bottle and poured him some wine. And then they all sipped their drinks, staring off into the lake. There was the sound of birdsong and the water gulping with the splashing of frogs. 'Who came up with that consequence anyway?' said Jolyon. 'I remember us talking about Jack's idea for Game Soc and what a huge coincidence that Emilia's father was a miner. How did we get from there to . . . ? Chad, wasn't it you?'

'It might have been,' said Chad. 'Honestly, I don't remember.'

XLVI(v) The sound, a harsh and sharp squealing, was so loud that Jack moved his hands to his head as if something were screaming down at them from the sky. Dee covered her ears. The noise lasted a few seconds and then came a crashing sound and a rumbling like rocks falling from a cliff.

'Jeez, what the hell was that?' said Chad.

Jolyon had already jumped to his feet. 'Brakes,' he shouted.

And then they were all on their feet, running, and Jolyon in front.

They ran across the grass and out through the gate. They ran up the lane. Some people had come out of their houses.

Jolyon was the fastest, he reached the end of the lane first and saw the jackknifed truck, its nose thrust into the front of a small stone cottage. The truck's trailer was blocking off most of the road. He kept running. First he saw the bike. And then further along the truck driver bending over her. She was lying in the road, her silk scarf fluttering in the breeze but her body motionless. He called out her name. Emilia. Emilia. He called it out again and again and again.

———

XLVII(i) *We pull up outside my apartment at five thirty. I dash up my steps eager to find Dee's reply. I have been thinking about our meeting all the way home. And that's when I have an idea. I have just enough time if I run. Casey's on Eleventh for my surprise and after that a drugstore.*

*

The afternoon's clouds have slipped from the smooth dome of the sky and the park is lush and loud, the East Village out and enjoying the gifts of an early summer.

A loudspeaker plays salsa, trombone sliding beneath Spanish words, horns stabbing the air. A path to my left is crammed with people, a prayer meeting, a preacher waving sunrise hands. The congregation is rapt, their heads like apples in a box.

And soon I am there, the middle of the park, out of breath. I scan our meeting spot and see no Dee, only the sunbathers who crowd the grassy knoll, pale flesh like matchsticks. This is good, I have time to prepare my surprise.

I conceal the gift, it takes only seconds. I have bought a picnic blanket on the way to the park. I spread it out and sit down.

While I am considering the worthiness of my surprise, I feel a tapping on my shoulder.

Hello, Jolyon.

Dee's voice, unmistakably Dee.

I look up and see her fringed with blue sky as she bends down and kisses me lightly on the forehead. Then quickly she sits and crosses her legs. Red lipstick, white shorts and a gauzy white shirt. She has a large tote with her, woven and straw-like.

Say something then, she says, rocking.

I look at Dee's simple clothes. You've changed, I say, you've become . . .

Boring, she says, stretching the word.

No, I was going to say refined.

Refined? Like sugar, *ugh*.

I always imagined you'd become more bohemian the older you got, I say. Headscarves and kaftans, cigarette holders.

Dee laughs. You know, when we were at college, I always thought I was going to be someone. Maybe I was even rehearsing to be someone. But instead I became bland. And all because I realised the time had come for me to hide.

Hide from what?

From failure. Like I told you, writing and writing and failing. And now I just want to disappear into the crowd. Who wants to stand out if they've achieved nothing?

Well, I think you look good, Dee, I say. And I like you as a blonde.

Dee looks happy. And I like you hairless, Jolyon, she says, pointing at her dimple.

I rub the smooth pommel of my chin.

I've been reading about how you lost your beard, she says.

I have become exceedingly forgetful of late, I reply.

She laughs. Well, yes, I've been reading about that as well.

I'm pleased to have made her laugh but now I can't think of anything witty to say. Instead I scratch awkwardly at the pattern of the blanket, palm trees splashed against pale blue sky.

So I have something for you, Dee says. She reaches into her bag and pulls out a large book as thick as a wedding album. It is old but well cared for, red leatherette. You haven't forgotten your promise, Dee says.

Of course not, I say, taking the book, touching it softly. I promise to keep it safe, I say.

Dee smiles at me gratefully. There are four hundred and ninety-nine poems inside, she says. I wrote another one today. And don't worry, I didn't write it to get closer to five hundred. I wrote a poem for you, Jolyon.

If I am quiet it is not only because I feel awkward holding a conversation with a woman for the first time in years. It is also because I feel close to tears.

Dee touches me kindly on the knee. Life should have been so much better to us, Jolyon, she says.

Maybe, I reply. Or better to you. This is probably all I deserved.

No, Dee says sharply. None of this was your fault. It's like you said, what happened was the result of misfortune.

I don't tell Dee that she's wrong. But I suppose if she keeps reading, she will have to find out eventually. Instead I say to her, I have something for you as well, Dee. Your present is under the Christmas tree.

Dee seems touched. Show me, she says, reaching out to me.

I pull her to her feet and lead her. On the lowest branch of the tree, attached with a piece of red ribbon, hangs a small gift bag. Dee opens the bag and removes the contents wrapped in tissue paper. Inside is an ink-pad and three rubber stamps. A silhouette of Jane Austen framed in laurel leaves, an illustration of Charles Dickens holding a quill and an ornate initial decorated with scrollwork and vines. The letter D.

Dee holds her hand to her chest and takes a single heavy breath. Oh how perfect, she says. *And the way she looks at me I feel a forgotten warmth returning to my heart.*

XLVII(ii) Dee gushes gratefully over my gifts. It feels good to remember how to perform an act of kindness. Every day I feel closer to my goal, the whole man.

Dee chatters about her recent weeks. The bumpy flight over, the sights she has seen, how much she is enjoying my story.

I listen patiently and then ask her, So can we meet every day? Why don't you come to my apartment? And then I correct myself. I mean, why don't you come to my apartment while I'm actually inside it? I say.

Dee laughs. Why don't we carry on meeting here? Six o'clock, every evening, and we'll meet for an hour. Perhaps everything else should stay the same, for now. You leave your apartment at twelve, return no earlier than two. We stick to our framework, right?

If that's how you want it.

It won't be for long, I promise. You have to finish writing your story, Jolyon. No distractions. The same routine. It's very important.

You're right, I say, the same routine.

Maybe I could become your trainer, Dee says, prepare you for your comeback.

I grin eagerly. Yes, I say, that's perfect.

And when does Chad arrive, how long have we got?

I don't know, I say, feeling a sudden panic. Soon, I say, but I don't remember. I must have written it down, yes, he told me on the phone. It was some time before . . . I stop and close my eyes, squeeze them tight and start to rock.

Jolyon, keep calm, Dee says, patting me gently. We'll start tomorrow, however long we have I'm sure you'll be fine.

I open my eyes and stop rocking.

What do you need training in? Dee says.

Sanity, I say, making Dee laugh. Well, maybe normal conversation would be a good start, I say, *wanting to add – and after that, the intimacy of women.*

I look up and notice the light beginning to drain from the sky. And then something comes back to me, a memory from years ago, just before I shut myself away. Already in Dee's presence my mind is beginning to open. I have another surprise for you, I say to her, but we have to wait a few minutes. And we have to keep our fingers crossed.

Dee sits tall and crosses the fingers of both hands.

And then it starts to happen. Slowly at first, a blink here, a flash there. But yes, the fireflies are emerging. There they are, bright strings, orange threads in the air. One by one the fireflies wake up and slide into the dusk.

Dee gasps, her head darts around. A blink here, a flash there. With her wrists together Dee claps, her fingers pattering with delight.

And soon the fireflies are aswarm. Gliding, unfolding. Their hearth lights puncturing every cupful of air.

I turn Dee around to point something out to her. Look, I say, spreading my arms. And for my next trick, I say, I have turned on the Christmas-tree lights.

The fireflies flash between the branches.

It's beautiful, Dee says, it's really beautiful.

XLVIII(i) They were shooed away when they arrived on bikes twenty minutes after the ambulance. The nurse told them to come back tomorrow.

The next day they took a bus to the hospital. They brought her music and books and Polaroids of the people who knew her at Pitt, everyone waving, blowing kisses or holding up 'Get Well Soon' signs.

'Sorry, don't know why she won't see you. Headstrong that one,' said Emilia's father. The nurse behind the desk shuffled some papers, pretended not to be listening.

'We had a fight,' said Jolyon. 'She didn't tell you?'

'Says she doesn't remember much.'

'And they're sure it's nothing more than the broken leg?' said Dee.

'That's what they reckon,' said Emilia's father. 'Other than that just bruises, scrapes, concussion. Say they'll hold on to her, run tests, keep their eye on her. Reckon if nothing more shows up she's fine to carry on for rest of term.'

'Tell her we're sorry,' said Chad. 'Sorry about the fight.'

'Whatever the fight were, don't worry, she was never one to hold grudges.'

'And tell her we love her,' said Jack, swallowing hard.

'Will do,' said Emilia's dad. And then he peered harder at Jack. 'Hang on, are you Jolyon, the boyfriend? She's been non-stop about you every time she rings.'

'No, I'm Jolyon,' said Jolyon.

'Oh, right,' said Emilia's father. 'Well, pleased to meet you, lad. Hopefully next time'll be different circumstances and we'll go for a pint.'

'I'd like that,' said Jolyon. 'Next time. Let's hope so.'

XLVIII(ii) Mark was waiting for Jolyon outside his room, sitting down with his back against the door and reading a newspaper. When he saw Jolyon on the stairs, Mark folded the newspaper, placed it under his arm and got to his feet.

Jolyon made an extravagant show of examining his watch. 'What happened to all that sleep you need so badly?' he said.

Mark shrugged. 'I now have a purpose in life,' he replied.

'To haunt me?'

'Haunt you?' Mark sneered. 'I'm not your ghost, Jolyon, I'm your mirror.'

'Come in,' said Jolyon, waving his door key, 'you might as well.'

Mark acted scared. 'So you can do away with me in private?' he said. 'I heard about Emilia. This thing is turning nasty, Jolyon, I can only think it must be your influence. Sounds like I got off lightly.'

Jolyon opened the door and went in. He sat on his bed pulling off his shoes. 'Why are you speaking to me, Mark? I thought the plan was a brooding presence and unnerving silence.'

'Yes, that's what I came to tell you,' said Mark. 'It's time for phase two. This whole escalation thing is actually really exciting. I have seven phases planned. And new ideas keep coming to me all the time. My mind's really come alive since you screwed me over, Jolyon. I should thank you. I understand now why you're so into all that fairness and equality stuff. A sense of injustice is quite a buzz. Almost better than drugs.'

Jolyon lay back on his bed and lit a cigarette. 'Well, thanks for serving notice,' he said. 'Very gentlemanly of you. But if you don't mind, the others will be here soon.'

Mark looked at the coffee table. The boxes of cards, the dice in their cup. 'Don't tell me you're going to carry on playing after you nearly killed Emilia. My God, you people are sick in the head. Winning really matters that much to you?'

'Thank you for coming, Mark. And phase two sounds like a blast.'

Mark looked closely at Jolyon's pile of mnemonics on the desk as he turned to leave. Looked closely as if he were studying them. But Jolyon didn't see, flat on his back and blowing his smoke at the ceiling.

'See you later then, Joe,' said Mark. And as he left he started to hum.

———

XLIX The first thing I want to do when I get home is read the poem Dee has written for me. But there are three whisky glasses staring at me from my kitchen counter. So much to plough through each night, their black lines so high like marks to commemorate record spring tides, legendary floods.

I pour as fast as I can, when I lose trust in routines, bad things can happen. And then I settle down on my bed, cradling the drink to my belly as I turn to the end of Dee's book and work my way back through the blank pages. And then I find it, poem number four hundred and ninety-nine.

CDXCIX (Jolyon)

(i)

His trust is the pressed willow bark
camphor, eucalyptus and menthol
His faith motherwort for the fluttering heart
and berries and herbs quintessential

(ii)

I first saw him . . . was it really?
fourteen years ago
Skin like dandelion milk
hair like its chaff
Cheeks piqued with blood
red clover bud
I loved him then
and he another

(iii)

And when stung, he is mellow green leaf
and in mourning the draught for my grief
my garlic, my grain and my fish
sweet liquorice

(iv)

We lived in the smoke
the many mirrors
of our youth
Such bliss to be young
indomitable
unshakeable
The family that plays together
stays together

(v)

Clove for sore tooth
and honey for throat
In fever my broth
Angelica root

(vi)

Our time was too brief
but I remember its musk
its flare
its thunder
And then time rent asunder
Dark days
ended
Dark thoughts
remain
Too many years
but I found him again

(vii)

My lavendered sleep
my soul antioxidant

Balm for my cheek

and my heart's smooth emollient

(viii)

So I will not go down in the water

And I will not go down in the air

And I will not go down in the fire

And I will not go down in the earth

(ix)

Love

salve

saved

I read Dee's poem and cry. I transcribe her poem for you and cry. I have never been anyone's saviour, only in need of one. And now we are each other's.

Love salve saved. Is Dee being merely poetic, referring to the love that exists between friends? Or do you think . . .? Could it be . . .? Is Dee still in love with me?

I want to read every poem but there isn't time, so I work my way back. I mark a few favourites but allow myself only thirty minutes of reading. There is still so much to write about. Partings, absences, escalations. And most of all, Jack.

Jack and the beginning of his end.

▬▬▬

L (i) While Emilia lay in her hospital bed they played on like the ship's band as the *Titanic* sank. They were English, after all, or most of them. And Chad had begun to think of himself as being closer to English than American. He thought of

Englishness as being defined by stoicism, determination, intelligence.

And Chad's play was undeniably smart. It was Jack who was sitting to his left on that occasion and therefore Jack who suffered from Chad's best hands, his careful strategies.

Several of Jack's consequences had been suggested by Dee and when the time came to pluck his fate from the pot, it was one of Dee's ideas that surfaced. She had intended the consequence mostly as punishment for Jack's dubious opinions. It would have pleased Emilia, it was a shame that she couldn't be there to witness it.

It began three nights later in the bar, Jolyon ready to begin the show, Tallest sipping sparkling water from a green pear-shaped bottle and now only four glasses on their table. But before they could start, Tallest cleared his throat and said there were a couple of trifling matters that needed taking care of first. He reached inside his jacket and placed an envelope on the table. Emilia's name was written on the front and you could see the outline of the stack of notes contained inside. Jolyon picked up the envelope but Dee snatched it away, suggesting it might be better coming from her. Jolyon nodded. And then Tallest continued with a statement. Middle would no longer be attending any sessions of the Game, he told them, and Game Soc would not be answering any questions on the topic. The matter was closed.

Chad acted as shocked as the rest of them while they peppered Tallest with questions he refused to answer. And then there fell over them a silence that started to gather weight, so Jolyon nodded to the table that, yes, it was indeed time to initiate Jack's consequence. He finished his drink, wiped his mouth and stood up.

L(ii) David sat alone and on the same stool most evenings in Pitt's bar. His homosexuality was something he wore awkwardly, the other gays at Pitt averse to his company, something starched and antiquated to his queerness. And the straight students preferred their gays cool and charismatic, David made them feel guilty.

He always had an old book for company in the bar, something by Wilde, a history of the Byzantine Empire, the Industrial Revolution. And nightly his eyes would hover the page, leaping up from time to time to survey the scene. Who was with whom tonight, where might he be wanted, with what sort of quip might he open?

Jolyon touched him on the shoulder to rouse him from his reading. 'David, why don't you join us for a drink?' he said.

'If you're sure I'm not too gauche for such esteemèd company,' said David.

'Can I be honest with you, David?' said Jolyon. 'I think we're all washed up tonight. Jack is resorting to fart gags and Chad has been telling us about his favourite episodes of *The Cosby Show*. Our conversation is in desperate need of an injection of genuine wit.'

David shut his book with a snap and followed Jolyon to the table. He had a large blond beard, its whiskers splayed out like the bristles of an overworked toothbrush. Jack's other nickname for him was the Bearded Clam. Such sprouting around so young a face made David's head appear shrunken and his eyes small among the wisps. He wore tortoiseshell glasses and often a cream fedora to match a cream linen jacket. He was wearing both that night over tight black jeans.

'Well, I'm surprised that Pitt's most guarded cabal has any time for little old me,' said David, sliding cautiously into the chair. 'I thought you were all quite strictly *entre vous* these days.'

Jack swallowed. 'You're always more than welcome to join us, David,' he said, playing his part without gusto.

David laughed. 'And this from the man who likens my face to a vagina. Which is just about the most ugly analogy one could choose for a man of my . . . *circumstance*. Oh, no offence,

Cassandra.' Dee waved away David's attempt at a look of concern. 'And just how, exactly, am I welcome?' David continued. 'The whole band of you guard the spots at this table like *les tricoteuses* their front-row seats at the guillotine.'

Jack sniffed. 'We'd love you to join us more often, David.'

'Oh, I'm sure,' said David. 'But only until eleven, one assumes. At which hour Brigadier Jolyon leads the parade to his room each night. And by and large the exact same group.'

'Well, you're more than welcome to come with us tonight,' said Jolyon.

'And what, may I ask, is the cocktail *de nuit*?' said David.

'I'm not sure,' said Jolyon, 'we're going to Jack's room and I have no idea what he has planned for us.'

Jack shrugged.

'Oh, Jack's room tonight,' said David, his voice vaguely suggestive. 'A sanctum whose walls I have yet to penetrate,' he added, archly.

Jack was not permitted to respond as he would have wished. Instead he forced an unconvincing laugh, but David didn't detect any falsity and looked rather pleased with himself.

'And am I to be let in on your secret?'

'What secret is that?' said Jolyon. 'There's no secret.'

'Oh, come, come,' said David. 'Everyone at Pitt is intensely curious. You must know there's a great deal of talk, you all seem to be behaving in peculiar ways since you became your own private sect.' David paused and sipped but could see that his mischief was not yet sufficient to provoke a reaction. 'Well, at least it gives the huddled masses something to chatter about at their *jejune* little gatherings for the rugby club or political discourse.'

Chad saw the danger and spoke quickly before Jolyon could say anything. 'People can talk a lot of BS, David, you do realise that, don't you?'

'Oh, don't worry, Chad,' said David. 'Let them have their idle fun. As Oscar Wilde said, the only thing worse than being talked about is not being talked about.'

Jack sighed, slipping out of his role. 'You do know you're not Oscar fucking Wilde, don't you?' he said.

David gave Jack a pitying smile. 'I believe that I said, *as Oscar Wilde said*. And I'm almost certain that quotation is not the same as transubstantiation.' He appeared pleased with the line and turned his attention to Tallest. While he did so, Jolyon threatened Jack with his eyes. Jack mouthed an apology.

'Meanwhile, you are a new member of the club, I believe,' said David to Tallest. 'Although I feel I've seen you around on other occasions. Tell me, how did you gain access to this cult? Is there space for part-time members? Please do tell, I'd pay good money to know . . .' he paused, before concluding triumphantly '. . . if such a thing as *good* money has ever existed.'

Now Tallest paused. He appeared to be measuring silence against a response. And then he said simply, 'Hello, David, I'm Tom.'

'A man of few words, Tom,' said David, and then he turned to address the whole of the table. 'Fair enough. And maybe that is my failing and Tom's appeal. But meanwhile there appear to be members missing. Whatever happened to Sleepy and Dopey? I thought Dopey had been released from hospital and was hobbling happily round.'

David's words were met with shock and blinking disbelief.

'So Mark is Sleepy, right?' said Jack, laughing at the severity of David's gaffe. David beamed. 'Very good. And obviously, from the hospital and hobbling, Emilia is –'

'Jeez, man,' said Chad furiously. 'Did I really just hear you call Emilia Dopey? What the heck? Do you ever wonder why people stay away from you up there on your stool all night long?'

David threw his hands to his head in panic. 'Oh, *mea culpa, mea maxima culpa.*'

Chad was turning red. 'Do you have any idea just how *rude* that is? She's lucky to be alive. What makes you think you can just sit there in front of Jolyon calling his girlfriend stupid?' he shouted.

'Oh dear, oh no,' said David. 'Oh, Jolyon, please do forgive me. I'm such an idiot, I'm sorry, I get so carried away sometimes.' David removed his glasses and started to thump his forehead with the heel of his hand. 'Such . . . an idiot . . . such . . . a stupid . . . idiot . . .'

Jolyon reached over and touched David on the shoulder. 'David, it's all right. David, that's enough now.' David stopped thumping himself, took a deep breath and rubbed at his moist eyes. 'Look at me, David,' said Jolyon, 'it's OK. It was only a joke, a harmless joke.'

'I don't think your girlfriend's a dimwit, Jolyon, I promise I don't. I mean, in this place –' David gestured around him – 'who is? No one, we're the –'

'David, stop,' said Jolyon. 'You don't need to explain.' Jolyon squeezed David's shoulder and, when David had nearly composed himself, patted him on the back. 'Good man,' he said. 'No harm done.' Jolyon took a drag of his cigarette. 'In any case, Emilia's not my girlfriend any more,' he said.

'She's not what?' said Chad, shocked.

'It's over,' said Jolyon. 'I went to see her and . . . Look, there are no hard feelings, she doesn't blame anyone for what happened. It was amicable enough. She just needs some time to herself, that's all.'

'Jolyon . . .'

'There's nothing to talk about, Chad.'

'Are you OK?'

'Of course,' said Jolyon, and he did appear to be in good spirits, it was true. 'But now the topic is closed, all right?'

So everyone became quiet because Jolyon had spoken. And after the necessary silence seemed to have lapsed, they all looked to Jack to lighten the mood, Jack the expert at shifting the gears of conversation. But Jack was making himself small and biting his nails, his imagination playing and replaying the scene to come.

L(iii) They left Pitt to buy cava and crème de cassis to make cheap Kir Royales. Kir Rochdales, Jack called them, his humour awakening in occasional bursts.

Jack walked alongside David, they were both studying history and they argued about the Glorious Revolution. Jolyon and Tallest walked behind them, listening in on their conversation to ensure that Jack said nothing untoward.

Jack's room was above the library, a long climb up several staircases. There was a small courtyard and a skylight for the library, raised like a wishing well. David tripped on a loose flagstone and the bottle of cava he was carrying smashed in the bag when he fell. He apologised anxiously, he said that he thought he might be a little drunk and suggested that if they were quick they could filter the drink from the bag into some sort of container. He was on his knees using his hands awkwardly to cover the holes that the broken glass had torn in the bag. The drink was draining away as if being tipped from a watering can.

Jolyon motioned to Jack and Jack helped David to his feet. 'Don't worry about it, David,' said Jack. 'It wasn't your fault.'

'My jeans are soaked through,' said David. 'I should go back to my room and change.'

'No, I'll lend you a pair of trousers,' said Jack. 'The others will wait outside. We'll go into my room and you can change there.'

'Only if you're sure I'll be quite safe alone with you and my trousers down, Jack,' said David.

Jack clenched his teeth. 'You're incorrigible, David,' he said.

David winked. 'Oh, but you have no idea, Jack,' he said.

L(iv) David was in a fresh pair of jeans and had been offered the room's only armchair. Jolyon mixed drinks in the plastic cups they had bought and apologised to David for Jack's disgraceful lack of glassware.

Tallest refused the offer of a drink and took the chair next to Jack's desk. He sat there in silence for almost three hours. The rest of them settled on the floor with their drinks, or on top of Jack's bed, and the night chatter started. They spoke about bullies they had known at school, Noam Chomsky's opposition to the Gulf War, *The Female Eunuch*, anorexia versus bulimia, football, *The Selfish Gene*, British seaside holidays, Orwell, early twentieth-century imperialism . . . And then at two in the morning, Kirs finished and several joints having circled the room, Jolyon initiated the final stage.

The armchair in which David was sitting was next to Jack's bookcase. Jolyon and Dee acted out a short debate over the meaning of the word *metonymy* and then Jolyon pointed to the bookcase. A thick red copy of *The Chambers Dictionary* was on the top shelf, at the bottom of a pile of history textbooks.

'David, pass me the dictionary so I can prove the supposed English Literature student utterly wrong.'

David tried to pull out the dictionary from the base of the pile but the pile threatened to topple. He groaned and stood up and removed the stack of history texts. Something behind the books caught his eye. 'My goodness,' said David. 'What's this I see here, Mr Jack Thomson?'

Jack pretended not to hear and stared at Chad. But Chad only smiled.

David picked something up. 'My oh my oh my,' he said. He held the thing close to his glasses and then grinned excitedly before revealing his discovery to the room.

It was a picture frame, an expensive frame, thick wood stained with a black lacquer. They had all seen the picture before, of course, but pretended now to see it as if for the first time. The photo had been taken in Jolyon's room one night, early on in their first term, several months earlier. Jack was in the photo, a cigarette slanting from the corner of his mouth. Red drunken eyes. In his right hand he was holding up and displaying for the camera his half-finished drink. His left arm meanwhile was around someone's shoulder, a fellow reveller. David's shoulder. David too was waving his drink for the camera.

'Well, I barely even remember this being taken,' said David. 'But then I suppose we do both look a little, shall we say, *ebriose*.' David moved his nose closer to the picture, screwed up his eyes as his spectacles almost bumped with the glass in the frame. 'Oh, now it's coming back to me, my sole invite to one of your parties,' he said. 'But the way I remember it, wasn't it Dee with the camera? And also I was under the impression that it was Dee's camera, not your camera, Jack.'

'You're quite right, David,' said Dee, 'it was my camera. But Jack asked me for a copy of that photo when I showed him the pictures.'

David turned gently pink. 'How very, very funny,' he said. 'And there was I thinking Jack not-so-secretly despised me.'

'What other photos does he have hidden up there?' said Chad.

David put the picture frame down on the seat of his armchair and shifted piles of books to peer behind them. 'There don't seem to be any more photos up here,' he announced. 'Jack, where are your other photos?' he asked.

Jack gulped. 'I don't have any other photos,' he said. He waved a hand dismissively. 'I look terrible in every photo I've ever seen. That's the only picture of me in which I look even half good.'

David picked up the frame again, held it at arm's length, and stared hard at the photo then Jack. 'I'm sorry to tell you this, Jack, but you don't look so terribly good in this photo. And neither do I. We are both undoubtedly the worse for several Hemingways.'

'Then let's take another one,' said Dee. 'A better one this time. Properly composed.'

'You have your camera?' said David.

'Of course,' said Dee, with enormous glee. 'I take it everywhere, don't I, Chad?'

'She never leaves home without it,' said Chad.

'And you'll make a copy for me as well this time,' said David.

'Absolutely,' said Dee. 'As many as you want.' She turned to Jack. 'Come on then, Jack, assume the position,' she said.

Jack moved slowly. David detected nothing but everyone else in the room could see it. The struggle for dignity, the urge to flee. Behind David's shoulder, Jack glared until Dee was ready to take the picture and Jolyon challenged him with a look.

'After three say cheese,' said Dee. 'One, two, three.'

'Cheese,' said David.

'Cheese,' said Jack.

L(v) When Jolyon returned to his room he found his door unlocked. At first this seemed no cause for concern. And then, as he turned to sit on his bed and take off his shoes, he saw an old white sock pinned to his door. On the sock the number four was written in green marker pen.

Sock four: lock door. Yes, he had placed it there to remember to start locking his door every time he left the room. It sometimes took a while for his mnemonics to bed in.

He went to his desk to find his evening routine and noticed the red folder in a curious position. It was sitting apart from everything else on his desk, which was where he left it if he had work to do. But he had done the work, there were three overdue essays for Professor Jacks in there, Jacks had demanded them by tomorrow. Jolyon opened the folder. Nothing inside, nothing. A panic surged through him. Three essays, three whole days' work. And he knew they had been there, he hadn't imagined working for three solid days.

He looked at the clock above his desk, nearly three in the morning. He remembered locking his door, didn't he? He had seen the sock as he left and had locked his door. Or was he constructing this memory? Did he only really remember going over and over the pilled surface of the sock with the pen to make the four stand out?

He sat at his desk feeling sick, pinching the bridge of his nose. Mark Mark Mark.

There were tears in Jolyon's eyes. He pulled them down his cheeks and then wiped his fingers over the desk. He opened the top drawer and took out some paper and a pen. He wondered how much of what he had written he could remember. His mind had not been so good of late. Not so very good.

He looked again at the clock. Nine hours to noon, three hours per essay.

And then he would kill Mark. Tomorrow he would find him and kill him. He should put something memorable somewhere to remind him to kill Mark.

LI I am full of my evening routine when I feel the same light kiss on my forehead as yesterday. Dee sits down on the blanket and crosses her legs, her shorts sliding gently over her thighs. How was your day, Jolyon? she asks. Tell me everything.

The park lounges all around as I glance here and there for reminders.

What is it? Dee asks.

But my head feels like a beehive deadened with smoke. I don't know, I say. Working, I suppose. There's so much to write about, I don't remember exactly.

Then tell me about your lunchtime walk, Dee says. Where did you go?

I pause to think. Left or right? I don't even remember. All of my walks have blurred into one. Just the usual, I say, tearing up handfuls of grass in frustration.

Dee sighs, leaning forward and gripping my wrist. Her hand is as cool as a stone and the grass slips away through my fingers. Oh, Jolyon, Dee says, you really do have a mind like a colander. She pats my wrist tenderly as she lets me go. But don't worry, she says, let's just chat about something else. Do you want to talk about your story?

OK, I nod. *I would like to lay my head in Dee's lap.* Yes, I nod again.

Dee does most of the talking, she seems to remember my words so much better than me. But I do at least contribute to the chatter, these are the early stages of my conversational training. As the discussion nears an end, Dee says to me, You know, Jolyon, your story makes me think of something D. H. Lawrence once said. Never trust the writer. Trust the tale.

And you trust my tale? I say.

There is not a single untrue fact, Dee says.

Then you like it?

How can I like it? It was the worst year of my life. Dee looks at me as if I have taken an absurdly wrong turn. No, that's over-simplifying everything, she shrugs. Maybe it was more like Dickens. It was the best of times, it was the worst of times.

Dee falls silent. And then I see her glance toward her book of poems beside me on the picnic blanket. Yes, let's talk about your work now, I say to Dee.

She hides a blush with her hands.

I love the poem you wrote for me, I say to her. Will you let me read it to you?

Of course, Dee says, that would be wonderful, Jolyon.

I marked two more as well, Can I read all three?

Dee looks embarrassed. Oh, Jolyon, really, you don't have to . . .

I silence her with a raised hand. We're here to save each other, Dee. I love your poems and I'd like to read them for you.

Thank you, Jolyon. Dee says, her eyes glinting with moisture.

I open the book and begin to read. First Dee's poem for me, then a poem about Nabokov's novel *Pale Fire*, and third a wonderful poem called 'Clean Slate'. It seems appropriate to end on this one, its closing lines –

> And when we clean the slate, her smooth dark face
> Is powdered white, our words are but a trace.

I close the book gently and say, I think your poems are beautiful, Dee.

Dee holds her hand to her heart and smiles gratefully. *Yes, cynical reader, this is indeed my chosen method of seduction. But I didn't lie to Dee. I love her poems, they remind me of puzzle boxes, as if you could slide around their pieces and discover something beautiful inside.* And they're much less dark than I'd have expected, I say.

Dee looks surprised. How much did you read?

I worked my way back, maybe the last fifty or so.

Ah, my later work, Dee laughs. If it's dark you're looking for, just wait until you make it all the way back to my teenage years.

We laugh together in the gathering dusk.

The fireflies will soon be out, I say.

Dee lies back on the picnic blanket. Let's watch them together every night, she says.

I lie back on the blanket as well and the city holds us snug in its sleepy hollow. Soon the evening show begins. Blink flash blink flash. We breathe in deeply, our chests rising and falling in unison. Bright strings, orange threads.

And with Dee by my side, nothing bad can befall me.

———

LII(i) 'What?' said Mark. 'Come on, Jolyon, you're a liberal socialist pacifist, you're not going to punch me,' he said. 'What's up anyway?'

'Don't pretend you don't know.'

'Your eyes are all red, Jolyon. Have you been crying or just not getting enough shut-eye? And you're late, by the way. We've already missed the nine o'clock on M'Naghten Rules. And you could do with a lecture on insanity.'

'What did you do with my essays?'

'Why did the chicken cross the road?' said Mark, shrugging.

'There were three essays in a red folder on my desk and I know I put them there and . . .' Jolyon halted, resenting himself for explaining.

'Oh, now I see,' said Mark. 'You lost something and you think I'm to blame.' His fingers began to drum at his chin. 'And you say you know where you put them.' Mark looked fresh, showered and rested. 'Isn't this like the time we had to delay the game because you couldn't find the cards in your room? Hours later Emilia went to the fridge and hey presto, there they were, next to your milk.'

Jolyon glanced away and sucked his lips. And then he ran back to the top of staircase six.

LII(ii) The fridge, shared between eight rooms, was in the corridor. And there they were, underneath his butter.

At first it seemed obvious to him that Mark had moved the essays. But then another alternative jumped into his mind. He remembered finishing the third essay and becoming hungry. He went to the fridge . . . Did he have the essays in his hand? He could picture them in his hand but imagination wasn't the same as memory. And it had been so hard to concentrate on the last essay because his mind had been running over and over the break-up with Emilia, her coldness, the cast on her leg covered in messages and drawings. He had asked her if he should write something, a get well, and she had said no. No, Jolyon, just go. And he felt so guilty. And maybe the essays had been in his hand when he went to the fridge. And maybe . . .

No, it was Mark, of course it was Mark.

Emilia had been in tears at the end. But he should have been the one in tears, he was in the wrong, he was losing her for what he had done. He loved her, he should never have gone along with the miners' strike speech idea, he should have stood up for what was right. And he could imagine the feel of the essays in one hand, reaching for bread and butter, needing two hands.

No no no.

Jolyon was so tired. He had been awake all night long, had already rewritten two of the essays. But at least now he did not need to rewrite the third. And the way Emilia had looked at him when he left the room, Jolyon had seen in her eyes all the happiness that could have been his. And now that he had lost that happiness, he was slipping down beneath the light. And he wasn't sure he would ever find it again.

Jolyon dropped the essays on his desk. Of course it had been Mark, of course it had, hadn't it? He set the alarm to wake him for his tutorial at twelve. But he didn't get any sleep.

LII(iii) Chad crossed the drawbridge to Pitt. In fact it was a flag-stone path across a thin lawn but Chad liked to imagine it as a drawbridge. Pitt was a castle, his place of strength. He wondered if he should try someone's room. Jolyon would be at his lectures. Should he go and see Emilia?

He decided to walk around the college and gather his strength. Yes, he would go to see Emilia and apologise. Perhaps he would even tell her it was all his fault.

And then he saw Dee, reading, sitting on her favourite patch of grass by the ancient tree in the gardens. Her legs were crossed and she was wearing cut-offs and a cardigan. A man's cardigan, large and grey. The cuffs were frayed and there were holes just above them through which she had hooked her hands.

Chad said 'boo' because Dee didn't look up when he arrived. She didn't jump. She paused and placed a feather in her book. Shielding her eyes from the sun, Dee looked up at Chad and smiled. There was so much joy in her smile it caused Chad to blush. 'How many books do you get through a week?' he asked, hoping to distract Dee from the heat in his cheeks.

'Six,' said Dee. 'One per day. I'm like the Lord. On the seventh day, I rest.' Dee patted the grass beside her. 'How's everything with Mitzy these days?' she said, when Chad was beside her.

'She's enjoying torturing me,' said Chad. 'Although no one in the house is speaking to me, it is permissible to speak *about* me. Especially when I'm in earshot. She told everyone that I'm a virgin and whenever there's a bunch of us crossing paths in the kitchen, she'll say something like, "So, did anyone hear Chad say he was from one of the Virginias? Or, does anyone know Chad's star sign? I bet he's a Virgo." Oh, and her latest, "I'm going home for spring break, who do you think it would be better to fly with, American or Virgin?"'

'Oh dear, sounds like Mitzy's a minx,' said Dee, pulling her hands inside her cardigan. 'But never mind, Chad, you're too good for her anyway.'

'You never really met her,' said Chad.

'Didn't I?' said Dee. 'Well, I still think you're too good for her. And I'm hugely confident you're going to find the right girl very soon, Chadwick Mason,' she said.

'*Theodore* Chadwick Mason,' said Chad.

'Really?' said Dee. 'You've kept that quite a secret.'

'Jolyon knows,' said Chad.

'Of course Jolyon knows,' said Dee. 'It wouldn't be a secret if Jolyon didn't know.'

'I hate it,' said Chad, his fingers ripping up grass, tossing it aside.

'No, it's elegant,' said Dee. She shook her hair in front of her face, tossed it behind her and tied it with a red band. And then she said to Chad, 'Oh, here's something funny. Apparently David keeps bumping into Jackie-oh. Every time he turns a corner. And Jolyon's warned him that he can't be rude to him or he's breaking the rules.'

Chad looked admiringly at Dee. 'What made you think of it?' he said.

'Female intuition,' said Dee. 'You boys have such blind spots. Or should I say *spined blots*,' she added with a wink. 'But enough games and our ridiculous friends. I have an idea, Chad. It's such a nice day, how about we go punting together?'

'Punting?' said Chad. 'I thought you hated punting. That was the one expedition of Emilia's you all refused. You said it was outrageously pretentious.'

'Really? Are we always that boring?' said Dee. 'Well, goddammit, Theodore Chadwick Mason, you and I are going to punt. And we'll buy Pimm's and strawberries and I may even purchase a straw hat. Because, even though it's such a ridiculous phrase, *you should try everything once.*'

'That should be a defence for murder,' Chad laughed.

'Precisely,' said Dee. 'Then you'll come with me?'

'I have a tutorial over at Bethlehem at twelve,' said Chad. 'Will you still be here when I get back?'

Dee riffled the unread pages of her book. 'Absolutely,' she said.

LII(iv) Jolyon left Jacks' room just behind his tutorial partner, Prost. He felt so tired he had to steady himself going down. 'Bad luck in there,' said Prost at the bottom of the staircase. 'He's incredibly hard on you,' he said. 'Look, I haven't forgotten you lending me your essays on Roman law when I was struggling. If you ever want to borrow one of mine . . .'

'Thanks, Prost,' said Jolyon. 'I'll get through it, but thank you.'

Jolyon felt his tiredness like a weight in the back of his skull. Did he want his room, did he need breakfast? He plodded randomly around college. And then he saw Dee and his uncertainty dissolved. He swayed from the path and toiled toward the shade of the ancient tree. And then when he reached Dee, without saying anything, Jolyon curled up beside her and fell asleep right away.

Dee looked at him fondly. Jolyon's hands were between his legs and his knees tucked in. His breathing stuttered on the way in but was smoother going out. She wished she had a blanket to tuck around his edges.

Still asleep, Jolyon rolled over and his face fell against Dee's bare leg. Then his arm stretched out and soon his fingertips were resting against the inside of Dee's thigh an inch beneath the fray of her cut-offs.

It felt good, the tingle, the fingertips cool. Dee stroked the hair from Jolyon's eyes.

LII(v) Chad crossed the Bethlehem bridge. There were two punts drifting on the river below, shallow and draped with young limbs. Three swans, the sky cloudless. Chad's chest was light, the paths of his mind awash with delight.

He took his favourite route back to Pitt via the narrow winding lane. The wisteria growing inside King's College was slouched over its old stone wall. The lane twisted, turned and Chad passed beneath the old covered bridge that connected the two halves of Holyrood College. He could see the battlements of Pitt, felt himself nearer and nearer to Dee. He tried to rub the grease from his forehead with the back of his arm and wiped the shine from his nose with the hem at the neck of his tee.

LII(vi) When Chad reached the garden, they were still there, Dee and Jolyon. A rock and a pool.

Chad slowed down as he approached, as if he might be intruding.

But Dee beckoned him and then gestured shush. Chad enquired with a shrug and Dee responded with a shrug of her own. And then, when Chad was sitting beside her, she whispered, 'He came over, said absolutely nothing, and just passed out there and then.'

Chad stayed with them but he felt uneasy, a sense of intrusion. At least he had not bought strawberries or Pimm's already. So he didn't look completely foolish. But even so his heart was breaking.

When finally Jolyon awoke they asked him if anything was the matter. He looked at Dee's leg an inch from his eyes and did not seem surprised to see it there. Jolyon said no, nothing at all was wrong. He sounded very convincing. And soon Jack arrived.

LII(vii) Jack asked Dee what she was reading. She showed him the cover, *Animal Farm*.

'Great story. I loved the *analogy*,' said Jack, although he mispronounced the word as if the first syllables were pronounced *anal* rather than *annal*.

Dee decided not to correct him. 'You've read it then?' she said.

'No,' said Jack, lying back on the grass, 'but I did watch the porn version on video.'

It was Jack's final joke, that's how Chad remembered it. Within five minutes he would be gone. And along with Jack there would depart from the Game the last scrap of any lightness, any humour, any entertainment left in this world of their making.

LII(viii) It began with a tease. Jack lifted himself to his elbows and suggested to Dee that in her outfit she looked like a geriatric prostitute. Dee responded that he should be careful, lest she decided to make it her mission to drive him from the Game.

'Well, that's me shaking,' said Jack. It was a mild comeback for Jack and he spoke it without his usual thirst for the fight.

Dee pushed her cardigan sleeves to her elbows. 'You don't want to make an enemy of me, Jackie-oh. I'm in the book depository and your entire sense of self is sitting pretty in the car seat next to you.'

'You've fired your best shot, Dee. Next session it's me gunning for you.'

'Jack, that was nothing, believe me.'

'Yeah, sure, Dee, OK,' said Jack, trying to look bored.

'You see, the problem you face, Jack, is you know nothing about me. God, you're such a man. You never ask any questions, it's all just jokes and more jokes. So you've got nothing to go on. Whereas the things I sense about you, Jack, my female intuition, oh boy! I listen to you, Jack, hard though that sometimes might be. I actually pay attention to the things you have to say, I look out for your little twitches. Men can be such dimwits.'

'Dee, you're actually becoming tedious now,' said Jack, lying back again and putting his hands behind his head.

'The thing is,' said Dee, 'all of us here know that half your jokes are an excuse to tell your version of the truth, while the other half are a shield, a distraction from the truth.'

'That's right, Dee, it's all just a shield that lets me tell pretentious bitches when they're being pretentious bitches.'

Dee smiled slyly. 'No, I think it's a little more than that,' she said. 'Don't you want to know what's next up my sleeve for you?'

'Not really,' said Jack, yawning. Chad and Jolyon were staring down at him. 'But if you really, really want to,' he said, 'then just go ahead and *wow* us all.'

Dee licked her lips. 'So the next time you land yourself with your worst consequence – and let's face it, Jack, you haven't been playing so well recently and it can't be that long – I'm going to suggest for its replacement that you have to go out on a date with dear David.' Jack closed his eyes. 'You don't have to actually do anything,' Dee continued, 'that wouldn't be in the spirit of the

Game. You simply have to ask him if he'd like to go and grab a bite to eat one evening. And then after that one's performed, we'll replace it with one where you have to turn up naked at his room late one night. Again, it wouldn't be fair to insist you go through with anything you don't want to. But if you *should* want to . . . Do you see a theme developing here, Jack? I can keep going if you like.'

Jack's eyes were still closed. 'Oh, Dee,' he said, laughing, his voice pitched higher than usual, 'you're just too hilarious for words.'

'Oh, but I am, aren't I? So,' she said, turning to Chad and Jolyon, 'can I count on your support?'

'That's one vote from me,' said Jolyon.

'And that's a second from me,' said Chad.

Jack laughed again. 'Funny guys,' he said. He opened his eyes, sat up and then showed them his palms for the very last time. 'Such a fucking funny bunch of funny fucking fuckers.' He got awkwardly to his feet and pointed up at the tower. 'They keep that place locked up ever since Christina Balfour jumped. But I heard from Big Dave there's another way up. Apparently if you go up the organ stairs in the chapel there's a window. You can get along the roof of Great Hall and climb up from there. Big Dave said it was pretty easy, a bunch of them got stoned there one night. I don't know why, Dee, but I just remembered I've been meaning to pass that information on to you for a long time.' Jack looked at his watch and woodenly acted surprise at the hour. 'Funny guys,' he said, 'funny, funny guys.' And then Jack walked away, still laughing. Laughing and shaking his head.

LII(ix) The next day, half an hour after they had arranged, Jack had not arrived. While Shortest beamed periodically at his wristwatch, the three of them agreed they would give Jack five more minutes and would then consider his resignation officially tendered. '*In absentia*,' said Jolyon. And five minutes later, unani-mously, they accepted.

—

LIII *Disappointingly, she plants her forehead kiss no more firmly than on previous occasions.*

It is a brisker night than the last few and Dee wears a cardigan, large and grey, she has hooked her hands through the holes in its sleeves.

I think I remember this, I say, pulling at the cardigan as Dee sits down.

Oh yes, Dee says, inspecting herself. From the good old days. How many good old days did we have before the bad old days?

Hundreds, I say, more good days than bad.

But the score doesn't matter, does it? Dee says.

I decide a diversion is called for. *Gloom is not good for seduction.* Do you still see anything of the others? I say.

Oh, yes, I see Jack and Emilia occasionally. I didn't for the longest time but then I bumped into Jack quite by chance three years ago. And he was relatively easy to bump into – boy oh boy has Jackie-oh ballooned. So now we get together to cross tongues on occasion, the three of us have dinner sometimes . . .

The three of you?

Well, obviously Emilia's there as well.

Obviously?

Oh, of course, Dee says, putting her hand to her mouth. You don't even know that much, Jolyon, do you?

I shake my head urgently.

Sorry, Dee says. Well, they got married five years ago. Ms Emilia Jeffries has become Mrs Emilia Thomson, no P in Thomson.

But that's great, I say, *hoping I have not lost the ability to lie after so many years on my own.* And what else can you tell me? What do they do?

Well, Jack spent most of his early twenties writing film scripts – and according to Emilia, several of them even nearly got made. Comedies, of course. Meanwhile he made just enough money to live writing snarky film reviews for underground magazines. Along came the *Guardian* and offered him the chance to go pseudo-underground. A few years later the phone rang, an ITV screen test was arranged and he landed the job of television presenter. So now he bounces round the screen being spiteful about artsy films and gushing for the mainstream. I'm really quite worried that soon there might be conferred upon our Jack the status of National Treasure.

I pause to take this all in. And then I laugh. Well, I think that's great for Jack, I say, *and I think I nearly half believe this.* But how did he and Emilia end up together?

Emilia spent her twenties researching brain injuries, married to an enthralling Argentine. But that see-saw relationship ended in tears and she bumped into Jack at a Pitt reunion. So she never did get her vet named Giles. But maybe Jack became her safe choice. With his TV salary they moved into a big house in the country and Emilia was able to give up her research, which had been exhausting her. She became an interior designer, she special-ises in something she calls Neo-Rural. I think that means a lot of wood and plastic, she's very much in demand among the wealthier echelons of Hertfordshire. Jack's determined she should follow him onto TV. Last thing I heard, she's up for one of those home makeover shows. Well, Emilia always did have a face for TV. Secretly I think of them as the Chinese restaurant couple, sweet and sour.

I laugh at Dee's joke. Any children? I ask.

Nooo, Dee says, and then she gives me a wink. And where would you like to cast your vote as to why this might be?

My vote goes to – they prefer childless tranquillity, I say.

Dee looks at me as if I have disappointed her hugely. Oh well, what do I know, Jolyon? she says. And Jack even seems to have found some strange Jack-twisted form of happiness. But you could at least have given me the small pleasure of a vote for impotence, Jolyon, she says.

I'm so sorry, I say, *using my apology as a natural opportunity to touch Dee on the shoulder.* And how about Chad? I ask. Do you see anything of him?

No, Dee says, and I don't even have any idea what happened to him.

I try to think of a next line but suddenly I am stumped, all this talk of old friends and there is one name we're missing, of course.

I can see that Dee knows what I'm thinking. Jolyon, please, she says, there's one part of your story I have a problem with. This overwhelming sense of guilt. Look, I understand how you might blame yourself for what happened. But you're wrong, Jolyon, you're not to blame. If you're a murderer then all of us are murderers. We all chose to play, Jolyon. What happened to Mark wasn't in any way your fault.

And what am I supposed to say to this? Oh, Dee, you just wait. Keep on reading and you'll get there. And then you'll find out just how wrong you are. So instead I reach for Dee's book of poems, there are three more I have marked for tonight. Would you like me to read for you again? I say.

Dee looks as if her heart is breaking for me. She nods and I open the book to one of the pages I've marked.

When I finish, the fireflies have begun threading the air with their lights. And soon our hour is up.

Maybe we could stay a little longer tonight, I say to Dee.

Oh, Jolyon, I'd like to spend more time with you too. But you need your rest, you have to finish your story. And then after that we have as much time as we like.

After that. After that. Those words sound so sweet and thrilling to me. And Dee is right, there remains so much more to tell.

Mark's new abode. Emilia's return. My fight with Chad.

———

LIV(i) And then there were three. Chad, Jolyon and Dee. And they were happy, they were in the mood to celebrate their success and this fine thing, this game they had whittled with their minds. They played and no one pushed excessively hard.

The final three. Gold, silver, bronze. Had Jolyon known that Jack would not arrive then perhaps he would have bought Pol Roger for champagne cocktails. A sugar cube in each glass dissolving, throwing up sparks like Roman candles. But instead a burst of warm weather had prompted the buying of rum and Coke and a bagful of limes. They dealt and tossed dice, they drank Cuba Libres as they bickered playfully over the cards.

A bottle of rum between three and Dee fell asleep soon after they finished playing, soon after Shortest had left, taking with him his frenzied notes on Jack's departure. Jolyon recounted the story, it was a shame that Jack wasn't there to tell the tale himself.

Chad and Jolyon drank a little brandy and then when it seemed time to leave, Jolyon told Chad that perhaps he shouldn't wake Dee. She looked so peaceful in her sleep. And this was true, so Chad left resignedly on his own.

The next day, it simply became known that Dee and Jolyon were together now. There was no need for any announcement because gradually the news became apparent, like a distant billboard being driven toward in a car. A suspicion on the horizon and then very quickly it's there, looming large on a hillside, spelling out the truth in giant red letters.

LIV(ii) They performed a few trifling consequences over the next several days, during which time an envelope was pushed across a table by Tallest. Jack's name was displayed on the front, scrawled across a brown paper plateau sustained from within by a bulge of twenty-pound notes.

Meanwhile there was a lull in the play, as if they were all saving their strength for the finale. Jolyon was grateful for this pause and grateful for Dee to hold, Dee to stroke, Dee to love.

Because despite having someone to soothe him at night once more, Jolyon's days were entering one of their dark ages. The once placid pace of his routine was becoming a stumble. And the mnemonics that nudged his days down the right path were beginning to lead him astray. He had started to eat his breakfast cereal midway through the afternoon. He hadn't showered in three days and when at last he did cleanse his body, it was not an object that reminded him but Dee, a gentle suggestion that he might wish to consider a shower. And he had abandoned writing his diary, he didn't remember when, he must have tossed it deep in a drawer at some point. It had become a grind in any case, he liked to write his essays at night and the diary would cut into his work time.

These shifts in his life were making him feel increasingly uneasy. As a child Jolyon had noticed that while other children seemed perpetually sunny, he passed periodically through bouts of bleakness. During these black spells, he suffered from a sense as if entering a room only to forget why one is there. But for Jolyon this feeling could last for days at a time. Sometimes weeks.

Slowly he had learned that a structured life could help lighten his darker spells. At twelve, he had begun keeping the diary to record his days as a series of lists. Gradually his system of mnemonics developed and his diary was no longer needed. But writing it every night had become part of his routine, so he continued. Instead of a book of lists, Jolyon's diary became a more traditional record of the days. Its conversations, his observations.

Or somewhere to vent his opinions in secret, a way to cleanse himself of his darkest thoughts.

And so, while eating cereal at an unfamiliar hour would not be a concern for most people, for Jolyon it felt like a symptom. Or perhaps it was a cause. And then he realised that the sock was no longer hanging from its hook on the door. He thought about replacing it but perhaps he had removed it so that Dee could come into his room unannounced and surprise him at his desk with a kiss, could leave his room early in the morning to work for an hour before climbing back into his bed. Dee's sleek dark hair on his chest, her limbs like the key to his lock.

LIV(iii) Chad had told them he had work to catch up on, so it was just the two of them that night, Jolyon and Dee. They crossed Hallowgood Court hand in hand and took the steps down into the swirling currents of the bar, the sounds and the smoke and the crowd. They saw Jack right away, telling one of his stories to a full table, Dorian and Rory and several more first years. Jolyon knew all their names and which subject each was studying but little more than that. He let go of Dee's hand and waited awkwardly at the edge of the table while Jack finished speaking. Jack's shoulders had become stiff and he didn't turn once the tale was over. Everyone was laughing, slapping their thighs, the table.

Rory raised his glass to Jolyon. 'What do you think, Jolyon, a star in the making?' he said, shifting his glass in Jack's direction.

'Absolutely,' said Jolyon, but the table could sense his uncertainty.

'The major part Jack just landed,' said Dorian. 'Didn't you hear? He's going to play Vladimir in *Waiting for Godot*.'

'You're kidding me,' said Jolyon. 'Jack, that's amazing. Well done.'

'It's just a little student production,' said Jack.

'Little?' said Rory, incredulously. 'It's showing at the Guildhall.'

'Wow,' said Jolyon, 'the first rung of many, Jack.'

'Whoever would have guessed that you're of the theatrical bent,' said Dee, inserting her words with a wink. But Jack took a sip of his drink instead of looking up at her.

'Let me buy you a pint to celebrate,' said Jolyon.

'No, I'm good,' said Jack, his glass almost full.

'Then come to the bar for a quick chat anyway,' said Jolyon.

Jack stood up but without any enthusiasm. He shuffled past three sets of knees on the bench alongside him while Jolyon touched Dee on the arm and asked her to wait.

'Sorry to interrupt, Jack,' said Jolyon. 'But I thought I should return this to you.' He pulled the brown envelope from his pocket.

Jack took a stool at the bar and tore open the envelope discreetly between his legs. He removed the money and pushed it quickly down into his wallet.

'Well done again,' said Jolyon, '– the theatre thing, I mean. When did you start auditioning?'

Jack, not looking up, stared at his hands pressed together around his wallet. 'I didn't think I'd get it,' he said.

'Are you sure I can't get you that drink?' said Jolyon.

'No thanks, Jolyon. Too much celebrating already,' said Jack. He held his hand to his chest and winced.

Jolyon ordered two drinks then turned back to Jack. 'Just one more thing then,' he said. 'Oh, by the way, we're still friends, right?'

Jack nodded. But he was still looking down.

'The thing is,' said Jolyon, 'we probably won't see much of each other . . . but only for a short time. The three of us and the consequences, you know. It's all meant to stay completely in house, right? So please don't think we're deliberately avoiding you. Anyway, I really can't see it taking too much longer now.'

'That's fine with me,' said Jack. He looked over to where he had just been sitting, the merry faces, Dee standing at the end of the table looking alone as the conversation circled beneath her. 'And you know, Emilia was right. It wasn't fun any more. We forgot we were friends. Sometimes it felt like we'd cut ourselves off completely from the rest of the world. And anyway, Jolyon, I'm going to be really busy with all this theatre stuff, you know?'

'I understand,' said Jolyon.

'That's all it was,' said Jack. He paused for a moment and then, with a jolt as if coming out of a daydream, he looked up at Jolyon and waved the empty envelope. 'So if anyone's taking bets, my money's on you. Good luck, Jolyon,' he said, and then he extended his hand.

They shook and Jack slid off the bar stool and began to work his way through the crowd. And then Jolyon, a strange feeling inside him, looked down at his hand. He frowned and picked up his change and the drinks from the bar. And then he realised it was the first time he and Jack had ever shaken hands.

LIV(iv) It was hard for Chad to find a moment when Jolyon and Dee were not together and his feelings built and built, his sense of anger fermenting.

It was not until five days had passed that the two of them were alone together. They were in the Churchill Arms, Dee having left for the library, a tutorial in three hours' time and her essay not yet finished.

As Dee departed, Jolyon felt a waft of discontent, a weight in the air around him. He took a gulp of his beer and decided it was safe to confide in Chad. 'Chad, do you mind if I tell you something?' he said. 'The thing is I, well, I'm just going through a bit of a difficult time right now, you know?'

Chad looked sour. 'I think you'll live, Jolyon,' he said.

Jolyon felt pricked by the response. How many times had he listened to Chad unburden himself? 'I know I'll live,' he said sharply, 'Obviously I'm not saying I think I'm about to die, Chad.'

'Shut the hell up, Jolyon.' Chad sounded weary. He took a large drink, leaned back and glowered at his glass.

Jolyon took a small sip of beer. He picked up his cigarettes and lit one.

Chad waited and waited but Jolyon only smoked and enough was enough. And so Chad began to shout. 'It's a goddamn conflict of interest.' It was a restrained shout, a voice half raised in a crowded place. 'It's an injustice, Jolyon.'

'OK,' said Jolyon, nodding and blowing his smoke. 'What is?' he said.

'You and Dee together,' said Chad. 'There are three left in the Game and two of them are now screwing, so how exactly is that reasonable? Tell me one thing that won't make me feel like I'm being cheated, I'm pretty confident it can't be done.'

Jolyon looked down and thought hard. 'OK then,' he said, not feeling any appetite for a fight. 'Yes, I can see what you mean.'

'So what the hell are you going to do about it?' said Chad.

Jolyon considered the problem, taking several drags from his cigarette. 'I think . . .' he said, 'No, I would *certainly like to think* that you trust me. Because I would never take advantage of any relation-ship outside of the Game. I promise you, Chad.' Jolyon marked his solemnity by putting out his unfinished cigarette, pushing its stub in the ashtray until it bent in two. Then he looked up at Chad.

Chad met his friend's look and Jolyon thought that soon they would buy more drinks and everything would be right between them again. But instead Chad tore himself free of Jolyon's gaze and exhaled hard as if he had been holding his breath. 'Jesus, Jolyon, that's just not good enough. You promise? Sure then, well, that's me totally over the moon.'

'Look, I've promised you, Chad. What else can I do? What happened between me and Dee can't be undone.'

'It was bad enough with Emilia,' said Chad, 'but at least that was only two out of six. Two out of three is a way bigger problem, Jolyon. A *majority*, it's an outrage.'

Jolyon was shifting uncomfortably in his seat but he chose to say nothing.

'It's way beneath you as well,' Chad said. 'I can't believe that you of all people would pull a stunt like that.'

Jolyon jerked back his head. 'A stunt?' he said. 'You don't actually think me sleeping with Dee is some kind of tactic, do you, Chad? I really don't care about winning so much that I'd whore myself just to score a few points.'

Chad said nothing, only looked away.

'Exactly what is it you think I should do?' said Jolyon. 'Why don't you tell me *your* solution, Chad?'

'OK then,' said Chad. 'You have to break it off.'

The response made Jolyon's body twitch. 'Break up with Dee?' he said, blinking hard. 'Don't be ridiculous, Chad.' Now Jolyon was loud. 'I mean, if that's what you think, you can really go fuck yourself.'

'Then I'll break it off,' said Chad.

'How can you break it off?' Jolyon leaned in across the table, his restraints beginning to snap. 'This is between me and Dee and you're not invited. No matter how much you'd like it, Chad, it's not a *ménage à trois*.'

'That's absolute crap, Jolyon. That's screwed up in the head.'

'I saw how you used to look at Emilia,' said Jolyon, leaning back in his chair. 'And recently I've seen you start to look at Dee the same way.'

'Well, if that's what you believe, Jolyon,' said Chad, 'if that's what you truly think, then why the heck would you go right ahead and sleep with them both? If we're supposed to be friends then tell me exactly what kind of a friend would do that?'

Jolyon lit himself another cigarette and dragged hard. He began shaking and shaking his head so that the smoke came out in ripples. 'It's women, Chad,' he said. 'It's different rules.'

'No, Jolyon, I'll tell you exactly why you did it. It's because you have to be the big man, the top *frickin* horn-dog.'

'I have absolutely no idea what you mean.'

'Alpha Jolyon and everyone else, the whole secret clan, has to bend to his will.'

'That's utter bullshit, Chad.'

'Really? Then tell me why. Tell me why you would do that. And don't give me that different rules BS.'

Jolyon blew his smoke carefully from the side of his mouth. 'OK then, I slept with Dee because I could, Chad, that's why. Just because I could.'

Chad snorted. 'That's pathetic, Jolyon. You could. And that's it? And I suppose I couldn't. That's what you're trying to imply, is it?'

Jolyon sighed. 'Chad, whatever self-worth issues you have going on here have got nothing to do with me. Go tell a shrink how your dad never loved you, blah boring blah, and leave me the fuck out of it. You're behaving like a bitter, spiteful little kid. And I've always tried my best with you, introduced you to all these people, and the rest of it is your problem now. I wash my hands.'

'My God, you arrogant prick.' Chad pressed his fingertips to his temples. 'Who on earth do you think you are? My *frickin* messiah? Go to hell.'

Jolyon's lips vanished, his mouth barely a slit in the flesh of his face. 'I've had enough of this,' he said. 'I've got more than enough to worry about without having to play nanny to all your immature insecurities, Chad. If you really need someone to shout at, why don't you just go home to Mitzy and spill all this pent-up rage over her.'

'And just what the hell is that supposed to mean?' Chad's voice was unleashed now, other people in the pub began noticing them.

'Go home, wait for Mitzy to make one of her virgin cracks and then stand up to her for once. And don't take it out on me any more. Go back to your own people, shout at Mitzy, fuck Mitzy, either or both, I truly don't give a shit.'

Chad frowned furiously. 'How do you know about Mitzy? I haven't mentioned her to you in weeks.'

Jolyon slumped back theatrically in his chair. 'How do you think I know, Chad? Dee told me. She told me in bed. Is that what you want to hear? That I fucked Dee and held her and we whispered sweet nothings in each other's ears? Because that's what people do after they've fucked, they tell their secrets to each other. Maybe you should try it some time, Chad, the fucking I mean. And then you won't have to share all your tales of woe with me night after night after over and over . . .' Jolyon's voice trailed away wearily while he shooed Chad away with a dismissive wave.

Chad's body was rigid. He stared hard at Jolyon while he thought what to do. And then, studiously, he stood up and walked slowly to the bar. When he returned to the table he had only a single drink. He sipped from the pint, stared at Jolyon and said nothing.

After perhaps a minute, Jolyon also got to his feet and went to the bar. And when he returned, he too had bought a single drink from which he took only the barest of sips.

And they sat there in their silences, Chad and Jolyon, waiting each other out. Chad's body was stiff, like a boy determined not to lose a staring contest, but Jolyon seemed loose and relaxed. Sitting at a nearby table were six or seven students in boat-club hoodies, loud and laughing at everything. Jolyon smoked another cigarette and then another and barely touched his drink.

Fifteen minutes later Chad finished the half a pint that was left in his glass in one gulp. He wiped his mouth with the back of his hand and shook his head bitterly. He stood up, waited a few seconds, and left.

LIV(v) The table at which Jolyon was sitting was beside a wall – or not so much a wall as a short partition, the pub was full of nooks and holes and hidden snugs. There were black-and-white photographs on the wall. There was one of the Queen, fifteen years younger. She was standing behind the bar of the Churchill, the landlord showing her how to pour a pint of beer.

Jolyon looked at the photo, drank half his pint in one go and let out a deep breath. And then, from the other side of the wall, Mark appeared.

He took the seat opposite Jolyon. 'And to the victor the spoils,' said Mark, smiling gleefully. He pointed to Jolyon's glass. 'Can I freshen you up?'

'What do you want, Mark?'

'We're best friends now, aren't we?' said Mark. 'I mean, we spend all this time together. And I'm enjoying our law lectures so much, I think I might put in a request to change courses. Maybe I'm like Chad and secretly I want to be just like you, steal all your best bits. Anyway, after what just took place I'm your only remaining candidate for best friend. So why shouldn't I buy you a congratulatory pint?'

'To congratulate me on what exactly?'

'Oh, I don't know. So many things. Ridding yourself of Emilia, getting Dee in the sack, making it to the final three. But perhaps most of all, your points victory just then over Chad. I could hear it all from the other side there. Your willpower truly amazes me, Jolyon, I could feel the crackle and buzz, all of that cold stony strength. Of course, it now makes me realise what a tough nut to crack you are. Which means that we're going to have to move swiftly onto phase three.' Mark leered, making Jolyon feel sick. 'So what about that drink then?'

'No thank you, Mark,' said Jolyon.

Mark sat back. He said nothing for some time and then he laughed. 'Oh, this is funny,' he said. 'Look, we're into another of those stand-offs like the one you just won against Chad.' He tapped a finger against his lips. 'Or a sit-off, actually, that's what we should call it.' Mark acted thoughtful. 'So what are the rules of a sit-off, Jolyon? Is talking allowed? You know what, how about some role reversal? My turn to make up the rules as I go along. Yes, talking is definitely allowed,' he said, and then he boomed out, with mock authority, 'Like mighty Jolyon, I decree it so.'

'Just go away, Mark.'

'Oh no, going away is automatic loss of game. And loss of deposit as well.' Mark tapped his lips again. 'So what shall we talk about? Emilia? Have you seen poor old Em hobbling about on her crutches? I think that would crush me, seeing Emilia's leg in a cast and knowing it was all my fault. I paid her a little visit to find out what happened. Oh, I played it ultra sympathetic. At first she said an insect flew into her eye and she should have just stopped pedalling . . . And then poor little Em started to cry. You could tell she just wanted someone to talk to at last. And that's when she told me that actually it wasn't an insect that caused her accident. No, it was you, Jolyon, you made her cry. But don't worry, Emilia's so sweet she wouldn't even judge you too harshly. She simply told me the facts, how she thought you would've protected her, and wouldn't allow anything like her miners' strike consequence. It was disappointment in her voice, she really is the forgiving type. I think she might even still feel a great deal of affection for you, Jolyon. Only now you've moved on to Dee, haven't you? And how's that going to make poor Em feel? Not even a fortnight since you almost killed her by breaking her heart, you've decided to finish the job. Already got the next girl in the sack. Although I must say, you've been keeping it very quiet, this thing with Dee. Even I didn't notice, and I'm your best friend.

'You know, I'm probably going to bump into Emilia tomorrow. I wonder what we should talk about? But enough about that. Where was I? Oh, phase three. Actually it was going to visit Em that gave me the idea. As you know, they let her swap rooms after the accident so that she's on the ground floor. And soon after seeing Em in her room, well, that's when I suggested to your neighbour that he might like to swap with me. I mean, I got so lucky in the room ballot with my palatial place on Hallowgood Court. And those rooms at the top of staircase six are a little poky. I told him I liked the view better from your floor. He jumped at the chance. So that's my news, Jolyon. Best friends and now neighbours as well.' Mark raised his glass to offer a toast. 'Cheers, Jolyon, you know I think we're going to have a lot of fun,' he said with a wink.

LIV(vi) Chad didn't go home. Jolyon had told him to go home, so he didn't. Instead, when he left the Churchill, he turned toward Pitt.

He wanted another drink but the bar in college didn't open till six. And so, glancing frequently behind as he walked, he headed for staircase six. He judged that if he ran up the stairs and was quick about it, even if Jolyon had already left, he would still have time.

The door to Jolyon's room was unlocked. Chad found a bottle of gin and left quickly. As he passed the fridge at the top of the stairs, he took from it a bottle of water. Down on back quad he hid behind a shrub, emptied the water and poured in the liquor. And then he went to sit in the gardens.

When Chad had drunk perhaps a half-bottle of gin, he saw Emilia on her crutches heaving herself along the gravel path. She paused when she saw Chad and waved at him, so he smiled and beckoned her over.

Chad got to his feet, took Emilia's crutches for her and held her hands to help her sit. She was wearing a slip of a top, her blonde hair kissing the tops of her shoulders.

Chad sighed. 'I'm sorry I haven't seen you since the accident,' he said. 'We came to the hospital. And then I thought you wanted nothing to do with us . . .'

Emilia nodded uneasily and then with more vigour. 'I needed some time,' she said, 'But now I'm good, really good. And you, Chad?'

Chad's skin was cool, the gin had numbed his nose. But deeper down, his rage lingered on. 'I'm just on top of the *frickin* world, Emilia.'

Emilia paused and the silence became awkward. Eventually, she broke it. 'So how's your silly game going?' she said.

'Silly? How can you say that after what Middle told us?'

'Told us when?' said Emilia.

'Just before your . . . Never mind,' said Chad. If the accident had caused her to forget then he was the only one who knew. And in that case . . . He pinched at the grass, ripped it up, tossed it over his shoulder. 'Look, Em,' said Chad, 'you know I can't talk about the Game.'

'Yes you can. You can talk to me about it.'

'I especially can't talk to you.'

Emilia lowered her chin and lifted her eyes. Chad felt his resistance diluting. 'OK, OK. Look, I can tell you this much but only this. Jack's out of the Game,' he said, and then leaning forward, 'it's down to the final three. Dee, Jolyon and me.'

Emilia put her hands together, fingers writhing, ecstatic snakes. 'Ooh,' she said, 'how on earth did Jack go out?' She screwed up her eyes speculatively. 'Please, Chad,' she said, 'you have to tell me now. It wouldn't be fair to tease me like that.'

'No way, Em, you know I can't tell you. But you can go and ask Jack, if you like. Come on, Emilia, whatever gets you in the end is a deeply personal thing.'

'So you're saying it was a deeply personal thing then?' said Emilia, her eyes narrowing further. 'How titillating. Oh please. I'll keep it to myself, Chad, promise.' Emilia moved her hand to her chest. 'Cross my heart,' she said.

Chad watched the X being drawn over Emilia's breast. 'I wish I could tell you,' he said. His mouth was dry. 'But it's the rules,' he said, 'I can't.'

'Oh, but Chad, *pleeease.*' Emilia ran her fingers up and down Chad's bare arm. 'Please, Chad. Please?' Chad was shaking his head. And then Emilia said, 'But Chad, I thought you loved me.'

Chad flinched. The snap of his body could have been Jolyon's gesture, his eyes could have been Jolyon's eyes. 'Get the hell off me,' he said, swatting Emilia's hand from his arm. 'Jeez, Emilia, love you? Don't be dumb. Is there something the hell wrong with you? I was drunk when I said that, I was steaming drunk.' Although Chad's resistance was diluted, his rage was distilled. 'Don't you remember, Emilia? You were part of the crew pouring whisky down my neck. Love you?' he snorted. 'Emilia, I couldn't love you. Because I don't even respect you. And you want to know why?' Chad licked his lips and pinched the bridge of his nose. The words were about to spill out of him just as before, words he had thought but denied. 'I'll tell you why I don't respect you, Emilia. It's because you're *blah*. You're not one thing or another. You're so permanently on the fence, you're just so . . .' He tried to think of another word and couldn't. '*Blah*, Emilia, *blah blah blah.*'

Emilia's eyes began to fill with tears. She tried to get to her feet but the cast held her down.

'Don't worry,' said Chad, 'I'm going.' He stood up and took a swig from his bottle. His words felt harsh now, yet the rush of release remained, a fresh wind that whipped all around.

LIV(vii) Jolyon left Mark leering in the pub, taunting him as he left. 'One–nil. Fifteen–love. That's a hundred points above the line, *Joe.*'

Jolyon longed to be alone in his room. When he got there he curled up on his bed and fell asleep.

He woke to a light knocking sound, turned and wondered if

he had locked the door, or if he should have done. The door began to open.

In came Emilia, or the upper half of her body, her shoulders bare but for the lacy straps of her top. She was not crying but it seemed as if she might have been only minutes earlier. 'Do you mind if I come in, Jolyon?' she said.

Jolyon wondered briefly if Emilia had come to confront him about Dee. But no, she was blinking and confused. 'Of course you can come in, Emilia,' he said. And when she moved into the room on her crutches, he thought about the stairs. 'My God, Emilia, how did you get up here?'

'It took a while. But you get used to it,' she said. 'My shoulders are going to look amazing by the time the cast's removed.'

The comment cast an uneasy silence between them. And then Emilia's body shook with a sudden shiver.

'What's wrong? Are you cold?' said Jolyon. 'It must be almost seventy today.'

'No,' said Emilia. 'Yes. I don't know.'

Jolyon jumped off his bed. Emilia was shaking as if sheathed in wet clothes. He took her crutches and led her to his bed, peeled back the duvet and helped her climb in. She crossed her arms and another chill ran through her. 'What's wrong, Em?' he said.

'Nothing, Jolyon, nothing,' said Emilia. 'Probably just the painkillers.'

Jolyon held the back of his hand to Emilia's forehead. 'Em, I'm so sorry,' he said. He felt his face bunching, tears squeezing to the surface. 'Please, I'm so sorry, I should never . . .' but the words were silenced as he started to cry.

'Shh, I believe you, Jolyon,' said Emilia. 'It's all right, really, it's OK.' There were tears in her eyes as well. She lifted the covers. 'I just want you to hold me, that's all I want. To be held, Jolyon. I promise, nothing more.'

Jolyon got under the covers and Emilia rolled against him, her warm breath pooling in the hollow of his neck. He wrapped his arms around Emilia and held her. Only held her. And then Emilia said, 'We can be friends again now, can't we?'

'Of course we can, Em,' said Jolyon.

Emilia wriggled against him beneath the covers until more of her was touching more of him. And in a few minutes' time they were both asleep.

LIV(viii) Chad stumbled around Pitt until he finished the gin. This, he had ordained, was the signal for action, the starter's gun at a race. He threw the bottle into the bushes at the bottom of staircase six.

He did not knock when he got to Jolyon's room, he was furious and ready with challenges. And then he stopped and looked at the two figures asleep in the bed. He turned around, he closed the door gently. And then Chad headed for the library.

LIV(ix) 'I'm seeing him after my tutorial,' said Dee. 'What's so urgent it can't wait?'

'I'm not supposed to say,' said Chad. 'I don't know.'

'I want to read through this essay one last time.'

'It's amazing, Dee, it's bound to be. You're amazing. Just go now, it'll only take a few minutes.' He turned off her reading lamp and closed the three large books on the desk. 'I'll return these,' he said. 'You just get going.'

Dee sighed, doubtfully, but then packed her things as fast as she could.

There was a spring in her step as she hurried over back quad toward Jolyon's room. She had been working on a poem for the last three days and now she knew how it would end. There was a wonderful inevitability to everything, if you only had the right light.

—

LV(i) *This is our fourth Christmas-tree meeting and yet the greeting kiss lands on my forehead just as lightly as ever. Perhaps my tactics require adjustment. Maybe the time has come for me to make my move.*

Dee appears to be in a jocular mood. She is bouncing above me on the balls of her feet. Come on, Jolyon, she says, let's do some real training. She makes fists and starts to hum boxing music. Come on. She pulls me to my feet.

I laugh and play along but I can't seem to work out which foot to lead with. Dee's music swirls, she opens her fists to offer me two targets weaving sparkler patterns in the dying light. I try to swap my feet, see a flashing white streak and swing. Sights blur and sounds muffle. Feelings slide.

And then I feel such a pain in my nose. Has Dee hit me? Why would she . . . ?

My face is pressed up against something, taste of earth in my mouth. No, it wasn't Dee who hit me. It was the ground.

I roll onto my back. Dee is brushing my face, wiping the grass from my lips. Oh, Jolyon, what happened? Does anything hurt?

The pain in my nose is immense. I'm fine, I say. I think my foot got caught in a rat hole. Don't worry, Dee. *She looks so hurt for me that it makes my heart leap. Perhaps one day she will kiss all the sore parts of me better.*

Dee fusses over me and I push her away, embarrassed. After spitting out more grass, I say to Dee, Maybe we should hold off on the skipping rope for a couple more days.

But Dee doesn't laugh at my joke, she starts rummaging through her bag and I feel the first trickle on my lips as she fishes out a packet of tissues.

The nosebleed lasts for twenty minutes, a magician's handkerchief display. Dee rubs my back, passes me tissues. When the bleeding stops a gory mass of paper is piled up next to the blanket.

And that's when I feel it, the jolt. That's when it comes to me –

Tomorrow, I say. JFK airport, 12.35 p.m.

Dee gives me a curious look.

That's when Chad arrives. Tomorrow, I say. And then the last of the information buzzes into my mind. Virgin Airlines, I add with a snort, wiping the last crust of blood from my nose with the back of my hand.

LV(ii) We are silent for a while. Then Dee tries to tell me not to worry, everything will be all right. And so on and so on.

She stares down at the blanket for a new set of words, the ones she really wants to say. Jolyon, I'm sorry, she says, but I can't help noticing a certain aroma on your breath whenever we meet. How much whisky are you drinking each day?

Perhaps more than usual, I say. But everything's under control, I add frantically, worried at the thought of anyone interfering with my routine.

And the pills?

I need them, I say, thumping the blanket.

It's OK, Dee says, touching me gently. No one's taking anything away from you, Jolyon. I just want you to cut down a little. Can you do that? For me? Will you promise?

I feel my nose, the lightest of touches and yet still my head swims. OK, I say, I promise, Dee. Less of everything.

Less whisky and pills, she says. The same walking and writing, meeting in the park, poetry reading.

Yes, the same routine, I say. Meeting in the park, poetry reading. I half turn to look for it beside me at the corner of the blanket.

So have you committed tonight's poem to memory? Dee asks me. Where is it?

It's OK, Jolyon, you don't have to read to me every night. Where is it?

Jolyon? Jolyon, is something wrong? Jolyon, tell me what's wrong?

———

LVI(i) Jolyon woke in the night, *tap tap tap* on his window. Half asleep, impossible. There could be no tapping on his window, no trees, four floors up. *Tap tap tap.* Still half asleep he thought of Dracula movies and jumped up out of bed. He pulled the curtain, nothing. He opened his window and leaned out. There was nothing to see in the darkness, except for his neighbour's window open, a faint light from within. And then he remembered, his *new* neighbour.

He went back to bed, held the pillow over his head and fell asleep again.

And then with a start he was awoken once more. For a second he thought that the world was ending, a great roaring of the earth being torn apart. And then the panic subsided as he realised that the sound was music, loud and distorted, and coming from the wall beside his bed. He held his hand there. The source of the din was only inches away, he felt it pump into his fingers. And then it stopped.

An hour later the tapping. An hour later the roaring. An hour later the tapping . . .

LVI(ii) Dee played a low card. Jolyon knew she had higher. Two against one.

Chad won with another low card, the six of clubs. And when Jolyon had to play next, he knew they would screw him again.

They did. Jolyon picked up the dice, five dice, and dropped them into the cup. Hard to roll low with five dice and he didn't. He rolled very high.

Dee and Chad looked pleased with their work.

Tallest looked less satisfied than Jolyon would have thought. When the five dice fell showing a total of twenty-one, Tallest removed his glasses to his jacket pocket and looked at Jolyon, squinting and blinking. Perhaps it was pity, or maybe Tallest was tired, just like Jolyon after his sleepless night. Maybe Tallest had been enjoying late nights drinking with other men who looked like accountants, or soirées with girls in nice floral dresses.

Jolyon yawned and held his head in his hands. Dee started to clear away the dice and the cards. 'How can you trust someone like that?' he said.

'What I trust,' said Dee, 'is my own eyes.'

'Chad sent you here,' said Jolyon. 'He sent you here to see whatever you thought you saw and he's playing you, Dee, don't you get that?'

'Chad did the right thing,' said Dee. 'Unlike you, Jolyon. I saw you with my own eyes, and . . .' As Dee tried to finish her sentence, Chad put an arm around her shoulders. He squeezed and out came her tears.

Chad didn't look at Dee as he made gentle shushing sounds. He soothed Dee but he stared at Jolyon.

Dee cried some more and then sniffed. 'I hope you don't quit too soon, Jolyon,' she said. 'I really think you should suffer for this.'

LVI(iii) No, he wouldn't quit. How could he quit? What had he done? He held Emilia when she was hurt. Only held her.

He was innocent. And now he was wronged. He would not quit. It would be a dreadful injustice were he to quit, it would be a terrible, terrible wrong.

LVI(iv) The next day, after another sleepless night, Jolyon had to carry out his first consequence. It was the last remnant of Jack in the Game and so it bore Jack's fingerprints, the schoolboy smut, the seedy performance.

Jolyon had spent the morning being shadowed by Mark who, despite his late-night escalation, looked well rested. When later he met Chad, Dee and Shortest in the bar, Jolyon's few hours of law lectures spent alongside Mark felt like relief, the three lightest hours this day had to offer.

Chad handed the magazine to Jolyon. Chad had come prepared. Good old Chad.

There were certain practicalities regarding this consequence. Dee and Chad had agreed that Jolyon couldn't be expected to perform, so to speak, under pressure. And who knew how long it would take. So no, he need not actually *do it*, he need only pretend. The magazine was both prop and shield, it was enormously sensitive of them.

They chose the toilets nearest to the bar. Shortest took the first stall and locked the door. Chad took the second stall and locked it. Jolyon took the furthest stall and left the door unlocked.

They did not have to wait long. There were three visitors to the urinals before the arrival of someone who needed to use one of the stalls. It was a first year called Colin, studying medicine. He was whistling the Beatles. Dee had wanted every last scrap of detail, but Chad wasn't sure which song. 'Was it *Come Together*?' she would later joke.

Chad had a small mirror. By holding it in the space beneath the wall that separated the stalls, he could ensure that Jolyon acted the role properly. He had forewarned Jolyon about this, the information delivered in a thoroughly businesslike fashion.

When the stall door opened, Jolyon was sitting there with jeans gathered around his ankles and his underpants stretched beneath his parted knees. The magazine was resting in his bare lap covering his flaccid state, his penis shrunken and ashamed. They had chosen a magazine called *Asian Babes* and behind its cover, Jolyon was pumping his arm. He pumped and he pumped and he pumped. He didn't look up. But he did hear that Colin had stopped whistling.

Chad, having ascertained that Jolyon had acted the role sufficiently, tilted his mirror and saw on Colin's face the appropriate shock and disgust. And then Colin recoiled, throwing up his hand to shield him from what he had already seen. 'Fucking hell, Jolyon,' he cried out, 'lock the fucking door next time, for fuck's sake, man.'

LVI(v) The news spread quickly around Pitt.

Over the next few days, Jolyon was shouted at outside lecture halls, jeered from the bar, spat on several times, called a racist many hundreds of times, a pig, fascist, wanker, porn junkie, misogynist, porno pimp, 'Tug', sex fiend, Nazi, paedophile and, by Nadia Joshi, chairperson of the Asian Students' Association, a crypto-Klan Paki basher.

Mark suspended his tailing of Jolyon for a short time, not wanting to be associated with such a vilified character, the taint of 'racist' perhaps the very worst to be marked with at Pitt. He walked into Jolyon's room to tell him as much and also to express his admiration for Chad and Dee. He suggested it would soon be necessary for him to step up his own game, although he also continued to employ his sleep-deprivation tactics. Jolyon, wide awake at two o'clock one night, had discovered that the window tapping was achieved by use of a drawing pin pushed into the end of a bamboo cane.

As his notoriety swelled, Jolyon spent more and more time alone in his room, waiting for the *tap tap tap* and the music like a splintering earth. He lay on his bed feeling the weight of Pitt's hatred for him being piled on his chest like vast slabs.

Jolyon had never taken any pleasure from that fact that he was universally adored at Pitt. He had felt only the vague impression that, yes, he was mostly liked and being liked was probably better than not being liked. But the sense of being hated was a sickness infecting every cell of his body. Love was something that had vanished without leaving its mark on Jolyon. But being hated was a feeling he would never shake. A feeling that gathered and calcified. And formed its thick mass at his heart.

———

LVII Dee is curled up on my sofa, no more tears for now.

I am opening cupboards I have opened two or three times already. The cupboards are empty, their contents strewn across the floor.

It's not here, Jolyon, it's not *here*.

It has to be, I say, picking up a rug, throwing it into a corner. It's not here. *It's not here!*

Dee, you've been coming to my apartment, do you remember –

Don't you dare! Don't even dare try to blame me, Jolyon.

No no no, Dee, no blame. Your memory's so much better, maybe I left it in the same spot every day. My hands fly all around me, pointing and waving, finally gripping the back of my skull.

You've lost it, Dee shouts, quickly sitting up, her sandals loud on my floorboards. The only thing I cared about, Jolyon. *Gone.*

Was it in here? That's all I need to know, I say, moving in circles now, trampling photographs, memories. Maybe I took it with me when I went out walking, I say.

What do you mean *took it with you?* Dee cries. You mean it could be *anywhere in New York?*

No, I don't know. I'm not saying I took it. I don't know. I don't . . . My nose is throbbing, the floor is a mess, my life scattered, misplaced. I fall back against the wall and slip down to the floor holding my hands to my face.

And then I hear Dee standing above me, her voice raining down on my shame. Unless you find my poems, Jolyon, you will never, ever see me again. *Never.* If I see you in the park by the Christmas tree at six one night then I'll know you've found them. Otherwise, don't bother, you won't see me. How could I forgive you, Jolyon? Why did I ever forgive you?

I look up at Dee expecting to see anger on her face, thinking that I must meet her gaze. I deserve her rage, my punishment. But she doesn't look angry, she looks immensely sad, Dee looks as if I have broken her.

She turns her head away from me and crosses her arms as if to ward off a chill. Her feet begin to pick out a path among the mess of my ransacked apartment, the shapeliness of her calves receding as I close my eyes.

And then I hear the door slam. I feel its shiver in the wall. My nose is definitely broken.

———

LVIII(i) Jolyon was caught in a pincer movement, the Game on one side and Mark on the other. But Hilary term was ending and Mark, at least, was returning home. He came to see Jolyon to deliver a parting line. 'Make sure to get some sleep then, Jolyon. Phase four begins next term.'

But still Jolyon couldn't sleep. He was staying on at Pitt, the Game would continue to be played throughout the six-week break. A vote had been taken on the matter, two votes in favour . . . Jolyon hadn't even bothered to acknowledge the procedure.

And so they played on. Chad and Dee continued to conspire and Jolyon continued to lose. But with most of the student population absent for six weeks, his opponents had to find their humiliations for Jolyon in the broader life of the city. At working-class pubs, cheap eateries, supermarkets . . . anywhere students were despised in the city. Day after day it was a mixture of the banal and excruciating. Public nudity, a one-man demonstration against immigration, street performance – unicycle, mime, Shakespeare – and a consequence to which they gave the name 'Nuptials Interruptus'. Jolyon had to sit in on the wedding of two strangers and rise to proclaim just cause as to why the bride and groom should not be joined in holy matrimony. He was in love with the bride, he said, they were engaged in a torrid affair. He was chased from the church, threats being yelled as he fled. There was exhibitionism, heckling, rap, pretension, cross-dressing, auditioning, money-burning, experimental dance, snobbery, solicitation . . .

He lay in bed at night reliving the looks in strangers' eyes. He could recall their faces with greater clarity than their words, their abuse. And so for the first time in Jolyon's life, strangers were becoming something to fear, his days beginning to warp and crack, being shaped by the opinions of people he knew nothing about.

LVIII(ii) A week before Trinity term was due to begin, Jolyon made an appointment to see the college doctor, an affable gentleman wearing a regimental tie.

The doctor weighed up the creature before him and started to jot merrily on his prescription pad. Yes, it was very brave of Jolyon to come. And one could actually do things about insomnia and depression these days, old chap, medicine had made remarkable leaps and bounds. The doctor handed Jolyon a prescription for three types of pharmaceutical. No need to fret any longer. Jolyon should be sure to return if he required anything more. Anything at all, old chap. He made Jolyon promise. And Jolyon promised he would.

LVIII(iii) He pulled his scarf up to his nose as he left Pitt. It was a college scarf, the one they had bought for Chad to wear in the early days of the Game. But there would be more to Jolyon's day than the simple wearing of a scarf.

He took a bus and met the others outside. Tallest was there, several feet away from Chad and Dee, who handed Jolyon his ticket. Jolyon's seat was two rows in front of the others, they didn't want to be associated with him once everything began.

In they went and Jolyon took his seat wearing the red-and-white scarf, which stuck out sharply surrounded by so much yellow and blue. Yellow-blue scarves, yellow-blue shirts, yellow-blue banners.

When the football match started, so did the singing and screaming. *United, United, United. Fucking blind. Fucking cheat. Fucking nail 'im.*

They had given Jolyon ten minutes to stand up and chant his first song, a familiar football tune but with a new set of lyrics. The opposition goalkeeper, Philippe Gherab, had been purchased from Le Havre. Chad and Dee had done their research.

Seven minutes into the match, when Gherab miskicked a back pass so that it hooked out of touch and the home crowd jeered, Jolyon got to his feet and started to sing, '*Vous êtes merde et vous savez que vous êtes, vous êtes merde et vous savez que vous êtes . . .*'

The crowd around him fell into a bristling silence. And then a voice shouted, 'Who the fuck are you?' and then hundreds of voices were chanting, 'Who are ya? Who are ya? Who are ya?'

Jolyon, the nausea sloshing in his stomach, began to protest. 'Because he's French, their keeper is French. It's *you're shit and you know you are.* But in French.'

Some voices were abusing him, other voices were shouting, 'Sit down, sit the fuck down.' And then everyone was shouting it, '*Siddown, siddown, siddown!*'

He sat down. The eyes, the eyes. Jolyon stared out at the game as if he couldn't sense the feeling of the crowd, the weight of their hatred.

He had until the twenty-minute mark to complete his next challenge, which was based around the fact that the United captain had the same name as a romantic poet.

And so in the nineteenth minute, Jolyon rose again. He felt faint as if he were caught in a cloud of gas. And then he began his second song, the tune taken from Beethoven's *Ode to Joy*, his voice quavering over the rippling of the crowd. '*We've got John Keats / And the best seats / He plays football potently / Like the ode / Composed to a bird / Keats is striking poetry.*'

A stunned silence was followed by a torrent of vicious abuse.

The crowd's agitation was rising, their blood pulsing. 'Look, he has the same name as a romantic poet,' Jolyon pleaded. 'And the ode to the bird is *Ode to a Nightingale*. And there's a double meaning to striking poetry . . .'

And that's when it happened, the opposition scored, the United fans threw their hands catastrophically to their heads. Part three now had to be performed. '*Goal!*' Jolyon cheered. '*Goooooal!*'

Something struck him from behind, Jolyon felt an explosion of sparks behind his eyes. And next the sound of shattering as the bottle broke against the back of his head. He stumbled down onto one knee, palms hitting the backs of the men in front who were pushed forward with a jolt. Recovering, they turned and stood and one of them threw a punch. Jolyon felt the blow at the side of his head, the heat in his ear. And then there were more blows from behind. Fists and feet. Jolyon pulled himself into a ball on the ground, tried to protect his head with his hands. And now someone was stamping, a boot crushing his fingers, then more boots stamping his ankles, his knees.

Just as he thought he would pass out, the rain of blows began to slow and Jolyon was pulled to his feet. More punches were thrown but the worst was over. Someone was shouting at his assailants, 'Enough. Stop. That's enough now.'

It was Tallest dragging him to the aisle. And then Chad was there, Jolyon's arms across two sets of shoulders. Up into dark-ness, down steps and cold corridors, out into the broken-glass light. They lowered him onto a bench.

Chad looked like he was about to be sick. 'Jolyon, oh God, I'm . . . It wasn't supposed to go like that.'

Jolyon felt his teeth grinding something hard and gritty like a small rock in his mouth. And then, prodding it with his tongue, Jolyon realised the small rock was a tooth. He spat it out into his hand along with his blood and phlegm. He stared at the tooth for some time, prodded it, turned the tooth over and over in his palm.

The others were making sounds, asking questions, but he didn't hear them.

'I know what this is,' thought Jolyon, 'the moment of *tooth*!' And he started to laugh. He cleaned the tooth against his thigh and dropped it in his pocket. And then he looked up at them, three horrified faces, and started to laugh even harder. 'Now you get it, right?' said Jolyon, noticing that he could see through only one eye. 'There's no way you can beat me,' he said. 'There's nothing you can do.' The blood was bubbling from his nose as he snorted with laughter. 'Nothing at all.'

LVIII(iv) Chad pleaded with Jolyon but Jolyon stared into the distance as if unable to hear, his fingers feeling like they had been crushed in a car door.

'Please, Jolyon. And not so I can win,' said Chad. 'but so we can stop. If you refuse to give in, it has to get worse. What other choice do we have?'

Jolyon looked up with his good eye. 'Well, *you* could quit,' he said.

'You do understand I can't do that, Jolyon,' Chad scoffed. 'Which means anything more that happens to you is as good as self-inflicted. Logically, you're pretty much doing this to yourself. Come on, this isn't the time to make your big stand in life. You've already had your way with Emilia and Dee, so I get it, you're the big man. You won, Jolyon, OK? But you have to let me have just *one* thing. Because if you don't . . . Jolyon, what just happened was terrible and I'm sorry, I swear I mean that. But from now on, no apologies, we're not responsible. Please, for everyone's sake. There's nothing more you need to prove.'

Dee crouched down and laid her hands on his knees. 'Please, Jolyon. Listen to Chad,' she said, tears gathering in her eyes.

Jolyon stood up and decided he could limp well enough. Tallest tried to take his arm but Jolyon pushed him away. 'Why don't you all get back to the game?' he said, looking across at the stadium. 'I was really enjoying it but things took a turn for the worse. And I think I should leave now.' He started to limp away but then turned, looking thoughtful, and added, 'Oh, Dee, you know I just realised something.' Dee wiped her eyes and Jolyon gave her a grim smile. 'You're the only one who can stop this,' he said. 'It's really all up to you now, Dee.' He put his hand in his pocket as he turned again and left.

LVIII(v) In front of the mirror in his room, Jolyon decided he wouldn't go to the dentist. The tooth was one of the lower molars and you could barely notice its absence, not unless he opened his mouth very wide.

He placed the tooth inside the mug with his pills and his toothbrush, the fork and the photos. And then Jolyon drew his curtains, lay down on his bed and closed his eyes. Tomorrow was the first day of Trinity, Chad's final term.

———

LIX(i) I lost Dee today. Chad arrives tomorrow. A fine symmetry.

LIX(ii) And where was routine when I needed it? Dee's book, the most important thing of all and I failed to find a place for it in my life. And now routine has abandoned me.

Did I take it on my walk? I don't remember.

Where did I walk today? I don't remember.

If I took the book out with me then it is lost. It must still be inside this apartment, it must be. It has to be.

Feebly I cast around my apartment as if the same old looking in the same old places might not have the selfsame result. But all I find is the destruction of my daily bread. Mnemonics scattered, life overturned. The only things I fish out from the stew are a whisky bottle and pills, prompted to find them by an itching beneath my skin. And laughably, amid all the wreckage, my evening routine ice-cube tray has held on to my pills as if cupped in a mother's outstretched palm. Four pink pills, three yellow, three blue. I swallow them with swigs of whisky straight from the bottle. I have only my cravings to remind me how to live now.

This apartment, this miserable machine of my life, its laughable ticky-tacky parts discarded and strewn.

Curtains closed, blinds lowered. The hermit returns. Long live the hermit.

———

LX(i) Third term began with an act of generosity. They pushed a note under Jolyon's door to inform him a vote had been taken, the Game was in hiatus, they would skip a round. And perhaps the extra time would give him a chance to reconsider his position.

Jolyon screwed up the piece of paper, returned to his bed and with a sudden gasp began to cry. Warm tears of relief flowed down his bruised cheeks, over his swollen lips.

And so, temporarily, the battle could be fought on only one front. A new term and Mark had promised a new phase. But the start of Trinity term didn't lead to the abandonment of his sleep-deprivation tactics, although there was no longer much sleep to deprive. The doctor's pills could send Jolyon only into fogs, sleep-like hazes but not sleep itself, and the tappings and roarings became mere annoyances. Soon Jolyon began to regard them only as distance markers in the slow race for the night to be over.

In the daytime Jolyon sometimes thought about stoicism, facing hardship like a man, like Santiago in *The Old Man and the Sea*.

And because manliness was a notion that appealed to him, he clung to the thought of not surrendering until he didn't know whether his refusal to surrender was genuine determination or merely a literary reference.

On the fourth day of term, Jolyon returned to the college doctor. Yes, there were indeed further options, old chap. Simply a case of finding the right combination apropos the particular patient – he began to scribble excitedly on his prescription pad – and they could bump up the doses, of course. Not to worry, the ship would right itself in time. No need to wave the white flag quite yet, old chap.

LX(ii) The first act of phase four was played out the next day. When Jolyon went to the bathrooms at the bottom of staircase six in the morning, there were two sheets taped to the wall. The *Pitt Pendulum*, as usual, but also a photocopied page from Jolyon's diary. It was a copy of an entry he had made two weeks after arriving at Pitt. Mark, helpfully, had provided a title.

Excerpts from the secret diary of Jolyon Johnson no. 1
Met a guy called Dorian today. Clearly an Etonian. He tries to convince himself and everyone else he's clever, as opposed to well trained, by learning answers to a quiz machine in the Churchill. Like a parrot. And with a parrot's capacity for understanding the information being blandly recited. I think they actually teach them charm at Eton and some of them wear it well. But on others it sits uneasily. Dorian is in the second camp.

Jolyon tore the sheet from the wall and checked the next bathroom where he found the same taped-up piece of paper. He went to the bathrooms on staircases seven and eight. And then he realised it was futile and hurried back to his room.

He wondered how he might avoid ever seeing Dorian again

and pinched the bridge of his nose, there was such a knot of pain there. He tried to think about who else he had written about negatively in his diary. The pain flared as names flashed through Jolyon's head. He curled onto his bed and pushed his forehead up against the coolness of the wall.

LX(iii) Jolyon stopped attending lectures the next day and started to leave his room only in the middle of the night. In the library at three in the morning, he would photocopy the cases and articles he had to read and then hurry back to his bed. And when he visited the bathroom at four in the morning, Jolyon found that, every day, another page had appeared.

Excerpts from the secret diary of Jolyon Johnson no. 2

Two of the most ludicrous characters at Pitt go by the names Jamie and Nick. Jamie is the son of a renowned Cambridge scholar but acts like one of the street urchins from *Oliver Twist*. His accent changes wildly according to the company he keeps. Conversing with any of us, he starts dropping and morphing his consonants, saying things like 'it's a bit fin on the ground, mate' or 'what do you fuckin fink?' He's good-looking, insecure and utterly insincere.

Nick, the sidekick, doesn't hide his accent so carefully but he does conceal his name. On the room board he's N. Risley. But on a tip-off from Jamie, I peeped at a letter in his pigeonhole. It was addressed to 'The Hon. Nicholas Tower Wriothesley'. Apparently, Wriothesley is pronounced Risley, and he's officially 'the honourable' because he's the son of a baron. Meanwhile, the honourable Nick has had a string of girlfriends at least sixty or seventy points higher than him on the scale of attractiveness. Maybe they use Jamie as bait. Or perhaps everyone's now heard tell of the £250 million family fortune the honourable Nick stands to inherit. The girlfriends never last more than a week. But I'm sure he treats them all honourably.

And what was Jolyon to do but hide? He thought about making a statement, pasting his own sheets to the walls, explaining that any diary was a place of secret thoughts. That his own diary was simply a way of purging these thoughts. He considered appealing to everyone's secret self, don't we all have dark thoughts from time to time? The only thing that matters is how we behave, how we *act* on those thoughts.

But Jolyon did nothing, only hid in his fog of pills and doubled the dose. As he lay on his bed he became very good at picturing everyone at Pitt. In his mind he could hear their accents and mimic their verbal habits, he could imagine their physical tics as they spoke. Jolyon was able to create puppets of everyone he knew inside his head. And he spent hours pulling their strings, acting out their hatred in intricate detail.

Sometimes he held the tooth clenched tight in his palm. And although he constantly fantasised about breaking down Mark's door, taking back his diary, attacking Mark, punishing Mark, Jolyon knew that his body had no more strength to give.

The truth was that suffering in silence was no longer only a romantic notion. Suffering in silence was now Jolyon's only remaining choice.

——

LXI(i) My hangover and the pain in my nose wake me at five in the morning, eight hours before I have agreed to meet Chad at JFK. I fall out of bed and stumble around looking for something to tell me what to do. But the sprawling mess of my apartment is like a thousand instructions yelling themselves at once.

My story, my pills, my whisky. These are the only voices that rise above the roar.

Just before I leave, I notice a distinct absence of clothes on my body. But there are clothes everywhere across the floor, how could I forget?

The few minutes it takes to dress give me enough time for one more whisky.

And now I must face him.

LXI(ii) I am watching the passengers emerge into the arrivals hall when there is a *tap tap tap* on my shoulder. I jump, a brief panic, and then I turn and see him. For a while I stare stupidly as if Chad's is the last face I would have expected to see in this place.

He is still young-looking, his hair smooth, not receding. He offers his hand to shake but I am caught unawares and fail to respond. Chad laughs, a gentle laugh, not a scornful one. And then he speaks. Should we hug instead? Chad's voice is softer than I remember, not English exactly but less acutely American.

I shake his hand quickly, my fingers limp in the firm grip of his palm.

You were late, he says. Or maybe I was early.

The arrivals board said you landed on time, I say.

Chad points down to his small carry-on case. No waiting at baggage, he says, I zipped on through. Then when I didn't see you, I got some coffee. Chad squints at my face and says, Man, what happened to you?

I touch my nose. Christmas-tree accident, I say.

Christmas tree? Chad says. Jolyon, it's *May*.

I can't think what to say, how to avoid mention of Dee. There is a great tranquil presence about this older Chad, an aura that makes me nervous. I blurt out the first thing I can think of. Great weather, I say. No humidity yet.

Chad only nods with a trace of bemusement.

I thought about making you one of those name signs, I say, feeling myself beginning to blush. And why did I say this? It's not even true.

Hey, you should have done, Chad says, with a genial laugh. A sign with my name, that would have been great, I've never had one of those.

But you wouldn't have seen it, I say.

No, he says, I guess that's true.

I try my best to listen for clues, to feel for invisible currents. I used to be good at this but I can tell nothing more about Chad than what lies on the surface. Good-looking and happy, at peace with himself.

Chad puts his hand on my shoulder. It truly is good to see you, Jolyon, he says.

His touch makes me flinch inside. I should go, I say.

Go? Chad says. But you only just got here. Jolyon, I asked you to meet me at the airport because I thought we might catch up. At least share a cab with me, that'll give us an hour to chat. I'll drop you off at your place on the way to my hotel.

I flinch when Chad talks about *my place*. It reminds me that he has found me here, has hunted me down like a fugitive from justice. I really think I should take the subway, I say.

I'm paying, Chad says.

I just bought a Metrocard, I say, quickly blushing again.

Sure then, Chad says. We can play this any way you want to, Jolyon. Chad looks muscular and tanned, he doesn't even look tired after his flight. We really do need to talk though, he says. Can I come to your apartment tomorrow? What time's good for you?

Any time, I reply, I don't think my schedule's especially hectic tomorrow.

Good, Chad says, see you tomorrow then. He shakes my hand firmly again. But then, as Chad is about to leave, he turns back and says, Oh, I nearly forgot, I have a present for you, Jolyon. I mean, it's dumb really. He reaches into his suitcase and hands me a small gift in silver wrapping. But don't open it here, he says, you'll embarrass me.

I am shaking the gift next to my ear, feeling its weight.

Come on, I'm like beetroot over here, Chad says. But this isn't true. He swipes paw-like at the air. It's really great to see you, Jolyon, he says. And then as Chad walks away, not looking back, he raises an arm as high as it can stretch. He points at the sky with his forefinger, waves a loose farewell. When he lowers the arm he is lost in the crowd.

LXI(iii) I open the present while I ride the Air Train to Howard Beach. Inside I find, folded up so that it is no bigger than a deck of playing cards, a small tablecloth. It is round and white, made of delicate lace. Also there is a box. I remove the lid and peer inside. The box is lined, foam rubber with two cut-out holes that nestle two eggs. Chad has carried with him, more than three thousand miles across the Atlantic Ocean, a tablecloth and two hard-boiled eggs.

I think about the gift for some time and how genial Chad seemed in the airport. And I wonder if I am mistaken about the purpose of his visit. Perhaps he wants everything to be finished between us, a renewal of friendship, remembrance of happier days.

Two eggs. Old friends. So much potential.

——

LXII(i) Jolyon's diary extracts counted out his days for him like a prisoner's scratches, the marking of time on the cell wall. No. 3, no. 4, no. 5, no. 6, no. 7 . . .

And then he could take no more, he kept his eyes low in the

bathroom, ignored his final humiliations written up there in his own words.

Saturday arrived, the Game's hiatus would be over the next day. Again they had pushed a note beneath his door to inform him.

Jolyon lay on his bed looking up through his window all day. The darkness was falling into his room. And that's when a new sensation suddenly flooded his chest, a feeling that broke over him even before the words. He whispered it out loud, the words turning a feeling into truth. 'I can quit,' he said. 'In the morning, I'm going to quit.'

Jolyon jumped off his bed, he should write it all down immediately, his formal resignation from the Game. To have such a letter waiting on his desk would be a release from everything. Maybe he wouldn't need the pills any more. Game Soc would return his deposit and he would give the thousand pounds to Mark right away. The solution was simple. Everything would be over in only a day or two.

He wrote the letter hurriedly, offering congratulations to his opponents. He was leaving without any grudges and wished them the best of luck. And when Jolyon finished and read the whole thing over, he started to laugh. He laughed at the silly lines he had strung together from all those silly letters looped into even more ridiculous words. Words like *sincerest*, *wholehearted* and *aforementioned*. The pomposity was hilarious. And then he realised, while reading the letter, that his fingers were playing with something they had idly picked up from the desk, turning the small thing over and over.

Jolyon looked down and there it was, his tooth. He placed it in front of him on the desk. 'The tooth, the whole tooth and nothing but the tooth,' thought Jolyon, everything now so amusing. His lucky charm stood there, casually leaning on the tips of three of its roots, and suddenly he began to hear a voice. He could almost see the regimental tie. 'Have you noticed, old chap, how the dentist always arranges the most painful procedures to take place at two thirty? Ha, *tooth hurty*, every time.' Jolyon smiled at this joke – yes, he had noticed the same thing. And then the tooth spoke again, but this time in a deep and serious voice. 'Remember, old chap,' it said to Jolyon, 'you can't be beaten. There's nothing they can do to you. Nothing at all.'

Jolyon blinked and looked around the room. He felt disorientated, as if he had just awoken from a dream. He stared hard at the letter as two choices jostled inside him. A minute later, he picked up the letter and started to tear it to pieces.

When he was done he took one of the strips of paper, rolled it into a ball and popped it into his mouth. Jolyon chewed until the ball became a soggy pellet which he manoeuvred with his tongue to plug the gap where his tooth had been. He piled the remaining strips of paper into an ashtray and set them alight.

When the letter was nothing but ashes, Jolyon got up from his desk and moved to the spot on the wall that roared in the night-time. And he started to tap with his head there, gently and rhythmically at first. Then harder and harder and harder. And was it the sound of his head, the beat of a song? Or maybe someone was knocking on . . . Yes, someone was knocking on his door.

Jolyon staggered across the room. He had to lean against the wall to keep himself upright as he opened the door just a crack, just enough to see her standing in his hallway.

LXII(ii) He had not seen Emilia for two months. Not since Dee had come into the room and spoken their names, two loud exclamations. 'Jolyon! Emilia!'

Dee had run from the room. And Emilia, her eyes brimming with her wounds, would have run from the room too were it not for her leg in its cast.

LXII(iii) His head didn't hurt. It must have been the new pills. Emilia was flickering in the half-light of the corridor. Jolyon shook his head and managed to steady the picture. 'Emilia,' he said, sounding delighted to see her.

Her nostrils were flaring and the track of a single tear marked one of her cheeks.

'What is it, Emilia, what's wrong?'

She began to lift her hand, her fist was holding something. When her arm came level with her face, she opened the hand. And out fell a piece of paper.

Jolyon looked down. He saw the *no. 10* and the fragment of her name vanishing into a crease. 'Oh, Emilia, no, no, I . . . I didn't mean any . . . It was just lashing out, venting, like therapy, you know, I felt awful . . .'

When Emilia turned, Jolyon noticed that the cast was gone from her leg. But just as before, when she left him, she left slowly. The picture was flickering. But his head didn't hurt him at all.

██████

LXIII(i) I write, I drink, I take pills. When I get home from the airport, when I wake up at five the next morning. I write, I drink, I take pills. Rewind and repeat.

So much to tell and so little time.

The intercom buzzes. Chad's voice.

LXIII(ii) Excuse the mess, I say, turning to lead him from one end of my sty to the other.

Jolyon, maybe you should put on some clothes, Chad says.

I look down. OK, I say. You wait in the living room, Chad. Anything else I should do?

You could offer me a drink.

I have only whisky.

I'll take a water.

So I dress, I find a glass among the swill of my apartment, I pour water for Chad and then take it, along with the whisky bottle, into the living room.

Chad inspects the filth-encrusted glass, its rim blackened with Magic Marker like the salt on a margarita. He places it on the table and pushes it away.

Have you come here to gloat? I say, indicating the mess all around.

You know that's not why I'm here, he says.

No, I know why you're here.

Well, it has to end, Chad says. He is sitting on my writing chair wearing crisp, dark jeans and a bright cerulean shirt with sleeves rolled up past the elbows. Chad now possesses forearms in the sense that Popeye the Sailor possesses forearms. He sighs as I fall onto the sofa. I feel bad, Jolyon, he says.

Fuck you, Chad, I shout. *I feel bad.* You feel guilty.

No, he says, I don't feel guilty.

Well, good for you, I say, that's probably what makes you such a winner.

I haven't won anything, Chad says. Not yet, Jolyon.

I laugh and take a swig of whisky. The chair creaks as Chad arranges his muscular frame into a fresh position of refined easy-goingness. What the hell do you *do*? I ask, moving my hands as if measuring the breadth of his shoulders, his chest. Do you work out for a *living*, what is this?

Chad chuckles. Just diet and exercise, Jolyon. Living well, you know. And how about you? Did you become a lawyer in the end? Crusader for justice, defender of the poor and innocent, that was always the plan, correct?

I pursued other avenues, I say.

Chad laughs and waves his hand. Oh well, we have more

important matters to discuss, he says. Three more days, your birthday. Shall we say two thirty?

Two thirty? I say, starting to laugh. Two thirty, tooth hurty? And then I laugh so hard that my body convulses, I have to slap my thighs. I'm sorry, Chad, I say, recovering slightly. It's just . . . it's a private joke, don't worry.

Chad starts to get up. His smile looks forced, his eyes uncertain. OK then, Jolyon, may the best man win, he says, offering me his hand.

Reluctantly I respond and we shake.

And just as I think Chad will turn and leave, he takes a deep breath, holding on to my hand a moment too long before letting go. And then he says, Jolyon, whatever happens later, you do understand that none of this is personal any more, right? I want to make sure you know that.

You mean it *was* personal? But it isn't now?

Chad sits back down. I guess it must have been, right? he says, leaning his elbows on his knees. God knows it wasn't the money, the money was never enough to explain anything. Perhaps it was something to do with Emilia, or something to do with Dee. Or maybe I just wanted to beat you more than anyone else. That's not so unusual, is it, Jolyon? You know, like fathers who flat-out refuse to let their sons ever beat them. Or someone who'd rather lose to any person in the world other than his own brother. I suppose that's personal, right?

And now? I say.

You know what it's all about now, Chad says. It's all about escaping from Game Soc, of course.

We could make a pact, I say.

Chad laughs. I wondered that too, he says. And if I thought it would work . . . but they'd just come after us both, Jolyon. Anyway, what do you even stand to lose here? He waves his hand at the filth and the wreckage. I'm sorry, he says. And then Chad stares off to one side. Honestly, I wish I'd just lost the whole thing fourteen years ago without knowing what I know now. And then he turns back to face me. Did they send you the green-ink letters as well?

What letters?

You're kidding me, right? Chad snorts. What letters? Tell me, Jolyon, what do you know about Game Soc?

Nothing, I say.

Nothing? Then what do you have to be afraid of, Jolyon? What are you hiding from?

This is what I think about saying in reply – Oh, I have my reasons, Chad, trust me. I have plenty to hide from. I'll let you read all about it one day. Skip straight to the chapter that follows this encounter, you'll find out soon enough.

But instead I say to him, What letters are you talking about, Chad?

Anonymous letters, he says. Bundles of letters written in green ink making certain grand intimations about Game Soc. Almost certainly from Tallest or Shortest, is my guess. And they were clearly intended to frighten me, so Tallest is the most likely, I think. What with him being such a fan of yours, Jolyon.

A fan of . . .? What? Chad, I don't have the faintest idea what you're talking about.

Chad blinks several times at me. And then he throws himself back in the chair. You've got to be kidding me, Jolyon. You don't know what we were to them? Because if you don't know even that much then you know almost nothing at all. He looks at me and waits to see if I comprehend any of what he's saying.

I shrug.

Chad holds his head in his hands. He starts to mutter and shake his head. Muttering, muttering, shaking. When he drops his hands from his face, he says to me, We were *their* game, Jolyon. They were playing and we were just their little pieces. Knights, bishops, pawns. Tallest backed you and Shortest backed me. So if you win, Tallest wins as well. If I win, then it's Shortest who gets the prize. You didn't even know that much?

I shake my head. But how do you know all of this? I say.

The letters, of course, Chad says, although there is something hesitant to the way he says it and this makes me wonder if he's telling me the truth. There were nine of them originally, Chad continues, all members of some rich boys club. Rich and bored and kicking around looking for something fun to do. And it was Tallest who came up with it. An astonishing, life-changing game. A game just like one he and some friends had played at boarding school to pass the time.

The details were never revealed to me, Chad says, but I know a few things. I know about the prize for winning. And I know Game Soc weren't the winners. That's why they had to find someone. Someone else to play, that was the price for losing.

Then who were the winners? I say.

I have no idea. But they were all rich, all from wealthy families. They were young and smart and well connected. And money meant nothing to them. So instead they played for something much more valuable. They played for power. Those who lost would be beholden to the victors for the rest of their lives. Whatever positions they reached, whatever stations in life, they would owe favours. Be they government ministers, influential bankers, publishing magnates, captains of industry . . . they would all look out for the winners, they would support them utterly and without any questions. Jolyon, you have to understand, our game was *nothing* compared to any of this.

And they had their own form of deposit as well. Money might not have mattered to them. But their standing in the world meant everything to them. And so that's what they all deposited. Their reputations.

So when Middle walked away . . . Look, like I say, I'm really not sure exactly how it all went down. Maybe the rest of them, whoever the rest of them are, simply decided that he needed a gentle reminder of his obligations. Anyway, a few years after we were done playing, Middle was doing very well climbing the greasy pole of a prestigious private banking house. Until one day he was arrested for the possession of a particularly large quantity of cocaine. He managed to wriggle out of serving any jail time, but he lost his job. And after that, no one in the banking world would touch him.

The letters told you this? I say. But how do you know any of it's true?

The information about Game Soc's game? I don't know if it's true. But Middle? Along with the letters I was sent a whole bunch of additional reading material – we'll come to that in a bit. But one of the things that was included was a bundle of press clippings, news stories all about Middle's arrest, the trial . . . and one of the press clippings had a note written in green pen. It said something like, Middle is aware there are considerably worse crimes on the statute book than possession of class-A drugs. And that was it. Chad claps his hands in sarcastic delight. In the very next letter, I was sent another bundle of press clippings. Can you guess what the story was this time? Let me see if I can remember one of the headlines – Oxford Student's Suicide Offers Grim Reminder.

Chad covers his eyes, I hear him sniff. And I want to tell him what really happened to Mark, I want to help him. But how can I tell Chad now? What if he were to use it against me? His body shakes gently between the arms of the chair.

Chad takes one long last sniff and then looks at me again. Let me tell you about some of the other things I got sent, Jolyon, he says. I have boxes full of this stuff back home in England, more press clippings, magazine stories, books . . . One time it was a story about a drinking club in Poland, all these tough guys who got together to down bottles of vodka and play games. One night, after a particularly vigorous session, things got a little out of control. They ended up cutting off each other's hands with axes.

Or another time I'd tear open the envelope and pull out an eighteenth-century essay about gentlemen gangs who roamed the streets of London slashing and stabbing and gouging out eyes. Pamphlets produced by fringe groups about American high-school shootings and video games, a long investigative piece about a secret collegiate society at Yale, another one about the Bilderberg Group, an entire book on the history of Russian roulette. And all of these things were covered in notes, every time in the same green pen. Notes or phrases that were circled, whole paragraphs underlined. Anything about games, about rules and punishments, consequences, conspiracies, secret societies.

Oh, I tried not opening the letters. But somehow I couldn't make myself destroy them. The idea that I was a part of all this, something so big, something . . . it was grotesque, it was ludicrous even. But at the same time I was fascinated. The secrecy, the hidden gears, it felt like a drug. Some nights I'd go to where I'd hidden the letters and open whole stacks in one go. And then I'd spend all night reading them over and over and over.

Chad looks up at the ceiling as if he can see the words of those letters hanging over his head. And you really knew nothing about any of this at all? he says. Chad slumps back in his chair looking suddenly exhausted.

No, nothing, I say. I am looking at Chad for a sign, a tell. Is this the truth or is he just trying to scare me? I can't imagine the Chad of fourteen years ago making up such a story and telling it with so much conviction. But how much has he changed? He looks tired and uncertain, he looks like a younger Chad wearing an ill-fitting disguise. His muscles seem foolish now, a thin and worthless shield. I feel the whisky surging inside me, the pills whirling away. I remember my story and my mind pushes Chad away. He belongs somewhere else, this all belongs somewhere else, somewhere later.

I swing my legs off the sofa and face him. Well, thank you for coming, Chad, I say. But as you can see, I'm really quite busy here.

Chad looks confused. That's all you have to say, Jolyon? You're really quite busy?

I have a lot of work on, I say. My head swims, the room lurches. Would you mind seeing yourself out? I say.

Chad looks spurned. Sure then, Jolyon, he says, getting to his feet. Sure, I can tell how busy you are. He turns and leaves the room. A few moments later I hear him call out, Thursday, Jolyon, two thirty!

The front door clicks shut.

LXIII(iii) Am I afraid that I might become trapped in a game I never wanted to play? I don't know. And I don't have the time to be scared of ghost stories. I don't even have the time to consider whether I believe in the existence of ghosts.

Perhaps Chad wanted to scare me. Maybe he made it all up. But anyway, I have my own reasons to fear Game Soc. More specifically, I have my own reasons to fear one particular member of their threesome. But we'll come to that soon enough.

No, I don't have time to consider either the present or the future. Because now the moment, fourteen years ago, has arrived.

The reckoning. An elegant solution. My endgame with Mark.

———

LXIV(i) His head didn't hurt. No, his head didn't hurt him at all.

Jolyon could feel each grain of wood as he hammered his fists against Mark's door, could sense his weight gathering at the soles of his feet. When the door opened, Mark's face was bright, his lips dry and parted. 'Jolyon, good to see you,' said Mark. 'Can't imagine what could bring you so urgently to my door.'

'You *really* want to beat me?' said Jolyon. 'You want to win so much you'd hurt Emilia just to get at me? OK then, Mark, just remember whose choice it was to raise the stakes. Come on then, let's play.'

Jolyon turned and started to leave but Mark stayed where he was. 'I don't have to do anything, Joe. Nothing that comes out of your mouth ever again.'

Jolyon stopped at the edge of the stairs. 'No, but you'll like this game, Mark.' he said. 'The odds are stacked in your favour.' The words were written inside him, Jolyon only had to move his lips. 'Look,' he said, 'I don't have a thousand pounds to give you right now. But I will, one day. And I'll give you back your thousand pounds plus another thousand if you can beat me today. Plus, I'll admit you were right all along. You'll enjoy that even more than the money.'

Mark looked uncertain. 'What's the trick?' he said.

'There's no trick,' said Jolyon. 'You win, you get two thousand pounds. I'll use next year's grant or I'll work through the summer. You have my word and you know I'll keep it.' Mark shrugged. 'But if I win,' Jolyon continued, 'you call off this vendetta. Double or nothing. And it's a game of physics, Mark. A game of gravity and acceleration.'

'OK then, I'm listening, Jolyon. But if this is a trick –'

'If it's a trick, Mark, if at any time you call the trick, you can pull out and you win, I give you my word. But you pull out for any other reason, you lose. Sound fair?'

'Fine, Jolyon, go ahead and tell me your game.'

Jolyon laughed through his nose. 'It's simple, like I told you, a game of physics,' he said. 'Tell me, the equation – the square root of two d over g – what does that describe?'

Mark spoke hesitantly even though he found the question childishly simple. 'The time . . . the, um, time, t, taken for an object to fall . . . to fall the distance d.'

'And how tall would you say the college tower is? Loser's Leap?'

'Maybe eighty feet,' said Mark, beginning to warm to the task.

'Feet, Mark, feet?' said Jolyon, sounding like a scolding professor. 'Come now, *Marcus*, did I not state this was a game of physics?'

Mark sighed heavily. 'Twenty-five metres,' he said sharply.

'And therefore the value of t is . . . ?'

'Twice twenty-five is fifty. Gravity is nine-point-eight. Divide them, about five-point-one. The square root of five-point-one is . . . approximately two and a quarter.'

'So that means it would take about two and a quarter seconds for an object falling from the college tower – Christine Balfour for example – to hit the ground, correct?'

'Correct,' said Mark.

'Good, so here's the game,' said Jolyon. 'I say I won't hit the ground for ten seconds when I jump off the tower. No, let's have some real fun, let's make it twenty.'

Mark snorted. 'Jolyon, you're being ridiculous.'

'So you're taking the position that I'll hit the ground before twenty seconds elapse.'

'*Obviously* you're not going to jump off a tower, Jolyon.'

'If that's the case, you win. Two thousand pounds. Come on then, Mark.'

Jolyon started to skip down the stairs, Mark calling out after him, 'This is stupid, what's the trick, Jolyon?'

The old stairs creaked and groaned. 'I already told you, Mark, there's no trick. And if there is. And you call it. You win.'

LXIV(ii) As Jolyon crossed back quad he glanced up through the darkness at Loser's Leap. It looked like a rook in a chess problem. He didn't need to turn, he could sense Mark at his back, the mounting discomfort, here was a problem to which he had no solution.

Back quad, front quad, the chapel. And it was just as Jack had said, a set of stairs leading up to the organ loft, a small window. As Jolyon climbed through the window, he heard Mark reach the top of the stairs. 'Just how far are you planning to take this, Jolyon?'

There was a thin space between the roof of Great Hall and its parapet wall. Jolyon jumped down. 'All the way, Mark,' he called out, 'all the way. How about you?'

Jolyon made his way toward the tower. The roof was steep but there was a crust of dry lichen on the tiles that made the climb easier. And then from the apex of Great Hall, Jolyon heaved himself onto the tower roof.

Mark rested his hands on his knees after he pulled himself up there. They were both out of breath and Mark looked even more confused than before. 'OK then,' he said, 'so what now?'

Jolyon crossed to the other side of the roof and faced out onto back quad. He leaned over the edge, the parapet wall queasily short where he stood, and saw beneath him the flagpole stripped for the night. It was a warm evening and in the pale light breaking from the windows he could make out a small group of people smoking and drinking on the grass below. 'Good,' thought Jolyon. And then he called out over his shoulder, 'Did we say ten seconds, or did we say twenty, Mark?'

'This is ridiculous,' said Mark. 'OK, you said twenty. But it doesn't matter, you're not actually going through with it, we both know that.'

'Twenty it is then.'

'What's the point of this, Jolyon?'

Jolyon spoke slowly, a broad spacing between solemn words. 'Do you agree to the game, Mark?'

'Fine then, Jolyon,' said Mark, rubbing his face in his hands, 'go ahead.'

'Excellent,' said Jolyon. He put one of his feet up on the short wall, leaned against his knee and gazed out like a tourist. The tower wall had been constructed as decorative battlements and Jolyon tapped the taller block beside him. 'Do you know what these higher parts are called?' he said, but Mark didn't reply. 'The taller parts of battlements are called merlons and these lower parts of the wall, the gaps, they're the crenels.' The crenels were only shin-high. Jolyon lifted his other foot so they were now both on the wall. He stood there rocking precariously on the balls of his feet as he breathed deeply into the night. 'What do you think, Mark? Twenty-five metres from the top of the merlon, or from down here on the crenel?'

'Jolyon, I know you think you can walk on fucking water but not even you believe you can fly. So just tell me the trick and let's get down from here.'

'I told you, Mark, there's no trick,' said Jolyon. 'And I don't need to fly in order to beat you. In fact, I don't even need to jump. Because you're going to pull out before it goes that far. You see, all I need to do is call out your name as I fall. Two and a quarter seconds, you said? That should be plenty of time.' Jolyon looked at his watch – 'Maaaa-aaaaa-rk –' moving his head to its tick. 'So even if you can live with my death on your conscience, there are plenty of witnesses down there. And when the police arrive and hear whose name I was calling out . . . and then someone's bound to tell them about the excerpts from my diary being posted round college. Even if no one has actually seen you doing it, I'm sure there'll be something forensics can find.' Jolyon pulled out a cigarette, lit it and blew. 'However, if at any point you want me not to jump, just say the word, Mark. Oh, which means you lose the game, remember. We did agree that if either one of us pulls out, it's a forfeit.'

Mark started to laugh. 'Brilliant, Jolyon,' he said, 'I mean, that's really very impressive. Except for one thing. Your grand plan to defeat me is based entirely on a false assumption. That I somehow believe you might jump.'

Jolyon looked out past the rooftops of Pitt and rested his hand on the merlon beside him. He could see all of the towers and domes of the city glowing yellow beneath the soothing black of the sky. And his head didn't hurt. No, his head didn't hurt him at all. He flicked his cigarette out into the night and it whirled away like a dying Catherine wheel before diving into the light. Then Jolyon lifted his arms above him and placed his palms together, a high prayer, a tall steeple. Slowly he lifted his foot and shifted it forward, held it out over the void. 'Velocity equals gravity multiplied by time. So what's my speed when I hit the ground, Mark? Let's do it in miles per hour, just for fun.'

Mark was quiet a while. And then, uneasily, he said, 'Just a fraction shy of fifty miles per hour.'

'A fraction shy? Let's round it up, friends shouldn't argue over trifling amounts, don't you agree, Mark?' He took a loud, sharp breath. 'Fifty should be fast enough,' said Jolyon.

And then he stepped down into the night.

They were laughing hard on the lawn below and they didn't hear Mark's panicked cry as Jolyon's weight began to pull him down, as his foot dropped beneath the edge of the tower. And his head didn't hurt him at all.

▬

LXV(i) No, it can't be done. I can't go on telling you what took place that night as if it were only a story, the climax to some distant thriller. My confession must come from the heart, there is no literary distance I can put between me and what happened back then. Because I live with it in the here and now. Not on the page. I live with it every second of every day.

First person. Singular. Me.

LXV(ii) Here is the worst of my guilt. He tried to save me. Mark tried to stop me from falling to my death.

Perhaps he believed I *would* shout his name. But this doesn't matter. No, he called out to me – Jolyon, no! All I had wanted was for him to believe I would go through with it, for Mark to surrender.

From where he was standing, he couldn't have seen the flagpole beneath my hovering foot – Jolyon, no! – daring him, trying to convince him I was mad enough to go through with it. And who knows, perhaps I was. But at that moment, I was only trying to plant my foot on a flagpole. So Mark ran at me, he leapt, he tried to save me. And then two things happened at once. My foot landed on its target, and Mark, with a lunging dive, caught hold of my trailing leg. And as he grabbed hold of me, Mark knocked me off balance.

My foot came away from the pole, there was nothing beneath me but death. The whole world seemed to lurch in my chest as time began to stretch, constant becoming variable. Suddenly there were no thoughts in my mind – gravity was claiming me and my thoughts were all feelings. Panic, regret, life, fear, death. And then the weight of me, gravity's scream, pulled Mark quickly over the low parapet wall. Somewhere in this jumble of feelings and instincts, my arms had started to move, had somehow found a way to wrap themselves around the flagpole. With a sharp jerk I stopped falling. I felt the slick surface of the pole and quickly became aware of a great burden attached to my leg. And as my fingers started to slip, I didn't think. There was no motive, no thought but survival. Life not death.

I kicked, electric, instinctive. I bucked like a killer at the end of a noose. Something was taking me down and I fought for life, I shook death off.

And that's when Mark pleaded with me to stop, or at least that's what I think those three quick words were supposed to mean, just before I managed to kick him away.

Jolyon, you win.

LXV(iii) As Mark's body fell slowly into the light I saw that he was trying to twist through the air, instinctively steering his body to keep his skull from shattering against the earth. And he didn't call out my name, Mark didn't cry out at all as he dropped from the tower. He simply fell, down and down for two and a quarter seconds. At the end he managed to turn his body enough that I could see his face before he hit the ground. And in that moment of impact, Mark's wide eyes seemed to call out to me that he was very scared of dying but also that this was a terrible injustice. And it was true, he was absolutely right.

And now I see his face every morning, every day. First Mark's wide and afraid and accusing eyes. And then I hear the horrible crumpling sound, I feel his spirit fly up like a cold wind biting through me. And then I see the blood pooling around Mark's body in the pale light. The blood was very black and the eyes very suddenly shut.

LXV(iv) It was quiet below as if the people down there couldn't comprehend this sudden appearance of death on the gravel. A silent pause. No one saw me as I scrambled up onto the roof.

And then the screaming started.

First the screaming of women and then the yelling of men, the men shouting out the words God and Jesus over and over. More screaming and I was scrambling down the roof of Great Hall. What was I thinking, what words were running through my mind? I don't know, I think there were only impulses. Run away, hide. I pulled myself through the chapel window, ran down the stairs and out onto front quad. I slowed down so as not to be seen running. And that's when I saw someone coming into college through the front lodge. And I shouldn't have stopped, I shouldn't have stood there frozen by guilt.

And then, distantly across the lawn, the figure making its way into Pitt stopped as well, as if it were he who'd been caught and not me. He turned around quickly, started to hurry away. His squat limbs, those small, furtive features. Shortest.

I gasped so hard the air stuck in my chest like a stone. And then the impulse to escape took over again. I didn't have time to think about Shortest, I had to keep moving. I had to cross the end of back quad to get to staircase six.

Already a crowd had gathered, some of them hugging, the rest of them smoking, hands jittery and tight around their cigarettes. And no one saw me, they were all looking elsewhere. Not at the body, no one could bear to look at the body for more than a moment or two. They were looking up vacantly, staring out into the night.

I could hear sirens as I ran up the stairs. Some part of me must have been thinking clearly, some awful part of me, because soon I had discovered Mark's door unlocked. I found my diary. It was under his pillow, ten or twenty pieces of bright yellow paper poking out from the top.

And then I was back in my room, shivering in bed, the pillow over my head to muffle the sounds of more sirens. And that's when I started to think, when words finally began to form in my head. The horror, the guilt.

And not only the guilt but the fear. Fear of Shortest. Fear of being caught.

LXV(v) So there you have it, my confession. And perhaps this is why I have been mnemonically upping my measures of whisky, my pills. Not because of Chad, not because of the Game, but because I knew that this moment would arrive. The time for confession.

And yes, I do confess to it. I killed him, Mark, it was me.

But it was never supposed to be that sort of game.

———

LXVI(i) There was a knock on Jolyon's door. He opened hesitantly, wondering if it might be the police. But it was only Dee and she flung her arms frantically around him. 'Oh God, Jolyon, Mark's dead, he's dead. Have you heard? He's dead, Jolyon, Mark's dead.'

'Oh my God, Dee, no.'

'He threw himself from the tower, Loser's Leap, it's so awful, it's so . . .'

Jolyon pulled Dee closer to him, if he clung to her tight enough he might squeeze out a drop of his guilt. And while Dee sobbed hard on his shoulder, Jolyon cried as well. But nothing could diminish the guilt.

'I phoned Chad,' said Dee, 'I told him what happened. He's on his way now.'

'OK, Dee, it's OK,' said Jolyon. And then the seed of Jolyon's guilt began to grow. Seed sprouted shoots. Shoots scrambled through soil and surged up through the earth, out into the light. The feeling that he wanted to confess.

Dee was in his arms and he was safe here. But he had to tell her before Chad arrived. Dee would understand, Dee would tell him what to do. Hadn't she loved him – even if only for a few days? And he had been lonely for so long and her tears were so warm on his shoulder.

He kissed Dee on the forehead and they broke away from each other's embrace. Dee, still in tears, collapsed into the armchair and Jolyon knelt down before her. Yes, he would tell her, everything was going to be all right. But quick, before Chad arrived. He placed his hands lightly on her knees and blew out his breath. 'Dee listen,' he said, feeling his fingertips on her flesh, 'Mark didn't kill himself.'

But Dee didn't flinch, she didn't recoil from him. Instead Dee spoke quickly. 'Don't say it, Jolyon.' She gave him a threatening look. 'Don't you *dare* say Mark didn't kill himself because of the Game. We both know the Game is to blame for this, it was the Game that sent him off the rails.'

'No, you don't – ,' said Jolyon.

'Christ, that's what Chad kept saying to me on the phone. "The Game didn't kill him, Dee, that's not why Mark did it." But it's not true. It's not true and I won't listen. I won't hear it from you as well, Jolyon, don't you *dare* say it, don't you . . .' Dee put her hands to her face and started to cry again.

Jolyon let his head fall close to her lap. Dee had to listen to him, she had to hear his confession before Chad arrived. 'Dee, please listen to me.' The words were sharp inside him, were trying to cut their way out through his skin.

But Dee pushed him away. 'No, Jolyon, I won't listen to either of you. We killed him. We all killed him and now it's over. I'm out. I quit. I told Chad already, I don't care what he says to me. It's finished, you both have to see that. And if you don't, then I don't care about either of you.' She looked at Jolyon for confirmation that he understood but Jolyon was looking down at the ground, his eyes darting back and forth as if following his thoughts while they fell in neat piles all around him. Dee was out, the worst was over. And maybe he didn't need to confess, perhaps he had the strength to fight the words, to hold them in.

'I hate you,' Dee cried out, 'I hate you both,' she said. And then Dee threw herself against him, at first with her fists to his chest, but then her hands began to climb. Up to his neck, his chin. And then Dee held Jolyon's face between her hands and kissed him desperately. He felt her teeth sharp against his lips, the taste of her tears. And finally Dee pushed him away. She sat back in the armchair, not looking at him, wiping her lips with the back of her hand. 'I'm sorry, Jolyon,' said Dee, 'I'm sorry.'

But Jolyon didn't know whether Dee was sorry for all she had done to him or sorry for kissing him. And he never did get to ask her, it was the last time they would speak for nearly fourteen years. Because just then there was a knocking on the door. And before Jolyon could answer, Chad was coming into the room.

LXVI(ii) Dee glared at him as he stood by the door trying to find somewhere to place his hands. Hips, pockets, the back of his head. 'This is terrible, just terrible,' said Chad. And then he became angry. 'But there are people out there who barely even knew him,' he said, pointing distantly. 'You should see them, the wailing and . . . they barely even *knew* him.' Jolyon was sitting on the floor by his bed, knees apart, head hung low. 'I spoke to Shortest,' said Chad, 'and obviously we're not going to go through with anything tomorrow.'

'What?' said Dee accusingly. 'You did what? You're already making plans? And why Shortest?'

Chad swallowed. 'He's just the one who answered the phone,' he said. 'They gave us a number a long time ago. You weren't there, Dee.'

'And was he upset? Or was he worried about getting caught up in something?'

'No,' said Chad, 'I don't think he was. Neither.'

Dee wiped her eyes, shook her head.

Jolyon looked at them looking at each other, his tormentors. Neither of them had seen his face, had noticed his fear and his horror, when Shortest's name was mentioned.

Chad's tongue hovered on his top lip. 'So, we're all going to meet next Sunday,' he said. 'Here at four, I guess. We have to . . . we have to wait a bit, let the dust settle.'

'Let the *dust* settle?' said Dee. 'Oh, that's nice, Chad. You mean post-cremation?'

'No, I . . .' Chad scratched the back of his head.

And Jolyon was watching them, watching. If Shortest had told Chad, then wouldn't he say something? Or look at him knowingly? But Chad wasn't looking across at him at all, Chad was only noticing Dee.

'I already told you, I'm out,' said Dee, hugging her shoulders. 'How dare you even talk about this right now?'

'Look, Dee,' said Chad, 'I'm really sorry. What I said to you on the phone, I shouldn't have . . . I mean, we're all just crazy upset right now.'

Jolyon locked his hands behind his head. Had Shortest really said nothing to Chad? Then perhaps he had a little more time, there might be a way out. And if Shortest had said nothing, what did everything mean? What was Shortest doing at Pitt?

'Oh really, Chad?' said Dee. 'You're *crazy* upset? And why's that exactly?'

'Because of Mark,' said Chad, as if there were only one possible answer. Dee said nothing, she only stared hard at Chad. 'Of course because of Mark,' he repeated, 'why else would I be upset?' And then, although it seemed to Jolyon that Chad might be about to cry, something else happened. Instead of tears, Chad let out a short laugh. It was a wet sort of snort as if Chad were a schoolboy who had just spotted a double entendre in a textbook. And Jolyon had seen men at funerals laughing nervously like this – into the crooks of their arms, behind shielding hands – a diversion of emotion, the only alternative to breaking down, breast-beating and wailing, the public unleashing of all of their pain.

But as Jolyon looked at Dee he could tell that she did not see any ambiguity in Chad's laughter. Dee looked shocked and appalled. What sort of a human being was this? What sort of monster? She got up hurriedly from the armchair and ran toward the door.

'Dee?' said Chad, catching her arm as she passed.

And then Dee turned and with a wild swing of her hand she hit Chad hard across the face. The sharp sound of the slap rang through the room.

Chad, his eyes wide and shocked, instinctively raised his hand and it seemed for a moment as if he might strike back. Dee looked at him, dared him to, and then Chad lifted his hand to his bright stung cheek. And Dee was gone.

LXVI(iii) Chad stood motionless by the door. He looked like a small boy who had been shamed by a teacher. Jolyon stared at him. He still felt guilty and yet he wanted to see Chad in all his humiliation. Chad glanced only momentarily back at Jolyon but this was long enough. He started to shuffle from the room.

Jolyon waited until Chad was halfway through the door. 'You win,' Jolyon called out after him. 'I'll quit next week, Chad. Congratulations, the best man won.'

Chad only paused, not turning around. His shoulders rose and then fell as he moved out into the hallway, as he disappeared gradually down the stairs.

LXVI(iv) Jolyon didn't sleep. He lay in his bed picturing Mark's eyes. The moment before, the moment after. Moment after moment after moment. And then, very early in the morning, Jolyon went down to the phone at the bottom of his staircase and dialled the number.

'Hello?'

'It's Jolyon.'

'Aha.'

' . . . '

' . . . '

'What were you doing at Pitt?'

'What were you doing coming out of the chapel?'

' . . . '

'You see, I heard that's the way Mark got up there. Through a chapel window, that's what they say, Jolyon, up via the roof of Great Hall. How about you?'

' . . . '

'So shall I tell the police what I saw?'

'No.'

'Good. But will they find any evidence? Might anyone else have seen you?'

'No.'

'Very good. Then I suggest we both hold on to our information like playing cards. Very close to our chests.'

'Why would you do that, Shortest?'

'Let's just call it a sense of fair play.'

'How do I know you won't say something later?'

'Respect the Game, Jolyon, and the Game will respect you.'

'Is that what you were doing skulking round Pitt late at night, Shortest? Respecting the Game?'

'Do we really have to spell it out, Jolyon? Oh dear, I was hoping we might be a little more English about the whole thing. Your erstwhile transatlantic friend has had an adverse affect on you.'

'. . .'

'Fine then, Jolyon. You have something over me and I have something over you. Should we continue to circle or are we done now?'

'It was an accident, Shortest.'

'I don't doubt it for the merest second, Jolyon.'

'. . .'

'Was that all?'

'Yes.'

'Excellent. See you next Sunday then.'

LXVII(i) No one ever asked me. No one ever said to me, Jolyon, did you kill Mark? Something extraordinary happened instead. In the small world of Pitt, I was pardoned.

In the eyes of almost everyone at college, Mark and I had been close friends. And not just close but inseparable. Wherever I went, Mark went. Mark had swapped rooms just to live next door to me. The *Pitt Pendulum* had even run a cartoon. Me as groom, Mark as demented bride, a congregation of jealous faces.

Yes, that's how it looked to Pitt. Six friends, a falling-out, my twinship with Chad left in tatters. But until his death, Mark and I had remained close. And perhaps Mark's depression – surely it must have been depression – was in some way related to my behaviour. I must have been under a great deal of strain being close friends with someone depressive enough to take his own life, someone who found the world such a strain he preferred sleep over consciousness. And perhaps, now that everyone thought it through with the benefit of hindsight, my public enjoyment of *Asian Babes* was not so indicative of racism after all. And really those diary entries only revealed the sort of dark, unkind thoughts we all have from time to time. Let he who is without sin cast the first stone. And no one thought to link the non-appearance of any further diary entries with the death of Mark. It was clear that whoever had been taping them to the walls had decided to stop out of respect for my grief. I think most people assumed my torturer to have been Jack.

For the next several days, girls stopped me and hugged me as I made my way around Pitt. Boys slapped my back, rubbed my shoulders. People who barely even knew me would tell me how sorry they were to hear about my friend.

One time I spied Jack and Emilia in a large group of people across back quad. They were walking toward me. Jack saw me and then cast his eyes quickly down. A moment later he appeared to have a sudden idea. Everyone nodded and shrugged and changed direction. I watched them all disappear through the Hallowgood gate.

Meanwhile I had spoken to the police who assured me that, while the circumstances of Mark's death were in no way suspicious, with any such death they had a duty to make inquiries, they hoped I understood. I nodded solemnly. Perhaps they were testing me as we spoke, feeling for leads. If so then I passed. It wasn't hard to act the grief-stricken friend, I was already broken. The police were very sensitive and understanding. It makes me sick to think of the lies I told.

LXVII(ii) But now the present must briefly interrupt my confession. Because there is still a life going on in this railroad flat. Only the barest scratch of a life but a life nonetheless.

Sometimes while writing I pause to wonder if Dee will come, if Dee will knock on my door and forgive me. But of course she won't forgive me, how could she forgive such a thing? And then it occurs to me that perhaps losing her book was no accident. Maybe some terrible part of me has chosen to lose her poems, a secret piece of my mind that refuses to let her know about Mark. I have lost Dee's book so she would flee from me, so she would never find out, never hate me for what I have done.

And it has worked. I sit all alone with my story. Only the past, the distant past.

———

LXVIII Emilia looked spectacular in black, a perfect Hitchcock widow among the candles and stained glass. Jolyon's eyes fell first on her and Jack sitting together when he entered the church. Jack looked uncomfortable among the pews, there could be no jokes in this place. Jolyon thought he saw them holding hands during one portion of the ceremony but perhaps he only imagined it. Seated on her own, a few rows behind Emilia and Jack, was Dee. Black sat very naturally on Dee. And Chad also was sitting apart from his friends, across the aisle in a borrowed suit two sizes too big for him. But Chad looked otherwise composed, a monochrome study of stoicism.

Jolyon looked up at the ceiling of the church. It reminded him of the bar at Pitt, as if he were staring up at the undersides of enormous stone parasols. He could almost hear the chatter and bubbling laughter.

He had taken the train to London on his own and remained alone in the church, sitting as far back as he could. As far as he could from the coffin, the grief.

But it was impossible for Jolyon to remain alone at Mark's mother's house where everyone gathered after the funeral, the house crammed with so many bodies. And being there reminded Jolyon guiltily of how, with delicate flutes of champagne, they had toasted Mark's nineteenth birthday only three months earlier in that house. Now he made small talk with people he only half knew. They ate sandwiches and said all the appropriate things. Shocking, tragic, so young.

The ceiling seemed to descend slowly around and around like the lid of a screw-top jar as a palpable grief began to evaporate from the dense welter of bodies. Grief gathered on the insides of the windows, trickled down the panes, collected in droplets on the window frames. And Jolyon stood there trying not to see the pain in everyone's eyes but felt their hurt seeping into him, wordlessly drenching his heart.

And when Mark's mother came to him, Jolyon thought he might shatter into a million black stars. Only her arms, which Mark's mother wrapped around him as she might once have done her son, held Jolyon together. And then she said to him, 'Mark told me all about you, Jolyon.' She held him by the shoulders and looked into his eyes. 'And I could tell that he loved you the most. So that's why I'm asking you. Please, Jolyon, if you know anything, anything at all. Why did he do it? Why did my beautiful son . . . what made him . . . ?'

Jolyon's throat was coarse and sore. He looked at Mark's mother, her trembling lips, her sleepless eyes. If he were to say to her 'I really don't know, Mrs Cutler' then it would all be over, they would hold each other again and he would say how sorry he was for her loss. But how could he do that? He had already taken her son. How could he leave Mark's mother alone with the torment of wondering *why* every haunted second of every night and day?

Their game had been such a pale imitation of life, such a blunt and childish thing. Because only life had real consequences, only life could cause real pain. There was nothing Chad and Dee could ever have dreamt, no consequence imaginable, that Jolyon could less have endured than what he had to do now. He led Mark's mother to the side of the room and they sat together at the very edge of a sofa, as if to sit any further back would be an insult to the memory of Mark.

A young man of great promise had died and no one deserved any comfort. No one deserved to rest or even to sleep or breathe. And Jolyon least of all.

———

LXIX(i) Sitting here now in New York, fourteen years after that funeral, I can still hear every word I said to her, each and every lie I drizzled over Mark's mother.

She looks at me with such a heartbreaking mixture of pain and gratitude, wiping her eyes tenderly as I tell her that her son was the cleverest person I ever met, the brightest at Pitt without any doubt. She squeezes my hand when I tell her that Mark wanted to be the very best. And he was the best, I say to her. But he couldn't see it, he was hard on himself, so hard. When we started, we all found ourselves suddenly surrounded by so many intelligent people, the brightest in the land. And Mark was a perfectionist. Yes, yes he was, she nods. If he couldn't do something perfectly he'd rather not do it at all. His work began to suffer. And there's such pressure at a place like Pitt to perform, I have friends at other universities who barely have to work at all but at Pitt they start to hound you if you begin to slip. Her grip tightens on the handkerchief balled in an unsteady hand. Mark became paralysed by the pressure from without as well as the pressure he put on himself to succeed. He was working on his own theory, something to do with dark energy, the invisible forces of the universe. I didn't understand the physics behind the theory and it was so frustrating to Mark that he couldn't share his glimpse of such beauty. He wouldn't take it to any of his tutors until the theory was complete and that might have taken years, decades even. She laughs with a small huff at the memory of her son, obstinate and proud. But I had no idea, I tell her, how heavily the burden of his work was weighing on him. Yes, I could see he was down. Sometimes he wouldn't get out of bed until late in the evening. She swallows hard, remembering the same thing. In the last week of his life, Mark said he'd arrived at a solution. He was wild-looking, excitable, and I thought he meant his theory on dark energy. But now, I say to her, I think maybe he was talking about something else. I am so sorry and I don't know if any of this makes any sense.

Mark's mother rests her hands on mine. Yes, she says, it's all so much clearer to her now. And she will always be so very, very grateful that Mark was lucky enough to meet such a good friend as me.

Such a good friend as me. Such a friend. Such a.

LXIX(ii) And there you have it, my entire confession. The truth, the whole truth and nothing but the truth. I cannot change the past but I can write it down, I can tell the world. And now, whatever happens to me, I am prepared.

Ready to face the consequences.

██████

LXX(i) Jolyon rang the brass bell. It was Sir Ralph Wiseman himself who opened the door. It was almost summer and the warden had abandoned the pullover beneath his tweeds. 'Jolyon, isn't it?' said Wiseman. Jolyon nodded. 'Good good, do come *een*.'

And so Jolyon's time at Pitt ended officially in the warden's parlour. The flowers in the garden were brushing brightly against the leaded windows. The two of them sat in meadow-patterned chairs sipping whisky dispensed from a crystal decanter. This is delightful, thought Jolyon, all in the very best of British tradition. The charm, the fellowship, the hospitality. It was almost as if he was not quitting Pitt but requesting reassignment elsewhere in the empire. Pastures new. Less blood, more sun.

Wiseman's words were stiff but he was well meaning. He told Jolyon that while he understood entirely his decision to leave, it really wouldn't be sensible to make everything too final. There would be no requirements for his re-entry, just say the word, take a year to think things through.

Jolyon wanted to say to him, 'But you don't understand, Warden. I'm not leaving because I can't handle Mark's death. And I'm not even leaving only because it was all my fault. I'm leaving because I *can* handle his death, I *have* handled his death. So I'm leaving because I deserve to be punished, I deserve no advantages or special treatment. I deserve nothing at all from the rest of my life.'

LXX(ii) When he reached the top of staircase six, he found that Shortest and Chad were there already, waiting outside his door. The time had come for Jolyon's second resignation of the day.

'Happy birthday, Jolyon,' said Chad.

LXX(iii) 'You didn't think I'd forget, did you?'

'Did you bring me a present?' asked Jolyon.

'The gift of good company,' said Chad, indicating Shortest with a broad sweep of his arm.

And then Jolyon laughed, he surrendered himself to gallows humour, there was nothing else left. Shortest was finding everything amusing as well. He swung himself into the armchair and dangled his legs over its side.

'Where's Tallest?' said Jolyon.

'Other plans,' Shortest replied. 'Sends heartfelt regrets.'

Jolyon took his customary spot on the bed and Chad the desk chair with wheels, rolling it back and forth while he looked at Jolyon. At least he had the decency not to smile.

'OK then,' said Jolyon, 'I have an announcement to make. I'm leaving Pitt,' he said, 'and also –'

Shortest interrupted with an exaggerated cough. 'Please do excuse me,' he said, 'but just one little thing. If you remember, Game Soc did reserve the right to insert into your game a single consequence, I'm sure you haven't forgotten. And before you say anything else, Jolyon, you should probably hear me out.

'The time has come, you see.' Shortest gestured regretfully toward Jolyon and Chad as they exchanged panicked glances. 'Our consequence is simple. It will be earned by whichever of you loses, obviously. And incidentally, we shall pursue our right to enforce performance with some considerable vigour, should the need arise. We have both the means and method for enforcement.' Shortest waved his hand in apology. 'But you are both honourable men in any case,' he said. 'Our consequence is as follows.' Shortest paused, taking an immense pleasure in the slow release of his words. 'The losing player will participate in another game,' he said. 'And that's really all I can state for now.'

Shortest shrugged gleefully. 'It was most important for us to find a very strong player,' he said. 'Shame we can't ultimately take the winner. Although that would hardly be fair. Anyway, once your game is complete, the loser will be provided with the necessary information. A welcome pack to Game Soc, if you like.' Shortest crossed his stubby legs in the armchair, removed the pillow from behind him and held it in his lap. 'OK then, Jolyon,' he said, smiling salaciously, 'why don't you tell us what it is you wanted to say?'

Jolyon blinked as his mind shrank rapidly around the truth – Game Soc had trapped them both.

Suddenly his bed felt very precarious as if it were a narrow ledge up high on a mountain. Jolyon had never been scared of heights but now he knew how it felt, his stomach rehearsing the fall, his head rushing wildly and beginning to spin. He was scared of Game Soc, he knew that now. And something else. The Game had not been fun for some time, that much was obvious. But now it was no longer even a game. Now it was simply a part of his life. And there were some things in life at which you couldn't afford to lose. There wasn't even such a thing as choice. Jolyon felt his lips peeling slowly apart as he opened his mouth to speak. One word, it seemed to take an age to heave it up from his chest. 'No,' said Jolyon, And then he felt a sickness in his belly, he was a plaything squeezed between the jaws of Game Soc. 'No,' he said, 'there was nothing else at all I wanted to say.'

Silence. Shortest leaned forward in his chair as he turned to look at Chad. And then Chad hammered his fist on the desk. 'No! You told me you'd quit,' he shouted. 'No, Jolyon, you've lost. You admitted I've won. You told me, you . . .'

Jolyon, somewhere far beneath his queasiness, felt a bitter sense of pleasure as he stared absently at Chad. 'I recall no such conversation ever taking place between us,' he said. The words felt automatic as if he had been programmed to say them by his helplessness.

Chad jumped to his feet and started to snatch up Jolyon's possessions from the desk, throwing them at the wall, glasses breaking, pills bouncing. He grabbed a book and tore out its pages, he threw the dried rose to the floor and stamped until its petals were dust. And then, when he was done, he collapsed back into the chair and held his hands to his face. Breathing heavily, Chad lowered his hands and stared hard at Jolyon. 'You're leaving Pitt,' he said, 'you can't continue. It's over. You're done.'

'I'm thinking of moving to London,' said Jolyon. 'It's not far on the train. I'm not quitting, I won't.'

'This has to be some kind of joke,' Chad shouted. 'Just look at you for *chrissakes*, Jolyon, you're finished. So you'll commute here to perform your consequences as well? Don't waste everyone's time.'

'Or maybe I could get a job in the car factory. I'll rent a place at the edge of the city.'

'The car factory? That's ludicrous.'

Jolyon's throat was parched and his voice began to crack. 'This isn't the end,' he said, the words almost as broken as Jolyon himself. He closed his eyes, his voice barely more than a scratch. 'I'm not quitting, Chad,' he said. 'I'm not quitting. I won't.'

LXX(iv) They stared at each other while Shortest remained motionless in the armchair, cross-legged and smiling like a lucky Buddha. Jolyon had made his final move and he waited.

When Chad broke the silence he managed to restore some calm to his voice. 'Then we're going to have to come to some kind of arrangement,' he said, glancing up at the ceiling. 'Unfortunately there is another factor to consider. It seems I have to leave Pitt early as well. I have to return to the States,' he said, shaking his head slowly. 'Possibly I could be gone for some time.' And then, Chad's voice becoming strained, he added, 'If you're allowed to distort the Game, Jolyon, then so can I. But I'll come back to finish this, you can be one hundred per cent certain of that. This is a temporary suspension. This is not the end, Jolyon, this is nowhere near the end.'

Jolyon brushed at his legs for a while as if they were covered in crumbs. 'How long is *some time*?' he said, looking at Chad with perfect calmness.

'A year might be enough,' said Chad, 'two years definitely.'

'And won't you return to Susan Leonard?'

'That's not your business,' said Chad. 'I suggest we meet again in two years' time.'

Jolyon threw up his hands slowly. 'Well, I suggest fifty years,' he said. 'No, no, I suggest a hundred.'

'Don't be an *asshole*,' said Chad.

'There are two of us now,' said Jolyon, 'that means you no longer control the casting vote, Chad,' he said. 'There *is* no casting vote.' Jolyon played at finding more crumbs to brush. 'So if I want, I can be all the *arsehole* I like.'

While Chad and Jolyon stared at each other, Shortest uncrossed his legs and got to his feet. 'Then I'm afraid Game Soc will have to intercede,' he said, pacing back and forth with his hands held together behind him. 'Waiting a few years is acceptable, perhaps even preferable. I mean, who knows what positions in life we'll all attain in ten years' time – which makes everything infinitely more interesting. But Game Soc can't wait forever, Jolyon. And anyway there's a wonderfully simple solution to your dispute.' Shortest picked up the playing cards from the coffee table. 'Your little game has been lacking in the element of luck for some time,' he said, fanning the cards. 'Let us allow the random its return'. 'One of you will cut the deck. The card's value is equal to the number of years you will wait before resuming your game. Mr Mason may require two years away, so let's say that aces are high. Jacks are eleven, queens twelve, kings thirteen and aces fourteen. Do you both agree?'

They looked at each other and nodded.

'Good, then,' said Shortest. 'Mr Johnson, why don't you cut?'

LXX(v) The ace of spades.

███

LXXI(i) Fourteen years ago, my birthday, the ace of spades. Fourteen years ago today.

LXXI(ii) My mind has been tumbling away from me for so long, ever since that night on the tower.

Jolyon, you win.

My memory, already not such an impressive piece of equipment, began to deteriorate daily from the moment of Mark's death. It was as if my brain had come up with a cast-iron plan to hold on to my sanity. If memory was the thing that could hurt me the most then my mind would cease to form strong memories. Instead it would paint for me only faint pictures, enough memory by which to survive, nothing more. Yes, my mind had to protect me from myself.

But there was an awful flaw in the plan. Sharp memories of Pitt had already formed, and they couldn't be easily erased. But what could be forgotten was the minutiae of life, the everyday, the world outside. And so now I live in a cage, trapped inside this story, a tale so vivid I feel it coursing through the circuits of my flesh every day.

Meanwhile, life goes on around me uncared for, unnoticed. Because instead of the world outside, every day I find myself wandering among towers and domes. I am surrounded by merlons and crenels, I live poised above a flagpole, my universe twenty-five metres high, an eighty-foot drop. The world outside is only distant chatter far below, some kind of happiness playing out on a faintly lit lawn.

Gravity, nine-point-eight. Time, two and a quarter. And the eyes very suddenly shut.

LXXI(iii) I have been working since I woke at five and at last Pitt is all written down. It is nine thirty now, it has been an abstemious birthday so far. A few sips, a light cocktail of pills. Chad arrives in five hours' time and then we will play. It seems to me that medication and celebration go hand in hand. I have such a hunger, a thirst.

LXXI(iv) Almost noon. Deliverance straight from the bottle. Would you like ice with that, sir? Pop pop pop go the rocks. Their pinks and their yellows and blues.

And now feel free to sing along. You know this tune?

For he's a jolly good fellow, for he's a jolly good fellow, for he's a Jolyon feh-heh-low. And now I think I should try to clear my head. *Which nobody can deny.*

Am feeling very muddy, so hard to concentrate. Fingers not finding these keys so well. But I must try to be ready, the day of the comeback fight has arrived. The fighter waits in his dressing room. He seems defeated before he has even stepped into the ring. The audience can only hope for some miracle.

LXXI(v) The phone rings.

Jolyon, it's me. Meet me by the Christmas tree, five minutes. Click.

LXXI(vi) I feel the stir of my youth for the merest moment, my memory roused by the sight of her. Dee's hair is dark again. Black and straight and sleek. She is hugging herself in the heat, beside the brief shadow of the tree.

I try not to stumble too much, not to lurch too wildly as I approach. I stop a few feet from her and Dee takes a step back.

So, did you find it? she says. Did you look, Jolyon?

Dee, you can't even begin to know how sorry I am.

I've been to the police, Dee says desperately. I've spoken to all the people who work in the park. I've stopped strangers in the street and put up reward posters everywhere within ten blocks of your apartment. Nothing, Jolyon, nothing.

What should I say to Dee? That I have been too busy with my own words to look for hers? How many forms of guilt can I juggle at once? I want to reach out and stroke the dark silk of her hair. Don't worry, Dee, I say. I'm going to find your poems. I'm going to find them, I say.

It's too late, Jolyon. It's too late. Dee's eyes dart down. She is holding an envelope creased in her folded arms. She notices me looking and reaches out slowly, the letter trembling, and hands it to me. Don't open it until you get back to your apartment, she says. Please, one last promise, Jolyon. I don't want you to read it in public.

I promise, I say, taking the envelope, my name written on its front in red ink. Please, Dee, just one last chance. Let me try.

She forces a smile. It's too late. It's not your fault, Jolyon, but it is too late, Dee says, wrapping her arms around her body. And please don't follow me. You won't see me again, she says, looking down at the ground.

Dee, please, no, I say. Dee, what is it?

She turns and she hurries away.

LXXI(vii) The posters taunt me as I stumble home. Stapled to trees, beneath missing cats. Large reward.

I fall into my apartment and steady myself on the kitchen counter. I tear open the letter.

LXXI(viii) Oh, Jolyon, I hope I'm not too harsh to you in the park, I don't want to be harsh. And please, I don't want you to feel guilty. Perhaps I have been downplaying how hard I've been finding life for the past several years. Your story is so important, I didn't want to distract you with the petty ins and outs of my own obscure existence.

Don't blame yourself, Jolyon. I had fourteen years to right myself. And the failure is mine, all mine.

Please would you find it in your heart to hold on to the second page of this letter? And then, if you ever find it, if anyone ever finds it, you can paste it straight into my book. I would like that very much.

It makes me enormously happy to think that you might do one final thing for me.

It's true, I never really deserved a saviour. I am so very, very sorry.

Dee x

LXXI(ix) While I read the note, I feel the grain of the second sheet of paper against my fingertips. Thicker, heavier, like a piece of old parchment.

Already I know what this is. The words don't matter. But I let Dee's note drop to the floor anyway.

The first thing I see, the first mark on the page, is a large and ornate initial decorated with scrollwork and vines. A stamp in red ink. My gift to her.

D (Black Chalk)

(i)
Six boys one day went running through the woods
inventing games while twisting through the leaves
Exhausted found a copse of old burned trees
and settled there to tally up the score
while feeling in their pockets for
the black chalk

(ii)
Aloft six clouds converged in breaking light
and flocks of angels grouped to form a list
debated who on earth was worthiest

But night had fallen when at last on high
they scrawled those names across the sky
in black chalk

(iii)

Six fledgling soldiers told to notch their guns
to keep engraved a note of every kill
were raising up their flag upon a hill
Then finding that the slate was deep within
they trembled as they filled it in
with black chalk

(iv)

And when soon comes the melancholy time
for you to speak of love, do not deceive
No love was earned and what did I achieve?
So draft upon the basalt tomb what was, what might have been
it is my final wish that you should write it in
black chalk

LXXI(x) Oh, Dee, no. Please, Dee, no. No no no.

———

LXXII Jolyon left Pitt and moved home to his mother's house
in Sussex. For the first month he spent most of his time sitting
listlessly in his bedroom. But then he decided to look for a job,
something to distract him before guilt sucked him under.

He found work in a factory that manufactured shrink-wrap
labels, plastic sleeves for bottles, cans, aerosols . . . For nine hours
a day he stood by a whirring conveyor belt onto which a cutting
machine disgorged labels. After every hundred a buzzer went off

and Jolyon had to scoop up the sleeves and pile them neatly together. But often there was a great build-up of friction and the sleeves would fight against his hands.

Once successfully gathered each stack had to be wrapped in a rubber band and placed in a cardboard box. When a box became full it had to be closed and taped shut. But the buzzer never stopped buzzing, so Jolyon had to learn to do this fast while still managing to gather and bind and fight with the static.

But once he mastered it, Jolyon felt soothed by the work. Rituals of repetition, a routine interrupted only by small and periodic challenges. And the rattling of the machines made conversation impossible and this soothed him as well.

When he wasn't working he read law books. Not because he had decided to return to Pitt but simply because law books were the only unread books he owned. And soon they started to comfort Jolyon just as the monotonous work of the factory comforted him.

Most of all he liked to read legal judgments. Jolyon enjoyed submitting to the opinions of appellate judges and law lords, men and women of learning and experience. He let their conclusions rain down on him like the warm spray from a shower head. He felt like a gatherer of truth, a piecer-together of fact from little fragments. You could find truth in order just as you might properly build a life that way.

Ten months after he had left Pitt he wrote a letter to inform the college he had decided not to return. Wiseman phoned a few days later. At first he tried to talk Jolyon around but Jolyon wouldn't budge. Jolyon told Sir Ralph about his job at the factory but mentioned that he still enjoyed reading law books. He could hear the regret in Wiseman's voice when he wished him well and said goodbye.

An hour later the phone rang again. Again it was Wiseman. He had pulled a few strings, if Jolyon was still interested in the law there was a legal newspaper in London looking for a junior writer. The job was his if he wanted it.

Jolyon acquiesced. Yes, he wanted to be told what to do now. How he wished he had had a Wiseman all along.

He moved to London, to a small flat in the Elephant and Castle where he lived alone. He was good at his job but remained distant from his colleagues.

And so it was in London, surrounded by the heartbeats of millions, that loneliness first became Jolyon's routine. Loneliness was the machine noise that cocooned him from life. And loneliness was not so bad.

———

LXXIII(i) I sit on the kitchen floor unable to get the image out of my head, picturing her all alone, her body not yet found. My darling Dee lying there, little blue doll rumpled and folded away. She looks discarded, carelessly left there for later, legs like stuffed cloth bent beneath her. My little blue doll, her wide stiff eyes, her ocean-coloured skin.

And I could have saved her. I could have . . .

Suddenly I pull a salad bowl out from the debris all around me. I retch. I puke violently, copiously.

LXXIII(ii) The intercom buzzes. Two thirty.

Happy birthday, Jolyon, Chad says when I open the door. He is carrying a black leather attaché case.

I say nothing. I turn and do my best to walk in a straight line. I want to get this thing over with. Perhaps I even want to lose, who knows what I'm thinking. Maybe I don't care about Game Soc, they can do what they like with me.

I have your present, Chad says. Would you like it now or later?

I keep moving forward. In the living room, I collapse onto the sofa and Chad takes the same chair he took three days ago. Already we seem to have fallen into a routine.

Chad lowers the attaché case beside him on the floor. He is dressed in the colours of flame, the crisp blue denim of four days ago and today an orange polo. Chad's boots imply a certain rough and tumble. Old and nicely scuffed as if an artist has burnished them just so.

And Chad's whole life in England begins to form before me. A home in Belgravia, Chelsea lunchtimes and horse riding in Hyde Park at the weekend. Weekdays in Zurich, Frankfurt, Brussels.

I look hard at Chad, feeling like a child. Chad has grown and I have stayed still. No, I have stagnated, I have regressed. How did you find me, Chad? I say.

Come on, Jolyon, Chad says, it wasn't exactly hard. You worked on a major newspaper.

My pieces appeared under a different name, I say.

I know, Chad says, you used your wife's surname. He looks at his watch and then he says, I guess we have the whole afternoon, right? No need to hurry. So don't you want to hear about my adventures as a tourist in New York these past few days? You know, I grew up only a hundred and fifty miles north of here and yet until this trip I'd been here only once. And that was years ago when I was just a kid.

I remember, I say, sounding bored.

Fine, then we can talk fondly of old times if you'd prefer, Chad says.

I grimace, the sarcastic imitation of a smile.

Chad waits as I let the silence lengthen. And then at last he shrugs and speaks. If you don't want to play small talk, Jolyon, then there was another game I had in mind. He picks up his case, rests it on his lap and snaps open its latches. These are your birthday presents, he says as he starts to unpack its contents.

Cards, dice and a blue cup. Chad even has a small square of green felt. He lays everything out on the coffee table, the green felt cut perfectly to size, and looks up at me. I took the liberty, he says. Or did you have your own paraphernalia you were planning to use?

No, I say, I clean forgot to contact my paraphernalia maker.

Chad laughs. Do you want to start now or would you like to chew the fat a little more?

Just deal the cards, I say.

LXXIII(iii) Chad wins. It is not even close. He wins and wins and wins. What are the words they use in sports reports? Carnage. Slaughter. Whitewash.

Although technically it is not quite a whitewash. But I lose spectacularly. I struggle to keep track of the cards that have already been played. I struggle to remember whatever strategy I once knew. At some points in the Game I even struggle to keep my eyes from closing. My head hurts. I am drunk, I am clouded by pills. The consequences of losing make me feel sick and weak. Chad intimidates me. I can't stop thinking about Dee.

And the dice fall unkindly. Everything is against me, everything except for the cards dealt during one solitary round. One round in which fate tosses me a bone, a hand so pleasing that it is hard not to win something. A crowded court of nobles, a diamond mine, a superabundance of spades . . . But I play this hand terribly, I play it like a Vegas lush. And then the dice fall kindly for Chad.

When this round of the Game is complete, I owe Chad three of the most serious consequences and two from the second pot. (I use the word pot symbolically as we have agreed to negotiate the consequences once the play is complete.) Chad, having fought off the onslaught of my single miraculous hand, owes only a single consequence. Yes, one minor scratch, a debt owed to the least serious pot.

LXXIII(iv) Why don't you go first? Chad says. Hit me, Jolyon, what will it be? He leans back smug in his chair, pulls out a piece of paper from his back pocket. I took the liberty of preparing a list of tasks for you already, he says, waving the folded page. You know, just in case I got lucky.

I hold my head in my hands. I don't know, I say.

Come on, Chad says, there must be something you want to do to me. Some minor embarrassment you've longed to see me suffer. You've had fourteen years, Jolyon.

Give me a minute, I say.

Sure, take as much time as you like.

LXXIII(v) I pace unsteadily up and down the length of the apartment. I pause before each turn hoping that something will have landed in my head, something simple yet devastating.

But I can only think about Dee. More blood on my hands. And nothing arrives.

The more I pace the harder it becomes, my head elsewhere and the room wheeling around me.

I stop in the kitchen. Maybe some of this light-headedness is not only because of whisky and pills. I start to wonder how long it is since I've eaten. How could I have forgotten to eat? I can't remember the last time I put anything in my mouth.

The fridge is empty and the cupboards are bare except for a few tea bags. Empty tins of chilli litter my kitchen counters, a jar of peanut butter that looks as if it has been licked clean by a greedy dog. I find a box of sugar on the floor and even that is empty.

There must be some food in here somewhere. I get down on my knees and crawl around, sifting through the mess, the dirty clothes, old newspapers, utility bills, empty whisky bottles, cutlery, crockery, a small mirror, so many green bottles, crushed eggshells, a Chewbacca mask, delivery menus . . .

And then I find something. Not much. But something.

I tip the bag and a few stale crumbs fall into my mouth. Brittle crunch. And then something softer, the sweet melt of a milk-chocolate chip.

I look at the wax paper bag, wet my forefinger, dab at the crumbs. I can hear Chad whistling *Auld Lang Syne* in my living room. I start to smile.

LXXIV(i) The kitchen table is bare. Old and scratched. She is throwing a tablecloth over it when I enter. The cloth is scorched in places. She wears a green pinafore over a white T-shirt. First she smooths the tablecloth, then the front of her pinafore.

This gentleman is from England, the farmer says. He takes the Ford cap from his head and hangs it on a coat hook by the door. You know, that country with all the famous queens, he adds.

The farmer's wife is flustered, she flaps toward her husband, turns him around. Why don't you go put on some bacon and eggs? she says.

Because I've eaten, the farmer says.

For our guest, his wife says, laughing nervously. Please, take a seat, she says to me. Has it been a long trip? From England?

Oh, I came up from New York City, I say.

Really? she says. She smiles but looks confused, as if she has many questions but is not sure which to ask first.

So I try to explain while the farmer studies me carefully. I was a friend of your son at Pitt College, I say. But I moved here to the States some time ago. I live down in the city. Anyway, unfortunately

I lost contact with your son for a long time. But we recently found each other, he's paying me a visit when he flies over in a few days' time.

How nice, Chad's mom says. She looks grateful for the explanation but still confused. When he flies over. In a few days. When he flies over from . . .? she asks, struggling hard to make it sound as if this is a normal enquiry for a mother to make of her son.

Oh, I say, right. Yes, Chad lives in England, I say.

Good, she says, good, then he went back there. Chad's mom pats at her chest. He clearly did love it so, she says.

The farmer is lowering a huge cast-iron skillet from a hook high above a kitchen counter. He is a large man, maybe once even larger, he looks almost seventy now. In the past I imagine he would have swung the heavy skillet over to the range with one hand but now he looks bitter as the skillet's weight takes him by surprise and he has to use two. The information that his son lives in England doesn't seem to affect the farmer, perhaps his ears are no longer so good. He opens the fridge door.

Man, the farmer says, stretching the word out, loud and angry. How is it we buy eggs every week and there are never any damn eggs in here? His bulk makes the minor complaint sound serious.

They're in a carton, Chad's mom says, in the drawer in the middle.

The farmer sighs and shakes his head. He snatches up the bacon.

Chad's mom flattens her hands on the tablecloth. Did my son send you to see us? she asks, trying to sound bright.

I wonder for a moment what I should say. Coming here today I had only a loose hope there might be something to discover. If I lie to Chad's mom now, if I suggest to her, yes, her son sent me, it might be presumed I know more than I do. But if I tell her no, perhaps the farmer and his wife will no longer trust me. So I say to Chad's mom, Your son always told me that if I was ever in the area . . .

She smiles at me. Oh, isn't that nice, Frank? she says, turning.

So you're just passing through, the farmer says to me, peeling bacon from a packet, slapping the rashers onto the skillet.

That's right, I say.

Where you headed? the farmer asks, slap.

I feel as if he is trying to trap me. I try to think back to my days upstate with Blair. The Catskills are south of here. Lake Placid is north. But now is hardly the season for skiing. Then I remember something else. Saratoga, I say to the farmer.

Races don't start for over a month, the farmer says. Can't think why else anyone would go to that place.

And now I am trapped.

Oh, then you're an artist? the farmer's wife says.

I pause uncertainly.

Or a writer? she says, making her eyes wide at me.

Yes, I say, yes, I'm a writer.

And just what in the hell has that got to do with Saratoga? the farmer says.

Oh, silly, Chad's mom says, the famous retreat. Yaddo, she says, it's a place for artists of all kinds. And I've always wanted to go, can't you just imagine all that creativity in the air? Well, I bet you could feel something like that. You know, like a tingle in your fingers.

The farmer snorts. Sounds like a place full of faggots, he says.

His wife flinches. Oh, Frank, she says, I've told you, you can't *say* that word.

LXXIV(ii) To support the Saratoga lie, I talk to the farmer's wife about my story. I give her only the barest details, nothing about the truth, nothing about her son. She nods along keenly as I make my tale sound like a series of light comic episodes.

The farmer, who has kept his back to us, is scooping slippery eggs onto a plate. Then he lifts the heavy skillet in which the bacon has fried. He tries to flick the rashers onto the plate below with a wooden spoon but he can't get the spoon beneath the bacon. You can see the frustration building inside him. The skillet begins to droop in his hand like an old flower in a glass.

He does not drop the skillet so much as hurl it down onto the plate. The plate smashes and the skillet hits the edge of the kitchen counter and falls noisily to the ground.

Chad's mother shrinks and puts her hands to her ears. Oh, Frank, she says.

The farmer turns to me, furious, and starts to yell. If my son says I made anything up then he's a damned liar, he shouts. You can't have made a thing up when you see it and it's nearly as big as a dime. And anything that happened after that was in everyone's best interest. And not just his. Born selfish and ungrateful.

There is a loud noise beside me that makes me spin around. It is the chair on which Chad's mom was sitting. She has risen so quickly she has knocked it over backward. She stands there clenching the edge of the table. Frank, I've had just about enough, she shouts, her voice straining, yearning to be fully unleashed. Don't you think it's bad enough I don't see him? She looks down at her hands and her voice tempers a little. Now you can just go, she says. God, please go. Go and do anything, go and just . . . feed the animals.

Animals don't need feeding yet, the farmer says, swallowing back his gust of temper.

The rage is released from Chad's mom now, it unspools as if a huge weight has been dropped. I will not listen to this for one more minute, she screams. Thirteen years and not a minute longer, she cries. Now leave the mess you just made and go feed the animals.

The farmer wipes his hands on the hips of his pants. His wife is breathing heavily and her head hangs low, not looking at him.

He takes his cap from the coat hook, drops it onto his head without pulling it snug, and leaves.

I'm so sorry, Chad's mom says. That can't have been at all nice for you to witness, she says. She picks up the chair. Let me make some more food, she says.

LXXIV(iii) In silence she cleans and she cooks and I eat.

From the kitchen window I can see a large cinder-block shed with a corrugated roof. A metal silo towers above the low building. The farmer crosses the yard to the building, sits outside and lights a cigarette. When he is finished he waits a minute before lighting another.

Chad's mom takes my plate and I thank her.

She washes up in the kitchen sink. I imagine she can see her husband from the window there. She stares out into the distance and says, I'd never leave my husband, no matter what he did. But I think he'd leave me. She scrubs the forks carefully, pushing the bristles of a brush between each tine. Oh, he wouldn't leave me for another woman, she says, even if he knew how to meet one.

She moves over to sit at the table again, drying her hands on a dish towel while she speaks. I'd like to see my son, she says. Without my husband around, I mean. And you can tell my son I said that. Anywhere he wants. I'll come down to the city, I don't expect him to make any effort himself. She finishes rubbing her hands with the dish towel and looks up at me. Frank feeds the animals every day at noon, she says. She looks up at the clock, five to twelve. If you could phone me one day at exactly five past, she says, then I would know that it's you with an answer. Could you do that? she says.

I don't know, I say. And Chad's mom looks so heartbroken that I add quickly, I just mean that I don't know what's going on here.

Oh, she says, Chad didn't tell you?

I shake my head. No, I say, and I don't want to talk to him and find myself in the middle of something I don't understand, or something I have no right to be in.

You're right, she says, sniffing and gathering the dish towel in her lap. But I don't know how far back I should start, she says. You really don't know anything? she asks.

I sigh. Chad used to speak about his school life, I say. And I knew he grew up on a farm. And I know he had to leave Pitt early but he didn't say why. And that's everything.

Oh, she says. OK then. Will you give me just a minute?

I say yes and she smears her cheekbones with the back of her hand.

Chad's mom gets up, goes to the stove and turns it on. She goes to the fridge and takes out a sausage-shaped cylinder. She opens a kitchen-cabinet door and takes out a bag of chocolate chips. Turning to me and holding the cookie dough and chocolate chips, she says, I just add extra chips to the store-bought dough, that's my secret, she says. But don't tell anyone.

LXXIV(iv) He's Chad's father all right, she says, there's no doubt or dispute about that. But maybe that shouldn't need saying. Oh, that's not a very good start.

Frank and me got married old, she says, for people our generation at least. Both past thirty. Even older by the time I fell pregnant with Chad. So he was our only one. She looks up toward the ceiling. Perhaps I should just say it more simple, she says.

She takes a deep breath. Frank never loved him. And I don't know why. Maybe he never should've had children, or maybe it was something about Chad. But I adored him. I did, I still do.

Chad was smart as anything at school, I was so proud. But Frank wasn't proud. I think it only made him jealous. Frank is a smart man, it's true, he likes to watch the news and talk back, tell them what he thinks. He has all this knowledge, who knows where from, I certainly don't. But once Chad was old enough he liked to talk back as well. But he talked back to his father talking back to the news. Anything Frank said was challenged. So that's part of it maybe. And they didn't just disagree on the news, they disagreed on *everything*. Even about facts, even about things as silly as the longest river in the world. So whenever they argued, Chad would bring back a book from school and point to the bit that, you know, said he was right all along. And Frank always said the book was wrong. Every time, the book's wrong, the book's wrong. The *Webster's Dictionary*, the *Encyclopaedia Britannica*.

Frank never thought Chad was tough enough, you know, that he wasn't growing up to be a real man. Money's always been tight around here, so Chad had to help out on the farm and he hated it. He'd rather be doing his homework instead, which to Frank was perverse, a kid who likes homework. So he gave Chad harder and harder jobs to toughen him up. But all Chad ever got better at was schoolwork. He didn't even play sports except when he had to at school. Not that Frank was ever such a star but he did like to watch and offer his thoughts.

But this is just stuff, you know, and I'm not saying it makes the rest of it make any sense. But there has to be something to everything, doesn't there?

Anyhow, you get the idea. They didn't seem to like each other much and then Chad went to college. Well, with such a good scholarship it didn't matter what his father thought. He didn't need us for the money all of a sudden. And I don't think Frank ever said well done. Probably not. But anyway, that was the two of them parted for a while and perhaps for the best.

When Frank heard Chad was to spend a year in England all he did was snort and say it figured. I didn't even ask what that meant and if I guessed I'd rather not say.

One day Frank was clearing weeds and he thought he'd probably got rubbed by some poison ivy around the side of his forearm.

Well, Frank never really suffered much from poison ivy and it didn't really itch him much. I just rubbed on some calamine and thought nothing more about it. But then this blister wouldn't go away. Even two weeks later it was still there. So I made him go see the doctor.

Well, long story short, it was skin cancer. Skin cancer on the same arm he always hung out the truck window, I won't let him do that any more. I was terrified, you hear such frightening things. I mean, *cancer*. I think even Frank was scared, not that he would ever say anything. But he went and borrowed all these books from the library, that's how I could tell. Every day another few. He must have been through hundreds. But Frank keeps it all in, you know. He's just a guy like that, typical man. He wouldn't even let me come with him to see the doctor.

But they'd caught it and so they arranged to remove it and that's when Frank agreed we had to tell Chad. Because how was I supposed to cope with everything? A husband with cancer. This place hardly makes enough for the two of us, we couldn't hire any more help. And Chad wanted to be here anyway, that's what I think. He may never have loved his father, and maybe he had no reason to, but we taught Chad right from wrong.

So he came back and took over the running of this place. We thought maybe a year would be long enough, we told him, just for a year. And he may not have liked the work but he knew what to do. The two of them even talked more than before. And while Frank didn't want to tell me anything, Chad would ask him questions, so at least I learned a little that way. I didn't even know there were different types of skin cancer until I heard them talking, right here at this table over dinner, Chad's first night back. It's a melanoma, Frank says. Now we have to wait and see. Chad tells him not to worry and not to think about doing anything. Frank says he feels fine but Chad insists. Tells his father he's long earned a rest and he should save his strength. And I was so proud of him, you could see it just the way he held himself, my little boy all grown up. It was like when our daddies returned from the war, came back men.

So we waited, and Frank had to go back over and over for treatment, and then one day he comes home and says it's not good news, the cancer's back. Who knows what he was planning to do next, how far he would have taken it. But I thought that was it, the end. Frank went up to his room as if he was climbing up there to die and I fell face down on this table and cried with my son. And that's when it came out. I suppose Chad must have read as many books as his father. Because when I said, how can a man die of such a little thing? And I said that I should have done something earlier but it looked like just a little red blister . . . Well, that's when he started asking me questions. I was just so confused. Was it a blister or a mole, Mom? What colour was it? Was it round or irregular? So I described it, like a little red button, and that's when suddenly Chad runs up the stairs and starts yelling all these obscenities at his father.

I have to go slow here to get the words right. Chad was shouting, Is it basal cell or squamous, basal or squamous? over and over. Yes, that was it. Well, I had to look up all the words later on. And Frank is yelling how he has no right and what does he know about anything anyway. And then Chad is yelling, I bet it's not even squamous, it's not, is it, you . . . and I won't say the word he called his father, and whatever happened that word wasn't right. It's not even squamous, you . . . it's definitely not a . . . melanoma and I bet it's not even squamous.

Chad runs to his room and starts to pack right away. Frank meanwhile won't say a single word to me. I'm in such a state here about my husband dying and now my son is shouting at him and leaving. So I run to my son's room and he's so angry he can barely speak. But eventually he grabs me by the shoulders. There was such a look in his eyes like I won't forget. And he says to me, Next time he goes to the doctor, you go in with him, Mom. Dad had a basal cell carcinoma, not a melanoma, he's a liar. You go and you ask the doctor the difference, Mom, almost no one has ever died from a basal cell carcinoma, it's a whole different thing. Even if it's squamous cell then it's very low risk. You find out the facts, Mom, and then you can decide if you ever want to see him again. That's your choice. But I will never ever come back to this place, you understand me? I will never come back unless that man is dead or gone.

Frank was at the door to the room. He starts saying things. Oh, don't worry, you'll be back, Mommy's boy. That's what he kept calling him, Mommy's boy this, Mommy's boy that. And you won't stay away from your mommy for long. Just like when you were a boy. You'll be back. And he had this look of . . . just this absolute horrible certainty. Sneering like he pitied his own son. And then he reaches out with his hand and says, A hundred dollars says you'll be back. Chad doesn't flinch so Frank keeps taunting him. You'll be back, I'll stake my life you'll be back. And then Frank said, I always knew you were a little . . . and this time he didn't say Mommy's boy. And I won't even use the word he said.

Well, Chad just finished packing all the while this was happening. And he refused to even look at his father while those vile things were coming out of his mouth. Frank was blocking the door and Chad had his bag ready. And then he walked to the door and just stood there, six inches shorter than his father. Just stood there and looked up at him slowly. And Frank I think tried to stare him down. But then he looked away, looked past him at me and said, He'll be back, just wait and see, he'll be back.

I thought someone was going to hit someone. But Frank stepped to one side. And that was the last time I ever saw my own son.

LXXIV(v) As I listen to Chad's mom I try to picture the farmhouse rooms upstairs, I think of needlepoint roses and orange wood. I see the door frame that the farmer filled, Chad's room full of the books in which he searched for all those facts to prove his father wrong.

I try to picture Chad in his room. But instead of one Chad I see two of him standing there, squaring up to the farmer. The first Chad is the boy who stumbled over his words while I rubbed my sore hands that first day on front quad. And beside the first Chad stands a second, the one who stared at me across the coffee table when the Game was down to three, the Chad in whose eyes I had seen the daily surge of resolve, the gloss of his strength.

And while I picture this, the second Chad grows immensely clearer than the first. The scene becomes very vivid indeed. And then the farmer, six inches taller than his son, steps to one side.

LXXIV(vi) Chad's mom starts to weep softly. A buzzer goes off. She gets up and takes a tray of cookies out of the oven and transfers them to a cooling rack.

Mrs Mason, I say, I promise I will speak to your son. I'll do whatever I can.

She turns around. Her tears flow harder and she nods at me. She tries to smile.

———

LXXV(i) Chad looks at me like a doctor waiting for a frail old lady to begin listing her complaints.

I respond with my own look, a tuck of the chin, a puffing out of the cheeks. And then I say to him, Go home and see your parents, Chad.

LXXV(ii) He tries to act as if my words are only the well-meaning advice of a friend. Well, thanks for the suggestion, Jolyon, Chad says, his cheeks flushing. Obviously it was already part of the plan, he adds innocently. But thanks all the same.

I stretch out on the sofa like a starlet in a silk dressing gown.

Oh no, I say, I don't think you quite understand, Chad. Or perhaps you're being deliberately obtuse. What I mean is that you *must* go and see your parents. That going to see your parents is your consequence. And then I laugh gaily. I mean, it's hardly a consequence at all, Chad. Although obviously I'll have to accompany you to ensure fair performance, I say. And then I add, I seem to remember it's quite a charming drive up there. To the old farmstead.

He stares at me. When at last he speaks his voice is low, a guttural threat in the back of his throat. You can't do this to me, Chad says.

I scratch behind my ear. That's funny, I say, because I think I can. It was you who offered me first move. And I don't think there's anyone would try to argue that a simple visit to the very people who gave birth to you belongs anywhere but the least serious pot. We must remain objective here.

The threat is rising in Chad's voice. This isn't happening, he says. And then, louder still and his fingers stabbing the air, Chad says, You can't do this to me, Jolyon. It's not right. Because I've won. You have no idea.

I remain perfectly calm. I have no idea of what? I say.

And at last his rage rushes out. Of *everything* I've done to you, Chad shouts. He pushes down on the arms of his chair as if he's about to rise, as if he might attack. But instead Chad falls back, and suddenly his strength is gone. When next he speaks it is as if there has been a key change, the slide from major to minor. You don't understand, he says. You have no idea of all the ways I've beaten you. So you can't do this to me, Jolyon. I'm winning. I'm . . . Chad closes his eyes and his voice trails away.

I'm sure you're right, Chad, I say, nodding thoughtfully. So it's simple. Just go and see your parents.

No, Jolyon, Chad says, his anger pitched quietly now. This can't be happening. This is not how it ends.

Chad falls silent. He stares over my head, out beyond my windows, his arms flat at the sides of the chair as if he is waiting, as if he wants to feel the earth turn beneath him and the truth will have drifted away.

I say nothing. I watch Chad's chest heaving up, falling back, as little by little the heaviness in his breathing subsides.

Finally he tips back his head. Jolyon, this is what you don't understand, Chad says, his voice turning bitter-sweet now. I haven't been in New York for four days. I've been here since before I called. I've been beating you *every single day and night* since that phone call. Chad lowers his head to stare at me. Jolyon, I've been running your life for five weeks.

And now it is my turn to pause, to think everything through. And the earth doesn't turn beneath me, it lurches wildly. It feels as if I am staring through the side window of a speeding car and I can't turn my head, I can't find anything on which to focus. Snatches of the last five weeks go spinning through me. My routine, my story, my life. Until gradually everything begins to slow – the world, my thoughts – and my eyes find something on which to focus. I am looking at Chad, his mouth foreshadowing a smile. I stiffen at the sight of it, remembering my edge, recovering my game. Bravo, Chad, I say. That's really very impressive. Yes, I understand now. So why not simply go and see your parents . . . ? I reach out my hand as if offering him a gift.

Chad's smile dissolves. No, you really don't see, he says, beginning to sound impatient. Don't for one single second make out you understand what I've done, he says. I've . . . Chad is rubbing his forehead in disbelief . . . I've been leaving your *notes* for you, Jolyon. I've been inventing and placing mnemonics, writing half your book. I've been pulling the strings of this pointless life of yours every day for five weeks.

Chad begins to look desperate. If you're high on pills, Jolyon, that's because of me. More whisky every day? Me! Don't pretend you understand. I've beaten you every single day. Who took away your water? Me! Well, except for the one glass you kicked over yourself, I'll admit you provided the spark for a good number of the ideas yourself. And who made you drink whisky instead of your water? Who kept gradually changing the line on your glass? And more pills as well, more drugs whenever we felt like it, whenever we thought you were starting to get suspicious.

Chad sees me flinch.

Oh, what's that, Jolyon? he says. Did you mishear me or did I say *we*? Yes, *we*, Jolyon! Me and Dee, both of us together. So you can't do this to me, you haven't won, because everything I've done, everything I've . . . Chad runs out of words as he fights to take in enough air.

I try to hide my feelings. Dee as well? I want to leap up and attack him, I want to punch and kick and choke him. But I know this isn't the way to defeat Chad. Instead, I lift a knee to my chest and rub the sole of my foot in circles as if fighting off an impending cramp. I applaud you, Chad, I say, feigning a distracted air. I'm truly impressed. If anyone were keeping score, how much do you think they'd say you were winning by? A thousand points? A million? But, to use an old sporting cliché, it ain't over till it's over, right? I suppose I'm like a boxer in one of those movies. Bloody and reeling, only one punch left in me. I throw it. And out of the blue, smack. You fall. The count begins, one two three . . . Will you make it up? Seven eight nine . . .

Please, Chad says, spare me your metaphor. I've read it a thousand times. The boxer, the fighter. He rolls his eyes.

Wow, I say, smiling appreciatively. You know, using Dee as well. That's really very clever. I had no idea.

Of course Dee was part of it, Chad says, outraged. And do you have any idea as to *why* she did it, Jolyon, any guesses? Chad taps at his head with his forefinger. Because she's married to *me*, he says. Because she's my wife, Jolyon. *I'm* her saviour, not you.

I can't stand to look at him any more. I turn away. Married? Chad married to Dee. Jack married to Emilia. And where am I? They loved me first. I can almost smell Chad's pleasure at having wounded me and quickly I turn back to face him. Then I suppose my invite got lost in the post, I say.

Chad snorts.

Seven eight nine . . .

And now I think it is time to end this. So when we head upstate, I say, obviously Dee should come with us, right, Chad? A family outing. I suppose now it's clear that the whole suicide poem thing was just another part of the act. A truly audacious move, I really am impressed. But yes, definitely bring Dee along. Because don't you think your wife should meet her in-laws? Your mother would find her charming. Your father also, I bet he'd just love her. What do you think about your father?

Chad's head drops and he puts his hands to his eyes. Soon he is rubbing his face as if trying to work soap into a lather.

Seven eight nine . . .

Chad? I say, as if perhaps he didn't hear me. Chad, I said, *what do you think about your father?*

He sits up stiffly and blinks several times. It takes him a minute to gather himself. A minute during which I try to piece together Chad's revelations of the last five weeks.

My shoes and WALK NOON. Dee's framework and my strict adherence to a fixed schedule. Mnemonics and routine. Pills and whisky.

I cannot say with utter certainty that all of the words in this story have been written by me. It seems that some of them may not have been my own.

Perhaps I am not the washout who stumbled pathetically through his life every day of his comeback. Maybe I am stronger than I thought.

Chad takes a sharp breath and I look up at him. And then, in a voice no louder than a whisper, Chad says to me, OK then, Jolyon. You win. God knows how, I truly have no idea. But you win.

I feel a weight departing my body, the everyday strain of it, fourteen years of dark accumulation. And now the slate on the wall is scratched one last time, the tally complete, its final black line.

Chad tries to look brave. Well, I guess that's it then, he says. Except for one thing, Jolyon. Please, will you grant me one favour? Hear me out, let me explain it all to you properly, the whole thing. Chad's shoulders slump a little, and then he says, It was beautiful, it really was something to behold. And you know, I think that of all people, you will actually appreciate it more than anyone else. Honestly, Jolyon, I do.

I nod at Chad. I feel life in my veins, a lightness returning. And I settle back comfortably to listen to his tale.

LXXV(iii) One of the letters told me where to find you. There it was on an index card, your address written out neatly in green pen and clipped to a few of your pieces for the newspaper with some helpful annotations. Six months ago.

So, we arrived nearly a week before I phoned you. I rented an apartment across the street, hoping to spy on you, I hadn't decided what I was going to do. But we couldn't see into your place, Jolyon, you never once opened the curtains. You didn't even go out. Correction, you left just once to go to that store on the corner. Early, of course, but I was jet-lagged and couldn't sleep so I saw you. By the time I got dressed and ran down the stairs, you were already on your way back with a bag of rice, some tins of chilli.

That's why I had to phone you, just to shake the tree a little, see what fell down. Then we waited.

And you opened the curtains. It wasn't much but at least it was something. The next day I knew I'd hit the jackpot. Out you went for that first walk. *The outside world is my medicine* – one of *your* lines, by the way. Well, I knew it was going to be easy after that, as soon as I started to read your story.

You again – *I leave the apartment in something of a trance.* Exactly right, Jolyon, the sort of trance that meant you didn't lock your door. So Dee followed you while I went through your things. I didn't have long. You saw that airplane, HELL ONE, and Dee phoned me to say you were running back home.

But that was long enough to take some files from your computer, your precious story. And also long enough for me to see all those objects arranged around the place, your strange little reminders. Well, of course I remembered what they were right away. So there I was in your apartment, you running back, I had some of your files, and suddenly on a whim I decided to take away one of your glasses from the floor. After I left, I thought I'd been stupid, you were bound to notice. But actually that was the spark for the next stage. You didn't notice at all. That's when I knew what to do, when I realised just how far we could go.

Back across the street, I read your story. And it was clear how to begin. I had to get into your apartment on a regular basis and I had to rearrange your life. When it came to the final round I wanted you vulnerable, drugged, traumatised . . . Well, I achieved my goal, everything and more. And in the end, even that wasn't enough.

Remember you wrote how you wanted to go outside but your water glasses stopped you. And then on that second day you were brave enough to go out for a walk. Well, at that point I thought, right, this is perfect. From here on I can do whatever I like while he's out – read his words, do whatever I want with his mnemonics. So I waited. But you didn't leave. And day four you didn't go out either. Well, this started to worry me.

But you gave me the idea for my next trick yourself, Jolyon. Remember inserting a note into your story? *Note to self: Must remember to place some trinket on the breakfast plate to remind me to breakfast al fresco.*

So I thought, how about if I augment his sense that regular walks would do him the power of good? And then I got really brave. I decided to insert my own note into your story. *Note to self: Remember to place your shoes on the bed, post-lunchtime walks*, and so on and so forth.

And what happened next? Within a couple of days you had those sneakers in place with a reminder scrawled on their toes. It worked, I mean, it worked literally like a charm. And that was going to give me a lot more time in your place.

Then came the snag. Your next walk, you locked your door. I mean, come on, Jolyon, how to ruin the best-laid plans . . . And maybe you'd have kept on remembering to lock your door, who knows, you were writing about how you were getting stronger all the time. The boxer, the fighter, blah blah blah. I decided it was time to give the tree another shake.

That was the night your buzzer sounded. You answered the call and there was a woman screaming through the intercom for help. And it was such a dilemma for you. Gallant Jolyon at the parapet, the maiden in distress down below. I have to say, I was very disappointed in you. What if it had really been a maiden in need of your help instead of Dee? But never mind, halfway down the stairs gave me just long enough. I was a neighbour fumbling for keys. You passed me on the way down and I ran upstairs with my fingers crossed. And bam, in your panic you'd left the door unlocked. All I needed was a few seconds to plant the pill in the appropriate hollow of the ice-cube tray. And we're not talking here about one of the varieties of drug that can be found in your own collection, Jolyon. No, this particular pill came from another family of pharmaceuticals altogether, a family not unknown to certain unpleasant and predatory males.

So we waited a while for the pill to take full effect. And then Dee turned up at your door, knock knock knock. And off you plodded to ACE bar. ACE bar, Jolyon, the joke was so lost on you. Fourteen years and that's where I sent you. Anyway, Dee kindly held on to your keys for you, dropped them at our prearranged spot, I got your keys copied and went up to your apartment.

Everything we'd done to you up to that point had worked. All we had to do was continue. It was like training a dog, Jolyon. Repetition repetition repetition. Once we had you walking regularly, we were free to do whatever we liked. We had a few hours in your apartment each day, left more notes, played with your mnemonics, increased your pills and whisky whenever we wanted . . . We even rewrote your book to our own ends, filled in some of the gaps. But I suppose you get the final say, Jolyon. History is written by the victors, isn't that what they say? Oh, but it was so flawless, Jolyon, it was as if we had this zombie we could move around by remote control. It was easy, it was all just so perfect.

Another little shake and out of the tree falls Dee. Behold the old flame.

Anyway, I'm sure you can fill in the rest yourself.

It was all falling perfectly into place. It was beautiful, it truly was. And I'm sure you can see that. You understand how perfect it was, Jolyon. You know that now, right?

LXXV(iv) I am quiet for some time. Chad's words whirl high in my head and I wait for them to trickle down, to offer me some essence of emotion. And then I surprise myself. I am not angry. And further back in my mind there is even a trace of admiration. The gallant winner should always make the effort to praise his opponent's game.

Yes, Chad, I understand now, I say. You know, I think I got lucky, I add.

Chad smiles. Thank you, Jolyon, he says. Thanks, I appreciate that.

And now more emotions settle inside me, the small flutter of victory, a vast sense of relief. It feels as if my whole body can breathe for the first time in years. Even in the lighter moments of the last fourteen years I always felt a sense of unease. Clenched jaw, stiff chest, balled fist. A feeling that if my body wasn't fighting to hold itself together, then I could simply fly apart, I could be scattered like ashes in the wind.

Chad has taken his phone from his pocket, is tapping out a message. His knees are parted and the phone is small between his legs. He looks up at me. Remember the green-pen letters I told you about? he says. Well, the last one provided me with a phone number to which I was instructed to send the result of our encounter. But screw them if they think I'm going to send them a play-by-play. Chad holds up the phone and presses send with a sarcastic flourish.

When Shortest finds out, he says, I guess he's going to be very disappointed. There is the twitch of a grin at the corner of Chad's mouth. Look, Jolyon, he says, I might as well admit something else to you now. I already told you that Shortest was my backer. Oh and Dee was his other runner, by the way, just imagine his smug delight at the composition of the final three. Anyway, Shortest helped me, Jolyon. I could never have thought of all those things to do to you on my own. Like the soccer match stuff. What do I know about soccer? How could I ever have thought of that on my own? But we lost, both of us, so now it doesn't matter. Back into the Game. I guess I'm going to be seeing a whole lot more of Shortest.

No, Chad, I say, I think whoever sent you those letters is a fantasist and a liar. There's nothing left for you now. You don't owe them anything.

Chad is pale, his arms limp slabs against the sides of the chair. I wish I could believe that, Jolyon, he says.

And do I believe it? I don't know, maybe not. Because for the last fourteen years there has been something troubling me about

Game Soc. If Shortest knew I was on the roof with Mark and decided not to tell anyone, then he must have been scared of something, right? Maybe he was just scared of becoming embroiled in the story of a death. What if I'd been arrested and told the police everything, right from the start? What if the newspapers got hold of the story? So maybe Shortest was only worried how Game Soc's behaviour would reflect on him, affect his future. But what if it was more than that? What if Shortest was terrified that Tallest would find out about him being at Pitt that night? And if so, if such a trivial and simple piece of information was enough to keep Shortest quiet, there would have to be something larger at play, something worth being afraid of, wouldn't there?

I don't know. I can't decide what Shortest's silence means. But whatever it means, I can see Chad is afraid.

You know, I think it's time for a cup of tea, I say.

Chad explodes with an enormous laugh. Fine then, let's have tea, he says. Sure, let's break out the best china, invite the vicar, the Queen.

Strong, no sugar, just a thimbleful of milk? I say.

Oh, perfect, Chad says. Christ, that's perfect, Jolyon, just how you trained me to take my tea. Jolyon my guide, my mentor. Chad smiles as if he has just said something enormously droll.

LXXV(v) As well as carrying mugs into the living room, I bring something else with me, something that caught my eye among the wreckage spread across the kitchen floor. I have to put the mugs down at Chad's feet. And then I unfold it, round and white, made of delicate lace. I spread the tablecloth over the square of green felt that lies on the coffee table and place our tea on top.

How very civilised, Chad says. We both stare at the tablecloth, then reach for our mugs at the same time. We blow at our drinks and take small noisy sips of the too-hot tea.

Chad, will you answer me one question? I ask.

Anything, he says. I mean, sure, you deserve that much at least.

Why did Dee go along with everything? I understand why you did it. But why Dee?

Chad stares at me, a trace of bitterness returns to his eyes. Go along with it? he says. Dee didn't know half the stuff that was going on. I came up with everything. Dee even fell in love with your story, she wasn't lying to you about that. But she's my wife, Jolyon, she loves me. And I've done very well in life, *very* well, and I've looked after her for years. When I told her I was coming here, when I explained it all to her, I suggested we might need some kind of an umpire. That if things got really bad between us, we would need someone else around, someone who understood what was going on. And she always felt guilty about what happened at Pitt between you and me. As if she should have stepped in earlier.

And then, when she still wasn't sure, I told her I was scared. I said to her I was trying to protect us both, you and me. That you were in no fit state to survive if Game Soc got hold of you. I had it all worked out, I said. She trusted me. She's *my* wife.

And then, once we got here, I didn't even tell her half the stuff I was doing. She was busy sinking down comfortably into your words and I was moving around your apartment, thinking up what to do next. I didn't tell her about your whisky and pills, how much I was increasing them. And she was even worried about you, she wanted us to find a way to make you stop, or cut down at least. She didn't know, she didn't see me washing your glasses, drawing new black lines that crept higher and higher every few days. And while the two of you were meeting in the park at night she had no idea what I was doing in here.

Chad looks briefly victorious again. But then his smile drops. He picks up his attaché case and places it on the coffee table. And Dee didn't know about this, he says, snapping open the latches.

I feel really bad about this, Jolyon. Chad reaches into his case and pulls out a large book as thick as a wedding album, red leatherette. He places it between us on the coffee table. He hangs his head low but then looks up at me. And then came my final assault on you, the five hundredth poem, he says. Dee did a great job, don't you think? She didn't want to write it, not at first. But I told her you needed some kind of a jolt to help you remember where you'd left her book. Everything went down *precisely* as I planned it.

I pick up Dee's book from the table and start to flick through its pages covered in red ink until I pass poem four hundred and ninety-nine. The rest of the pages are blank. Suddenly I realise something. I look up sharply at Chad. So Dee never finished reading my story? I say.

Me neither, Chad says. Well, you stopped going for your walks after you thought you'd lost Dee's book. And I thought I'd done enough by then, it didn't matter to me any more. Anyway, we all know how your story ends. Mark jumps and you leave Pitt, Chad says. And we're all just as much to blame as each other.

He pinches the bridge of his nose and then takes a sip from his mug. Chad doesn't see me looking up and breathing out hard, offering my silent prayer of thanks.

I slap my hands on my thighs. You know what I feel like right now? I say to Chad. I feel like going for a walk. Let's blow off the cobwebs. Would you like to take a walk with me?

A walk? Chad says. You mean one of your medicinal strolls? Shouldn't I stay here and rewrite your life for you? he says.

LXXV(vi) We turn left out of the building toward the park.

Chad's hands are pushed deep in his pockets. So how much do you know about what happened with my father? Chad asks.

The cancer story, you mean? Your mother told me everything, I think.

Chad sighs. The one thing in the world I wouldn't do, he says. Unbelievable.

Your mother wants to meet you, Chad, I say. Without your father there, you don't have to see him. She said she'd come to the city, or anywhere you want. She's waiting by the phone every day. Five past twelve, she said to call then and she'll answer, your father won't ever know.

Still feeding those damn pigs at noon every day, Chad says. I don't know. She stayed married to him, didn't she?

Going and seeing your mother doesn't mean your father's won, Chad, I say. Anyway, I promised her I'd pass on the message.

Thanks, Jolyon, Chad says.

We fall silent for a moment but I can sense there is something Chad wants to tell me. He pushes back his hair, begins to slow down. Jolyon, there's something Middle said to me back at Pitt. I never told you, I never mentioned this to any of you. Just before he left Game Soc, he said to me it's possible we would be told things. Not about Game Soc but something much larger. And he said he didn't know if it was all just ghost stories but the only sensible way to behave would be to act as if it were true. He said, the longer you stay in the game, the more dangerous things become. I thought about what he said every time I opened one of those letters in green pen.

Our pace has slowed to a standstill. Chad turns and drops down onto a stoop, he sits with his legs wide apart.

Why didn't you tell us? And why was Middle talking to you? I ask.

He told Emilia as well, Chad says. I suppose he assumed we'd pass on the message. Half an hour later Emilia got hit by a truck and she only remembered the dare we had planned for her. So I had this whole can of worms to myself. Chad stares off to the side. Truthfully? he says. I think perhaps it gave me a secret thrill. It was as if the whole thing were an adventure. But then I grew up. And I'm happy with where I got to, Jolyon. I don't want any more adventures.

Chad looks small now, hunched down on the steps.

I think Shortest is a sadist, Chad, I say. The only game still going on is the one inside his twisted little mind.

That's easy for you to say, Jolyon, you won. There's nothing left for you to be afraid of any more. Anyway, I always thought it was Tallest behind the whole thing. Why Shortest?

Come on, I say, pulling Chad to his feet. This was supposed to be a medicinal stroll, remember? Let's not talk about the Game any more.

We walk on in silence until we reach the end of the block and cross the road.

Around the grassy knoll? Chad says.

It is gloomy beneath the trees at the entrance to the park. Clouds have gathered overhead, hot clouds, and the air is pushed low.

No, I say, let's just keep going on Seventh.

So you married an American, Chad laughs.

Worse than that, I say, I'm a bone fide American citizen. Four years now, it came through just before my divorce.

Then you beat me to it, Chad says. I got my British citizenship three years ago. He bites his lip, makes a sucking sound. Man, look at us, he says. You an American, me now a Brit. It's almost as if we swapped places.

We walk on and begin to talk about old times. The day we first met, my strangled hands. Named after a Third World fucking country. Country and western singer, suede tassels, big hooters. *Hooh-durrs*, I say, mimicking Chad.

A decade in this country and you still can't do the accent, he jokes.

I feel a spot of rain hit my nose and a few seconds later the first great gush of the downpour lands all at once as if a large bucketful of water has been thrown from a tall building nearby. We look at each other and then toward the shelter of the trees in the park. We both start running in the direction of a grand old elm. It is not far but when we reach the tree's cover already we are soaked to the skin. I lean back against the elm tree and we both begin laughing. We laugh together like we used to before some other kind of life came along.

And then Chad puts his arm around my shoulders and looks up at the canopy sheltering us. Man, look at this huge gnarled old thing, he says.

Garlands of dried flowers hang from the trunk. Chad slaps his hand affectionately against the back of my neck and turns away. He begins to trace his finger around the bark, beneath the string of flowers. As Chad moves around the tree, I get down on my haunches and start rubbing my hair, my back fitting smoothly into a hollow in the trunk. I wipe the rainwater from my face. It feels good to be happy and wet. I let my head flop back against the tree and close my eyes.

I'll help you, Chad, I call out. Whatever it is you have to do for them, if it's anything at all, then I want to help you. Please, promise you'll let me help you.

Chad doesn't answer me. I open my eyes but can't see him. I stand and I circle around the tree, following the garlands of flowers.

But he is gone. The rain is steady now, a maze of beaded curtains. And Chad is nowhere to be seen.

———

LXXVI(i) I stare at the clock, waiting for its final digit to change from a four to a five. And then I make the call.

Her gratitude is overwhelming, before I can ask her a question she is full of thank-yous and tears.

When did you see him? I ask.

Just a few days ago, Chad's mother says.

Where? I ask her. Down here in Manhattan?

No, she says, a Johnny Rockets in a mall near Albany. It was only for a few hours. He said he had some important matters to take care of back down in the city. You haven't seen him since he got back?

I'm sure I will, I say.

We talk some more. I let her tell me about her son, that she baked him cookies, they were always his favourite, he hasn't changed one little bit . . . And then I tell her I have to go.

We say goodbye, Chad's mother thanks me some more. And I hang up.

Dee looks at me, all of the hope gone from her face, and I shake my head. He went to see her near Albany, I say. Then he said he was coming back here.

Maybe he just needs some time, Dee says.

Maybe, I nod.

But that's not what you think, is it, Jolyon?

I don't know, Dee. I don't know if he believes in them or not.

Oh, Chad believes in them, Dee says.

Did you see any of the letters?

He showed me a few. And he admitted it was perfectly possible the whole thing was ridiculous, a sadistic game.

And what do *you* think, Dee?

What do I know, Jolyon? The only things I know about the world I got from reading books. Good people do good things, good people do bad things, bad people do worse things. What more is there? My husband was scared, that's all I know.

So what will you do? I say.

Continue to wait for him.

And if he doesn't come back?

I'll find him. I'll look and I'll never stop looking. Dee picks up one of the cushions from my sofa and hugs it to her belly. And how about you, Jolyon, what will you do?

Stop drinking, I say. Stop taking pills. And start working.

As simple as that?

No, probably not, I say.

And now I think the time has come. In the corner of the room there hangs a white sheet draped over my surprise.

She hasn't asked about it but Dee watches me curiously when I kneel down and feel for the electrical cord, when I plug it into the socket.

The lights show faintly through the fabric. I stand up and pull the sheet off with as much flourish as I can muster. And there it stands, a four-foot artificial Christmas tree, green wiring wrapped all around and the red lights ablaze.

The fireflies are out, I say to Dee.

She sniffs and half laughs at my silly game.

And look, I say, there's a present underneath the tree for you.

What is this, Jolyon? Dee says. A reminder of all the lies I told you in the park?

I make shushing sounds. That's not what this is about, I say. I told you I understand what you did. The present is for you, Dee. Open it.

I have overwrapped the gift, trying to conceal my surprise with layers of bubble wrap and now it looks as big as a pillow.

Dee pulls away the paper, rips through the layers of wrap. And there it is, the large book as thick as a wedding album, red leatherette.

She blinks in amazement. She has to open it to be sure, to see her words inside.

Oh, Jolyon, she says, throwing her arms around my neck and starting to cry.

I hug Dee tight to me, rub circles on her back.

But how did you find it? she asks.

It doesn't matter, I tell her. And don't worry about anything, Dee.

But I'm scared, Jolyon.

No no no, I say. Everything's going to be all right. I promise, Dee.

LXXVI(ii) Because what should I have said to her? Do you think I should have told Dee the truth? That I don't think she will ever see her husband again? The truth about Mark? Should I have told her that, two days ago, when I returned to my apartment from a walk, I found a small package outside my door? And that the package bore only my name and no address, no stamps? Should I have told her that inside the package I found twelve thousand pounds in cash beneath a sealed envelope? And that when I opened the envelope I found the following note written in green ink?

Dearest Jolyon,

First of all, heartfelt congratulations. Please find your prize money herewith. We agreed upon ten thousand pounds, of course, but the other two thousand pounds represent the monies deposited by yourself and Mark Cutler. (The tragic suicide of young Mark remains one of Game Soc's overwhelming regrets. However, it was agreed, if you remember, that the deposit of any defaulter would be added to the prize fund. And the rules are the rules, we suppose. That was certainly always your position, Jolyon, if memories serve us correctly.)

There is one final matter: Game Soc is still in possession of a final one thousand pounds, the deposit banked by Theodore Chadwick Mason. Please do have a good hard think, Jolyon, and perhaps you might let us know the precise location at which Mr Mason might be found. There remains, alas, the awkward question of unfinished business.

Other than that, Jolyon, good luck. Good luck, and our very best wishes.

G.S.

No, I have told enough truth, I have played by their rules, I am free.

So I hold Dee, only hold her, old friends who have spent too long apart. I have hidden myself away from everything for too long. I have a small amount of money now, a gentle itch for something new.

But as I let Dee go, I start to wonder – how much did he love her? Did Chad love Dee unreservedly or did a part of him want her because, in having her, he imagined he was defeating me?

Acknowledgements

I always used to believe lengthy and rambling acknowledgements at the ends of novels to be an author showing off his number or quality of friends. Then I wrote one. And now I realise that so many people have been such an enormous help to me that it would be an act of unpardonable rudeness not to thank them all.

Therefore, thank you so very much to all the following:

For everything, my wife Margi Conklin. Not a single page of this novel would have been written were it not for her unwavering and loving support.

For reading me stories while curled on her lap, for encouraging me in my own story-telling and for her constant cheerleading, my mother, June.

For her unflagging support, shrewd suggestions and for never giving up, my extraordinary agent Jessica Papin at Dystel & Goderich.

For her inspiring, tireless insight and innumerable improvements, my editor Alison Hennessey at Harvill Secker.

For their enormous professionalism and kind support, Lauren Abramo, Arabella Stein and Michelle Weiner.

For their relentlessly intelligent reading, re-reading and invaluable suggestions, Jemima Rhys-Evans, Katherine Gleason, Paul Manes, Sarah Crawford, Shaun Pye (thank you for ideas as well), Jeffrey Williams, Jonathan Brown and May Kuckro.

For his help, twenty-three years ago, with the conception of the Game (which thankfully we never played), Chris Winslow.

For help with attention to detail, Ted & Sue Conklin and Jason Kohn. For publishing advice and support, Lisa Thompson. And thank you also to the following for their various and much-appreciated contributions – Andrew Cresswell, John Lee, Adam Lewin, Stefanie Cohen, Brian Sampson, Jillian Straus, Jon Luke, Sharon Wright, Dorothy Koomson, James Jones, Kathy Fry, Simon Rhodes, Ben Fowler and Felicity de Chenu.